FRANK MUIR presents

The Book of Comedy Sketches

FRANK MUIR
Presents

THE BOOK OF COMEDY SKETCHES

Edited by Frank Muir and Simon Brett

ELM TREE BOOKS
London

First published in Great Britain 1982
by Elm Tree Books/Hamish Hamilton Ltd
Garden House 57-59 Long Acre London WC2E 9JZ
in association with EMI Music Publishing Ltd
138-140 Charing Cross Road London WC2H 0LD

Cover photographs by Beverly Lebarrow

British Library Cataloguing in Publication Data

Frank Muir presents: the book of comedy sketches.
1. English wit and humor
I. Muir, Frank II. Brett, Simon
827'912'08 PN6175

ISBN 0-241-10852-7
ISBN 0-241-10870-5 Pbk

Filmset by Pioneer
Printed and bound in Great Britain
by Billing & Sons Ltd, Worcester

Contents

Acknowledgments

The author and publishers would like to thank the following for their kind permission to reproduce copyright material in this book:

Samuel French Ltd for: *Gloom* by E. Preston from 'Play Bits' (1922); *Footsteps* by Herbert C. Sargent from 'Bits and Pieces' (1924); *Wow Wow* by Basil Charlton from 'Green Room Rags' (1925); *The Green-Eyed Monster* by Dion Titheradge from 'The Prompt Corner' (1925); *The Great White Sale* and *He Who Gets Sacked* by Dion Titheradge from 'Folly To Be Wise' (1931); *The Judgement of Parrish* by Dion Titheradge from 'Written on Foolscap' (1933); *Caught in the Act* by Ronald Jeans from 'The Review of Revues' (1925); *Incredible Happenings* by Ronald Jeans from 'Sundry Sketches' (1924); *Road Tests for Pedestrians* by Ronald Jeans from 'After Dark' (1934); *Off the Lines* by Ronald Jeans from 'Bright Intervals' (1927); *The Tragedy of Jones* by Maurice Lane-Norcott from 'Try One of These' (1927); *A Man of Letters* by C. B. Poultney from 'Pulling the Show Together' (1928); *Yes and No* by Harold Simpson from 'Airy Nothings' (1927); *When Television Comes To Town* by Harold Simpson from 'He Dines Alone' (1931); *Saved?* by Harold Simpson from 'On and Off' (1944); *Glad To Have Met You* by Douglas Furber from 'The Favourites of the Stars' (1948); *Laughing Gas* and *The Influence of Thesaurus* by Douglas Furber from 'The All Star Cast' (1931): *Moment Romantique* by Reginald Beckwith from 'Sketches from Nine Sharp'; *Directory Enquiries* by Julian Elliston from 'The Management Regrets' (1939); *Bicycling* by Hermione Gingold from 'Hermione Gingold Wrote These' (1942); *La Plume de ma Tante* by Simon Phipps and *Tie Up* by Ben Gradwell from 'La Vie Cambridgienne' (1949); *The Trouble With Miss Manderson* and *Restoration Piece* by Alan Melville from 'A La Carter'; *We Come Up From Mummerset* by Peter Myers, Alec Grahame and David Climie from 'Intimacy at Eight-Thirty' (1956): *No Ball* by Arthur Macrae from 'Living For Pleasure' (1960);

Reynolds Music Ltd for: *Motoring* by Harry Tate; *Nicholas Knox of Nottingham* by Charles J. Winter; *Business As Usual* by Robert Rutherford; *The Never-Idle Apprentice* by Scott and Whaley; *The Mother, The Careful Wife* and *The Prize* by George Arthurs; *Fanny Writes a Book* by Stanley C. West;

W. H. Allen & Co. Ltd for *Nobel Prizes* and *Naked Films* by Steven Vinaver; *Internal Combustion* by David Nobbs and *But My Dear* by Peter Shaffer, all from 'That Was The Week That Was' (1964) and for *Nows At Ton* by Barry Cryer and Peter

Vincent and *Sketcherism Spoon* by Dick Vosburgh from 'The Two Ronnies Sketchbook';
Alan Bennett for *Take A Pew* and *The Great Train Robbery* from 'Beyond the Fringe' and *The Telegram* and *The Defending Counsel* from 'On the Margin' (Polydor 582 D37);
Bob Bloch for *Narcissus* from 'The Frost Report';
Rob Buckman and Russell Davies for *Chippenham Wrexham*;
John Cleese and Bill Oddie for *BBC BC* from 'Cambridge Circus' (Parlophone PMC 1208); *John and Mary* and *The Doctor* from 'I'm Sorry I'll Read That Again' (Parlophone PMC 7024) and *Butterling* by John Cleese from 'The Frost Report';
Peter Cook for *Hand Up Your Sticks* and *Not An Asp* from 'Pieces of Eight'; *Critics' Choice* from 'One Over the Eight' (Decca LK 4393); *One Leg Too Few* from 'Beyond the Fringe'; *Are You Spotty* from 'The Misty Mr Wisty' (Decca LK 4722); *The Ravens* by Peter Cook and Dudley Moore; and *TVPM* and *The Great Train Robbery* from 'Beyond the Fringe';
Dr Jan van Loewen Ltd for *Sorry You've Been Troubled; Growing Pains* and *The Order of the Day* by Noel Coward from 'Collected Sketches and Lyrics' (Hutchinson, 1931);
Mrs Phyllis Winifred Cranston for *The Home Guard* by Robb Wilton on 'Music Hall to Variety Vol. 3. Second House' (World Records SH 150);
Barry Cryer for *Chancellor of the Exchequer* from 'The Frost Report';
Ian Davidson and Neil Shand for *Strangers When We Meet* from 'Frost on Sunday' and Ian Davidson and Robin Grove-White for *Attitudes* from 'Monty Python';
Essex Music for *Six of the Best* by Peter Cook on 'Once Moore With Cook' (Decca LK 4785);
Marty Feldman and Barry Took for *Educating Alec* from 'Not So Much A Programme';
Doug Fisher for *Tennis* from 'The Frost Report';
John Gould and David Wood for *First Performance* from 'Four Degrees Over';
Granada Publishing for *French for Beginners* from 'The Best of Bentine' by Michael Bentine;
Irene Handl for *Shadows on the Grass* from 'Songs for Swinging Sellers' (Parlophone PMC 1111);
David Higham Associates Ltd for *Please Captain Eversleigh* from 'Diversions'; *Long Distance Divorce* from 'Sketches at Nine Sharp' and *Snaps* from 'Spread It Abroad', all by Herbert Farjeon;
Roger McGough for *TIM* from 'The Scaffold' (Parlophone PMC 7077);
Methuen London Ltd for *Trouble in the Works* by Harold Pinter from 'Sketches from One to Another' and *At The Art Gallery* by Peter Cook and Dudley Moore from 'The Dagenham Dialogues';
Chris Miller for *How's Your Father* from 'The Two Ronnies';
Mrs Munro-Smith for *Party Political Speech* from 'The Best of Sellers' (Parlophone PMD 1069) and *Lord Badminton's Memoirs* from 'Songs for Swinging Sellers' (Parlophone PMC 1111) by Peter Munro-Smith;
Frank Muir and Denis Norden for the four *Take It From Here* sketches; *Balham* from 'Third Division' and *Common Entrance* from 'Songs for Swinging Sellers' (Parlophone PMC 1111);

David Nobbs for *Repeats* and David Nobbs and Peter Vincent for *Orgy and Less* from 'The Two Ronnies';
Michael Palin and Terry Jones for *Hendon, Forgery, Report on the Village Fete* from 'The Frost Report'; for *Hello* from 'The Two Ronnies' and Michael Palin for *Christmas Oath* from 'The Frost Report';
Nigel Rees for *Yes Folks It's Obituary Time!*;
David Renwick for *Mastermind* from 'The Two Ronnies';
Myles Rudge for *Traveller's Tale* from 'And Another Thing';
N. F. Simpson for *Gladly Otherwise* from 'Sketches from One to Another';
Peter Spence for *Lost For Words;*
Peter Vincent for *Sandwich Board* from 'The Frost Report';
Dick Vosburgh for *Secretary* from 'The Frost Report';
Keith Waterhouse and Willis Hall for *Boy Scouts* from 'Not So Much A Programme';
Gerald Wiley (Ronnie Barker) for *Doctor's Waiting Room* from 'The Frost Report';
Douglas Young and Tim Brooke-Taylor for *Pots and Puns* from 'I'm Sorry I'll Read That Again'.
And special thanks for their invaluable advice and generous sharing of their private collections for sketch material to: Ian Davidson, Doris Donnellan, John Gould, Denis Norden, Amanda Smith, Denis Stokes and Peter Titheradge.

Every effort has been made to trace copyright owners of material used in this book. Should any errors or omissions have been made, we apologise and will be pleased to make the appropriate acknowledgment in any future edition.

Introduction

At first thought it might seem a waste of good trees to print a collection of old sketches. The very word 'sketch' is defined in dictionaries as something 'unfinished', 'rough'. The OED dismisses it as 'a short play or performance of slight dramatic construction'. One is left with the feeling that sketches are superficial, unmemorable little concoctions which may give amusement, but are not worth bothering about as a dramatic or humorous form; that a sketch is to a full-length comedy what a toffee is to a four-course dinner.

There is a certain amount of truth in this, but not much. Sketches are by their nature brief, often slight and trivial, but they are an essential and valuable part of comic entertainment, and always have been. The tradition of presenting a short comical, witty, satirical or obscene dramatic piece is almost as old as comedy itself. And during the dark centuries, when for something like a thousand years the performing of public plays was suppressed, it was the *mimi* — the wandering groups who set up their platform on greens and streetcorners and sang and juggled and performed sketches lampooning the gods, lords and magistrates — who kept a tiny flickering flame of drama alight.

The birth of English drama is often believed to be the playing of Interludes during gaps in the interminable meals of Tudor times. These Interludes were short plays and sketches.

The traditional Mummers plays were broad, comical sketches.

The Mystery Plays, usually performed in segments, kept their audiences' attention by relieving the high drama and deeply religious sequences with knockabout sketches. One of these was invariably the story of Noah's Ark, in which Noah was depicted as a cheerful drunk and Noah's wife as a nagging shrew.

When, during the Civil War, the Puritans closed down all theatres and forbade the performing of plays, once more it was the 'slight', 'unfinished' sketch which kept drama going. These Civil Wartime sketches were called Drolleries and their leading light was 'the incomparable' Robert Cox, who cobbled together a mixture of dancing, mime, buffoonery and funny bits from Shakespeare. He ducked under the Puritan ropes by calling his performances a demonstration of rope-dancing. Some of his sketches, most of which he wrote himself, were happily bawdy (there is a print of Cox doing something surprising with a French loaf. Of this, Cox's publisher wrote, 'I have frequently known several of the female spectators . . . to long for it.').

During the eighteenth century the After-Piece became a part of the theatrical evening. This was a short, amusing playlet put on to send the audience home happy after sitting through, say, a five-act verse drama. It was, in essence, a sketch.

The development of pantomime and Music Hall in the nineteenth century brought about a brisk demand for sketches and, until the arrival of radio and television in our century, was perhaps the time when more sketches were played to more people than ever before.

This book is an attempt to bring the story up to date; to assemble a collection of sketches which bridges the gap between the Music Hall comedy of Harry Tate and the television comedy of The Two Ronnies, via 'little' revues, radio, LPs and *Beyond The Fringe.* It represents the sketch humour of our time (*my* time, anyway — I saw Harry Tate).

Toffee, anyone?

Frank Muir

The Book of Comedy Sketches

Harry Tate's famous sketch, *Motoring*, was hugely popular in its day and is now looked upon as a classic of the Music Hall.

It is a good example of the type of sketch which is not for general use but is material tailored to fit the style of one specific comedian.

Also it must be one of the last of the 'mini-farce' sketches which ran as long as a one-act play, had a full set, elaborate props, and a huge supporting cast all dressed up in colourful costumes.

Sketches like *Motoring*, like most pantomime sketches today, were not normally bought ready-made from a writer. They usually began with a simple idea, e.g., 'How about a sketch on golf? Pawn-shop? Haunted house? Fishing?' *Motoring* probably started life as a topical sketch: 'Motor-cars are all the rage these days – how about a sketch with a motor-car?' Harry Tate and his team would work out what could be done using a motor-car as their chief prop. Bits of business would be devised. The sketch would be given some sort of rough shape. The comedy was broad and jokes, eccentric behaviour, funny walks, etc., would be worked in. The sketch would be rehearsed and take its place in Harry Tate's repertoire. Over many years and many performances the sketch would be fined down; new business would be added and bits which did not work would be dropped. The text we have now, dating from 1918, is probably a transcript of the sketch as it ended up.

It is as difficult to appreciate the comical effect of the sketch from reading the text as it is to enjoy the flavour of a meal by reading the recipe. When reading *Motoring* we have to summon up a mental picture of Harry Tate, vast, elaborately clad as the Gentleman Motorist in knickerbockers, Norfolk jacket, goggles, sporting a wholly unconvincing clip-on moustache which swivelled as he spoke. His voice was extremely loud, and peculiar. The man who played his son also had a very odd voice; high and piercing. One of their tricks, which audiences would await and greet with delight, was their eccentric pronunciation of the word 'goodbye'. The script merely reads, 'Friend (*off*): Goodbye. Tate: Goodbye. Friend (*off*): Goodbye. Son: Goodbye . . . (*Goodbyes ad lib*). In practice, Tate and his son let out tremendous shrieks of 'Goooood-BYEEEEEEEEEEEEE!!' which went on for minutes on end.

It is easy to understand the popularity with Music Hall audiences of this kind of grand theatrical production, before the cinema, radio and television diffused their need for a magical, escapist, hilarious Night Out.

MOTORING

by Harry Tate

SCENE represents a typical London street with battered old car outside Tate's house. Tate is in the driver's seat, his son beside him, and a supercilious chauffeur sits in the rear.

Friend (*off*): Hi! Hi! Hi! Hi!
Tate Hullo, old man, how are you?
Friend (*off*): Fine, thanks. Where are you off to?
Tate I'm just going down to Portsmouth (*localize*) taking my son back to the Naval College.
Friend (*off*): That's funny, I'm going down there too.
Tate Well, why not join us?
Friend (*off*): I can't very well, I've got the wife and family with me.
Tate Well, bring the wife too, there's plenty of room along the side of my son, we can put the family in the tool box. (*To* Chauffeur.) Open that box, will you?
Friend (*off*): No, no, no. Don't trouble, old man, I'll meet you down there.
Tate All right, I'll meet you down there.
Friend (*off*): How long will it take you to get there?
Tate Oh, I don't know; how many miles is it?
Friend (*off*): Oh, about ninety miles.
Tate Ninety miles, oh, about half an hour, I suppose.
Friend (*off*): Half an hour! That's a terrible speed, isn't it?
Tate Oh no, that's only half speed; of course if the roads were straight, we could do it in about a quarter of an hour or fifteen minutes.
Friend (*off*): Oh, I see. I suppose you thoroughly understand these cars?
Tate Every nut. What I don't know about it isn't worth knowing; besides I have a very reliable man here, if I tell him to do anything, I do it myself, and I know he's done it.
Friend (*off*): And what is your opinion of motoring?
Tate Oh, there's nothing like it.
Friend (*off*): Ah! but suppose you break down?
Tate Then there's nothing like it.
Friend (*off*): It's a wonder to me you aren't afraid of being killed.
Tate Oh, I don't care a d— — —
Friend (*off*): Well, goodbye, old man.
Tate Goodbye — I'll be down there long before you, I'll order lunch.
Friend (*off*): Thanks.
Tate What will you have, grouse or bread and dripping?
Friend (*off*): Oh! both thanks. Well, I'll see you down there.
Tate All right I'll see you down there.
Friend (*off*): Goodbye.
Tate Goodbye.
Friend (*off*): Goodbye.
Son Goodbye.
Friend (*off*): Goodbye.

} *These goodbyes are shouted.*

(*Goodbyes ad lib.* Tate *and* Chauffeur *biz, with levers, getting wild.*)

Tate It's all right, we've a self-starter.
Friend (*off*): Goodbye.
Son Good—

(Tate *turns round and knocks boy's hat off.*)

Chauffeur Why, sir, you've got the brakes on.
Tate Which is the brake?
Chauffeur (*points to a lever*): That's the brake, sir.
Tate (*laughing to* Friend *off*): Oh, I had the brake on. (*To* Son.) Why didn't you tell me, you little fool? We might have run into something. (*Biz pulling levers, etc. — all to no purpose.*) What's the matter now? Have you got any oil in that lamp?

(*Enter Motorist's* Wife.)

Wife Good gracious! Haven't you started yet?
Tate Yes, my dear, we've started and —
Wife (*very voluble*): I knew it — I knew it — you'll never get the boy there in time. I told you not to do it — I knew what would happen — don't say I didn't tell you, because I did. Here you are stuck in the middle of the road when you ought to be half way there by now.

(Son *laughs very loudly.*)

Wife Don't laugh — you idiot — you'll grow up to be as big a fool as your father.
Tate Madam, can't you see it's stopped?
Wife Of course it is — you'd stop anything. That boy is supposed to be in school tomorrow morning. He won't be there by tomorrow week. Do something, man — do something — twiddle it — turn the handle — turn the handle.
Tate Oh, turn the handle! — this isn't a barrel organ.
Wife I know that, because you're not on top — I'm going down to the school to let them know whose fault it is.

(*Going.*)

Tate Nonsense, we shall be there hours before you.
Wife No you won't, I'm going to walk it. (*Exit.*)

(Chauffeur *looks disgusted.*)

Tate (*to imaginary man*): Hi, get out of the way there, do you want to get run over, and then come on to me for damages? (*Revolver fired behind car.*) (*To* Son.) Did you touch anything?
Son No, Pa Pa.

(*Shot fired behind car.*)

Tate (*gets out of car: while doing so says*): It's no use, the whole thing will have to come down. (*Goes to front of car, and takes book off the bonnet.*) Have you been taking any friends out in this car?
Chauffeur No, no, no, no, no, no, no. Oh dear me, no, no, no, no.
Tate Brought it straight out of the garage?
Chauffeur Yes, yes, yes, yes. Oh, yes, yes, yes, yes.

(*Keeps on indefinitely.*)

Tate One yes is quite sufficient. I don't want a hundred and fifty answers to every question; we shall never get there.
Son Isn't it annoying, Pa Pa?
Tate Yes, it's more than annoying.
Son Pa Pa!
Tate Yes; my son, what is it?
Son Would you mind stopping while I pick up my hat?
Tate (*very annoyed*): Where's your hat?
Son On the floor.
Tate On the ground. Don't you know the difference between the floor and the ground? Pick it up. (*To* Chauffeur.) Hand me the screw hammer.

(Chauffeur *hands axe.*)

Tate Is this all you've brought?
Chauffeur Yes, sir.
Tate Where's the tool box?
Chauffeur Well, sir, to speak expleasantly, I forgot it.
Tate Thanks, I'm very much obliged. What's the use of this? I'm not out chopping wood.

(*Revolver shot behind car.*)

(*Note* — Chauffeur *can fire all shots without audience seeing him do so.*)

Tate (*picking up large book labelled 'How to Drive a Motor'*). What page is that?
Chauffeur Page eight, sir.
Tate It's torn out.
Chauffeur Try nine, sir.
Tate It's the same page.

(*Enter* Man.)

Man Hullo, what are you trying to do? Milk it?

(*Exit* Man.)

Tate I suppose he thinks it's a cow.

(*Goes in front of car and turns handle. Enter* Boy *with mouth organ, business round car.* Harry Tate *pushes boy away.*)

Tate Come out of the way, boy, how many more times, go home and tell your mother I hate the sight of you.
Son Isn't it annoying, Pa Pa?
Tate (*very angry*): If you say that again, you'll have to walk; put your hat on straight, boy; what have you been doing to it? It's too long for you, it's all full of dents.
Son The Chauffeur ran over it, Pa Pa.
Chauffeur I didn't do anything of the kind.
Son You did.
Chauffeur I didn't.

Son You did.

(*They keep on 'You did' — 'I didn't' as rapidly as possible till interrupted.*)

Tate How long does this conversation last? Did you run over the hat?
Chauffeur Certainly not, sir.

Son You did.
Chauffeur I did not.

(*Ad lib. as before 'You did' — 'I did not.'*)

Tate Don't start it again, I know it all by now, and don't you come out in that hat again, you look a damn fool in it, where did you get it? It's a rotten hat.
Son It's yours, Pa Pa.
Tate Well, I like your impudence, how dare you come out with my hat?
Son I found it in your study, Pa Pa.
Tate Well, kindly let it stop in the study. (*To* Chauffeur.) What is the matter with the confounded thing? Here have I to get this boy to college, and we are here looking at this pug-nosed monkey (*indicating urchin*). Where do you come in?
Chauffeur Well, sir, to speak expleasantly —
Tate To what?
Chauffeur To speak expleasantly.
Tate Are you aware there isn't such a word? (*To* Son.) Correct him, Roland.
Son It's expleasantplosh, Pa Pa.
Tate It's nothing of the kind, you're worse than he is.
Chauffeur Well, sir, it's the sprockets, they are not running true with the differential gear, and that causes the exhaust box to short circuit with the magneto ignition on the commutator, I don't think.
Tate What do you mean, 'I don't think'?
Chauffeur Well, sir, I don't think the sprockets are running true.
Son No, no, no, no, no, it's nothing of the kind, Pa Pa.
Tate What's nothing of the kind?
Son What he said.
Tate Well, he's said nothing yet. What's the matter with you?
Chauffeur With all due deference to your son —
Tate I don't want you to talk about my son, I want to know what's wrong with the car.
Chauffeur As I said before, sir, it's the sprockets, they are not running true with —
Son No, no, no, no, no.

(Son *and* Chauffeur *both go on speaking while* Tate *is holding axe to him.*)

Tate Don't all speak at once; can't you see I'm busy?
Son It is not so, Pa Pa.
Tate Well, what is it?
Son It's the wheels that are not round.
Tate Surely these wheels are round (*looking at wheels*).
Son Oh, yes, they are round.
Tate What do you mean they are round, and they are not round?
Son I mean they are not *going* round.

(Tate *gets mad — business with* Tate *holding his fist up to* Son, *etc.*)

Chauffeur Well, sir, I say once again, the sprockets are not running true with the differential gear, and that causes the exhaust box to short circuit with the magneto ignition on the commutator — I don't think.

Tate Oh, don't keep saying 'I don't think'. You want to say I don't think at the commencement of a sentence, not at the finish of it. I don't think it's this, or I don't think it's that. Fancy me going to college and saying to the head master, 'Oh, here's my son, I don't think.' Why the man would think I was a raving lunatic.

Chauffeur I know what I'm talking about.

Tate Yes; and so do I.

(*Enter* Man *who looks over car, etc., examines it very critically — walks off without speaking.*)

Boy (*very loudly*): That was my school teacher, Pa Pa.

Tate Well, he's an ass. (*To* Chauffeur.) You say this is short squirting?

Chauffeur No, no, sir, short circuiting on the commutator.

Tate Where is the commutator?

Chauffeur I don't know, sir, but I've heard 'em talk about it.

(*Enter two* Ladies.)

First Lady (*looking at occupants of car*): What extraordinary creatures.

Second Lady Hush! dear. Some of the circus folk I expect.

First Lady (*to* Tate): Pardon me, is this the way to the fair?

Tate (*perplexed*): Well — I — er — I —

Second Lady (*to first — aside*): This is the fair I expect.

First Lady Oh! of course. (*To* Tate.) What time do you start?

(Tate *is dumbfounded.*)

Son Papa, the lady wants to know what time we start.

Tate That's what *I* want to know.

First Lady Is this a merry-go-round?

Tate No! It's a *won't* go round.

Second Lady *I* know. It's one of those knife-grinding affairs. Oh! I wish I had a pair of scissors.

First Lady Shall we give the poor man something?

Second Lady I haven't any coppers.

First Lady All I have is a ha'penny.

Second Lady Never mind. I daresay he'll be glad of that.

First Lady (*giving halfpenny*): There you are, my poor man. Good-day.

(*Exeunt* Ladies.)

Tate (*with coin in hand*): Well, I'm — a ha'penny — a ha'penny. What did she mean by that?

Son She thought she was buying the car.

(*Enter* Son's Friend.)

Friend Hullo.
Son Hullo.

(*They shake hands.* Tate *looks worried, scratches his head.*)

Son (*introducing his friend*): My Pa Pa, Master Turvey.

(Son's Friend *and* Tate *shake hands.*)

Tate Oh! er — pleased to meet you.
Friend Bonjour.
Tate What?
Friend Bonjour.
Tate What did he say? 'What's yours'?
Friend Qu'est ce que c'est.
Tate What?
Son He's trying to speak French, Pa Pa. *Qu'est ce que c'est.*
Tate What is it?
Son Yes.
Tate Does he mean me?
Son Yes.

(Tate *goes after boy who retreats backwards.*)

Tate What is it, indeed; look at him, looks like a bottle of ink.
Son Pa Pa, will you give him a lift?
Tate I'll give you a lift in a minute.

(Son *motions to his* Friend *to get in car. He does so.*)

Tate (*to* Chauffeur): Something has got to be done.
Son I think I've found it out, Pa Pa.
Tate You have. Well, what is it? You ought to know something about it, being a submarine designer.
Son Well, I don't wish to say anything derogatory against Mr —

(*Meaning* Chauffeur.)

Tate (*introducing them*): Oh, this is my son. My son, Mr Gherkin Brownjohn.

(Chauffeur *and* Son *shake hands.*)

Son Well, I don't wish to hurt Mr Gherkin Brownjohn's feelings.
Tate Brownjohn is sufficient; leave the gherkin out.
Son Well, I don't wish to hurt Mr Brownjohn's feelings.
Tate No—o.
Son But by no meithorium of the colossal mathematics—
Tate Oh! My dear boy I simply want to know what's the matter with the car.
Son We're broken down, Pa Pa.
Tate I know that, you silly boy, isn't that the very point I'm driving at? What has broken down?
Son It's very difficult to explain, Pa Pa.

Tate Well, explain the difficulty.
Son It's the co-efficient of the tangent.
Tate Co-efficient of the tangent, what the devil are you talking about?
Son Yes, the co-efficient of the tangent, 3 Pi R. but yours are 4 Pi R.
Tate So we've got a Pie too many.
Son Yes.
Tate Then your friend had better get out. (*To* Chauffeur.) You heard what he said.
Chauffeur Yes, sir.
Tate Well, what do you think about it?
Chauffeur (*not sure of his ground*): They're very expensive.
Tate What are?
Chauffeur What he said.
Tate What did he say?
Chauffeur Ask him.
Tate Ask him! Do you think I pay you to ask him things?
Son They can't be bought, Pa Pa.
Tate Of course they can't. (*To* Chauffeur.) What a silly ass you are.
Son It's twenty-two over seven.
Tate What is?
Son Co-efficient of the tangent.
Tate I see.
Son You see, three sevens are twenty-one.
Tate What the dickens are you talking about?
Son Three sevens are twenty-one.
Tate Well, what's that got to do with twenty-two over seven?
Son Well, you can't go.
Tate Three sevens are twenty-one and you can't go?
Son No, you must borrow one.
Tate Borrow one?
Son You see, this car won't go.
Tate That's the very point I'm driving at; now we are coming to something.
Son Well, you must borrow one.

(Tate *goes for* Son, *knocks his hat off, etc.*)

Tate (*to* Urchin): Why don't you go home? Go home and tell your Mother I hate the sight of you.
Friend Excuse me, pardon me.
Tate Oh, is this fellow going to start again? I don't know what you want to bring him for, wearing the tyres out. What do you want?
Friend Might I ask a question?
Tate Well, I don't expect you are going to ask an answer.
Friend Could you tell me, what is that that turns and never moves?
Tate What?
Friend What is that that turns and never moves?
Tate How can it turn if it doesn't move?
Friend Milk.
Tate Milk?

Friend Yes.
Tate (*to* Son's Friend): Get out of the car.

(Tate *bends down in front of car,* Urchin *picks up motor horn and blows it. All look round to see who is coming.* Urchin *blows again.*)

Tate I thought he was coming this way.

(*Detects* Urchin *with horn, pushes him over. A revolver shot is fired.* Tate *kicks car.* Man *walks past, strikes a match on car and lights his cigarette and walks off.* Son *and* Friend *laugh loudly,* Tate *throws his coat at them, goes to front of car.* Son, Friend *and* Chauffeur *start singing.* Tate *gets up and threatens them.*)

Chauffeur There's no spark, sir.
Tate What?
Chauffeur There's no spark, sir.

(Tate *stoops down,* Urchin *puts cracker under his heel, cracker explodes.* Tate *rushes at* Chauffeur *and they spar.* Tate *gets under car, revolver fires.* Tate *gets up with eye blacked.*)

Chauffeur Why, whatever is the matter, sir?
Tate Matter! I got my eye in the gear box. It's no use, we'll have to push the confounded thing. (*To* Urchin.) Hi, boy, give us a push.

(*All get out of car and start to push.*)

(*Enter* Policeman.)

Policeman Stop!

(*All look in amazement.*)

Policeman Now then, sir, I want your name and address, licence and number.
Tate What for?
Policeman For furious driving.
Tate Furious driving? Why, my dear fellow, we've been stuck here for the last half an hour.

(*All argue.* Tate *pushes* Urchin *away. In doing so he gets hold of* Urchin's *cap and puts it on.* Urchin *puts* Tate's *cap on.* Tate *discovers it, pulls it off, puts it on over the* Urchin's *cap,* Urchin *kicks* Tate, Policeman *collars* Chauffeur. *Car falls over.*)

Curtain.

(*Note: In all cases the revolver shots are fired to represent explosions, back-fires, etc., in mechanism of car.*)

* * *

The English have always admired word-play, as Shakespeare was well aware. 'Admire' seems to be the right word, because the following concoction is admirable in its ingenious play on permutations of 'knock', 'knack' and 'knick' without reading very funnily. But it was written for performance rather than reading. From the groundlings of Shakespeare's days to the Music Hall goers of 1913, audiences respected a comedian who could juggle with the language. It was as though audiences felt that they were being complimented on their intelligence rather than being talked down to.

Unlike Harry Tate's *Motoring*, this is a sketch written by a professional writer of monologues and it stands up by itself; any comedian could have a go at it. If a comic had a particularly strong comedy character he might have a go at playing the piece slowly and realistically for laughs but most performers would have belted into it at breakneck speed and gone for a huge round of applause at the end.

NICHOLAS KNOX, OF NOTTINGHAM

by Charles J. Winter

Nicholas Knox — commonly known as Nick Knox — was employed at the shop of a knick-knack dealer in Nottingham named Nathan Knight, who was known amongst his friends as Nat Knight. Now as Nick Knox had to be early at Nat Knight's, he engaged a knocker-up named Nicodemus Noakes, to knock him up. Nicodemus Noakes, familiarly known as Nicky Noakes, knowing that knocking up required a knack, engaged another knocker-up who happened to be knock-kneed, to knock *him* up, so that being knocked up, he could knock up Nick Knox.

Well it happened that one morning the knock-kneed knocker-up, not knowing the time, did not knock up Nicky Noakes, and Nicky Noakes, not being knocked up by the knock-kneed knocker-up, failed to knock up Nick Knox, so that Nick Knox, not being knocked up, was not at Nat Knight's in time; thereupon Nat Knight knocked off some of the wages of Nick Knox, and Nick Knox next got even by nicking some of the knick-knacks belonging to Nat Knight. In addition to this, Nick Knox nagged Nicky Noakes for not knocking him up, and Nicky Noakes retaliated by knocking the knock-kneed knocker-up down, and the knocker-up who was knock-kneed, being knocked down, felt knocked up.

Some people said that no knick-knacks had been nicked from Nat Knight's; others could not say whether Nick Knox had nicked knick-knacks from Nat Knight, or Nicky Noakes had nicked the knick-knacks from Nick Knox, or whether the knock-kneed knocker-up had knocked at the knocker of Nat Knight's and next nicked his knick-knacks. But it was proved that knick-knacks *had* been nicked from Nat Knight, either by Nick Knox or by the knock-kneed knocker-up who never knocked up Nicky Noakes, the Nottingham knocker-up. The matter was taken before a magistrate.

Of course Nick Knox said that not having the knack, he had not nicked Nat Knight's knick-knacks, and Nicky Noakes said that he had nicked nix from Nick Knox, and the Nottingham knock-kneed knocker-up next said that he had not nicked never no knick-knacks neither from Nat Knight, Nick Knox, nor Nicky Noakes; so the puzzle was to find out how Nat Knight's knick-knacks had been nicked.

The magistrate said it was not for the jury to decide whether Nick Knox was as much to blame as Nicky Noakes, or whether Nicky Noakes was as bad as the knock-kneed knocker-up; the question was — had Noakes nicked? or had Nick Knox nicked? or were the knick-knacks nicked by the knock-kneed knocker-up? He would state the case clearly and lucidly — it was simply that the knock-kneed knocker-up had not knocked up Nicky Noakes, and the said Nicky Noakes, not being knocked up by the knock-kneed knocker-up, had failed to knock up Nick Knox, so that Nick Knox did not knock at the knocker of Nat Knight the Nottingham knick-knack dealer in time; and next it was found that knick-knacks had been nicked from Nat Knight either by Nick Knox, Nicky Noakes or the knock-kneed knocker-up who had not knocked Nicky Noakes up.

The jury, finding the matter so simple, came at once to an arrangement which suited all parties, and so now the knock-kneed knocker-up has acquired the knack of knocking up Nicky Noakes, who in his turn knocks up Nick Knox, and Nick Knox next knocks at the knocker of Nat Knight the Nottingham knick-knack dealer in good time every morning.

* * *

This sketch — what used to be called a 'skit' — must have been one of the first to mock Russian drama. It is dated 1922 and is probably a reflection of the popular reaction to a season of Chekhov's plays produced in London in 1919 and 1920. The critics and public thought the plays 'excessively gloomy'.

There have been many parodies of the gloomy Russian play since, but none have bettered this splendid piece.

GLOOM; OR, THE OLD GREY BARN

by E. Preston

Scene: A room in a Russian house.

(Maria *crouches by the fire, stirring a small saucepan.* Elizaveta *stands looking out of the window. There is a table in the centre of the stage.*)

Elizaveta. It is very cold outside.
Maria. It is cold in here. The fire is dying. (*They sigh. A pause.*) Is anyone coming yet?
Elizaveta. No, not yet.
Maria. They will not come till too late.
Elizaveta. The snow is very heavy. It reminds me of the day when Vladimir Vladimirovitch hanged himself in the old grey barn.

(*They sigh heavily. A slight pause.*)

Maria. The fire will soon be dead.
Elizaveta. Someone is coming. It is my brother and three others. I must welcome them to this unhappy house. (*Exit.*)

Maria (*stirring saucepan*). Dmitri Petrovitch and three others. (*Counting slowly on fingers.*) One, two, three, four, five, six. Six to supper. And Yonsky. There will not be enough. (*Sighs.*) There is never enough.

(*Enter* Elizaveta, Ivan, Nadia, Serge, *and* Dmitri. Nadia *and* Serge *stand by the fire,* Elizaveta *returns to the window,* Ivan *and* Dmitri *seat themselves at the table.* Ivan *buries his face in his hands.*)

Elizaveta. Why have you not brought Vassili Mikhailovitch?
Dmitri. He hanged himself yesterday in a barn.
Elizaveta. Whose barn?
Dmitri. The Copski's barn. (*They all sigh.*)
Nadia. It was very cold coming here. I am very cold.
Elizaveta. It is cold in here.
Serge. Put your hands to the fire, Nadia.
Maria. What is the use? It is nearly out.

(Nadia *crouches by* Maria.)

Nadia. That is a little better.
Maria. Now, I cannot cook the supper. It does not matter. (*Sighs.*) There will not be enough.
Dmitri. There is never enough.
Ivan (*raising his head*). I do not need much. I am not hungry.
Serge. Neither am I.
Elizaveta. Here is the postman. I expect he brings bad news. I will go and see. (*Exit.*)
Dmitri. It is getting dark. Maria, light the lamp.
Maria. There is no oil.
Dmitri. There is never any oil.
Serge. It is better in the dark.

(*A pause.* Ivan *sighs deeply.*)

Nadia. Elizaveta is a long time. It is bad news.
Ivan. It is always bad news.

(*Enter* Elizaveta, *reading a letter.*)

Dmitri. It is bad news?
Elizaveta. Yes.
Nadia. I said so. Who is it from?
Elizaveta. It is from the Letoff's. Seymon has hanged himself in their barn.
Serge. Which barn?
Elizaveta. The red one. (*They sigh heavily.*)
Nadia. Elizaveta, I must speak. I came here to ask you a favour.
Elizaveta. I have little to give, but I will do for you what I can.
Nadia. You know, Elizaveta, my parents live in the town. Our house is very small. We have no barn. (*Sighs.*)
Elizaveta. Well?
Nadia. I wish to hang myself, and I want to know whether I may borrow your barn — the old grey one.

Elizaveta. Of course you may, my dear Nadia. I am only too glad to be able to oblige you.
Nadia. Thank you, dear Elizaveta. Is it free now?
Elizaveta. I am not sure. I will find out. Maria, call Yonsky.

(Maria *goes to door and calls* 'Yonsky! Yonsky!')

(*Enter* Yonsky.)

Yonsky. You called me?
Elizaveta. Is the old grey barn empty?
Yonsky. Yes, quite empty, mistress. It has been empty since Vladimir Vladimirovitch hanged himself there last week.
Elizaveta. Thank you, Yonsky. You may go.

(*Exit* Yonsky.)

Nadia. Then I will go. Good-bye, Serge, Dmitri, Ivan, Elizaveta, Maria.
All. Good-bye, Nadia.

(*Exit* Nadia.)

Maria (*stirring in saucepan*). More room at the fire now. And one less to supper. Perhaps there will be enough.
Dmitri. There is never enough.
Elizaveta. It is snowing again.
Ivan. That snow comes from Siberia.
Serge. It has crossed the Steppes.
Dmitri. Think what a lot of barns it has fallen upon.
Ivan. And what a lot of people were hanging in them.
Elizaveta. It is getting darker.

(*A pause.* Serge *sighs, gets up and goes to door.*)

Dmitri. Where are you going, Serge?
Serge. I am going to hang myself in the old grey barn.
Dmitri. Very well. Good-bye.
Elizaveta. Shut the door. There is a draught.

(*Exit* Serge.)

Maria. One more gone. That leaves one (*counting on fingers*) one, two, three, four, five to supper. (*Examining saucepan.*) I believe there will be enough.
Ivan. Surely it is getting colder.
Maria. Yes, the fire is dying. Yonsky says it is much warmer in the old grey barn than in here.

(*A pause.* Ivan *sighs heavily and gets up.*)

Elizaveta. You are going to the old grey barn, Ivan?
Ivan. Yes, it is better. It is warmer there, and there will be more supper for you.
Dmitri. You are going to hang yourself?
Ivan. Oh yes.

Elizaveta. Good-bye, then.
Ivan. Good-bye. I will shut the door because of the draught.

(*Exit* Ivan.)

Elizaveta. It has stopped snowing. The wolves are howling in the forest.
Dmitri. They are hungry. Is supper ready, Maria?
Maria. Not yet, Master.
Dmitri. It is a long time. Hark at the wolves!
Elizaveta. Our guests are all gone, Dmitri. Is it right that we should stay on here?
Dmitri. It is not right. But must we go to the old grey barn?
Elizaveta. Why not?
Dmitri. Would not the white barn be better?
Elizaveta. No, it has no beams strong enough.
Dmitri. Very well, then. Let us go.
Elizaveta. To the old grey barn. It will be better. Good-bye, Maria. The rats will come out soon to keep you company.
Maria. Good-bye, Mistress. Good-bye, Master.

(*Exeunt* Elizaveta *and* Dmitri.)

(Maria *takes saucepan off fire, empties contents on two plates and places them on the table. Goes to door and calls:* 'Yonsky! Yonsky!')

(*Enter* Yonsky.)

Maria. Come. They are all gone.
Yonsky (*shaking his head*). I do not like it. It is too full.
Maria. What is too full? Your plate?
Yonsky. No, the old grey barn. There are too many. They are in rows.
Maria. Never mind. Come, eat your supper. There is plenty now. (*They eat.*)
Yonsky. Hark at the wolves!
Maria. Yes. It is very cold. (*They eat.*)

Curtain.

* * *

As the 'revue' form of theatre became increasingly popular in the 1920s, there was a brisk demand for sketches which could be played by any members of the company. This resulted in what might be called the Sketch of Ideas. The usual form was for the revue's compère to come in front of the curtain and explain the idea behind the sketch, which would then be played by the company.

Some of the ideas were distinctly odd and were, one suspects, born of desperation and whisky on the pre-London tour. The following depends on the proposition that the cast had been robbed of all costumes except shoes and socks.

FOOTSTEPS: A DRAMA IN SEVERAL FEET

by Herbert C. Sargent

Note: The Orchestra must play well-known appropriate airs throughout the explanation.

The Compère *enters in front of Tabs, and addresses the* Audience.

I am desired by the Management to crave your indulgence for any shortcomings in the next scene. There has been a most unfortunate contretemps.

(Turns as though addressing someone in stalls.)

Yes, sir, I *do* know how to spell that last word.

(To Audience.*)*

All the costumes for this scene have been stolen from the dressing-rooms, and all that are left are the shoes and stockings.

Now I am quite aware that, in some revues, costumes have been reduced to a minimum, but, even so, when it comes to only shoes and — well, I ask you!

Anyway, we've got to have this scene, so we have decided to play it in a somewhat unusual manner.

The performers will go through the action, but for obvious reasons the curtain will be raised only sufficiently to enable you to see the feet and — er — so forth of the actors and actresses. (*Confidentially.*) I call 'em actors and actresses because they're behind there listening, but they're only revue artistes really.

As you might find it difficult to follow the story with only footnotes, as it were, I propose to explain it as it goes along.

The play is a pathetic drama of real life, in six scenes. The title is *Footsteps,* or *From Nurse Maid to Crouch End,* by a well-known author who prefers to remain incog., and I don't blame him.

The first scene is a Quiet Corner in Hyde Park, where only the sound of plain clothes policemen's feet scrunching the gravel disturbs the calm.

(The curtain is raised about two feet.)

It is a beautiful summer morning. The birds are singing sweetly. They hop upon the grass, picking up worms and lost hairpins.

(A large pair of bird's legs are seen to hop across the stage.)

Our heroine, *Gertrude Gherkin,* enters wheeling her little charges in their pram.

(A pram is wheeled on by a Girl *wearing very smart shoes and stockings.)*

She is a poor, but honest nursemaid, who, out of her tiny pittance, contrives to support an aged mother, and silk stockings. The aged mother you must take my word for, but the — well, look for yourselves.

Gertrude is beloved by a Policeman. Wherever his beat may be, his heart beats only for her. Hark! he comes.

(A pair of Policeman's *feet are seen.)*

He sees *Gertrude,* and starts back with surprise and joy. She sees him, and is coy.

(Business with feet.)

He goes to her, and shakes hands. Once more he presses his suit, once more she is forced to tell him that she loves another. He writhes with anguish.

(Business.)

He drops a manly tear.

(Marble falls.)

Then, pulling himself together, he proceeds upon his lonely beat.

(Exit Policeman.*)*

Why, you may ask, or you may not, why does *Gertrude* spurn the love of this good man? Ah! *I* know. It is because she is enamoured of *Jack Turrett,* the bold A.B. of His Majesty's Navy. She is expecting to meet him, otherwise she wouldn't have turned the P.C. down so hurriedly. See! She starts! Can it be? It is!

(Aside.)

Of course it is. It is her lover, *Jack.*

(Enter Sailor's *feet.)*

He hastens to her. They embrace over the perambulator.

(The pram is seen to rock violently.)

Gertrude's little charges have a stormy passage. *Jack* has come to tell her that he sails at once, and that he will be away for at least three days.

(Aside.)

The Navy mustn't waste coal these times.

(To Audience.*)*

Duty calls!

(Bugle call.)

He leaves her.

(Business.)

No, he cannot tear himself away.

(He returns. Repeat bugle call.)

Ah! He goes.

(Business.)

No, he returns.

(Business, which can be repeated until Sailor *exits.)*

Thank goodness, he *has* gone this time.

Gertrude sinks on to a seat. She bursts into tears and then into a profuse perspiration at the thought that she may have to pay tuppence for the chair.

But who is this?

(A Man, *dressed in very smart socks and shoes, enters.)*

It is *Lord Stickphast,* the notorious roué. You can tell he is a roué by his socks. He sees the beautiful *Gertrude* in tears and a becoming uniform. In a moment his eagle eye observes the second chair, by her side. He seizes the opportunity, and regardless of the cost, takes the chair.

(Sits in chair near Gertrude. *She draws her chair away, about two inches.)*

See, the startled fawn, shrinks instinctively from the roué's ruse.

(She drops her handkerchief.)

Ah! The poor child has dropped her handkerchief.

(Addressing a member of the Audience.*)*

Of course it was an accident. How dare you suggest that —

(To Audience.*)*

Lord Stickphast seizes the handkerchief, and returns it to *Gertrude.* He speaks, she bashfully replies. You can tell she is bashful by the trembling of her glacé kids. The persistent peer proceeds to persecute her.

(Business. He presses her foot with his. She withdraws her foot, then advances it again.)

Alas! the simple maiden is in the Serpent's toils.

*(*Park Keeper *enters and collects money for chairs.)*

The reckless libertine squanders his gold upon her. He rises to his feet. He is about to leave her, but before he goes he makes her promise to go with him to a dance club. He describes this haunt of vice in glowing colours.

*(*Man *does a few dance steps.)*

Who is this that enters unobserved?

*(*Policeman's *feet enter.)*

It is the faithful P.C. He sees what is going on. Shall he interfere? No, it is no part of a policeman's duty to arrest one of the aristocracy for speaking to a lady in Hyde Park.

He creeps away to warn *Jack Turrett,* if he can find him, for he knows that *Jack* is his successful rival, and that it is *Jack's* duty to shield his sweetheart from harm.

The first scene finishes with the parting between *Lord Stickphast* and poor *Gertrude.* You may observe that the artful aristocrat has been successful in his evil plans by the jaunty manner in which he walks away from his victim.

(There is a short Black Out.)

The next scene is the Nonsuch Night Club. The midnight revels are at their height. Intoxicated with ginger ale, and air balloons, the reckless revellers are dancing to the strains of the Mississippi Music Mutilators.

(Curtain rises two feet. A jazz band is playing, and the feet of dancers are seen.)

Into this scene of guilty gaiety *Lord Stickphast* enters with the guileless *Gertrude*. The observant spectator will notice that *Gertrude* has changed her hose. But do not misjudge her, for many an honest corn throbs beneath a silken stocking.

He persuades her to dance, and such is her grace and skill that all the other dancers stand aside to gaze upon this fair unknown. It is a Terpsichorean triumph.

(Aside.)

My word, what a mouthful!

(To Audience.*)*

The faithful P.C. has been unable to find *Jack Turrett*, so, disguising himself as a Man about Town, he has followed *Gertrude*. See, he enters.

(Pair of enormous feet in pumps and striped cotton socks.)

Alas! His well-meaning efforts are in vain. The keen eye of the Manager has noted his feet. In a moment he realizes that the police are on his track. Instantly the place is plunged in darkness.

(Black Out.)

And his guests make their escape.
Lord Stickphast carries off *Gertrude*.

The next scene is the street outside the Club.

(Lights up.)

The dancers are making their escape.

*(*Girls' *and* Men's *legs are seen running across stage.)*

Lord Stickphast and *Gertrude* enter. He hails a taxi. It stops.

(Wheels seen.)

He almost throws *Gertrude* into the cab, and shouts directions to the driver.

At that moment the faithful P.C. enters, and overhears the address which *Lord Stickphast* has given.

Too late to stop the cab, he resolves to follow.

(Galloping movement of P.C.'s *feet.)*

At that moment *Jack Turrett* enters.

(Very drunken Sailor's *legs seen.)*

Jack has missed his boat, owing to being delayed by important business not unconnected with the licensed victuallers' industry,

The P.C. recognizes his successful rival and stops him. He urges *Jack* to pull himself together.

(Business.)

Jack does so, and the P.C. tells him where he may find *Gertrude,* and bids him waste no time or it may be *too late!*

*(*Jack *is seen to try to hurry in a very zigzag fashion. Black Out.)*

Our next scene is an Opium Den in Limehouse. On the right is the den. Across the stage from back to front is the wall of the room with a window in it, outside which is the dark and silent Thames. You'll have to imagine this, as we can't show you much of the scene.

(Lights up.)

It is night, and the opium smokers are indulging in their disgusting orgies. *Hop See,* the proprietor of the den, is attending to his customers.

*(*Chinaman's *legs seen.)*

Lord Stickphast and *Gertrude* enter. *Hop See* recognizes *Lord Stickphast* as an old customer, and welcomes him. *Lord Stickphast* draws him aside, and whispers some orders, while *Gertrude* stands in startled terror. The artful Asiatic is told what to do, and while the unsuspecting *Gertrude* is sitting with the wicked peer, eating bird-nest soup, under the impression that it is porridge, he creeps behind her, and claps a handkerchief soaked in chloroform to her mouth.

She struggles for a moment, but soon falls into insensibility. The wicked *Lord* laughs in triumph. No one can save her now, he murmurs. He takes the insensible girl in his arms, and carries her towards an inner chamber. But suddenly he stops. What was that? Someone at the window! There is a crash of broken glass!

(Glass falls.)

The iron bars are wrenched away like so many matches.

(About fifty iron bars fall on stage.)

And *Jack Turrett* springs lightly into the room. The Chinaman rushes at him with a knife, but *Jack,* with a smashing blow on his jaw, puts him to sleep, while his knife falls to the ground. *Lord Stickphast* has tried to creep away with his lovely burden, but *Jack* springs upon him, like an angry tiger. He seizes *Stickphast,* and a struggle for life ensues.

(A big struggle, furniture seen to fall, etc.)

Lord Stickphast snatches up the fallen knife, but *Jack* avoids his thrust, and with a superhuman effort lifts the villain off his feet and hurls him through the window into the river. It so happens that it is low tide, and we are therefore able to see *Lord Stickphast's* end. Head first in the mud, he meets a dirty death.

(A pair of legs are seen sticking up from the mud.)

Jack seizes his senseless sweetheart, and carries her off to safety.

(Black Out.)

We now arrive at our epilogue.

The scene is *Jack's* cottage in the little village of Crouch End a year later. It will be understood that he and *Gertrude* were married quite soon after the rescue from the Opium Den. Don't forget that *please.* It is 4 a.m. on a winter's morning.

(Lights up.)

This scene speaks for itself. In case you may wonder where our heroine is, I may mention that she is asleep in bed.

(Orchestra plays 'Jack's the Boy for Work.' The legs of a double bed are seen. There are two cradles. Jack's *bare feet and pyjamas or night-shirt are seen, as he sits between the cradles, rocking them. There is a sound of babies crying.* Jack *drops a feeding-bottle, and says 'Damn' as the* Curtain *falls.)*

* * *

This must have started out as yet another Ideas sketch, and an unpromisingly mechanical idea at that, in which every word of the dialogue had to begin with the letter 'w'.

In fact, perhaps because the Co-optimists were such a successful and gifted company, it turned out to be a very good sketch indeed; a model of what these things should be. The idea is ingeniously developed, there are lots of incidental laughs as the sketch builds up, and there is a satisfying payoff.

'WOW WOW!'

by Basil Charlton

Scene: Wheatsheaf, Woolwich. Winter. Restaurant tables laid for dinner in accordance to space.

Manager (speaking in front of the curtain). The sketch which is about to be produced is the outcome of a bet. A well-known manager bet the author that he could not write an actable sketch in which every word of the dialogue commenced with the same letter of the Alphabet. The letter chosen was 'W'.

*(*Walter *and* Winnie *discovered at table (centre).* Wilkins *is sitting in front of screen partitioned off from restaurant lazily reading 'Racing News.')*

Wilkins. Weathervane — Wragg — Werewolf — Weston — Waterwitch — Whalley.
Walter. Waiter, waiter, waiter.
Wilkins (yawns). Wonder what's wanted.
Winnie (has been examining wrist-watch, holds out arm to Walter displaying watch). Worthless wrist-watch!
Walter. What's wrong? Won't work? What? *(Catches hold of hand, kisses it, looks at*

watch, winds top.) Wants winding. Waiter, Wait*ar*! (*Thumps table,* Waiter *begins to stir himself, appears from recess.*) Waiter, Wait*ar*!

Wilkins. Well, what's won? (*Suddenly corrects himself.*) What's wanted?
Walter. Waiter, we've waited weeks — watercress — woodcock.
Winnie (claps hands). Winnie worships woodcock.
Walter. Welsh-rarebit — walnuts.
Winnie. Walter! Winnie wants whortleberries.
Wilkins. When winter, we're without whortleberries.
Walter. Well, waiter — watercress, welsh-rarebit — woodcock.

(Waiter *writes order.*)

Winnie (looks over pad). What writing!
Walter. Whitebait.
Wilkins. We're without whitebait.
Walter. Why?
Wilkins. Well, whitebaiters were wrecked Worthing while westerly wind washed whitebait where whales were.
Walter. Wonder whether whales wolfed whitebait.
Wilkins. Well! Whitebait went.
Walter. Went where?
Wilkins. Went west.
Walter. Waiter, wrecked whitebait wheeze won't work. What will Winnie want — winkles? Whelks?
Winnie. Winnie wants whiting.
Wilkins (with broad smile). We've whiting.
Walter. Well, waiter — whiting. Was Wilkins waiting when we were waging war?
Wilkins (proudly). Wilkins *was* waging war.
Walter. Where?
Wilkins. Wypers.
Walter. Wounded? (*Wilkins nods.*)
Winnie. Where?
Wilkins. Windpipe.
Walter. Wounded warrior, what?
Wilkins. Windy warrior.
Newspaper Boy (from outside). Winner! Winner!

(Wilkins *rushes to entrance, brings back paper.*)

Walter. Waiter, what's won?
Wilkins. Weathervane's won. (*Miserably.*) Wasted wages.
Walter. What'll win Wokingham? Will Wooten win?
Wilkins. With Wheesle wrongly weighted, Whispering Wind will waddle Wokingham. Willow Wren will win Windsor Wednesday.
Walter (makes note on cuff). Willow Wren Wednesday.
Wilkins. What wines wanted?
Walter. What's Winnie's wine?
Winnie. Winnie's wine's Worthington.

Wilkins (*whispers knowingly to* Walter). Wincarnis works wonders with widows.
Walter. Whist! Worthington — whisky. (*Whispers loudly in* Waiter's *ear.*) Whacking whisky?
Wilkins (going, then suddenly turns). What whisky?
Walter (pauses to think). 'Walker'!
Wilkins. What Walker?
Walter (slight pause). 'William Walker.'

(Exit Waiter.*)*

Walter (leans across table — whispers loudly). Winnie! Winifred!
Winnie. Well? What? (*Coyish giggle.*)
Walter (whispers loudly). Winifred — wonderful Winifred!
Winnie. Whisper, Walter.

(He does, they do, their heads almost touch over the table.)

Wilkins (entering and banging down dish, they part asunder quickly). Watercress — Watford watercress — wonderful watercress. *(Goes to fetch other dishes.)*
Walter. Winnie — wee — widdikins. *(Offers cigarette-case.)* Woodbine — Wills'.
Winnie. Willingly. *(Takes one, puffs smoke into* Walter's *face.)*
Walter. Wee wipsy wopsy.
Wilkins (with wallop). Worthington. *(With worse wallop.)* Whacking whisky. *(With worst wallop.)* Warm water. *(Holds jug about to pour.)* When? *(Pours water.)*
Walter (stops him suddenly — shrieks). Whoa! Why wasps wallowing within whisky?
Wilkins. Wasps want watching. *(Having removed wasp — absent-mindedly begins to drink whisky.)*
Walter (rescuing glass). Waiters want watching. Waiter! Woodcock!

(Waiter *fetches woodcock quickly.*)

Winnie. Weird — worrying waiter — what?
Walter. Well, waiter's *Welsh*. Welshmen *will* worry.
Winnie (coyly giggles). Winnie worships Welshmen.
Walter. Why wasn't Walter Welsh? Walter worships —
Wilkins (with bang). Woodcock. *(Moves to buffet.)*
Walter. Whopping woodcock. *(Carves.)* Wing?
Winnie. Wishbone!
Walter (tustling with tough bird). Wants wrestling with. *(Hits bird with fork.)* Woodcock's wooden.
Winnie (giggles — looks Walter *coyly in face*). Winnie wouldn't want *wooden* woodcock.
Walter. Waiter! Woodcock's wooden.
Wilkins. Wouldn't wonder. *(Takes bird up and exits.)*
Winnie. What wicked wit! Winnie wants walnuts. Winnie *worships* walnuts.
Walter. Walter worships Winnie. When will Winnie wed Wally? Wally wants Wednesday.
Winnie. Walter!
Walter. Walter's waiting. *(Facetiously.)* Waverer!

Winnie. Well, winter's wretched. Winnie wants warm weather — white wedding. We'll wait.

Walter. We won't — Walter wants —

Wilkins (entering and with wallop). Walnuts!

Walter. Waiter! Waiting's woeful. Watercress wet. Whisky weak, while welsh-rarebit was wishy-washy.

Wilkins. Well, what was wanted was Worcestershire — Worcestershire will work wonders with whiting, woodcock, welsh-rarebit — with weddings.

Walter. Why?

Wilkins. Well, Worcestershire warms.

Walter. Winnie, Worcester warms. We'll wed Wednesday — won't we?

Winnie. We will, Wally-wog, we will.

Walter (crosses in front of table to other side of Winnie *with joyful steps).* Walter's won! Walter's won! Waiter — wine!

Winnie. We wish waiter would wine wedding wishes.

Walter. Wil'st, waiter?

Wilkins. Willingly.

Winnie. Walter! We'll want waiter when wedding.

Wilkins. When's wedding?

Walter. We'll welcome Wilkins Westminster — Wednesday.

All (all three lifting glasses high to each other). Westminster — Wednesday.

Walter. Waiter — wrap *(puts wrap on)* — waterproof — walking-stick.

(Waiter *hands stick, etc.)*

Winnie. Walter, waiter's waiting.

(Walter *looks in every pocket — eventually brings out cigar-case — in ultra-lordly manner presents* Wilkins *with cigar — first having by grimace made it clear that it is a bad cigar.)*

Walter. Waiter, weed!

(Exeunt Walter *and* Winnie, *bowed off.)*

Wilkins. Wow — Wow! *(Very wobbly and full of wine comes down centre, holds on to chair-arm, drinks remains of whisky — catches breath — explains excusedly.)* Wind! *(Flops into chair, examines cigar, smells it, makes grimace.)* Woolworths!!!

Curtain.

* * *

Harry Tate became many things in many sketches — motorist, fisherman, business-man, broadcaster, aviator. Will Hay was only ever one thing — a schoolmaster. In Music Hall sketches and then in films the Headmaster of St Michael's, with his pince-nez askew, ineffectually harangued his pupils, including the incredibly aged Harbottle and the Fat Boy.

FOURTH FORM AT ST MICHAEL'S

by Will Hay

Will Hay, as Headmaster, addresses his class

Will Hay. Morning, boys.
Boy. Good morning, sir.
Will Hay. Well, where's old Jimmy Harbottle?
Boy. He's not here yet.
Will Hay. Not here?
Boy. No.
Will Hay. What, late again?
Boy. Yes.
Will Hay. Oh dear, oh dear, he's always late . . . Still, one must make allowances for his age; he's getting on now. Let's see, how old will he be now?
Boy. Eighty-five.
Will Hay. Eighty-five. Eighty-five and never left school. I don't suppose he ever will leave, either. Ah, here he is . . . Well, you're late.
Harbottle. Yes.
Will Hay. What?
Harbottle. Yes.
Will Hay. Yes, what?
Harbottle. Yes, I'm late.
Will Hay. You'll say Yes, sir, when you speak to me, will you. I want to know why you're late.
Harbottle. I've been having an argument with another boy.
Will Hay. With another boy?
Harbottle. Yes.
Will Hay. Who's the other one?
Harbottle. Me.
Will Hay. You don't call yourself a boy, do you? — And don't say *me*! What's the matter with your grammar!
Harbottle. She's ill.
Will Hay. Ill?
Harbottle. Yes.
Will Hay. Who is?
Harbottle. Me Grandma.
Will Hay. I didn't say your Grandma, I said grammar. Grammar! I am, thou art, he is, we ain't — that's grammar. Well, what was the argument about?
Harbottle. He said some nasty things about you.
Will Hay. Who did?
Harbottle. The other boy.
Will Hay. Oh did he?
Harbottle. Yes.
Will Hay. What did you do?
Harbottle. I stuck up for you.
Will Hay. That's right, always stick up for me. What did he say that was nasty?
Harbottle. He said you hadn't got the brains of a donkey.

Will Hay. He said that?
Harbottle. Yes.
Will Hay. About me?
Harbottle. Yes.
Will Hay. Mm, sauce. You stuck up for me?
Harbottle. I did.
Will Hay. What did you say?
Harbottle. I said you had.
Will Hay. That's right . . . Did you? Yes, well don't you stick up for me anymore. I'll stick up for myself. Er, we'll take Scripture.
Boy. Oh, yes, that reminds me — the other day you were telling us about Noah. (*He pronounces it 'Nor'.*)
Will Hay. Telling you about what?
Boy. Noah.
Will Hay. Nor.
Boy. Yes.
Will Hay. Nor what?
Boy. Nor nothing.
Will Hay. No, no, no, I couldn't tell you about nor nothing, I must have told you about nor something.
Boy. No, just Noah.
Will Hay. Just nor.
Boy. Yes — oh, but not what the mice do.
Will Hay. Not what?
Boy. Not what the mice do.
Will Hay. Not what the mice do.
Boy. No.
Will Hay. Well, what have the mice go to do with it?
Boy. Nothing.
Will Hay. Well, why mention them if they've got nothing to do with it?
Boy. I've got to.
Will Hay. Oh, you've got two.
Boy. Yes.
Will Hay. I see.
Harbottle. I've got three.
Will Hay. Uh?
Harbottle. I've got three.
Will Hay. Three what?
Harbottle. Mice.
Will Hay. No, no, no, you've got the rats, that's what's the matter with you. Listen, you say the teacher was telling about Noah, well, I was, not what the mice do, they've got nothing to do with it, you've got two and he's got three. Now where are we? Listen, we'll get this down on paper, and then we can sort it out. You take it down, Harbottle.
Boy. The teacher . . .
Harbottle. The teacher . . .
Boy. Was telling.

Harbottle. Was telling . . .
Boy. Us . . .
Harbottle. Us . . .
Boy. About Noah.
Harbottle. About Noah.
Will Hay. Let's have a look. About what?
Harbottle. About nor.
Will Hay. Well, why don't you put nor?
Harbottle. 'Tis nor.
Will Hay. No, how do you spell nor?
Harbottle. N. O. R.
Will Hay. No, no, no, no; K.N.O.R; k, the k is silent you see, as in soup.
Boy. But not . . .
Harbottle. But not . . .
Boy. What . . .
Harbottle. What . . .
Boy. The mice do.
Harbottle. The mice do. Yes?
Will Hay. Got that?
Harbottle. Yes.
Will Hay. Comma.
Boy. Well, you know what the mice do.
Will Hay. No.
Boy. They gnaw.
Will Hay. Who?
Boy. The mice.
Will Hay. Yes. I know that. Tell him, he's taking it down, I'm not.
Boy. The mice gnaw.
Harbottle. Yes.
Will Hay. Well, put it down, put it down.
Harbottle. The mice gnaw.
Will Hay. Semi-colon.
Harbottle. Which fire?
Will Hay. What?
Harbottle. Which fire?
Will Hay. What d'you mean, which fire?
Harbottle. You said put some coal on.
Will Hay. No, no, no, I said put a *semi-colon.* Put some coal on! It's a gas-fire, too, but he doesn't know. Go on, semi-colon.
Harbottle. How do you spell it?
Will Hay. Spell it?
Harbottle. Yes.
Will Hay. You don't spell it, you splash it. Don't you know what semi-colons are?
Harbottle. No.
Will Hay. Well, they're commas with knobs on . . . Well, we've got that, come on.
Boy. Well, not that gnaw, but Noah.
Will Hay. Oh dear, oh dear, oh dear, I don't know what you're talking about.

Boy. Noah — the fellow who built the ark.
Will Hay. Built the ark.
Boy. Yes.
Will Hay. You mean Noah.
Boy. That's right.
Will Hay. Is that who you mean?
Boy. Yes.
Will Hay. Well, why didn't you say Noah?
Boy. I did.
Will Hay. No, no, no, you said knor . . . a different family altogether. Cross all that out, Harbottle. Well, what about Noah?
Boy. Well, who was his wife?
Will Hay. Who was whose wife?
Boy. Noah's wife.
Will Hay. Who was Noah's wife?
Boy. Yes.
Will Hay. You want me to tell you?
Boy. Yes, please.
Will Hay. Yes, well, um, ahem . . . I think we'll go out to play now, shall we?
Boy. No, we won't. Come on, who was Noah's wife?
Will Hay. Well, Noah's wife was Mrs . . . er . . .
Harbottle. I know.
Will Hay. What?
Harbottle. I know Noah's wife.
Will Hay. You do.
Harbottle. Yes.
Will Hay. Yes, well you ought to, you were in the ark with 'em, weren't you?
Harbottle. Ah.
Will Hay. Well, you tell him who she was.
Harbottle. Noah's wife?
Will Hay. Yes.
Harbottle. Joan of Arc!

(Mirth)

Will Hay. Joan of Arc?
Harbottle. Yes.
Will Hay. No, no, that was *Lot's* wife. You know less than I do. Well, to continue with Scripture; we'll take the chief mountain ranges of the world.
Boy. Ha-ha. That's funny.
Will Hay. What's funny?
Boy. Mountains in Scripture.
Will Hay. Why, have you never heard of mountains in Scripture?
Boy. No.
Will Hay. Oh, yes. You've heard of Mount, er, let me see, Mount Ararat, surely?
Harbottle. I have.
Will Hay. What?
Harbottle. I have.

Will Hay. Yes, you would.
Harbottle. Yes, I like it.
Will Hay. What?
Harbottle. I like it.
Will Hay. Like it?
Harbottle. Yes.
Will Hay. Like what?
Harbottle. Arrowroot.
Will Hay. Who's talking about arrowroot?
Harbottle. You were.
Will Hay. Never mentioned it! That's not a mountain.
Boy. What is it?
Will Hay. What?
Boy. What is it?
Will Hay. Well, it's a piece of ground that, er, stands up higher than the surrounding country, and it's elevated to that position owing to the internal forces which, er, shove it up.
Boy. What, arrowroot?
Will Hay. Mm?
Boy. Arrowroot?
Will Hay. No, a mountain.
Boy. No, I mean, what is arrowroot?
Will Hay. Oh, what is arrowroot?
Boy. Yes.
Will Hay. Ah, that's different.
Boy. Yes.
Will Hay. Yes, much different, yes.
Boy. Well, what is it?
Will Hay. Well, it's, er, what, arrowroot?
Boy. Yes.
Will Hay. Well, it's like, er, it's like celery.
Harbottle. Yes, it's like celery.
Will Hay. What is?
Harbottle. Rhubarb.
Will Hay. Oh, listen, you go to sleep. We won't bother with you, we'll call you when we want you. Now, is the earth round or flat?
Boy. Round.
Will Hay. Good, how do you know it's round?
Boy. Well, flat then.
Will Hay. What?
Boy. Flat.
Will Hay. I thought you said it was round.
Boy. Well, I don't want any argument about it.
Will Hay. Argument?
Boy. No.
Will Hay. There's not going to be any argument here, my boy. If I ask a question I want an answer.

Boy. I gave you an answer.

Will Hay. No, no. I said is the earth round or flat; you said round. I said how do you know it's round, and you said flat. Now why do you say flat?

Boy. Well, if you don't want it round you can have it flat.

Will Hay. Have what?

Boy. The earth!

Will Hay. I don't want the earth at all. I want you to tell me how you know the earth is round.

Boy. Now, look here — how should I know if the earth's round? I'm not here to teach you — you're supposed to be teaching me.

Will Hay. I know that, and I'm doing my best to teach you.

Boy. Well, get on with it.

Will Hay. Now listen, when you answer my question I'll get on with it. I want to know how you know the earth's round, and I don't want any nonsense.

Boy. How should I know if the earth's round?

Will Hay. You should know.

Boy. The earth was made before I was born.

Will Hay. I know that.

Boy. Well, you ought to know, you're older than I am.

Will Hay. I ought to know?

Boy. Yes.

Will Hay. Why?

Boy. 'Cause you ought to know!

Will Hay. Because I'm older than you?

Boy. Yes.

Will Hay. Well, what about Harbottle here?

Boy. Just a minute — do you know if the earth's round?

Will Hay. Certainly I know.

Boy. Well, how do you know?

Will Hay. How?

Boy. Yes, how?

Will Hay. Well, it's round because, er, it's, er — what's it got to do with you how *I* know it's round?

Boy. You're supposed to be teaching us, aren't you?

Will Hay. Yes, and if I'm doing the teaching, I'll ask the questions. A lot of argument about nothing! All I said — you heard me, Harbottle —

Harbottle. I wasn't listenin'.

Will Hay. Well, why weren't you listening?

Harbottle. Got nothing to do with me.

Will Hay. What hasn't?

Harbottle. The earth.

Will Hay. You've come here to try and learn something. Not to sit there twiddling about with your fingers.

Boy. Now look, we'll take it this way. We'll suppose you're standing on the seashore, and you're watching a boat crossing the horizon.

Will Hay. Watching a what?

Boy. Watching a boat crossing the horizon.

Will Hay. Now wait a minute — I'm on the seashore, watching a boat going over the horizon, is that what you mean?
Boy. No, crossing.
Will Hay. No, no, you mean going over.
Boy. I mean crossing.
Will Hay. No, no, this is something I *do* know. Now wait a minute. When you speak of the horizon you mean a line which is on a horizontal plane, you see. You know what a plane is?
Boy. Yes.
Will Hay. What?
Boy. A thing you shave wood with.
Will Hay. Er, yes, yes . . . well, it's on that, you see, there it is. Now then, when a boat is crossing the horizon it's going along that line, you see, but when it goes over, it goes that way, out of sight, you see?
Boy. That's over?
Will Hay. That's over.
Boy. And that's crossing?
Will Hay. That's crossing.
Boy. Oh —

Together. Crossing — over — over — crossing —

Harbottle. Crossing —

Together. over

Harbottle. Over —

Will Hay. Nobody asked you to join in this, you go to sleep.
Boy. All right, the boat is going over the horizon.
Will Hay. The horizon, yes.
Boy. Well, if you watch closely, you'll see that the hull of the boat disappears first.
Will Hay. I'll see what?
Boy. That the hull of the boat —
Will Hay. The whole of the boat?
Boy. Yes.
Will Hay. No, no, no, I don't know where you were brought up, my boy, but you must learn to speak correctly. You mustn't say things like hull of the boat, y'know.
Boy. Why not?
Will Hay. Well, it's not right, that's slang. You want to say, if I watch closely I'll see that the *whole* of the boat —
Boy. No, no, the hull of the boat, hull, hull!
Will Hay. Yes, but what's this got to do with the earth being round or flat?
Boy. I'm trying to show you how I think it's round.
Will Hay. Well, Harbottle, you know the earth isn't flat, don't you?
Harbottle. It is where I live.
Will Hay. Ye — Oh, is it? Yes, well you take your cap and get out. You go off somewhere else. Think I want to waste my time teaching you? You go and do something else.

Harbottle. What shall I do?
Will Hay. What?
Harbottle. What shall I do?
Will Hay. Oh, go and put some coal on.

* * *

Dion Titheradge was a prolific writer of sketches for West End revues, and a master of the Idea.

This example, written for Jack Buchanan, required the first half of the sketch to be played straight, which must have mystified the audience somewhat. It then burst into life.

THE GREEN-EYED MONSTER
by Dion Titheradge

Scene: George's study. A nice room, well furnished. Bay window at the back. Doors R. and L. A small table down R. on which is a telephone and a telephone book. A Chesterfield in front of the window at the back and a desk above the door L. with a chair in front of it. A gramophone on stand above door R.

When the Curtain *rises,* Joblin *is sitting in the chair his feet up on the desk. He is smoking a cigar, reading the 'Pink 'Un' and has a drink in front of him.*

The telephone bell rings.

Joblin. Damn the telephone! *(He rises, puts paper and cigar down and stretching his arms, goes over to the table.)* Can't get a bit of peace no 'ow! *(Picks up receiver.)* 'Ullo? 'Ullo? Yes, I 'eard you — Mr. Trippitt. I'll tell the mistress you'll be 'ere at three o'clock. Yes — good-bye.

(He hangs up the receiver and turns quickly as George *rushes on door L.)*

George (loudly). Where's your mistress?
Joblin. Good 'evings, sir! I didn't know you was in town! *(Moves to* George.*)*
George (raging). I asked you — where's your mistress!
Joblin. Upstairs, sir.
George. Tell her I'm here!
Joblin (going to door R.). I will, sir.
George. Stop!

(Joblin *stops.)*

Where was she last night?
Joblin. Dancing at Lady Puddleduck's, sir.
George. Did she come home?
Joblin. I told you, sir — she's upstairs.
George. When — when did she come home?

Joblin. At eleven h'ay h'em, sir.
George (in agony). This is too much!
Joblin. Yes, sir. *(Looks off R.)* Here is the mistress, sir. *(He turns and crosses to above door L., where he stands.)*
George (taking in a deep breath). Ah!

(Jane *enters door R. A bright, pretty little thing. She stops on seeing* George.)

Jane. George!
George (calmly). Joblin, you may go.
Joblin. Very good, sir.

(He exits door L. Husband and wife face each other.)

Jane. George! What brings you back to town? *(Moves to* George.*)*
George (grimly). You!
Jane. I?
George. You — and your lover!
Jane. My lover — what do you mean?
George. Woman, I know all! *(Steps forward — grasps her hand.)*
Jane. George, don't be silly!
George. Whom were you with last night?
Jane. Lady Puddleduck.
George. Was *he* there?
Jane. Lord Puddleduck?
George. Lord Puddleduck be damned! I mean your lover!
Jane. George! George! You wrong me! *(Hands on his shoulders.)*
George (flinging her off in a fury). I will find out the truth — I swear it! *(He moves to table, grabs up telephone book and dashes it violently on the floor.)*
Jane. How can you be so jealous!
George (comes down to her — grabbing her by the wrists). Tell me his name!
Jane. There is no one — no one but you!
George. Tchah! *(He throws her off L.)* Keep out of my way — I warn you — keep out of my way!

(He exits violently through door R.)

Jane (stretching out her arms to his retreating figure). George! George! Listen to me!

(Joblin *enters at door L. and stands.)*

Joblin. Mr. Trippitt has called to give you your dancing lesson, ma'am.
Jane (turning). Show him in, please, Joblin.
Joblin. Very good, ma'am.

(Jane *powders her nose.* Joblin *exits L.)*

(Joblin *re-enters L.)*

Joblin . Mr. Trippitt.

(Trippitt *enters; an insignificant little man in tight-fitting clothes.)*

Trippitt (crossing to Jane *impetuously with hand outstretched).* Dear madam — I am charmed.
Jane (taking his hand). How are you? *(To* Joblin.*)* That will do, Joblin.

*(*Joblin *exits L.)*

Trippitt. You look a little tired. Shall we postpone our lesson?
Jane. Oh no, I'm quite all right, thank you.
Trippitt. Then, shall we commence?
Jane. Of course. *(Moving away.)* I'll start the gramophone.
Trippitt. No, no. First we will practise the correct position, Are you ready?
Jane. Oh, quite.
Trippitt. Then, I place my arm about you — so. *(Puts his arm round her waist.)* This hand here. *(Holds out her hand.)*
Jane. I see.
Trippitt. The other hand a little farther on my shoulder.
Jane. Like this? *(She puts her hand up on his shoulder.)*
Trippitt. Now come closer to me — closer. *(She moves towards him.)* That is charming.

*(*George *suddenly appears at door R.)*

George (exploding). Dirty dog! I've found you!

*(*Jane *and* Trippitt *turn.)*

Jane (flinging out a warning hand). George! Be careful!
George. Stand away from my wife!

*(*Jane *moves down L.* Trippitt *steps up.)*

Trippitt. I beg your pardon?
George (moving towards him). You snake in the grass, you!
Trippitt (taking a step forward.) Sir, how dare you!
George. Dare! Dare! *(He draws a revolver.)* I told her what I'd do! Take that!

(He fires and Trippitt *falls dead.* Jane *rushes to* George *R.)*

Jane. George! George! You've killed the wrong man!

Curtain.

When the applause has subsided, George *steps forward and addresses the audience. In the event of there being no applause (a very likely occurrence) he should not be deterred but proceed to deliver the following speech.*

Ladies and Gentlemen, in thanking you for this magnificent ovation, we feel that it is only right to respond with an encore. Not having another playlet ready we can only do the one which you have just seen. However, in an effort not to bore you, we propose to start where we left off and work backwards.

(The Curtain *rises.)*

*(*George *is standing with a smoking revolver in his hand. To him is clinging* Jane. Trippitt *lies dead on the floor.)*

Jane. Man wrong the killed you've! George! George!

*(*Jane *rushes backwards a few paces.* Trippitt *rises from the floor.* George *goes up backwards, turns, faces* Trippitt, *then fires the revolver.)*

George. That take! Do I'd what her told I! *(He puts the revolver back in his pocket.)* Dare! Dare!
Trippitt. You dare how, sir! *(He takes one step backwards.)*
George. You, grass the in snake you! *(He takes a step backwards.)*
Trippitt. Pardon your beg I?
George. Wife my from away stand!
Jane. Careful be! George! *(She brings her hand to her side.)*

*(*Jane *and* Trippitt *turn away from* George, Trippitt *holds her very close as if about to start to dance.)*

George. You found I've — dog dirty!

*(*George *walks backwards to door R., pauses a moment and then goes right off backwards through door.)*

Trippitt. Charming is that.

(She moves away from him a little.)

Closer — me to closer come now.
Jane (takes her hand a little from his shoulder). This like?
Trippitt. Shoulder my on farther little a hand other your.
Jane. See I. *(hand right off his shoulder.)*
Trippitt (letting go her left hand). Here hand this. *(Turns, takes arm from around her waist.)* So — you about arm my place I then.
Jane. Quite, oh. *(Takes a step or two backwards from him.)*
Trippitt. Ready you are? Position correct the practise will we first, no, no.
Jane (moving a couple of steps towards him). Gramophone the start I'll. Course of.
Trippitt. Commence we shall then?
Jane. You thank, right all quite I'm, no, oh.
Trippitt. Lesson our postpone we shall? Tired little a look you.

*(*Joblin *enters backwards door L. Stands up stage of facing* Jane.*)*

Jane. Joblin, do will that. *(Puts her hand in* Trippitt's.) You are how? *(Takes her hand away.)*
Trippitt. Charmed am I, Madam dear.

(With his hand outstretched he exits backwards through door L.)

Joblin. Trippitt Mister!

(He exits backwards through door L. Jane *hastily powders her nose from vanity bag.* Joblin *enters backwards through door L. and stands upstage of door.)*

Joblin. Ma'am good very.
Jane. Joblin please, in him show.
Joblin. Ma'am lesson dancing your you give to called has Trippitt Mister.

*(*Jane *turns to door R. and stretches out her arms.* Joblin *exits backwards through door L.)*

Jane. Me to listen — George, George! *(She drops her hands to her sides.)*

*(*George *enters backwards door R., turns as he gets near to her.)*

George. Way my of out keep — you warn I — way my of out keep! *(He grabs her hands.)* Tchah!
Jane. You but no one — no one is there!
George. Name his me tell! *(Goes backwards to table.)*
Jane. Jealous so be you can how!

*(*George *picks up telephone book from floor and puts it on table.)*

George. It swear I! Truth the out find will I. *(Comes backwards to her and takes her hand.)*
Jane. Me wrong you! George! George! *(She puts her arms on* George.*)*
George. Lover your mean I. Damned be Duckpuddle Lord!
Jane. Duckpuddle Lord?
George. There *he* was?
Jane. Duckpuddle Lady!
George. Night last with you were whom?
Jane. Silly be don't, George!
George. All know I, woman! *(Unclasps hand.)*
Jane. Mean you do what — lover my?
George. Lover your and you!
Jane. I?
George (grimly). You!
Jane. Town to back you brings what, George? *(Moving backwards.)*

*(*George *faces door L.* Joblin *enters backwards and stands above door.)*

Joblin. Sir, good very.
George. Go may you, Joblin. *(Walks backwards L.)*
Jane. George!

(She exits backwards through door R. quickly.)

George. Ah! *(He expels his breath heavily.)*

*(*Joblin *turns and walks backwards to above door R., turns and looks at* George.*)*

Joblin. Sir, mistress the is here. *(He looks off door R.)* Sir, yes. *(Looks at* George.*)*
George. Much too is this, no, no!
Joblin. Sir, h'em h'ay eleven at.
George. Home come she did when — when?
Joblin. Stairs up she's, sir, you told I.

George. Home come she did?
Joblin. Sir, Duck'spuddle Lady at dancing.
George. Night last she was where?

*(*Joblin *walks backwards towards him.)*

Stop!
Joblin. Sir, will I. *(He faces* George.*)*
George. Here I'm her tell!
Joblin. Sir, stairs up.
George (raging). Mistress your where's — you asked I!
Joblin. Town in was you know didn't I, sir, 'evings good! *(Going backwards R.)*
George (loudly). Mistress your where's?

(He rushes off backwards through door L. Joblin *walks a few steps backwards to small table and turns, taking off receiver.)*

Joblin. Good-bye yes. O'clock three at 'ere be you'll mistress the tell I'll. Trippitt Mister — you 'eard I, yes. 'Ullo? 'Ullo? *(Puts on receiver. As he walks backwards to desk.)* 'Ow no peace of bit a get can't!

(Stretches his arms above his head, turns, takes up cigar and paper, sits, puts his feet up on desk.)

Joblin. Telephone the damn!

(The telephone bell rings.)

Black Out.

* * *

This is a classic of the revue-sketch genre and has been played all over the world. It was written for Cicely Courtneidge.

THE GREAT WHITE SALE

by Dion Titheradge

Scene: Linen Department at a large store.

An inset showing part of a counter in a big store behind which stands the Assistant, *an immaculate young man with a high collar. The counter has, on each side, neat piles of white linen. On R. of the counter, a notice which reads:*

BARGAINS!
Sheets.
Pillow-slips.
Table-cloths.
Dinner Napkins.
DOUBLE DAMASK!

The Assistant *is idly manicuring his nails when* Mrs Spooner *enters briskly from L. She is a fussy suburban lady, dressed rather over-elaborately, with a perky hat and aggressive pince-nez. She approaches the counter.*

Mrs Spooner. I wonder could you tell me if my order has gone off yet?
Assistant (languidly). Not knowing your order, Madam, I really couldn't say.
Mrs Spooner. But I was in here about an hour ago and gave it to you.
Assistant. What name, Madam?
Mrs Spooner. Spooner — Mrs Spooner.
Assistant. Have you an address, Madam?
Mrs Spooner. Do I look as if I live in the open air? I gave a large order for sheets and table-cloths to be sent to 'Bacon Villa', Egham.
Assistant. Egham?
Mrs Spooner. I hope I speak plainly. *(With emphasis.) Egg-ham,* I said.
Assistant. I remember perfectly now, Madam. No, the order won't go out until to-morrow morning. *(Taking up his book.)* Is there anything further?
Mrs Spooner. Yes, I want two duzzle dummen damask dinner napkins.
Assistant (politely). I beg your pardon, Madam?
Mrs Spooner. I said two dummel dazzle dummusk dinner napkins.
Assistant. I'm so sorry, I didn't quite catch —
Mrs Spooner (sharply). Dinner napkins, man, dinner napkins!
Assistant. Of course, Madam. Plain?
Mrs Spooner (irritably). Not plain at all. Dabble dummusk.
Assistant. Would you repeat the order, Madam? I'm not quite sure —
Mrs Spooner (firmly). I want two duzzle dammen dubback — dear! dear! two *dozen* dammel dizzick danner nipkins.
Assistant (astonished). Danner nipkins, Madam?
Mrs Spooner. Yes.
Assistant. You mean dinner napkins.
Mrs Spooner. That's what I said.
Assistant. You'll pardon me, Madam, you said 'danner nipkins'.
Mrs Spooner. Don't be ridiculous! I said dinner napkins and I *meant* danner nipkins — ninner dapkins. *(Heated.)* I wish you wouldn't confuse me!
Assistant. I'm sorry, Madam. You want danner nipkins — exactly; how many, Madam?
Mrs Spooner. Two duzzle.
Assistant (sharply). Madam?
Mrs Spooner. Good gracious, young man — can't you get it right? I want two dubben duzzle damask dinner napkins.
Assistant (anxious to help). Not two 'dubben,' Madam; you mean two *dozen.*
Mrs Spooner (icily). I *said* two dozen — only they must be dammel duzzick.
Assistant. I'm afraid we haven't any of that in stock, Madam.
Mrs Spooner (in despair). Of all the fools! Can I find *anybody* with a modicum — just a modicum of intelligence in this store?

(The Shop-Walker *enters from R. An elegant figure in a morning coat; suave, unruffled and always anxious to please.)*

Assistant (indicating him). Here is our Mr Peters, Madam. Perhaps if you asked him –

(At a sign from the Assistant, *the* Shop-Walker *approaches.)*

Shop-Walker (R. of counter). Can I be of any assistance, Madam?

Mrs Spooner. I'm sorry to say it, but your assistant doesn't appear to speak English. I'm giving an order – but it might as well be in Esperanto for all he understands!

Shop-Walker (with a superior air). Allow *me* to help you, Madam. You require?

Mrs Spooner. I want two dazzen dabble dummusk dinner napkins.

Shop-Walker (starting). I beg pardon, Madam?

Mrs Spooner. Good heavens, can't *you* understand?

Shop-Walker. Would you mind repeating your order, Madam?

Mrs Spooner (pulling herself together). I want two dazzen –

Shop-Walker (interrupting). Two dozen.

Mrs Spooner. Didn't I *say* two dozen?

Shop-Walker. You said 'dazzen,' Madam – but I understand what you mean. Two dozen – in other words, a double dozen.

Mrs Spooner (relieved). That's it. A duzzle dubben of dabble dummusk dinner napkins.

Shop-Walker (smiling as one would to a child). Pardon me, Madam. You mean a double dozen of dummel dabbask dinner napkins.

Assistant (helpfully). Double damask, sir.

Shop-Walker (coldly). I *said* 'double damask'. *(To* Mrs Spooner.*)* It's danner nipkins you require, Madam?

Mrs Spooner. Please get it right! I want dinner napkins.

Shop-Walker. I beg your pardon. *(Laughing foolishly.)* How stupid of me. One gets so confused – dipper nankins, of course!

Assistant (correcting him). Dapper ninkins, sir.

Mrs Spooner (severely). Danner nipkins!

Shop-Walker (pulling himself together with an effort). I understand *exactly* what you want, Madam. *(A pause. He clears his throat – then his courage fails him.)* Will you repeat the order?

Mrs Spooner (wiping her brow and drawing a deep breath). I want two duzzle dizzen damask dunner nipkins.

Shop-Walker (taking a grip on himself). Allow me, Madam. *(He turns blandly to the* Assistant.*)* The lady requires – *(he takes a breath)* two dummen dazzen dimisk dunner napkins.

Assistant. Dunner napkins, sir?

Shop-Walker. Certainly. Two dizzen.

Mrs Spooner. Not 'dizzen' – dozen. I want two dozen.

Shop-Walker (keeping calm). Quite so, Madam. If I may say so, we get confused splitting it up, as it were. *(He clears his throat again.)* The *full* order is: two dazzen dibble dummusk ninner dupkins.

(From here on the action is at top speed.)

Assistant. You'll excuse me, sir. You mean two dummen dabble dimmick dizzy napkins.

Mrs Spooner. I don't want dizzy napkins at all! I want two dizzle dammen dussack –
Shop-Walker. No, no! Two dazzle dummen dizzick –
Assistant (excited). Two *dozen,* sir! Two dozen dimmel duzzick –
Mrs Spooner (staggering, wildly). Two damn dizzy duddle dimmer dapkins!
Shop-Walker. Madam, please, *please!* Your language!
Mrs Spooner. Oh, hell! Give me twenty-four serviettes!

Black Out.

*　　*　　*

We have two more examples of Dion Titheradge's skill.

In the revue *Folly to be Wise,* 1931, he had a leading actor/comedian, Nelson Keys, of great energy and versatility so he wrote sketches for him in which these virtues could be displayed.

HE WHO GETS SACKED

by Dion Titheradge

Scene: An office in a large Department Store.

A double set. The L. and larger part of the stage is taken up by the Manager's office. There is a flat-topped desk over L. with the usual writing paraphernalia and two telephones. Behind this is a swivel chair and on the other side a high-backed chair. A typist's desk with machine and chair is at the back up R. There is a door to a waiting-room up L. Another door (opening off) leads to the second room, which is part of the set. This is very small. On the R. wall is a row of pegs on which hang sundry clothes, including white and alpaca jackets, aprons, etc. At the back is a plain table holding a mirror and make-up. On each side are piled wig-boxes.

When the Curtain *rises the* Manager *is seated at his desk and the* Secretary *at hers. Standing C. is* 'He'. *He is dressed in the sober garments of a Shop Assistant, striped trousers, short black coat and a black tie.*

Manager. You're late.
'He'. So was the nine-twelve from Clapham, sir.
Manager. Oh, was it? Well, the waiting-room out there is full of people with their usual complaints. We'd better get at it.
'He'. I'm sorry there are a lot of people, sir. My throat is –
Manager. I don't want to hear about it. *(To* Secretary.*)* All right, Miss Beldon.

(The Secretary *crosses to door L.)*

Go on, Bodger. We've a lot to get through.
'He' (grumbling as he exits). Well, it's a bit hard on a man. I wouldn't mind if I had an understudy or even a day off now and then –

(*'He' suddenly hurries as he hears the* Secretary.)

Secretary. This way, Madam.

(*She opens the door L. and the* First Customer *bustles in. A fussy, perturbed suburban lady, very thin and angular. The* Secretary *goes back to her desk.*)

First Customer (crossing down, brusquely). Are you the Manager?
Manager. I am, Madam. *(He waves her to chair.)* Is there anything —
First Customer. I've come to lodge a complaint. One of your assistants in the Grocery Department has been disgustingly rude to me.
Manager (picking up dummy telephone and speaking in it). Give me Groceries, please.

('He' *immediately grabs white jacket and apron from pegs, which he proceeds to put on, through the following.*)

First Customer. I was buying half a pound of best back rashers, when he insulted me.
Manager. Could you describe him, Madam?
First Customer. I certainly could. I'll never forget his ugly face. He was elderly, baldheaded, with a horrible fringe of white hair, a nose slightly the worse for liquor and a scraggy grey moustache.

('He' *starts making up, back to audience.*)

Manager (in the telephone). Send up McTavish at once. *(He leans across the desk.)* Now as to the complaint, Madam.
First Customer. Well, as I told you, I was buying bacon — and, as this wretch was cutting it, I said I preferred it streaky. I distinctly heard him mutter: 'Ay, the old sow can do with a bit of fat!'
Manager. Disgraceful! The man shall be dismissed at once.
First Customer. I sincerely trust so.

('He' *knocks at door R., fully made up according to the description.*)

Manager. Come in.

('He' *enters. The* First Customer *glares at him.*)

(Sternly.) McTavish, I hear you have been extremely rude to this lady.
'He'. Weel, I'm no' sayin' I was an' I'm no' sayin' I wasna. I was terrible busy an' I canna remember.
First Customer. Repeat to me — just repeat to me what you said.
'He'. What was it ye might ha' been purchasin'?
First Customer. Back rashers.
'He'. Ah, then, I might ha ca'ed ye a'most anythin'.
First Customer. I want you to repeat before the Manager what you said to me!
'He'. It wouldna be that I called ye a cluckety old hen?
First Customer (to Manager). Am I here to be insulted further?
Manager. Now then, McTavish, that's enough.
'He'. Och! awa' wi' ye. Let's get to the bottom o' this. (*To* First Customer.) I'll thank

ye, ma'am, to tell me straight oot — wi'out any blether, just what it was I call'd ye?

First Customer (drawing herself up). You distinctly called me an old sow!

Manager. He was referring to the bacon, I'm sure, Madam.

'He'. I was referrin' to neether. I couldna ha' called this good wumman a sow for the reason I pronounce it 'soo.' (*To* First Customer.) The same way as if I would say 'coo' if I was to ca' ye a cow.

First Customer (aghast). He's calling me a cow, now!

'He'. I'm no' callin' ye a coo, noo!

Manager. That's enough, McTavish, that settles it. Draw two weeks' wages and get out. You're dismissed!

'He'. You mean it?

First Customer. Of course he means it. *Instantly* dismissed.

'He' (going R.). Ah weel, I'm for gettin' back to Aberdeen, where wummen is wummen a' no' a lot o' pawky, dried-up poll parrots. *(At door.)* That's the truth, an' a very good mornin' to ye!

('He' *exits. The* First Customer *has emitted a series of speechless gasps. The* Secretary *comes down to her and leads her to door L.* 'He' *is taking off his apron, etc., and make-up.)*

Manager. You were quite right to complain, Madam. The fellow will be out of here as soon as you. Good morning.

First Customer. Good morning.

(She goes out door L.)

Manager (sitting). Next, Miss Beldon.

Secretary (through door L.). Next, please.

(She holds the door open, and an irate man enters accompanied by a pretty, shy wife.)

Second Customer. Look here, Mr Manager, I've been in a few big stores in my time, but this one's run like a circus.

Manager. My dear sir, have you a complaint to make?

Second Customer. Have I? Why can't you employ decent, honest Englishmen? Yesterday I 'phoned up for someone to tune my piano. What happens? Along comes a fat German *and*, if you please, starts making eyes at my wife!

Manager (loudly). A fat German?

('He' *reaches for padded coat and waistcoat and starts dressing. The* Manager *takes up telephone and speaks in it.)*

Pianos, please.

Second Customer. He was one of those greasy, long-moustached, curly-headed old rascals.

('He' *starts to make up.)*

Manager. This is very serious. *(In telephone.)* Pianos? Send me up Herr Baumgarten. Yes, right away. *(To* Second Customer, *as he replaces telephone.)* You mean to say the man was actually *rude* to your wife?

Second Customer. Rude? I came in to find him sitting on the same piano stool.
Wife (sitting in chair, in a baby voice). He made eyes at me; my husband doesn't like men to make eyes at me.
Second Customer. Not only that, but he had the nerve to hold her hand.

('He' *enters as a German.)*

I'll break his neck!

('He' *immediately starts to exit.)*

Manager (loudly). Come here, Baumgarten. I sent for you.
'He'. If you occupied vos, I vill come a leedle later back.
Second Customer. This is the fellow. *(To* 'He'.*)* Now perhaps you'll tell the Manager what the devil you mean by flirting with my wife!
'He'. Mister Cripps, here we a gross misunderstanding have. I go to der flat of der gentleman der pianner to toon —
Second Customer. What did you do when you got there?
'He'. I tooned it.
Second Customer. Were you or were you not sitting on the same stool as my wife?
'He'. Mr Cripps, I my sits on the piano stool puts und, ven I turn round, there vas *two* sits on the piano stool.
Second Customer. Are you suggesting — ?
'He'. Unt I say, 'Here of parlour maids am a pretty one,' so I am permit myself to take her hand. Unt der gentleman in comes and kick me in the pant!
Manager. That will do, Baumgarten, you are dismissed!
'He'. Ach, so! Dot makes simple a lot of things. *(He crosses to* Wife.*)* Vere I live I got a nice pianner stool mit plenty of room for two sits!
Second Customer (furiously hauling him off). Get out of here!
'He'. Not again in der pant you kick me! I am sacked. Soon you will sing, 'Oh vere, oh vere has my leedle wife gone!'

('He' *exits R., still singing.)*

Second Customer. Does he *know* he's got the sack?
Manager. My dear sir, he will be thrown out of the building immediately.
Second Customer. Good! *(To* Wife.*)* Come along, my darling.

(The door L. bursts open and a big irate man wearing a bowler hat comes in violently.)

Third Customer. I can't wait any more — where's the Manager?
Manager. Just a moment, sir. (*Indicating door to other customers.*) Good morning, sir. Good morning, madam. Rely on me to attend to that matter.

(The Secretary *crosses to door L. and shows out* Second Customer *and* Wife, *then returns to her place. The* Manager *sits again and turns to* Third Customer.*)*

And now, sir?
Third Customer. You've got a nice Hairdressing Department here! Look at what the barber's done to my hair!

(He lifts his bowler hat. His hair is cut 'en brosse.')

Manager. Don't you like it that way, sir?
Third Customer. No, I don't. I went in for a haircut, fell asleep — and this is what I woke up to!
Manager (in telephone). Give me Hairdressing, please.

('He' *is getting into alpaca coat. The* Manager *turns to the* Customer.)

What was the barber like, sir?
Third Customer. A blonde idiot with a large quiff, rosebud mouth and as masculine as my Aunt Jemima!

('He' *starts to make up.*)

Manager. I understand. *(In telephone.)* Hairdressing? Send up Cuthbert at once. Yes. *(He hangs up.)*
Third Customer (sitting). What am I going to do until my hair grows properly again?
Manager. We have a very good Wig Department here, sir.
Third Customer. Yes, I'd look funny in a wig, wouldn't I?
Manager. Very.

('He' *steps swayingly through door R. made up as described, with an ultra-effeminate manner.*)

'He'. Good morning. Have I been summoned?
Third Customer (turning on him). Ah! I've already said a few words to you — now the Manager will tell you where you get off!
'He'. I'm sure Mr Cripps is welcome. All I ask is justice.
Manager. This gentleman says you've ruined his hair.
'He'. Oh, I never did! I put my whole heart and soul into my work and never before have I had a complaint, so there.
Third Customer. When I come to a barber —
'He' (interrupting). Barber! I didn't come here to be insulted. Surely, in a high-class establishment like this, one is entitled to be called an artist!
Third Customer. Call yourself what you like — but look at my hair!
'He' (laying his fingers on the customer's head and turning to the Manager*).* You see, Mr Cripps, it all depends on the architecture of the 'ead — if you know what I mean. This gentleman has 'ighly developed bumps — if you'll excuse my putting it that way, sir.
Third Customer. You leave my bumps alone!
'He'. I'm not being personal, sir. To me my work is my all. Every 'ead is virgin soil — if you understand me. Now, your bump of generosity, sir — if you'll excuse me — doesn't go with the flat style of 'air-dressing. It simply shrieks out for a place in the sun, as it were.
Third Customer. I don't know about bumps — all I know is you've made me look like a monkey!
'He'. I assure you, sir, that's purely a matter of opinion.

('He' *giggles inanely.*)

Manager. That's enough, Cuthbert. You've made a mess of your work, so don't argue. You're sacked!

'He'. Sacked! Oh, but you can't sack me, really you can't. I don't know what I shall *do.* I've got my white-haired mother to keep and three sisters and the little boy that lives down the lane. You wouldn't be so *cruel.*

Third Customer (mollified). Oh, well, that's different. I didn't know you were supporting a family. We'll look over it this time.

'He'. No, it's no use. You've cut me to the quick. I couldn't stay now, you've hurt my artistic soul. We'll starve and it'll be all your fault — both of you. (*He crosses R.*)

Third Customer. Now, look here —

'He' (*turning by door*). Not another word. You've ruined me, and you know it. I'll never come into this beastly store again — never, never, never!

('He' *goes out R.*)

Third Customer. I feel very sorry about that.

Manager (rising). Please don't worry, sir.

(*They go up to door L. together.*)

I trust your next visit will be more satisfactory. Good morning.

(*The* Third Customer *starts to go through door when he is pushed aside by a bustling, hysterical woman, who turns round.*)

Fourth Customer. Are you the Manager?

Third Customer. No!

(*He exits.*)

Fourth Customer (to Manager). Are you the Manager?

Manager (crossing to desk). I am. Madam.

Fourth Customer (following him down, speaking very quickly). I've been meaning to come in since the day before yesterday. Of all the incompetence and lack of system! I was in your Gramophone Department ordering records and a fool of a man was there. I know him well. He has a mop of red hair —

('He' *puts on red wig.*)

stands about six feet in his socks,

('He' *gets on to a chair.*)

and has a wart on the left side of his nose.

('He' *dashes to make-up table for nose.*)

But my complaint isn't so much against him as the other fool. I distinctly asked him for 'Just a little Something' and he gave me 'His hot lips that never blow cold!' You know the black-faced man —

Manager (blankly). Black-faced man!

('He' *starts blacking his face.*)

Fourth Customer. The singer who made the record – Johnson or Jolson or something. Well, your assistant –

Manager. Which one, Madam?

Fourth Customer. The other one with the fair hair and the white face –

('He' *changes his wig and tries to rub the black off.*)

– *he* was positively rude. But the man in the shirt-sleeves was even worse.

('He' *tears off his coat.*)

And then I got to the one I'm *really* complaining of. That silly-looking blonde girl in the white blouse and black skirt.

('He' *discards collar and tie.*)

And if your girls must wear skirts they should be a decent length, I say. Better no skirts at all than up to the knees!

('He' *starts to take his trousers off, stops, and takes up a black apron for a skirt.*)

And of all the peroxided blondes I ever did see –

('He' *puts on a woman's wig.*)

With rouge on her cheeks and a huge painted mouth.

('He' *takes carmine, dabs his cheeks and paints an enormous mouth.*)

Heaven knows what her private life is like! But the man I *most* want to complain about is the stout idiot with a black beard and bow legs and a horrible squint – I could see it through his blue spectacles. He may have been dressed in a frock coat –

(*By this time* 'He' *has got thoroughly confused and looks a positive mess, so he staggers through door R.*)

'He' All right, all right! We're ALL sacked!

Black Out.

* * *

THE JUDGMENT OF PARRISH

by Dion Titheradge

Scene: A Morning Room.

A smart, bright room. An armchair R.C. Over L. a desk with a chair against it.

At the opening of the scene George *is sitting in the armchair reading* 'The Times'. Ruth *is standing by the desk.*

Ruth. George, you can read your paper going to the City. I wish you'd listen to me.
George (still reading). Yes, my dear? Go ahead.
Ruth. I'm going to get rid of Parrish.
George (lowering his paper). Parrish?
Ruth. The new parlourmaid.
George. Oh, yes? Well, she's been here a month — that's almost a record.
Ruth. For a girl of her sort, I should say wonderful. She's too attractive.
George. Is she, by Jove? I must look at her again. *(He returns to his paper.)*
Ruth (crossing to him). Now, do listen. Don't you realize we've got grown-up sons?
George (looking up). You don't mean to tell me — ?
Ruth. Yes, I do. She has two nights out a week. She divides them between John and Arthur.
George (rising). Well I'm damned! *(He crosses her to L. and turns.)* Are you sure of this, Ruth?
Ruth. Almost positive — though I can't swear to actual dates. She'll have to go.
George (turning away again and putting paper on desk). Well, you know best, my dear, but you realize what these modern girls are, I shouldn't go making wild accusations.
Ruth. My dear George, I flatter myself I'm modern, too. She hasn't the slightest idea that I suspect, so I shall simply go straight to the point and hear what she has to say.

*(*Parrish *enters R. A very attractive maid, neatly dressed.)*

Parrish. The car is here, sir.
George (turning from desk). Oh, thank you, I'm just coming.
Parrish. Yes, sir.

(She exits R.)

George (putting letters into his pocket). Is that the girl?
Ruth. Of course.
George. M'm. I don't think much of her. *(He crosses.)* Well, I'm off, darling. I shouldn't ask too many questions, if I were you. I'd just give her notice.
Ruth. Leave it to me. *(Kissing him.)* Don't be late to-night.
George. No. 'Bye, my dear. *(He crosses R.)*
Ruth. Oh, and send Parrish to me as you go out, will you?
George. Right.

(He exits. Ruth *moves to desk and sits, sorting some letters.* Parrish *re-enters R.)*

Parrish. You sent for me, ma'am?
Ruth. Yes, Parrish. I wanted to ask you something.

(She rises and turns. Parrish *approaches.* Ruth *looks straight at her, then speaks slowly.)*

Which of my two sons do you prefer going out with?
Parrish (quite unabashed). Well, ma'am, Mr. John is quite nice — and Mr. Arthur dances beautifully — but for a real good slap-up time give me the Master!

Black Out.

* * *

Ronald Jeans, man-of-the-theatre and wit (he once defined an Actor-Manager as 'one to whom the part is greater than the whole') supplies our next four sketches.

My favourite is *Incredible Happenings* but take note of the idea behind *Off The Lines*, i.e., that one actor speaks his part a few lines behind the other, and compare with the last sketch in this book, *Mastermind* — which was written some fifty years later.

CAUGHT IN THE ACT

by Ronald Jeans

Preliminary Speech

Ladies and gentlemen, we've had a spot of trouble with the next scene. It was the last to be written — in fact, to be quite candid, it's not quite finished yet. However, we have to put something in here — and as we know the beginning we're going to start away. Meanwhile the author is working away on his typewriter and I've no doubt he will catch us up before we get to the end. But you will understand he is working at very high pressure and for any small deficiencies that may be apparent we crave your indulgence.

Scene: The scene is an interior showing a window (curtained) in back and door either side. A large safe stands in a conspicuous place. A table. At the rise of the Curtain *the* Comtesse de Grand Marnier *(wearing a pearl necklace) is discovered. She rings the bell.* Wilmott, *her maid, enters.*

(Note: *During the whole of the dialogue a typewriter is heard off.)*

Comtesse. I shall wear my puce ninon to-night, Wilmott.

Wilmott. Yes, madame.

Comtesse. Dear Aubrey is so sensitive to puce. You are sure my husband has gone out?

Wilmott. Oh yes, madame. I have just called him a taxi.

Comtesse. I've called him worse things than that. But, Wilmott, suppose he should return!

Wilmott. He will not return, madame. He borrowed five pounds from me as he went out.

Comtesse. You are a good servant, Wilmott. I don't know what I should do without you!

Wilmott. No, madame.

Comtesse. I shall change immediately. Aubrey may be here at any moment now. See that everything is ready for me!

Wilmott. Yes, madame.

(Exit Wilmott. *The* Comtesse *goes to the safe, unlocks it, and takes out a jewel-box. She then takes the pearl necklace from her neck and puts it in the jewel-box, returning the box to the safe, which she locks and puts key in drawer. She then turns off lights and follows* Wilmott *off. A momentary pause, and the curtains move; then they are pulled cautiously aside, disclosing the silhouetted figure of a man. He comes into the room, flashes a torch on the safe, returns to window, and whistles; a second figure enters through window.)*

1st Crook. Give me the keys! You guard that door! *(He takes keys from the other and goes to safe.)* If you hear anybody coming — lock it! See?

2nd Crook (at the door through which the Comtesse *has gone out).* There's no key in this door!

1st Crook (busy at safe). Hell! That means somebody's taken it away!

2nd Crook. Very likely. They're moving about in the next room. Somebody's coming. We'd better quit.

1st Crook. No time for quittin' — leave it to me, kid!

(The Comtesse *enters and switches on the light which reveals the two figures in the uniform of American police. She utters a stifled scream and steps back.)*

(Assuming a very business-like tone.) Comtesse de Grand Marnier?

Comtesse. At your service!

1st Crook. No need for alarm, madame. From information received we suspect a big-scale burglary is to be carried out in this house to-night. We came in this way 'cos we didn't want to scare you — but with your permission we'll take a look around.

Comtesse. Burglary — here — to-night?

2nd Crook. That's what he said — we've no time to waste — so if you'll excuse us, we'll see where we can place our men.

(They go out. The Comtesse *goes to door and calls.)*

Comtesse. Wilmott! Wilmott!

(Enter Wilmott.*)*

Wilmott, the police are here. They are expecting a burglary! Do you know anything about it?

Wilmott. No, madame — *(She puts a piece of paper on the table.)*

Comtesse. There is more in this than meets the eye, Wilmott. *(Suddenly inspired.)* Wilmott, *(dramatically)* could it be that —

Wilmott. What, madame!

Comtesse. I wonder. *(She has worked round to the table. She picks up the piece of paper and looks at it.)* Yes, I have it! There is no burglary expected — it is my husband — he has sent these men to spy on me! Detectives! and Aubrey may be here at any moment! What am I to do?

Wilmott. I don't know, madame. *(She looks about helplessly, then sees a slip pushed under the door. She picks it up and reads from it.)* I have it. Have you any money, madame?

Comtesse. Money? What for?

Wilmott. Give me what you have and leave all to me.

Comtesse. Yes! Yes! *(She goes to a door and is handed a bundle of notes.)* Here is all I have — thirty thousand dollars.
Wilmott (reading from the back of the notes). Now I shall know how to deal with them. When they return leave us alone!
Comtesse. Yes, yes!

(The two Crooks *return.)*

1st Crook. Now, madame, where are the valuables?
Comtesse. In that safe! Jewels to the amount of a million dollars.
2nd Crook. Good!
1st Crook. Then this is the room we've got to watch. You go to your bedroom. You'll be better out of this!

*(*Wilmott *signals her to go.)*

Comtesse. Whatever you think best!

(Exit the Comtesse.*)*

Wilmott (quickly to the others). Thirty thousand among the three of us if you quit right now!
1st Crook (snatches a note from her and reads from it). What? and leave the necklace? Not on your life!
Wilmott (getting key from drawer). Here's the key of the safe. You get the necklace while I count out the notes! *(She gives him the key — he goes to safe — she is counting the notes.)*
1st Crook (to 2nd Crook*).* You guard the door!

(2nd Crook stands looking into corridor. The sound of a door shutting. The 2nd Crook *shuts the door hurriedly and turns a scared face to the others.* 1st Crook *leaves the safe.* Wilmott *crosses to* 2nd Crook.*)*

Wilmott. What — what was that?
2nd Crook (taking the notes that Wilmott *holds out to him after consulting them).* Footsteps! *(He looks through the keyhole, still consulting the notes.)* A man — coming this way.
Wilmott. Her lover! Quick — hide!

(The two Crooks *hide behind curtains as* Aubrey *enters. He is in immaculate evening dress, and carries an evening paper.)*

Aubrey (throwing his paper on the table). Good evening, Wilmott. Your mistress expecting me?
Wilmott (picking up the paper and reading from it). She's in her room, sir. Will you come this way? *(She puts the paper down again.)*

(He hesitates and again picks up paper. After consulting it.)

Aubrey. No, Wilmott, I'll wait; just tell her I'm here. *(He puts the paper down again.)*
Wilmott. Very good, sir.

(A hand is thrust through window placing a 'tear-off' calendar on nail in wall.)

Aubrey (alone). The twenty-third of February! (*He goes to calendar, tears off slip and reads from back.*) It's now or never!

(*He puts the slip down on table, then furtively looking round goes to the safe, and drawing a bunch of skeleton keys from his pocket begins to fit one after the other; meanwhile the two crooks cautiously come out from behind the curtains. They look at each other questioningly — uncertain what to do. The* 1st Crook *takes slip from table, reads it, and tiptoes towards* Aubrey, *who is still fumbling with the safe.*)

1st Crook (confronting Aubrey*).* Well — if it ain't Jim Higgins!
2nd Crook (snatching slip from 1st Crook*).* We all thought you'd turned straight, Jim.
Aubrey (disconcerted). I don't understand!
1st Crook. Out of it! We've got the key. Shares?
2nd Crook (to Aubrey*).* Shake?

(*They shake hands. By this means* Aubrey *receives a slip from* 2nd Crook.)

1st Crook. Is it a bet?
Aubrey (having consulted slip. Immediately assuming the crook). Sure! (*To* 2nd Crook.) You guard that door — I'll take this.

(1st Crook *goes to safe once more.*)

(*At door*). Look out! She's coming!

(*He leaves the door as the* Comtesse *enters.*)

The Two Crooks (covering Aubrey, *who is between them, with revolvers).* Put them up!
Comtesse. Aubrey! (*She hands a slip to* 1st Crook.)
1st Crook (reading from it). Caught him red-handed, madame! At the safe with skeleton keys?
Comtesse. Aubrey — is this true?

(*She hands* 1st Crook *a slip — he passes it to* Aubrey.)

Aubrey (reading from slip). It's a lie — a foul lie! You cannot believe me to be a common thief.

(Wilmott *has entered and handed* Comtesse *a slip. All the characters are now in line.*)

Comtesse (reading from slip). No — no — Aubrey — I trust you — for I love you.

(Wilmott *hands her a slip, which is passed via* 1st Crook, *to* Aubrey.)

Aubrey (reading from it). And I love you — more than life itself.

(Wilmott *has handed another slip which is passed all the way down the line to* 2nd Crook.)

2nd Crook. Thanks — that's all we wanted to know!

(*He blows a whistle. The safe door opens and the* Comte de Grand Marnier *steps out.*)

Comtesse. My husband!

(*The* Comte *advances with revolver pointing at* Aubrey. *In his other hand he carries a slip of paper.*)

Comte (*consulting slip, sings*). Way down in Wallabaloo where the skies are blue . . .

(*Or any popular song of the moment.*)

Comtesse. Idiot! You've got the wrong bit!

Curtain.

* * *

INCREDIBLE HAPPENINGS

by Ronald Jeans

Preliminary Speech

Ladies and gentlemen, the next scene is an attempt on our part to give you something completely different from anything you can see in any other theatre in London. As you know, all the plays you've ever seen have set out to reproduce events which happen, or might conceivably happen, in real life; so we thought it would be rather a change for you to see a few things that never do happen in real life. The following episodes we have therefore selected because they have never actually happened, and what is more, we are willing to guarantee that they never will happen.

No. 1

(*A man and a girl, in evening dress, seated at a table. Enter to them a* Waiter, *bearing change on plate. The man takes the change, selects some silver, and hands it to the* Waiter.)

Waiter. It's very kind of you, sir, but I really couldn't take it. I have served your dinner both clumsily and slowly, sir, and I am about to report myself to the Head Waiter.

Black Out.

(*During which replace table covering with whisky bottle, siphon and glasses.*)

No. 2

(*A* Barmaid *discovered standing behind table.* Mr Smith *and* Mr Cameron *enter.*)

Mr Smith. Will you have a drink?
Mr Cameron (*in broad Scots*). Not for me, Mr Smith. But ye'll hae a wee drappie ye'sel'?
Mr Smith. Thanks, I don't mind if I do.

Mr Cameron. A large whisky, please, for my friend here. (*Puts half a crown on counter.*) That's all richt. Ye can keep the change!

Black Out.

No. 3

(Husband *and* Wife *are discovered seated. A* Maid *enters and hands the* Husband *an envelope.*)

Wife. What is that, darling?
Husband. It's the bill for that hat you bought last week. I'm so glad you decided to buy it after all.
Wife. I think it was very extravagant of me, Jack.
Husband. Not at all, darling — I'm only sorry you didn't get the dress as well.
Wife. I would have — but I thought we ought to spend the money on a new suit for you.
Husband. Absurd! What should I do with a new suit? I have only had this one ten years.
Wife. But I like you to look smart, Jack. That reminds me, I've asked that pretty Miss Willoughby in to-morrow night.
Husband. To-morrow night? I thought you were going to Aunt Emily's to-morrow night.
Wife. So I am, darling. That's why I asked Ruby Willoughby in to keep you company. I know you like her; you even noticed the dress she wore at the theatre the other night.
Husband. I couldn't help it — there was so little of it —
Wife. She promised me she'd wear it to-morrow night just to please you.
Husband. Good Heavens! I shan't know where to look!
Wife. Oh! yes you will, darling. And listen, Jack, I shan't be back till midnight — and I'm sending the maids to the pictures!
Husband. Now that's very kind and thoughtful of you, darling!

Black Out.

No. 4

(*A* Gentleman *discovered seated in a* Barber's *chair having his hair cut.*)

The Barber. Your hair's in splendid condition, sir, and if you take my advice, you'll never put anything on it!

Black Out.

No. 5

(*A* Bookmaker *is discovered, with satchel and board.*)

Bookmaker. To win or a place! To win or a place. I'll lay 3 to 1 bar one!

(*Enter harassed* Racegoer.)

Racegoer. I beg your pardon, but can you tell me — did Stoneflint win the last race?
Bookmaker. He did, sir. At 33 to 1.

Racegoer. Now, isn't that annoying? I meant to put £5 on it, and I forgot.
Bookmaker. You really did mean to, sir?
Racegoer. Certainly I did.
Bookmaker. All right. I'll take your word for it.

(*Pays out.*)

Black Out.

No. 6

(*A Motor-car — a* Salesman *and* Customer.)

Customer. I must say she looks a nice car. How about petrol consumption?
Salesman. I must confess, sir, she's not very economical. I think you will be lucky if you get ten miles to the gallon out of her.
Customer. M'h! that's not very good!
Salesman. No, sir. That's the great drawback to our cars — they do eat up the petrol.
Customer. Is she silent?
Salesman. When the engine's not running, sir, very silent — otherwise she is — yes, she's *rather* noisy — especially at high speed. You'll find she'll always begin to knock a bit at twenty miles an hour.
Customer. And over that?
Salesman. Oh, she won't do more than that, sir — except downhill.
Customer. Then you don't really recommend me to buy one?
Salesman. Certainly not, sir. If I was you I'd go somewhere else.

Black Out.

No. 7

(*A table, two chairs. On the table is a sign 'Inland Revenue'. The* Tax Collector *is seated at the table. Enter a* Taxpayer.)

Taxpayer. Good morning! Are you the Income Tax Collector?
Collector. I am.
Taxpayer (*heartily*). I'm delighted to meet you, sir.

(*They shake hands.*)

Do you know you never sent me a form to fill up?
Collector. I'm sorry. (*Handing one.*)
Taxpayer. Thanks ever so much. You know, I've had such a *prosperous* year. My income is about *trebled.* So I thought I'd just write you out a cheque for a hundred pounds in case I drop dead on the way home!

Black Out.

No. 8

(A. *appears one side of stage with telephone instrument.*)

A. Hallo! Gerrard 4856, please. Yes.
Operator (*appearing C.*). Gerrard 4856?
A. Yes, please.

(*Bell rings. At other side of stage,* B. *appears, also with instrument.*)

A. Is that Gerrard 4856?
B. It is.

Black Out.

No. 9

(*A* Bricklayer *discovered laying bricks.*)

Bricklayer (*sings*). Work, boys, work — etc.

(*A whistle blows. Enter his* Mate.)

Mate. Knock off, Bill! Dinner-time!
Bricklayer. Dinner be blowed! I'm going to finish this job!

Black Out.

No. 10

(*Tube Lift gate C., and Booking Office window down L. There is no queue at the Booking Office, but two or three people enter in quick succession, pay, and receive tickets. Then a* Lady.)

The Lady. Golders Green, please. (*She receives ticket.*) Do you know, I'm awfully sorry, but I'm afraid I've only got a ten-pound note!
The Booking Clerk. That's all right, miss. You can pay any time you're passing!
The Lady. Thank you so much. (*She joins the others waiting for the lift.*)

(*A* Newsboy *crosses with contents bill of 'Evening News' bearing the words: 'No News of Interest To-night'. A dirty* Old Woman *carrying a large bundle of old clothes, etc., addresses a* Young Knut.)

The Old Woman. Could you tell me if I'm right for the Elephant?
The Young Knut. Perfectly right, madam — I am going to the Elephant myself, so if you will allow me —

(*He shoulders her bundle, and they take up their position side by side waiting for the Lift. A* Navvy *approaches the* Knut *from the other side.*)

The Navvy. Got a light, guv'nor?
The Young Knut. Certainly, sir. But I hate to see you smoking that clay. Won't you have a cigar? (*Puts down bundle and hands cigar.*)
The Navvy. Thank you, sir.
American (*entering with friend*). Waal — I've travelled some — but I guess your little old London has Noo York beat to a frazzle!

(*The Lift gate slowly opens, and the* Lift Man *steps out.*)

The Lift Man (*smiling benignly*). At your service, Ladies and Gentlemen!

Black Out.

* * *

ROAD TESTS FOR PEDESTRIANS

by Ronald Jeans

Scene A. (*Front cloth.*)

(*Husband and wife, seated at breakfast-table.*)

He (*opening official-looking letter*). I'm afraid I can't drive you down to Roehampton this morning after all, darling.
She (*disappointed*). Oh! John! Why not?
He. I've got to go and see about my walking licence.
She (*reproachfully*). John! You haven't applied for a walking licence?
He. Yes, darling. I've just had this notice from the L.C.C. asking me to call and see about it.
She. But, John dear, why do you want a *walking* licence? Isn't the car good enough for you?
He (*hesitating*). Yes, of course, dear — it isn't that . . .
She. You promised me when we married you'd give up walking and stick to the car. What has made you change, John?
He. I don't know. I suppose every man needs the spice of danger in his life. I've been leading such a sheltered existence, May, driving you about London in the Bentley. I want to feel the thrill of standing poised on the curb of the Haymarket, proud in the knowledge that when the moment comes I shall go over the top with the best of them. I want to use my legs as God meant me to use them, for leaping smartly out of the way of swooping taxicabs. I want to go out into the wide open spaces of Piccadilly Circus and scent the blood-lust of the bus-drivers.
She (*proudly*). I know, darling. It's perfectly splendid of you and I admire you for it. But have you thought what would happen to me if anything happened to you?
He. If we walk close together, darling, the same thing will happen to both of us.
She. Could *I* get a walking licence, too, John?
He. I don't think so. One has to go through pretty severe tests, nowadays.
She. What sort of tests?
He. I don't know exactly. You'd better come with me and you'll see.

(*They go off, as the* Curtains *open to:*

Scene B. (Full stage.)

(*Down stage R. is a table, at which, facing the audience, is seated the* Inspector. *Down L. are two windsor chairs. At back of stage is a signpost, at present blank.*)

(He *and* She *enter L. and cross to this table.*)

Good morning!

Inspector. Good morning.
He (*handing card*). I got this card asking me to call.
Inspector. Ah, yes. You want to take out a walking licence?
He. Yes, please.
She. I don't want him to have one if it's da . . .
He. Sh!
Inspector. Do you want a licence under Section D, H or J?
He. I beg your pardon?
Inspector. Do you want a licence under Section D, H or J?
He. I beg your pardon?
Inspector. Do you want to qualify for walking in the Country, in the Suburbs, or in London?
He. London.
Inspector. That will be Section J. I must warn you that to obtain a J walking licence, you have to satisfy us that you are not only proficient in all forms of leaping, hopping, skipping and dodging, but are noise-proof, shock-proof and curse-proof. Do you think you can do this?
He. You bet your life.
Inspector. It's *your* life the law is concerned with.
She (*beseeching*). Oh, John! Give up this mad idea.
He (*brushing her aside*). Tcha! Tcha! Sit down, dear, and don't interrupt.

(*She seats herself.*)

Inspector (*taking a form*). I shall have to ask you for certain particulars for your proposal form. Your name?
He. John Bullradish. (*The* Inspector *looks up suspiciously.*) Must I repeat? (*The* Inspector *writes it down.*)
Inspector. Occupation?
He. Husband.
Inspector. Husband? You mean husbandry?
He. Certainly not. I've only got one wife.
Inspector (*writes*). Occupation — Married.

(She *looks at her husband and smiles proudly.* He *smiles back.*)

There are certain medical questions . . . (*gives the wife a look*) perhaps . . . ?
He. Darling, would you like to . . . ?
She. No, I'm going to stay right here and see he answers correctly.
Inspector. State how many limbs you have lost in the streets of London during the year ending fifth April last.
He. None.
Inspector. That's very good. To what do you attribute your remarkable immunity?
He. Living in Norfolk.
Inspector. That's not so good. Have you ever as a pedestrian suffered from giddiness, hesitation or vans in the back?
He. No.
She. John dear, you're forgetting . . .

He (*to the* Inspector). Don't take any notice of her — she doesn't want me to get a licence.
She. He *has* suffered from a van in the back — a year ago last November.
Inspector. One van in back. Give exact spot on which you were hit . . .
He. Must I?

(Inspector *nods.*)

(*After a moment's hesitation.*) Bird Cage Walk.
Inspector. What were you looking at when the van hit you? If member of opposite sex, produce photograph.
He (*after a look at his wife*). I was admiring the sunset across the Park.
Inspector. I see. (*Reprovingly.*) Well, you won't escape so lightly if you go about admiring sunsets nowadays. (*Threateningly.*) There are noiseless eight-cylinder cars being specially built to deal with you and your kind.
She (*frightened*). Oh, John! Please don't go on with this!
Inspector. Don't interrupt, please. (*To the man.*) Now, (*returning to the form*) have either of your parents died premature deaths, or were they just run over in the ordinary way?
He. My father died of faulty acceleration of a Minerva.
Inspector. And your mother?
He. Mother was hoist with her own Packard.
Inspector (*writing*). Both parents died natural deaths. (*Leaves desk.*) Now for the eyesight tests. Look at that sign! (*Indicating sign C.*) And act accordingly. One! (*The sign reads 'Look left'. He obeys.*) Two! (*The sign changes to 'Look Right'. He obeys.*) Three! (*The sign becomes 'Look Out'. He jumps behind the* Inspector.) Very good! Very prompt and agile. Now turn your back on me. (He *does so. The* Inspector *produces a revolver, which he points at him.*) What have I got here?
He. I can't see.
Inspector (*incredulous*). You can't see?
He. I can if I turn round.
Inspector. That's no good. They don't give you time to turn round. (*Calls.*) Doctor! (*He puts away the revolver.*)

(*Enter a* Doctor.)

Take his pulse.

(*The* Inspector *re-seats himself at the table, while the* Doctor, *watch in hand, takes the patient's pulse. The* Inspector *signals to an* Assistant, *who creeps up behind the patient and blows a devastating blast on a Klaxon horn. The patient jumps a couple of feet in the air — the* Doctor *rushes after him and seizes his wrist again.*)

Doctor. Pulse increased by fifteen.
Inspector (*writing*). Fifteen.
Assistant (*who has produced a two-foot rule and taken the lateral measurement of jump*). Two foot, three inches.
Inspector. Two foot three. Give him the ear tests, please!

(*The* Assistant *blindfolds the patient.*)

Now listen intently and tell us what you hear!

(*A series of spasmodic loud explosions.*)

He. A motor-bicycle obeying the silencer laws.
Inspector. Right!

(*A rattling noise, with broken-winded blasts on horn.*)

He. A taxicab.
Inspector. Right!

(*A sharper rattling, with very high-pitched, frequent horn.*)

He. A Paris taxicab.
Inspector. Right!

(*A siren.*)

He. A ninety-eight super-charged Mercedes passing by on a by-pass.
Inspector. Right! Now, listen very carefully to this one.

(*An almost inaudible sigh.*)

He. A Rolls-Royce passing by on the same by-pass.
Inspector. Wrong.
He. Wait a minute! I know.
Inspector. Well?
He. A baby Austin standing by the roadside in a breeze.
Inspector. Right! Now try the street-crossing tests. (*To* Assistant.) Bring in that island. (*He leads him to the back of the stage.*) Here you are on the pavement, which we'll imagine is down there. (*Indicating the footlights.*) Are you ready? Go!

(*A noise to represent traffic. The man starts for the island. From his R. darts across* an Assistant, *carrying a profile taxicab.* He *narrowly escapes it and makes for the island. As* He *leaves the island, two other vehicles swoop down on him from his L.* He *dodges between them and reaches the footlights in safety.*)

He. Well, what do you think of that?
Inspector. That's an easy one to start with. Once again. (Inspector *leads him back to the back of the stage.*) Are you ready? Go!

(*This time the same business is repeated except that the vehicles are more numerous and travel faster, also a very flashy* Girl *leaves the downstage corner, as the* Man *leaves the back and they therefore meet on the island, where they exchange glances. The* Girl *then continues to the back, the* Man *looks after her and then, after carefully looking to his left, he proceeds towards the footlights. Half-way across he turns to have another look at the* Girl *and his reward is to be bumped in the small of the back by a vehicle, which has approached from his R.*)

(*Triumphantly.*) Got him!
He. That's not fair — it came the wrong way.
Inspector. Ah! This is a one-way street. Besides, you weren't concentrating — you were looking at that girl's . . .

He (*frowns at the* Inspector, *then whispers*). I say, who was she?
Inspector (*whispers back*). She's broken more bones than any woman in London. Now for our final test. Our Piccadilly Circus test.

(*The* Inspector *and his* Assistant *take hold of the man's arms. The* Inspector *blows a whistle to the accompaniment of noises and hoots — a fleet of cardboard buses and taxis rush in from the corner. Corners and all begin to gyrate round the central island. The* Inspector *and the* Assistant *lift the man by his elbows and swing him to and fro.*)

One! Two! Three! (*They hurl him into the traffic.*) Get across that if you can!

(*In his attempt to cross,* He *is carried round with the traffic and after a few futile attempts to escape from the stream,* He *gives up and begins to run and finally settles down to a marathon. So engrossed does* He *become in keeping ahead of the vehicle behind that* He *does not notice that one by one the vehicles in front of him leave the race at different heats, until finally* He *is being chased by one solitary taxicab. The* Inspector *blows his whistle. The man sinks exhausted on a chair.*)

(*Comes up to him and pats him on the back.*) That's fine! Here's your licence!

(*Hands him paper.*)

He (*rising proudly*). Darling, do you hear that? I've passed!
Inspector. Wait a minute!

(*The* Assistant *fits a driving-mirror on his shoulders.*)

Turn round!

(*The* Assistant *fits a reflector on his back.*)

She. Oh, John, I'm so proud!
He. Come, darling! So the knights of old went forth to battle.

(*Proudly* He *walks out, his wife on his arm.*)

Inspector. Next applicant, please.
Assistant (*calls off*). Next applicant, please.

(*There is a scream, off, and the wife runs in, covering her eyes.*)

Inspector. What is it?
She. I knew it would happen — I knew it would!

(*The* Man *is helped in by a policeman — his mirror is bent, his collar undone and he has a black eye.*)

Inspector. Already?

(*He nods feebly.*)

What got you?
He. I walked into a lamp-post!

Black Out.

*　　*　　*

OFF THE LINES

by Ronald Jeans

(Written in collaboration with H. C. G. Stevens)

The Scene represents a breakfast room. Table laid for breakfast C. — two chairs. Door R. Window L. C. Telephone on small table L.

Version 1

Mabel (seated at table, rising and calling through door). Hurry up, George — you'll miss your train!

(*Enter* George *R. She places his chair for him L. of table.*)

George. Don't worry — there are plenty of others! (*He sits in the chair.*)
Mabel. There's your tea, dear. You've got a good five minutes — don't bother to talk, darling. I've buttered your toast for you! I wonder what you would do without your little wifie!
George (patting her hand). She's a darling!
Mabel. I must really tell Jane to call you earlier. She's getting so slack about getting up in the morning.
George. And Cook is too!
Mabel. I think you had better tell her that, George dear. It will come better from you!
George. Better wait till to-night!
Mabel. I think so. You will have to tell her so tactfully, George, but firmly.
George. Yes, dear. I'll show her I mean business!
Mabel. And I'll remember to mend your pyjamas for you.
George. Yes, dear, all of them.
Mabel (rises). Shall I get your umbrella?
George (goes towards door). I don't think so. It's cold and dry as usual.
Mabel. Come and let me kiss you good-bye, then. (*They kiss.*)

(Mabel *goes to him, holding out overcoat.*)

George. How sweet you are to me!
Mabel. Of course I am. There you are — here's your hat.
George. You are the most devoted wife man ever had.
Mabel. Good-bye darling!

(*Exit* George. *She goes to window and waves to him. Telephone bell rings.*)
Hullo! That you, Dickie? What a narrow escape — George has only just gone. Yes, of course I love you. Romano's at one — right!

Black Out.

Tabs On.

Lights Up.

Compère *appears in front of* Tabs.

That, ladies and gentlemen, is how this playlet should be played. Unfortunately, one evening the Actor playing the part of the husband was half a minute late for his entrance, and the Actress who played the wife, being rather inexperienced, failed to rise to the occasion, with the result that he was several lines behind her throughout the sketch — as you will see.

No Black Out.

Tabs Off.

Version 2

Mabel (seated at table, rising and calling through door). Hurry up, George — you'll miss your train! (*She goes to table and sets his chair for him, then addressing the empty chair.*) There's your tea, dear. You've got a good five minutes — don't bother to talk, darling. I've buttered your toast for you. I wonder what you would do without your little wifie!

(*Enter* George.)

George. Don't worry, there are plenty of others.
Mabel. I really must tell Jane to call you earlier. She's getting so slack about getting up in the morning.
George. She's a darling!
Mabel. I think you had better tell her that. It will come better from you.
George. And Cook is too.
Mabel. I think so. You will have to tell her so tactfully, George, but firmly.
George. Better wait till to-night.
Mabel. And I'll remember to mend your pyjamas for you.
George. Yes, dear, I'll show her I mean business!
Mabel (rising). Shall I get your umbrella for you?
George. Yes, dear — all of them.
Mabel. Come and let me kiss you good-bye then.
George (rising and kissing her). I don't think so. (*Re-seating himself at the table.*) It's cold and dry as usual.
Mabel. Of course I am! There you are — and here's your hat. (*She crosses towards 'phone.*) Good-bye, darling. (*She waves to him. He is still seated at breakfast-table. Telephone bell rings.*)

(George *takes coat and hat from chair and struggles into them.*)

Hullo! That you Dickie? What a narrow escape — George has only just gone. Yes, of course I love you.
George. How sweet you are to me!

Mabel. Romano's at one — right!
George. You are the most devoted wife man ever had!

Black Out.

* * *

The following sketches are early Noel Coward, written when he was making his mark with words and music in London revues.

The three are interestingly different.

SORRY YOU'VE BEEN TROUBLED

by Noel Coward

(*When curtain rises* Poppy *is discovered asleep in bed. A breakfast tray is on a small table on her left, and a telephone on her right. Sunlight is streaming across the bed — the telephone rings violently.* Poppy *slowly wakes up.*)

Poppy (sleepily). Oh damn! (*She takes off receiver and speaks with a pronounced Cockney accent.*) 'Allo! 'Allo! Who is it, please? Mr Pringle — No, sir, I'm afraid Miss Baker isn't awake yet . . . Oh no, sir I daren't, sir, she'd sack me on the spot, sir. Yes, sir. Good-bye, sir. (*She slams down receiver crossly.*) Old fool, waking me up!

(*She takes the breakfast tray from side table and rests it on her knees. She proceeds to pour out coffee, she sips some of it and then begins to eat a little toast. The telephone rings again. She takes off receiver and speaks with her mouth full.*)

'Allo, 'allo — who is it speaking? (*Abruptly changing her voice.*) Maggie darling, is it you? Yes, I thought it was old Potty Pringle — twice this morning, dear, really it is the limit, he ought to be at home dandling his grandchildren — Oh yes, dear, orchids as usual — very mouldy-looking with rude speckles all over them, but still they *are* expensive — what! No! — You haven't got your Decree Nasty or whatever it is? — Darling, I'm frightfully glad — Well, if dragging you to the Beggar's Opera fourteen times isn't cruelty, I don't know what is — You'll have to be awfully careful now for six months, won't you? — Well, you'd better leave Claridge's and go to the Regent Palace, you'll be safer there — Do you mean to say the Judge actually said that to you in Court? — What a dreadful old man — but they're all the same, dear, no respect for one's finer feelings — Fanny? Oh no, it was quite different with her, she won her case on points like a boxer — No, nothing was ever proved because though she started for Brighton four times with the worst possible intentions, she never got further than Haywards Heath — Well, dear, I really am most awfully glad — I suppose they'll give you the custody of the Daimler — What? Oh no, darling, no such luck, I heard from him yesterday — he won't let me divorce him — Beast! — It isn't as if we were fond of one another, I haven't set eyes on him for five years — Yes, he's with Freda Halifax now, she got him away from Vera — I believe she's driving him mad — serve him right — what I think of husbands! — Oh no, Bobbie's different — besides, he isn't yet, I don't suppose he ever will be. (*She sniffs.*) You know, I love him terribly — Don't go on giggling — All right, Ciro's at one o'clock.

(*She puts receiver on and resumes her breakfast. Her expression is rather pensive and she occasionally sniffs pathetically. The telephone rings again, she answers it.*)

Hallo — Hallo — Yes, who is it? — What? — I can't hear. What? Oh the line's buzzing — Yes, yes, speaking — Police Station! Why — what's happened? — Yes — Last night — Oh, my God! — this is terrible — Yes, at twelve o'clock — I say — listen — Oh, they've cut me off!

(*She puts the receiver on again and sits in stricken silence for a moment. She bites her lip and dabs her eyes with her handkerchief — then a thought strikes her — she grabs the telephone.*)

Hallo — Exchange — get me Mayfair 7160 at once — Yes — Claridge's? — Put me through to Mrs Fanshaw, please — Oh, quick, quick, it's urgent — Hallo — Maggie — Maggie, is that you? — Oh, my dear, listen, the most awful thing — the police have just rung me up — Jim jumped over Waterloo Bridge last night — No, darling, I don't know what time — Yes, I knew you'd be sympathetic — That's a little callous of you, dear; remember he *was* my husband after all — I'm wretched — utterly wretched — Yes, naturally they communicated with me first, how were they to know we hadn't seen each other for years? — Oh, it's awful — awful! Yes, Ciro's one o'clock (*She hangs up receiver for a moment, then bangs lever violently.*) Hallo — Hallo — Kensington 8712 — yes, quickly. Hallo, is that you, Flossie? Poppy speaking — My dear, Jim's dead! (*She sniffs.*) Thank you, darling, I knew you'd be a comfort — No, dear, he jumped off Waterloo Bridge — Yes, the one next to Charing Cross — No, no, no, *that's* Blackfriars. Don't be so silly, Flossie, you know perfectly well Westminster comes first, then Charing Cross — the one with trains on it, *then* Waterloo — Oh, how *can* you — you do say the most dreadful things, you'll only make me break down again in a minute — I'm having such a struggle — such a bitter, bitter struggle — (*She sobs.*) Anyhow, I'm quite successful enough without that kind of advertisement — Look here, lunch with Maggie and me at Ciro's one o'clock — All right — *thank you,* darling. (*She hangs up receiver again. Then after a moment's pause she calls up.*) Hallo, hallo, Regent 2047, please — yes — I want to speak to Miss Hancox, please — Yes, it's important — Hallo, is that you, Violet? Poppy speaking. You know when you told my cards the other day you told me something dreadful was going to happen? Well, it has! — Oh, no, darling, not *that,* anyhow I haven't seen him since Tuesday — no, no, much worse — Jim's dead. Yes, dead — I know, dear, I try to look at it in that light, but it's very very hard — you see, after all he was my husband — I know three months wasn't long, but still — You do say divine things — it wasn't very kind of him, was it? — Well, dear, Maggie and Flossie and I are lunching at Ciro's at one — come too, and we'll talk it all over then. Good-bye.

(*She hangs up receiver and then rings up again.*)

Hallo, hallo, Exchange — Mayfair 6773, please — yes — Hallo, is that the Guards' Club — yes, put me through to Lieutenant Godalming, please — yes, please — (*She puts receiver down for a moment while she takes puff from under her pillow and powders her nose — then she speaks again.*) Hallo, is that you, darling? — Oh, I'm sorry, Higgins, I thought it was Lieutenant Godalming — in his bath? — Please, please get him out of it, Higgins, it's frightfully important — Yes, I'll hold on — (*There is a pause.*) Darling — something too fearful has happened — yes, absolutely appalling — Jim's dead. What — who's Jim? He's my husband, of course — yes, he jumped off Waterloo Bridge last night — *He jumped off Waterloo Bridge last night. No! Waterloo Bridge!* Your ears must be full of soap — Isn't it dreadful? — Now, Bobbie dear, you mustn't be naughty — No, darling, I won't listen to you — I'm very, very miserable — it's been a terrible shock — Very well, I'll forgive you — Kiss me, then. (*She responds to his kisses over the telephone.*) Yes, to-night — somewhere quiet — really quiet — I shan't have any appetite — No, that would be too heartless — No, that would be too dull — Say the Embassy — All right, good-bye, darling — Bobbly wobbly —

(*She hangs up receiver and rings up again.*)

Hallo — Brixton 8146, please — Hallo, is that you, Mr Isaacstein? It's Miss Baker speaking — will you fetch my mother down, please — Yes, it's important. (*A slight pause.*) Is that you, Mum? — What do you think, Jim's been and drowned himself — I don't know — I expect Freda drove him to it — No, mother, I won't have you saying things like that — besides, he's too young to marry yet — Look here, Flossie, Violet, Maggie and I are lunching at Ciro's — One o'clock — come along too and we'll talk it all over — You can wear that old one of mine — All right.

(*She rings off and screams for her* Maid.)

Lily — Lilee — come here —

(*She pushes breakfast-tray to the end of the bed and is just about to spring out when her* Maid *enters, sobbing bitterly.*)

What is it? What's the matter with you?

Lily. It's dreadful, dreadful —

Poppy. What's dreadful?

Lily. That poor dear upstairs —

Poppy. Mrs Straker?

Lily. Yes, Mrs Straker — she's just heard that her husband jumped off Waterloo Bridge last night.

Poppy. What!!

(*The telephone rings violently.* Poppy *snatches up the receiver, listens for a moment, then hurls the instrument to the floor.*)

(*Through clenched teeth.*) Sorry you've been troubled!

Black Out

* * *

GROWING PAINS

by Noel Coward

The atmosphere and period are mid-Victorian. The scene is a refined English home.

(Mamma *with chignon and bustle is discovered weeping while* Papa *with mutton-chop whiskers towers over her.*)

Papa. The boy must be told.
Mamma. Humphrey, Humphrey.
Papa. He has reached the age of — of —
Mamma. But only with the greatest care, Humphrey.
Papa. There comes a time when a mother's tender solicitude must give place to a father's worldly influence.
Mamma. My son, my son. (*She weeps again.*)
Papa. Where is the lad?
Mamma. Learning his Collect for Sunday.
Papa. Call him.
Mamma. But Humphrey —
Papa (*sternly*). Call him, Marion — and be brave.
Mamma (*going to the door*). Herbert! Herbert! Your father wishes to speak to you. Oh, Humphrey, Humphrey — he is my babe, my unsullied blossom — I cannot bear it.
Papa. Life is life, Marion — the boy must be told.

(Herbert *comes running in — he is a well-grown lad, dressed à la Little Lord Fauntleroy. He is sucking a pink sweet on a small stick.*)

Herbert. You call me, Mamma?
Mamma. Herbert — I — we — your father — oh dear, oh dear, oh dear! (*She goes out weeping.*)
Herbert. Poor Mamma! She seems slightly hysterical this morning.
Papa. Herbert!
Herbert. Yes, Papa.
Papa. Be seated.
Herbert. Very well, Papa. (*He sits down.*)
Papa. The time has come, Herbert, for you to be informed of certain facts of life which hitherto have been veiled from you.
Herbert (*with a leer*). Yes, Papa?
Papa. You have reached an age when — er —
Herbert. Oh yes, Papa.
Papa. I feel that my duty as a father towards you lies in the — er — revelation of — er — er —
Herbert. Yes, Papa.
Papa. Put that sweet down.
Herbert (*laying it on the table*). Very well, Papa.
Papa (*clearing his throat nervously*). There are in life, Herbert, certain strange elements which as a growing lad it is only right for you to know — for instance —
Herbert (*smiling*). Go on, Papa.

Papa. For instance — er — you may often have wondered during your childish frolics in the garden and in the meadows — how the — er — flowers and — er — birds —
Herbert. Oh yes, Papa. (*He takes up the sweet again.*)
Papa. Well, Herbert, I will go even further.
Herbert. Very well, Papa.
Papa. Has it ever occurred to you to question the appearance of a flock of tiny golden chicks or a young calf or a —
Herbert (*wriggling delightedly*). Go on, Papa.
Papa. Stop sucking that sweet.
Herbert. Yes, Papa. (*He puts it down again.*)
Papa. Where was I?
Herbert. It's not for me to say, Papa.
Papa (*pompously*). Your mother and I, Herbert —
Herbert (*leaning forward*). Oh, Papa!
Papa. Your mother and I have decided after a great deal of thought that there are certain facts of life which should be made clear to you.
Herbert. You've said that before, Papa.
Papa (*irritably*). Never mind whether I've said it before or whether I have not said it before — that is not the point.
Herbert. What is the point, Papa?
Papa (*clearing his throat again*). The point is this, Herbert — have you ever noticed a litter of little pigs in the sty — ?
Herbert (*with slight boredom*). Oh yes, Papa. (*He takes his sweet again.*)
Papa. And, Herbert — has it ever occurred to you to ask yourself — er — er —
Herbert. I'm waiting, Papa.
Papa. The little pigs — er — grow and grow and grow until one day they — er — become — er — big pigs.
Herbert (*eagerly*). What then, Papa?
Papa. When they are big pigs they are sometimes sold and killed for bacon and — er — sometimes they are — er — not killed.
Herbert. Obviously, Papa.
Papa. And the ones that are not killed sometimes — er —
Herbert. Go on, Papa.
Papa. Will you stop sucking that filthy sweet!

(*He snatches it out of his hand and throws it across the room.*)

Herbert. Why are you so nervous, Papa?
Papa. I am not in the least nervous, Herbert, but that which I have to tell you is rather delicate — and — er — rather difficult.
Herbert. What is that you want to tell me, Papa?
Papa (*with a gulp*). My boy — there is no Santa Claus!

Black Out

* * *

THE ORDER OF THE DAY

by Noel Coward

The scene is a front cloth of a street with, on the right, three steps leading to the front door of a neat little house.
(*The* Husband *and* Wife *come out — he is wearing a business suit, bowler hat, etc., and carrying a little bag.*)

Wife. Well, good-bye, dear.
Husband. Good-bye.
Wife. Be home in good time for dinner.
Husband. I always am.
Wife. Have you got everything?
Husband. Yes everything. Good-bye. (*He kisses her and walks off L.*)

(*When she has waved to him she goes into the house and comes out again with a pail of water and a scrubbing brush — she kneels down with her back to the audience and proceeds to scrub the steps. The* Husband *comes on again L. tapping his pockets, obviously having forgotten something. He sees his wife, smiles and, meaning to surprise her, creeps gaily up behind her and gives her a playful slap.*)

Wife (*without turning her head*). Only half a pint this morning, Mr Jones.

Black Out

* * *

A curiosity. Early in 1982 the writer Brian Aldiss invented a literary game in which authors were challenged to write what he called a Mini-saga, a novel in exactly fifty words.

Before the last war Maurice Lane-Norcott wrote an eight-act play in exactly forty-three words.

THE TRAGEDY OF JONES

by Maurice Lane-Norcott

Preliminary Speech

We now come to our great eight-act play. This, of course, is a remarkable achievement, because a complete play has never been presented in revue before. Now the difficulty in fitting a whole play into a revue is that whole plays are always so long. This struck the producer at once. Accordingly he limited the author to only a very few words. 'What we want,' said our producer, 'is a gripping play with a strong love interest in not more than 50 words.' 'I see,' said the author. '50 words. Must it be as long as that?' 'Well, say not more than 45 words,' replied the producer. So the author went away and wrote his play. The result we are now going to show you in 'The Tragedy of Jones' — a play written in 43 words and eight acts, with one central character; this giving an average of one-eighth of a character and five and a half words per act. 'The Tragedy of Jones.'

(*Up small* Curtain. *The* Announcer *remains on the stage.*)

Scene: *This is a girl's boudoir throughout, and is sufficiently represented by a table and chair. In each act the* Girl *is discovered in the process of composing a letter. She bites the end of her pen thoughtfully and reads aloud what she is writing as she writes it. Between each act she makes some slight change of clothing in order to show the passing of time. The scene should be an inset scene with a small* Curtain.

ACT 1

Girl (*reading*). 'Dear Mr Jones, I . . .'

(*Lower small* Curtain.)

Announcer. One week later.

(*Up small* Curtain.)

ACT II

Girl (*reading*). 'Dear Harry, You . . .'

(*Lower small* Curtain.)

Announcer. A second week later.

(*Up small* Curtain.)

ACT III

Girl (*reading*). 'My very darling Harry, You — and I . . .'

(*Lower small* Curtain.)

Announcer. A week has elapsed.

(*Up small* Curtain.)

ACT IV

Girl. (*reading very affectionately*). 'My beloved own angel darling Harry. You — and I — *and* Mother . . .'

(*Lower small* Curtain.)

Announcer. Seven days have slipped by.

(*Up small* Curtain.)

ACT V

Girl (*reading coldly*). 'Dear Harry, You . . .'

(*Lower small* Curtain.)

Announcer. Another week has glided away.

(*Up small* Curtain.)

ACT VI

Girl (*reading very coldly*). 'Dear Mr Jones, — I . . .'

(*Lower small* Curtain.)

Announcer. The space of a week has dragged past.

(*Up small* Curtain.)

ACT VII

Girl (*reading very icily*). 'Miss Smith presents her — *compliments* to Mr Jones and . . .'

(*Lower small* Curtain.)

Announcer. We now come to the last act. Fourteen days have passed.

(*Up small* Curtain.)

ACT VIII

Girl (*reading ecstatically*). '*Dear Mr Anstruther!*'

Black Out.

* * *

The sketch based upon word-play had become somewhat subtler since our second item, *Nicholas Knox, of Nottingham.*

How subtle it had become can be judged by the following which takes us admirably through the alphabet.

A MAN OF LETTERS

by C. B. Poultney

They are seated at the breakfast table. Mr Alfy Bett, *who is a small sad man, is reading the morning paper.* Mrs Ethel Bett, *who is larger, is trying to make conversation.*

Mrs Bett. Any noos? (*No answer.*) *Any noos?* (*No answer.*) Oh, thanks very much! Upon my word, it's fair sickening, that it is. I might as well be married to a blessed mummy as you. There you sets, and not a blessed word can I get out of you but a grunt. Blest if I know if you *can* talk or not, straight I don't. In the morning you sets and reads the paper, and in the evening you sets and goes to sleep. Do you *know* any words of more than one sillybul — I've never 'eard you use 'em. (*Getting all worked up.*) Hi! I'm talking to you.

Mr Bett (*looking up slowly*). Eh?

Mrs Bett. There you go — A! I wonder you don't use the deaf and dumb language when you talk to me. Or the alphabet.

(Mr Bett *hastily takes a drink of tea, and chokes.*)

Now wot's the matter with the man? Swallered a tealeaf or somethink? Well, why don't you swear? Anything to 'ear you say something.

(Mr Bett *fishes in teacup with spoon.*)

Well, what is it?

Mr Bett (*peering*). Bee.

Mrs Bett. A bee, you fool? How can it be a bee? There's no bees about at this time of the year. Don't be so soft.

Mr Bett (*holding out spoon in triumph*). See!

Mrs Bett (*rather discomforted*). Why, so it is a bee. How in the world did it get there? Anyway, it won't 'urt you; you ain't even swallered it. The fuss you make about a mere trifling bee! Why, I'm sure you swallered whole 'oneycombs in the Army and never complained. Personally, I wonder you ever left the Army at all; I'm sure it was a bad day for me when you was ex-mobilized, or un-mobilized, or wotever you called it.

Mr Bett (*briefly*). De.

Mrs Bett (*impatiently*). Well, *de*-mobilized, then. Tell me I'm wrong, do. Why can't you behave a bit more decenter, and not be for ever arguing? Look at that Mister Burkin next door — you never 'ear *'im* always complaining.

Mr Bett (*contemptuously*). 'E —

Mrs Bett (*sharply*). No 'e ain't, then; he's a gentleman, 'e is, and knows how to *treat* a wife. Not like you, you hulking great brute.

Mr Bett (*hurt*). Eff!

Mrs Bett. And I'll trouble you not to call me Eff — my name's Effel. That's one of your slang tricks wot you picks up from that low friend of yours — the American bloke — and I don't like it. American slang, in my opinion, is nothink less than perishing, blooming iggerance.

Mr Bett (*drawing back*). Gee!

Mrs Bett (*enraged*). There you go again; will you stop it now? I tell you I don't like it. Nor I don't like your friend, neither, and as for 'is wife —

Mr Bett (*who has been listening gloomily, suddenly sneezes*). *Aitch!*

Mrs Bett. 'Ullo, caught a cold now, 'ave you? Well, I don't wonder. I suppose that's standing at the gate saying good-night to 'er.

Mr Bett (*protestingly*). I —

Mrs Bett (*accusingly*). Don't attempt to deny of it, now.

(Mr Bett *subsides.*)

Well, I always *thought* there was something between you two. Mrs Smallweed said only yesterday that I ought to watch you.

Mr Bett (*with contempt*). Jay!

Mrs Bett. Don't you dare to call my best friend a jay. She's a lady, she is, and very different from your Mrs — Mrs — wot's 'er name?

Mr Bett (*sulkily*). Kay.

Mrs Bett. That's it — Kay. Sadie Kay. Huh! There's a nice name to walk about with. Fast cat! But there. I s'pose you like 'em fast.

Mr Bett (*fed up*). 'Ell!

Mrs Bett (*in resigned tones*). Now he's swearing at me. Wot a *nice* 'usband to 'ave. Never speaks but wot he swears. How you can be so cruel I do not know; I'm sure I've always been a good wife to you, ain't I? Wasn't it only yesterday I sewed a new 'em on your shirt?

Mr Bett (*puzzled*). 'Em?

Mrs Bett (*impatiently*). Oh, well, I don't know wot you call it; it was the part where — Anyway, it was the part I sewed on. (*Changing subject.*) And wot about the lovely breakfast I've give you this morning. New-laid egg straight from the duck.

Mr Bett. 'En.

Mrs Bett. Duck, I tell you. Anyway, the man said it was a duck's egg and charged according. But don't mind me; call me a liar at once, and 'ave done with it.

Mr Bett (*protesting*). Oh —

Mrs Bett. No use you saying you didn't, now, cos I 'eard you. (*Sobs.*) And me slaving night and day to make you comforbal. Look at wot I'm going to give you tonight. A nice surprise — soup.

Mr Bett (*showing signs of interest*). Pea?

Mrs Bett. Ah, I shan't tell you, or it'd spoil the surprise. Besides, if you knew you mightn't come 'ome at all. (*Hastily, as* Mr Bett *looks at her suspiciously.*) Ready for some more tea?

Mr Bett (*pushing over cup*). 'Kyou.

Mrs Bett (*trying to rouse him*). *'Kyou.* I s'pose you mean *thank you.*

Mr Bett (*deep in paper*). Ah!

Mrs Bett (*indignantly*). Then why not say so? Too much trouble, I suppose?

Mr Bett (*nodding absently*). 'Es.

Mrs Bett. I thought so. Too much trouble to be decently perlite to your poor wife. Like 'aving a statoo for breakfast, you are. Nodding and grunting, and never —

Mr Bett (*stretching out hand*). Tea.

Mrs Bett (*pettishly*). Well, there you are; take it, for goodness' sake. (*Hands tea. As she does so Postman's knock is heard at door.*) There's the postman.

(Mr Bett *reads calmly on.*)

Oh, don't bother, I'll go myself. (*She goes and fetches letter.*) 'Ullo, it's for me; now p'raps he *will* say something. (*Returns to table. As she does so* Mr Bett, *without looking up, stretches out his hand.*) Oh no, you don't my lord — this is for *me.*

Mr Bett (*looking up*). You?

Mrs Bett. Yes — *me.* Is there anything strange in me 'aving a letter now and then, may I ask? (*Turns letter over in her hands.*) Now I wonder who *this* is from? Can't make the postmark out. Can you? (*Holds letter in front of him.*)

Mr Bett (*peering*). V —

Mrs Bett (*snatching it away again*). V? V? I know — Ventnor. Why, this'll be from Aggie. You've 'eard me speak of Aggie, ain't you? My cousin, y'know. (*Opens letter rapidly.*) Yes, it is . . . *What.* . . . Well, fancy that, now — she's engaged. Well, I'm blessed. Aggie engaged. Lor! Well, they say wonders will never decease. But fancy

Aggie, of all people. Why, I bet she's as big as a house now, if she's gone on increasing. Why, even when she was sixteen she was double my size.

Mr Bett (*incredulously*). Double *you*?

Mrs Bett (*sharply*). Yes, double *me*. And why not, pray? There's nothing remarkable in that, is there? I'm only — but never mind wot I am, Aggie is a very charming girl. I won't 'ear a word against 'er. After all she *ought* to make a good match, considering as her father, my uncle, is a jockey.

Mr Bett Ex.

Mrs Bett. Yes, of course I mean *ex*-jockey — don't be so finicky. Anyway he was a man oo always got on very well, and Aggie being 'is only child you can quite understand 'er getting off. Great friends we used to be, 'er and me. People used to call us the two Graces.

Mr Bett (*staring*). Why?

(*Before she can reply a whistle is heard outside.* Mr Bett *glances at clock, springs uup, grabs his hat, and rushes out, banging door behind him.*)

Mrs Bett (*gazing after him*). Well, I'm blessed. There's a nice way to go off. He might at least 'ave said Z!

Curtain.

* * *

During the Golden Era of lavish revues, the 20s and 30s, a tendency grew towards shorter sketches, perhaps because musical scenas became more elaborate and longer, and the light comedians were allowed a smaller slice of the available time.

The following five sketches are typical of this move towards expressing the idea of the sketch as briefly as possible.

YES AND NO

by Harold Simpson

Preliminary Speech

Ladies and Gentlemen — there have been many complaints lately that people are too fond of using the same hackneyed, stereotyped phrases over and over again. Well, why not? Economy is a good thing — even in words. We will show you how a young man of limited conversation came successfully through the most trying ordeal in the world — asking a father for his daughter's hand — by the use of two little ordinary everyday words.

Scene: A sitting-room.

When the Curtain *rises the* Father *is sitting in a chair reading a newspaper. Enter* Maid.

Maid (*announcing*). Mr Palethorp!

(Young Man *enters.* Maid *exits.*)

Father (*throwing down paper and rising*). How are you, my boy — all right?
Young Man (*nervously*). Yes.

(*They shake hands.*)

Father (*playfully*). You've come to see me about my daughter! Am I wrong?
Young Man. No.
Father. I understand that you want to marry her.
Young Man. Yes.
Father. I hope that there's nothing in your past that — er —
Young Man. No.
Father. Still, I suppose you've sown a few wild oats?
Young Man (*grinning*). Yes.
Father (*heavily jocular*). Ah well, I've been young myself.
Young Man (*as though expressing surprise*). No!
Father. Won't you sit down?
Young Man. Yes. (*Sits down.*)
Father. Now, you don't mind if I discuss business?
Young Man. No.
Father. But one has to be careful.
Young Man. Yes.
Father. Not that I care about money.
Young Man (*questioningly*). No?
Father. Still, I feel bound to ask the question — is your income a good one?
Young Man. Yes.
Father (*rubbing his hands*). Capital! (*With studied carelessness.*) Is it true that your uncle left you part of his fortune?
Young Man. No.
Father (*disappointed*). Oh! (*Hopefully.*) Perhaps he left you everything?
Young Man. Yes.
Father (*pleased*). That's *very* satisfactory. (*Anxious.*) You haven't — er — squandered it?
Young Man. No.
Father (*rubbing his hands*). Then — er — shall we consider it settled?
Young Man (*rising*). Yes.

(*They shake hands.*)

Father. I suppose you've no doubt as to what my daughter will say?
Young Man. No.
Father (*aghast*). No?
Young Man. Yes.
Father (*laughing*). Oh, I see what you mean. You young dog! (*Slaps him on the shoulder.*) Well, good luck! (*Exit laughing R.*)

(*Enter* Daughter *L.*)

Daughter. Well — had a row?
Young Man. No.
Daughter. Was father nice to you?
Young Man. Yes.
Daughter. Then he doesn't object to you as a son-in-law?
Young Man. No.
Daughter (*coming to him with outstretched arms*). Oh, you darling! Don't you think you're the luckiest man in the world?
Young Man (*looking at her critically*). Yes *and* no!

Curtain.

* * *

WHEN TELEVISION COMES TO TOWN
A Sketch in Two Parts
by Harold Simpson

PART I. BEFORE TELEVISION

Scene: An Office.

Hilary Dexter *is discovered sitting at his desk. A clock strikes six.* Hilary *throws down his pen, yawns, and stretches himself. Enter* Maisie Fothergill, *a very pretty typist.*

Maisie. Do you want me any longer, Mr Dexter?
Hilary (*looking at her*). No . . . er . . . yes. Shut the door, please.

(Maisie *goes and shuts the door, then comes back.* Hilary *rises.*)

Do you mind working overtime?
Maisie. Not if it's business.
Hilary. It depends what you mean by business.
Maisie. Well . . . all this. (*Indicates desk.*)
Hilary (*coming closer to her*). Don't you get sick of business sometimes?
Maisie. Oh, I don't know. It's something to do.
Hilary. Yes . . . but there are lots of other things one can do.
Maisie (*looking at him innocently*). Are there?
Hilary (*coming closer still*). Especially when a girl's as pretty as you are.
Maisie (*turning her head away*). Oh, Mr Dexter!
Hilary. Hilary . . .
Maisie. Hilary!
Hilary. Maisie! (*Suddenly takes her in his arms and kisses her passionately.*)
Maisie (*struggling*). Oh, you shouldn't!
Hilary. Why not . . . don't you like it?
Maisie. Yes.
Hilary. So do I. (*Kisses her again*). Doing anything this evening?

Maisie. Nothing particular.
Hilary. Then how about making a night of it?
Maisie. Oh, Mr Dexter!
Hilary. Hilary . . .
Maisie. Hilary!
Hilary. Dinner, theatre . . . supper if you like. Then I'll see you home.
Maisie. I live with mother.
Hilary. How old-fashioned! Where?
Maisie. Golders Green.
Hilary. Couldn't you make it Barnet?
Maisie. Why?
Hilary. Farther to drive.
Maisie. Oh, Mr . . .
Hilary. Hilary . . .
Maisie. Hilary!
Hilary. Then that's settled! (*Embraces her again.*) Run and get your things on.
Maisie. All right. (*Moves off, then stops and turns.*) But aren't they expecting you home?
Hilary. Oh, my lord . . . so she is! I must ring up. What's the number?
Maisie (*coming back*). Can't you remember your own number?
Hilary. I can't remember anything when I look at you.

(*He sits down, pulls her on to his knee, and hugs her. She pretends to expostulate.*)

Maisie. Oh, you really mustn't!
Hilary. Can't help it . . . seems to come natural. (*Reaching out for 'phone.*) Now for it!
Maisie. What excuse are you going to make?
Hilary. Oh, the usual one.
Maisie (*playfully*). Am *I* the usual one?
Hilary. You're one in a thousand! (*Hugs her, then prepares to take off receiver.*) Now, what the devil is the number? Oh, I know! (*Takes off receiver and speaks in 'phone.*) Hullo. Give me Hampstead 0-seven-0-one. Yes. (*Listens.*) Is that you, my darling? I say, dearest, I'm most awfully sorry, but I can't possibly get home to dinner. (*Listens.*) No, not till rather late, I'm afraid. (*Listens.*) Yes, in the office. Something's cropped up quite unexpectedly. (*Listens.*) Oh, yes . . . business, of course. I've got my hands full.

(*He hugs* Maisie, *who squeals.*)

(*In 'phone.*) What's that, dearest? No, *I* didn't hear a squeak. I expect the line wants oiling. (*Listens.*) No . . . I couldn't very well ask my typist to stop after hours. (*Listens.*) Yes, it *must* be done to-night. (*Listens.*) Oh, I don't mind . . . it's a bit of good luck, really. (*Listens.*) Yes . . . fell right into my lap. (*Playfully.*) I shall be able to buy little wifie that new hat she wanted. (*Listens.*) I thought you'd like that! Good-night, my angel. Don't sit up for me. (*Listens.*) *Darling!*

(*He blows a kiss into the 'phone, hangs up receiver, then puts his arms round* Maisie *and hugs her.*)

Black Out.

PART II. AFTER TELEVISION

Scene: The same Office.

Hilary Dexter *discovered dictating a letter to his typist, who is standing by him taking it down in shorthand. The typist is a forbidding-looking person with hair brushed straight back and wearing a blue overall and blue glasses.*

A clock is striking six.

Hilary (*dictating*). With reference to your letter of the 16th inst., I beg to inform you . . . (*Breaks off.*) Just a moment! I'm afraid we shall be working late to-night. I must ring up my wife to say I can't get home to dinner. (*Picks up telephone and takes off receiver.*) Hullo. Give me Hampstead 0-seven-0-one. (*Listens.*) Is that you, my darling? I say, dearest, I'm most awfully sorry, but I can't possibly get home to dinner. (*Listens.*) Oh, yes . . . business, of course. Miss Salt has kindly consented to stay on late and help me out. (*Listens.*) You can see for yourself, can't you? What a blessing this television is, to be sure! (*Listens.*) Goodnight, my angel.

(*He hangs up receiver, then rises and holds out his arms. With a little laugh,* Maisie *whips off her wig and blue glasses and flies into his arms.*)

Black Out.

* * *

SAVED?

by Harold Simpson

Compère. We are now going to take you back a long, long way — to the days of the Indian Mutiny, in fact. I must ask you to imagine that we are in a room in the Colonel's quarters. The Colonel is manning the defences with the rest of his depleted regiment. The mutineers are getting nearer and nearer. They are yelling like fury and shooting like mad. (*Appropriate noises off.*) The Colonel's Wife is pacing up and down the room in an agony of dread, when . . .

The Tabs open. A sofa is on the stage. Noises off continue.

The Colonel's Wife *is discovered pacing up and down. Enter the* Major.

Wife. Oh, Major Andrews! Any hope?
Major. None. We're nearly down to the last man.
Wife. My God!
Major. We've been promised relief — the Highlanders. But there's no sign of them.
Wife. So this is the end?
Major. I'm afraid so.
Wife. What are we going to do?
Major. That's what the Colonel sent me to tell you. (*He produces a revolver.*) Two bullets!

Wife. What d'you mean?
Major. One for you and one for me.
Wife. As bad as that?
Major. Not so bad as falling into the hands of . . .
Wife (*nodding*). Quite. (*A dramatic pause*.) Ronald!
Major. Yes?
Wife. You know I love you.
Major. I . . . I guessed.
Wife. And *you* love *me!*
Major (*nodding*). You may as well know . . . now.
Wife. How long have you loved me?
Major. For years.
Wife (*exultingly*). I knew it! (*Reproachfully*.) And you never told me!
Major. You are the Colonel's wife and . . . (*He makes a gesture*.)
Wife (*bitterly*). The old school tie! (*He goes and sits on the sofa*.)
Major. We were at Eton together.
Wife. Otherwise . . . ?
Major. Perhaps . . . (*He approaches the sofa*.)
Wife. There's no perhaps about it.

(*She pats the sofa beside her, and after some hesitation he comes and sits by her*.)

We've only a few minutes to live!
Major. Looks like it.
Wife. Then let's *live* them!
Major. You mean . . . ? (*He edges closer*.)
Wife (*passionately, holding out her arms*). Ronnie!
Major. My darling!

(*He throws his arms round her and his lips seek hers. Suddenly we hear the sound of bagpipes, faint at first but gradually becoming louder. He lifts his head and listens. As the music grows louder and nearer he frees himself and jumps up*.)

The Highlanders! We're saved!
Wife. Oh, HELL!

Black Out.

*   *   *

BUSINESS AS USUAL

by Robert Rutherford

Scene: The Registry Office. A desk with papers and books, also a calendar. Chairs, etc. The Registrar *is seated at desk. Enter the* Clerk.

Clerk. You rang, sir?

Registrar. Yes, Jones, I did. Is there any news of that man Nobbs, yet?
Clerk. No, sir, not a word.
Registrar. Most extraordinary! In all my thirty years' experience as a Registrar of Marriages I have never known anything like it. The man comes here in the ordinary way, makes all arrangements to be married on Monday morning — and doesn't turn up. Now it's Friday, and not a word of explanation of any kind.
Clerk. Perhaps he came to his senses in time, sir.
Registrar: Jones, don't be facetious. The matter is serious. I can only think that the man has suffered some accident which has prevented . . . (*The door opens and in comes the* Bridegroom, *dressed loudly for the part.*) Good gracious! Here is the very man we're speaking about. Well, Mr Nobbs?
Bridegroom: Good morning! I know I'm a fool, but I've come to be married.
Registrar: Are you aware that you are four days late?
Bridegroom: Can't be helped. I got ready to come on Monday, but I was called away on another rotten job.
Registrar: And may I enquire where is the other contracting party?
Bridegroom: What?
Registrar: Where is the lady you wish to be married to?
Bridegroom (Thunderstruck): Oh, Ellen!!! Strewth! I've forgotten her! I'll have to go back for her. (*He makes for the door.*)
Registrar (Sternly): My good man — are you a drunkard?
Bridegroom: No, I'm a plumber!

Black Out

* * *

GLAD TO HAVE MET YOU

by Douglas Furber

The Scene *is a sitting-room in any seaside hotel.*

She. The moment I saw you walking along the promenade I fell for you at once — although we'd never met before.
He (fatuously). I blush when I think of it, but — but — I hope we meet again.
She. And so I brought you *here* — to this quiet hotel — and registered our names as 'Mr and Mrs Bingham-Bingham.' We've had four heavenly days!
He. How clever of you to invent a name like Bingham-Bingham.
She. Well — you see, I recognized you at once. You're the famous Mr Justice —
He (nervously). Please! *Please* — not so loud! I'm a married man!
She. And so I invented 'Bingham-Bingham' on the spur of the moment because I knew that at all costs you must avoid scandal. (*She kisses the top of his head.*) And now I'm going to slip out of here alone. It might cause talk if we were seen leaving here together. I'll tell the manager to bring you the bill, then you must slip away too. We've had four perfect days together and it's a secret between us two. Good-bye, my sweet!

(*She kisses him lightly and runs off.*)

He (fatuously). Foolish little woman. I hope we meet again.

(*The* Head Waiter *enters, bearing a folded bill on a salver.*)

Head Waiter. Mrs Bingham-Bingham has just left in a taxi, sir. She asked me to bring you the bill.

He. Ah, yes, the bill. (*Taking the bill, glancing at it and registering complete consternation.*) Nine hundred and eighty-seven pounds, fourteen and six! But — But — *I've only been here four days!*

Head Waiter (coldly). I know, sir. *But Mrs Bingham-Bingham has been living here for four years!*

Black Out.

* * *

And so to another 'classic'. Nobody who saw Cicely Courtneidge as The Widow ever quite forgot either her performance or the sketch. When the sketch was revived recently on television in a slightly cut version a great number of letters were sent to the producer bewailing the loss of favourite lines which viewers had remembered for over fifty years.

Douglas Furber was one of the best of the revue writers and *Laughing Gas* is pure theatre. The simple — brilliantly simple — idea of arranging for laughing gas to escape during the reading of a disagreeable will meant that the sketch ended up with howls of laughter from the entire cast, and laughter is infectious . . .

LAUGHING GAS
by Douglas Furber

Scene: *A Doctor's Consulting-room.*

Notes: *All the characters, with the exception of the workman, should be elderly, sour-looking and funereal. The Butler* (James) *should be the last word in solemn dignity and staid perfection, so that the effect of the laughing gas upon him is a complete metamorphosis.*

When the scene opens, James (*the Butler*) *is discovered bringing a table down C. and preparing it for the reading of the will.*

There enters to him a working man carrying on his shoulders a cylinder of 'Laughing Gas'.

Workman. What'll I do with this?
James. What is it?
Workman. 'Laughing Gas.' (*He takes the opportunity to put his heavy burden down, and he now reads its label aloud.*) 'Dr Harley — Fragile — With Care.'

James (absently). That's right. (*He busies himself placing chairs around the table.*)
Workman. Where'll I put it?
James. Put it anywhere for now. Er — on that pedestal. (*He indicates a pedestal up-stage.*)
Workman (doing as he is bid). All right. (*A slight pause while he puts the cylinder into place.*) I say —
James (absently, and still fixing his table). Um?
Workman. I suppose it'll be safe? Nice 'ow-d'yer-do if it got knocked over.
James (a trifle impatiently). That's all right.
Workman. Well, Goo' mornin', Sunshine. Don't say I didn't warn yer.

(*Exit.*)

(*The family solicitor,* Mr Preedle, *bustles in, carrying a brief bag.*)

Preedle. The table is there . . . good. I am ready to read the will the moment they all arrive.
James. Yes, sir.
Preedle. You will bring the ladies and gentlemen in here.
James. Very good, sir.

(*A feminine voice is heard off.*)

Preedle. The widow!

(Preedle *and* James *move up-stage solicitously to meet the widow and her daughter. The lady is wearing a mourning which she rather hopes becomes her and she carries, and frequently resorts to, a black-bordered mouchoir.* Preedle *and* James *bring her down-stage and place her gently into a chair; then* James *exits.*

The daughter (Ramona) *is a nosy, unmanageable creature of perhaps* 14 *or* 15 *years of age.*

The widow discards her pretence of grief the moment James *has gone.*)

Widow (icily addressing her child, who is nosing and peeking around the room). Ramona, come you here.
Ramona (shuffling forward a step or two). Yes, mum.
Widow (icily). I will trouble you to weep a little when they're reading your father's will. He was a good father to you, when he was not at Brighton.
Ramona. Yes, mum. (*By cylinder.*) What's this 'ere?
Widow (completely at a loss). Which ear?
Ramona (pointing at cylinder). That there?
Widow. That there? (*She glances casually at the cylinder.*) I don't know.
Ramona. It says 'Laughing Gas', oo-er!

(Preedle *looks up from his business of arranging the contents of his brief bag upon the table.*)

Widow (puzzled). 'Laughing gas oo-er?'
Preedle (warningly). That's your uncle's — Dr Harley's, y'know. I wouldn't touch it if I were you —
Ramona (with a pretence at obedience and humility). No, Mr Preedle.

Widow (distantly). Also, Ramona. (*The child comes nearer.*) Now that your father has gone to heaven, a'hem (*she coughs doubtfully*), you will no longer say 'This ear' or 'That there'. You will copy me instead of Daddy. There are three aitches in 'Olly'ock, one in 'Astings, none in *H*eligoland —

Ramona (bored and rudely interrupting her). All right, mum.

Widow. Now run along for five minutes, like a good little girl. Mummie wants to talk to Uncle Preedle.

Widow (after Ramona's *unwilling and inquisitive exit).* You've brought the will?

Preedle. I have it here.

Widow. You know the contents?

Preedle. Er — oh — yes. (*He coughs with extreme nervousness and embarrassment.*)

Widow (rambling on). I'm sure James has done the right thing. He was not a good husband, but we understood one another.

Preedle. Yes.

Widow. And now he has gone, twenty chorus ladies have gone back into circulation.

Preedle. Chorus ladies? I always thought James was so open — so *frank* and so *earnest.*

Widow (tartly). He *was. Frank* in Paris and *Ernest* in London.

Preedle. Poor James!

Widow. But *I* knew how to manage him. You see these pearls?

Preedle. Yes?

Widow. You know what they cost?

Preedle. No?

Widow. One kiss.

Preedle. You gave *him?*

Widow. No, *he* gave the maid.

James (re-entering and announcing). Miss Bedlington.

(*Exit.*)

Widow (aside to Preedle *as* Miss Bedlington *enters).* James's sister — how I loathe that woman! (*Aloud to* Miss Bedlington.) *Darling!*

Miss Bedlington (a breezy and somewhat eccentric-looking spinster). Hullo, Agatha.

Widow (faintly). How are you?

Miss Bedlington (heartily). I'm *fine!*

Widow (acidly). I'm glad somebody thinks so.

Miss Bedlington (flicking her sister-in-law's black-bordered mouchoir). Haven't you pulled yourself together yet?

Widow (pretending to be aghast). Pulled myself *together!*

Miss Bedlington. Why not? You didn't love each other.

Widow. Emilia!

Miss Bedlington. Hypocrite. Don't *I* know why he gave you that last lot of sables?

Widow. To keep me warm.

Miss Bedlington. To keep you *quiet.*

Widow (sniffing her handkerchief and completely outraged). Oh!!

Miss Bedlington. I'm single — thank the Lord. No one wants to kiss *me* under the mistletoe.

Widow (icily and sotto voce). They wouldn't kiss you under an anaesthetic.

(Miss Bedlington *moves away.*)

(From sheer force of habit.) Ramona, if you're *there,* come you *here.*

Ramona (re-entering but remaining by the gas cylinder, which seems to fascinate her). All right, mum.

James (re-entering and announcing). Mr Mitcham.

(Exit.)

Mitcham (entering). I'm not late, am I? *(Like the rest, he is elderly and gloomy-looking.)*

Preedle. Not at all. *(He picks up the will, then calls.)* James!

(James *re-enters.* Mitcham *crosses to the widow and condoles with her.*)

Will you all be seated?

Widow. Ramona —

Miss Bedlington (cattishly taking the words out of her mouth). Oh, come you *here.*

Ramona. Half a tick, mum. *(She fiddles with the gas cylinder.)*

Miss Bedlington. Isn't she sweet?

Widow. Brrr. *(To* Ramona.*)* You will get no egg to your tea.

Ramona. Yes, I will.

Widow. That settles it. You will have no egg today *or* tomorrow.

(Ramona *puts out her tongue; then she deliberately switches on the gas, leers at the audience, and shuffles down to her mother's side.*
Ramona *is now seated next to her mother on the R. of the table.* Preedle *is in the C.;* Miss Bedlington *on his L. and* James *on her L.*)

Preedle (clearing his throat). Er — Dr Harley, the deceased's brother, who has kindly loaned our poor friend this house, is unable to be present; but as he is not a legatee it does not matter. I will now read the will, and I will ask you all to remember that in the midst of life we are in death.

All (cheerily). Yes.

(A broad grin spreads very gradually over all their faces. Then they pause for a second, beaming full at the audience.)

Widow (smiling at Miss Bedlington*).* So witty — for a solicitor. *(She gazes upwards, beaming at* Preedle.*)*

Preedle. This is the last will and testament of James Endicott Goulick —

James (the butler). 'Goulick' — what a name!

(All chuckle.)

Widow (beaming at James*).* I wonder I married him.

Preedle. 'To my dear friend, Ernest Mitcham, I bequeath a sum of one thousand pounds —'

Mitcham. One? He promised me five. What a sense of humour! *(He chortles delightedly.)*

Widow (gaily, to Mitcham*).* You thought you were going to get five thousand and you only got *one?*

Mitcham. *Ye-es!!! (He giggles delightedly.)*
Widow. Damn funny!!

(*All laugh.*)

Preedle (with handkerchief). This is the funniest will I ever read.

(*All laugh.*)

Preedle. 'To our old family butler, James Smith —'
James. I can't bear it!
Miss Bedlington. He can't bear it!! (*She wipes her eyes.*)
Preedle. '— I bequeath a sum of ten thousand pounds.
Mitcham (amused beyond measure. To James*).* *You've* got ten thousand pounds!
James (shrill with mirth). Ye-es!
Mitcham (with unrestrained delight). And I've only got *one*!
James. *Ye-ES!!!!!*

(Mitcham *and* James *treat this as a superb mutual joke,* Mitcham *forgetting that he should be bitterly disappointed.*)

Widow (to Preedle*).* *Go on.*
Preedle (coyly). I don't like to. (*He hugs the will to his bosom.*)
James (his appearance of the perfect butler has dropped from him and he has now become — completely belying his dignified mien — the gayest of them all). Stick it, Preedy!!! *(He slaps the solicitor on the back.)*
Preedle. 'To my solicitor, Robert Preedle, I bequeath my best wishes.'
Widow. The old blighter!
Preedle. Yes, isn't it amusing?

(*All laugh.*)

Preedle (resuming the reading). *Ooooo I say* — this is a good one — (*Ladling it out.*) 'I bequeath the remainder of my fortune, in equal parts, to my sister, Emily Bedlington Goulick — on condition that she has her face lifted (*all laugh unrestrainedly*) — and the only offspring of my marriage, Ramona.'
Ramona (chanting again). I-*shall*-have-an-egg-for-my-tea;
I-shall-have-a-hegg;
I-shall-have-a-hegg —
All (joining in once). She-*shall*-have-a-hegg-for-her-tea!

(*All laugh.*)

Preedle (resuming). 'To my dear wife, Agatha —'
Widow. This'll be good, boys.
Preedle. '— to my dear wife, Agatha, who promised to make my life one long heaven and made it one long hell —'
Widow (tickled to death). Wasn't he a witty man?
Preedle (continuing). 'I bequeath — I bequeath —' (*He peers closely at the will.*) What's this? — Oh — oh! (*He laughs loudly.*)
Widow. Show *me.*

Preedle. I don't like to — (*He hugs the will closely to him, while overcome by amusement.*)

Widow. Oh, let's have a look.

Preedle. I really ought not to.

Widow. Sez you! (*Laughing, she snatches the paper from* Preedle, *glances at it, then tries to speak. Owing to her peals of laughter, in which everyone joins, it is several seconds before she can manage to articulate*). Ramona —

Ramona (chuckling). Yes, mum?

Widow (delightedly reading sentence in will). Naughty daddy has left us four little brothers and three little sisters!

(*At this they all set up the loudest and most infectious laugh of all, mounting on a gradual crescendo.*)

Black Out *when the laugh is at its height.*

* * *

Another rock-solid sketch by Douglas Furber.

Note how he manages to give the actors some suggestion of character which they can work up, even in a piece in which the idea is everything. Note, too, how most of the speeches, which are really only long lists of words, end with the strongest, most laughter-inducing word.

THE INFLUENCE OF THESAURUS

by Douglas Furber

Scene: At Margaret Smith's (*any room*).

John Brown *speaks before the Curtains.*

Ladies and Gentlemen, we propose to give you one of these triangle plays.

Now in the *old* triangle play the villain entered, proposed to the girl, *she* refused him, there was a struggle; the hero arrived in the nick of time to knock the villain down; a challenge followed, and then Curtain:

Now our triangle play would be exactly like that but for the influence of Thesaurus, better known as 'The Crossword Dictionary'. For every word we used to know, Thesaurus has given us a dozen alternatives. And we are better educated.

Why not glory in our knowledge? Why use only *one* word when we know a *dozen*?

Our little triangle play will show you what I mean. (*Exit.*)

(*The* Maid *ushers in* John Brown.)

John. Is Miss Smith in, at home, visible, see-able, indoors, chez elle, right here, or in the bosom of her family?

Maid. Yes, certainly, unquestionably, undoubtedly, definitely, decidedly, of course, *sure*, you bet, *ra-ther*.
John (handing her his hat). My hat, chapeau, cady, sombrero, tam-o'-shanter, billycock, headgear, Dunn, bonnet, turban, fez, shako, helmet, busby, tile or lid.
Maid (taking the hat). I will tell, inform, acquaint, apprise, advise, enlighten, awaken, intimate, notify, and specify Miss Smith.
John. I am tickled, obliged, grateful, beholden, merci, thank you, thumbs up, ta.

(Margaret *enters. The* Maid *exits.*)

Margaret, Meg, Peggy, Peg, *Maggie*!
Margaret. John, Jay, Jack, Jackie, Jean, *Jacko*!

(*They shake hands.*)

John. We are alone, solus, apart, on our own, solitary, q.t.?

(Margaret *nods affirmatively.*)

Margaret (sitting on sofa and patting a place by her side). Sit, squat, relax, anchor, rest, bivouac, park yourself.
John (taking the place by her side). There is something I must say, aver, affirm, declare, state, remark, observe, propound, contend, and get off my chest.
Margaret. Continue, go on, attaboy, carry on, go right to it, spill it, stick it, and shoot.
John. Will you be my wife, better half, she, female, missus, beau, squaw, nymph, grisette, mate, whoopee, wench, or bit-of-all-right?
Margaret. This is so sudden, quick, fast, rapid, instantaneous, slick, swoop, immediate, gee whizz, zowie, oh my, and lor lumme.
John. Say 'Yes' or I kill myself, destroy, suicide, slay, massacre, lapidate, butcher, do in, slaughter, puncture, nip in the bud, or bump myself off!
Margaret (nervously endeavouring to gain time). Have you seen mother, mum, mater, ma, mither, mammy?
John (grimly). No, but I've seen father, dad, papa, pa, old man, pater, papa, pop.
Margaret (querying). Um?
John. He asked about money, splosh, cash, spondulicks, specie, coin, rhino, stivers, dibs, dough, and the doings.
Margaret. Oh!
John. Then showed me his boot, shoe, slipper, moccasin, Saxone, Sorosis, sandal, hobnail, welt, Wellington, or clog.
Margaret. They dislike, abhor, loathe, despise, detest, abominate, execrate, yah-boo, rasberry and hate you!
John. Why, eh, gee, no, pourquoi, query?
Margaret. They wish me to wed, marry, tie-up with, splice, espouse, and mate another.
John. Damn, blast, curse, bother, tut-tut, *who*?
Margaret. Lanchester, peer, lord, undergraduate, public-school, Ciro's, Embassy, scion of nobility, M.P., aristocrat and gent.
John. You love, worship, breathe hard, pant, desire, long for, accept, adore him?
Margaret (sympathetically). Yes. This is your end, finish, dismissal, close, stop, termination, curtain, envoi, conclusion, finale, dénouement and *sock*!

John (*bitterly, rising and parading the room*). That idiot, greenhorn, fool, numskull, zany, dunce, simpleton, witling, ass, ninny, dolt, booby, imbecile, nincompoop, oaf, lout, loon, sawney, clodhopper, and *pie-can*?

Margaret (*rising indignantly*). He is not portly, stout, corpulent, fleshy, chubby, lumpish, whopping, swollen, elephantine, Paul Whiteman-ish, enormous, fat, bulbous and obese!

John (*sneeringly*). No, he is thin, exiguous, tenuous, skinny, emaciated, bony, shadowy, lantern-jawed, spindle-shanked, lean, meagre, gaunt, weedy, scrawny, slinky, shrivelled, raw-boned, herring-gutted, wafer-like, and Hannen Swaffer!

Margaret (*indignantly pointing to the door*). Go, depart, leave me, fly, pop off, beat it, buzz off, bunk, 'op it, *git*!!!

John (*hurling discretion to the winds and seizing her in his arms*). I must be your love, amour, beau, sweetheart, inamorata, swain, sweetie, cutie, duck, Novarro, Buchanan, Hulbert, Nares, Tearle, du Maurier, Astaire, Merson, or Grossmith!

Margaret (*struggling with him*). I shall scream, cry, bellow, yell, shout, yap, yelp —

John (*interrupting her, pulling her closer, and shouting exultantly*). Three's a crowd, multitude, pack, gang, legion, host, galaxy, peck, bushel, shoal, swarm, bevy, flock, herd, drove, covey, litter, and hell of a lot!

(*The struggle is brought to a sudden end by the entrance of* Lanchester, *who seizes* John, *tears him away from* Margaret *and hurls him to the ground.*)

Lanchester. Cad, viper, roué, scallywag, loafer, churl, debauchee, Lothario, Don Juan, Bluebeard, Henry the Eighth, ruffian, hell-hound, jailbird, vagabond, rapscallion, rip, *chorus boy*!!!

John (*venomously spitting forth the words*). Infant, seedling, babe, bantling, youth, juvenile, papoose, bambino, bairn, pickaninny, brat, whipper-snapper, hobble-dehoy, sap, cub, whelp, olive-branch, calf, puppy, foal, kitten, and *cradle mark*!!!

Lanchester (*rounding in his turn*). Veteran, seer, greybeard, Methuselah, patriarch, ancient, grandpa, old 'un, gaffer, dotard, and *baa*! (*With the word 'Baa' he plucks at an imaginary beard and brays like a goat.*)

(John *strikes him across the face with one of his gloves.*)

John (*handing him a visiting-card and querying choice of weapons*). Swords, sabres, cutlasses, rapiers, scimitars, claymores, krisses, dirks, poniards, hatpins, stilettos, foils, blades, tomahawks, assegais, carving-knives?

Margaret (*stepping between them to plead*). Fists, hands, knuckles, Mary Anns, truncheons, bludgeons, shillelaghs, sandbags, catapults, bricks, horseshoes, gloves.

Lanchester (*brushing her aside*). Revolvers, guns, colts, six-shooters, Chicagoes, howitzers, carbines, Maxims, blunderbusses, flints, Big Berthas, Lee Metfords, Lee Enfields, Lee Ephraims, Lea and Perrins.

(John *bows mockingly, then crosses and picks up his hat.*)

John (*with venom*). I wish you halitosis, palsy, paralysis, indigestion, dyspepsia, heartburn, acidity, dizziness, gout, plague, ague, asthma, bronchitis, housemaid's knee, goitre, St. Vitus, shingles, hiccups, lockjaw, and croup!

Lanchester (*dramatically throwing one protecting arm around* Margaret, *then pointing to the door). To Hell, Satan, Heat, Fire, the Styx, Lucifer, Mephistopheles, Bradford, the Potteries, and A HEATED HEREAFTER!!!!!!*

(John *cringes out.*)

Curtain.

*   *   *

During the late 1930s revues began to get smaller. Lavishly produced shows with star comedians and singers were still presented, but there was also a move towards taking a small theatre and dispensing with spectacular musical numbers and elaborate scenery. There was usually a small company of players, all of whom could sing and dance a bit as well as play the sketches. Scenery was minimal. The emphasis was upon wit and charm.

One of the pioneers of this intimate style of revue was a dramatic critic and playwright named Herbert Farjeon. During the late 30s and early 40s he — sometimes with his sister Eleanor — wrote a great number of sketches, and indeed whole revues. One of these revues, *Herbert Farjeon's Little Revue,* 1939, gave this new kind of theatrical production a name, 'little revue'.

Herbert Farjeon's little revue sketches lacked Douglas Furber's robustness but had instead a sharper wit and a subtler approach.

The next three sketches demonstrate Farjeon's range. *Long-Distance Divorce* had fun with film-star interviewers and has a good, strong payoff. *Please, Captain Eversleigh* was a monologue of some delicacy written for Edith Evans. *Snaps* was one of the most successful little revue sketches ever.

LONG-DISTANCE DIVORCE
by Herbert Farjeon

(*Film-Star asleep in bed. 'Phone rings.*)

Sunbud (*sleepily*). What's that? Aw! get off the damn set! (*'Phone rings.*) See here; Mr Eisenstein, if you think I'm going to play Scarlett O'Hara, *and* supply my own wind — (*'Phone rings.*) Oh, it's you, is it? (*Takes up receiver.*) Hullo! . . . Yes . . . Long-distance call from *where*? . . . London, England? . . . Oh, I suppose so . . . put 'em through.

(Pressman *and* Colleague *with notebook spotted R.*)

Pressman. Hullo! Stand by. Is that Hollywood One Million?
Sunbud. Yes, who's that?
Pressman. This is the 'Daily Badger' 'phoning from Fleet Street. I want a word with Miss Sunbud Snowflake, please.
Sunbud. Sunbud Snowflake speaking.

Pressman. Is that you, Miss Snowflake? (*To* Colleague.) Got her! (*At 'phone.*) Sorry to trouble you, Miss Snowflake, but I fancy we may be some use to you. 'Course, we're all crazy 'bout that new picture of yours.

Sunbud. Well, it's very sweet in you to say so, but as it happens to be three o'clock in the morning —

Pressman. That's funny. It's not three o'clock in the morning here. How time flies!

Sunbud (*mirthlessly*). Har, har.

Pressman. Now look here, Miss Snowflake, about this divorce of yours —

Sunbud. Divorce? What divorce?

Pressman. That's a good one. Don't tell me you don't know you're going to divorce Roderigo? We hear it's all practically settled —

Sunbud. Settled? There's *nothing* settled.

Pressman. Nothing settled at all, eh? (*To* Colleague.) Everything unsettled.

Colleague (*writing*). 'I do feel terribly unsettled . . .'

Sunbud. What the heck are you getting at?

Pressman. We don't want to be inquisitive, Miss Snowflake, all we want is the truth, the whole truth, and anything we can get besides the truth. Now isn't it the truth you want to divorce Roderigo?

Sunbud. Say, now, what business is that of yours?

Pressman. Here, here, kindly remember you're talking to the 'Daily Badger'. I'm not going to be personal, Miss Snowflake, but I take it, after two whole months of married life, to put it delicately, you and Roderigo aren't exactly doing a close-up any more. Not exactly in the honeymoon stage.

Sunbud. Depends on what you mean by the honeymoon stage — there *are* subtleties.

Pressman. Well, anyway, you're not *on* your honeymoon any more, are you?

Sunbud. Correct for once.

Pressman. Thank you. (*To* Colleague.) Honeymoon with Roderigo a thing of the past.

Colleague (*writing*). 'No more honeymooning with Roderigo for *me*, thank you . . .'

Sunbud. If you think I'm going to sit up all night . . .

Pressman. You seem to forget you're a public figure, Miss Snowflake. Good heavens, all we want is the facts, that's all. Kindly tell me, quite impersonally, just what exactly are your present relations with Roderigo.

Sunbud. Well — really — I never did!!

Pressman. Really — never did. (*To* Colleague.) Never *had* any relations with Roderigo.

Colleague (*writing*). 'Husband in name only. I demand an annulment . . .'

Pressman. I shan't keep you much longer. I just want a plain answer to a plain question. Are you in love with Tyrone Power?

Sunbud. No, I am *not* in love with Tyrone Power.

Pressman. Can I deny it in print?

Sunbud. I'd rather you didn't.

Pressman (*to* Colleague). Rather not deny she's in love with Tyrone Power.

Colleague (*writing*). 'I won't deny Tyrone and I are contemplating a tie-up . . .'

Pressman. Have you ever had an affair with Charles Laughton?

Sunbud. Oh, gee, not that I'm aware of.

Pressman. Why not? Don't you like Charles Laughton?
Sunbud. Listen, lollipop, I've only met him once, and never thought about him since.
Pressman (*to* Colleague). Only met him once, never thought about him since.
Colleague (*writing*). 'After our last parting, I put Charles right out of my mind . . .'
Pressman. Will you definitely state that there is nothing between you and Freddie Bartholomew?
Sunbud. Only just about twenty years. Say, who the Metro-Goldwyn-Mayer do you think I am —
Pressman. If you think I'm going to stand this sort of thing from a lousy film-star, you're very much mistaken. When did you last see Roderigo?
Sunbud. Oh, go to Hell! (*Slams down receiver.*)
Pressman. Hullo! hullo!! (*To* Colleague.) She's rung off.
Colleague. What a cheek!

(*Two* Pressmen *are faded out.* New Pressman *spotted L.*)

New Pressman. Hullo! hullo! Is that Hollywood One Million?
Sunbud (*sitting up in bed, taking receiver*). And who in the Garden of Allah are you?
New Pressman. Oh, this is 'Daily Backchat' speaking. I want a word at once with Roderigo.
Sunbud. With Roderigo? Well, thank God for that! Hi! Roddy, wake up. Your turn, sweetie-pie.

(Roderigo, *who has up to now been covered by the bedclothes, sits up in the bed and takes the receiver.*)

Black Out.

*   *   *

PLEASE, CAPTAIN EVERSLEIGH

by Herbert Farjeon

At the back, a full-length mirror. On the left, facing the stage, a dressing-table, with articles of toilet, a telephone, a stand-mirror and a hand-mirror. In front of the dressing-table, a chair, with an evening cloak over the back. On the right, another chair, with shoes beside it. A Lady *is discovered standing sideways to the long mirror, regarding her figure critically over her shoulder, turning this way and that. The stage directions accompanying the dialogue are only indications from which departures may be freely made; the essential is to keep the business going, this business consisting of putting on lipstick, shoes, perfume, what you will, in the way of completing an elaborate toilet — all as much counter to the affected simplicities of statement as possible. After a turn or two in front of the mirror, the day-dream begins.*

Lady (regarding herself in the mirror). Good evening, Captain Eversleigh, I'm so sorry to have kept you waiting . . . (*She turns and regards herself from a different angle.*) Good evening, Captain Eversleigh, I *am* so sorry to have kept you waiting . . . (*She walks up and down before the mirror to observe the set of her skirt.*) You poor, poor thing, and in the rain, too. . . . (*Ditto.*) And in the rain, too, you poor, poor thing. . . .

(*She sits on the chair R. and regards the shoes on her feet.*) I've been so rushed all day, I haven't had a moment to make myself fit to look at. . . . (*She takes off one shoe and tries one from another pair.*) But not a moment, Captain Eversleigh. . . . (*She regards her foot, kicks off the shoe, and puts on the first one again.*) No, not a moment. . . . (*Walking over to the table.*) I just had to *fling* myself together, put my trust in God, and come as I was. . . . (*She sits and examines her features critically.*) Just — as — I — was, h'm. . . . (*Relaxing.*) So you'll have to pretend you're quite an old friend, Captain Eversleigh, instead of quite a new one. . . . (*Looking for her powder-puff.*) That will be delicious, I *adore* old friends, Captain Eversleigh. . . . (*Powdering her arms and her nose.*) I'm *rather* an old-fashioned girl, Captain Eversleigh . . . up to a point. . . . (*Taking up the eye-black.*) Well, I *do* believe in being absolutely natural and . . . (*She applies the eye-black to her lashes*) well, absolutely natural, do you know what I mean? . . . I can't help it, I just do, Captain Eversleigh, I suppose I happen to be made that way. . . . (*She takes up the lipstick.*) Well, it's very sweet of you to say so. . . . (*She applies the lipstick.*) Yes, but it is. . . . (*Lipstick.*) It's very . . . (*lipstick*) very . . . (*lipstick*) very-sweet-of-you-to-say-so.

(*Relaxing.*) Of *course* I could bear the Dorchester, I don't care *where* we go. . . . All the same. . . . (*She takes up the scent-spray.*) All the same, Captain Eversleigh, I *did* rather imagine the Dorchester was reserved for Millicent Andrews. . . . (*Spray.*) *Dear* Millicent Andrews. . . . Oh, don't you? . . . Not a teeny bit? . . . (*Spray.*) *Poor* Millicent Andrews. . . . (*Hair.*) Well, I don't care what people say about her, I always stand up for Millicent Andrews. . . . (*Hair.*) No, *not* like 'God Save the King', aren't you horrid? . . . (*Hair.*) I know she is. . . . (*Hair.*) I know she does. . . . (*Hair.*) All the same, I always stand up for Millicent Andrews . . . whatever she may say about me. . . . (*She finishes her hair.*) Dear Millicent Andrews, I suppose she's just a girl's girl. . . .

(*Putting on a ring.*) I suppose you know that happens to be my hand. . . . (*Another ring.*) Yes, Captain Eversleigh, and that happens to be my hand, too. . . . Captain Eversleigh, *please*. . . . I suppose you know you're hurting? . . . (*Putting on a bracelet.*) Well, you *are*. . . . I'd never have come if I'd thought you were like that — you *needn't* believe it, but I *wouldn't*. . . . (*Putting on a necklace.*) Well, I *am* cross. . . . I'm very, very cross indeed — you don't seem to realize I'm not like that. . . . (*Taking up the hand-mirror.*) I'm *not* smiling. . . . I don't feel in the least *like* smiling. . . . (*She smiles slowly into the mirror.*) But I can't *help* smiling when you say things like that. . . . Do I? . . . I suppose everyone looks rather nice when they smile. . . . (*Gazing into the mirror.*) Is it, Captain Eversleigh? . . . And what else is my smile like? . . . Anything else? . . . Do go on, I adore it. . . . Well, I defy you to say anything pretty about my nose . . . poor nose. . . . Even my chin? . . . No, I suppose that *is* true, I'm not insipid. . . . (*Looking into the stand-mirror.*) But I should rather *like* to be insipid, Captain Eversleigh. . . . I should like to be rather vain, and rather foolish, and rather insipid, I think it would be adorable. . . . And that is *still* my hand, Captain Eversleigh. . . . (*Looking on the table for something.*) Yes, Captain

Eversleigh, quite as much my hand as it was to start with. . . . Well, almost, almost as much — *please*, Captain Eversleigh! . . . Well, just for five more seconds. . . . No, only five. . . . Captain Eversleigh, I'm going to count, and I trust to your honour as a gentleman and a soldier. . . . (*Putting the things away in the drawer.*) One . . . Two . . . Three . . . Four . . . (*Getting up and regarding the table.*) Captain Eversleigh! . . . How dare you, Captain Eversleigh. . . . (*Moving over to the chair.*) Of course I'm furious — you just don't begin to understand me. . . . (*Putting on a cloak.*) You think I'm just like other women and I'm not. . . . And I didn't think you were just like other men and you are. . . . I'm disappointed in you, Captain Eversleigh. . . . (*Moving over to the table again.*) I don't care whether my eyes look fine when they flash or not, I'm disappointed — bitterly disappointed. . . . (*She sits down to the 'phone.*) I thought you were nice. . . . (*Dial.*) I thought you were decent. . . . (*Dial.*) I thought you were safe. . . . (*Dial.*) And you're weak. . . . (*Dial.*) You're common. . . . (*Dial.*) You're cheap. . . . (*Dial.*) And I'm going straight home. . . . (*Dial.*) Is that the taxi rank? I want you to send a taxi to Number Forty-four Culverton Square, please. . . . (*A last look in front of the long mirror, then moving forward with her hand extended, her voice very gentle again.*) Good evening, Captain Eversleigh, I *am* so sorry to have kept you waiting. . . . You poor, poor thing . . . and in the rain, too. . . .

Fade Out.

*   *   *

SNAPS

by Herbert Farjeon

She, *continuously enthusiastic, is presiding at a small tea-table L.C. There is another small table L.* He, *grimly submissive, is seated on the sofa R.C.* She *is talking as the* Tabs *part.*

She (enthusiastically). Not a drop of rain the whole time — not a single drop — sugar?
He. Three, please.
She. Sweet-tooth! And the *sunsets! (Handing him his cup).* I never *saw* such sunsets — simply every colour you could *possibly* imagine. What with the bathing and the tramps over the downs and the honey and the chickens and everything — honestly, I never *had* such a holiday.
He (stirring his tea). You're looking fit enough.
She. So I should! We just put on our oldest clothes and turned into *complete* gypsies — you never *saw* such a crew of ragamuffins — I must have looked a perfect *sight. (Picking up a plate of sandwiches.)* Gentleman's Relish?
He. Thanks.
She (handing the plate). I *do* so like to feel free and — and elementary and all that on a holiday, don't you?
He. Yes, rather.

She (sighing). Oh dear, you *would* have enjoyed it! (She *puts down the plate again.*)
He. I expect I would.
She (jumping up). I'll tell you what — would you like to see my snaps?
He. Er — oh — yes, of course I would.
She (going over to the small table L. and taking up an envelope — the double-sided kind, so favoured by 'D. and P.' merchants). I'm so glad I took such a lot. *(Returning below the tea-table to C.).* It's always worth while in the end, isn't it? (She *sits L. of him on the sofa*). Of course, they're rather small. (She *takes the snaps from the folder.*) Have you got good sight?
He. Yes, I think so. (He *balances his cup on his knees.*)
She (fingering the snaps lovingly). Well, now, let's see — where shall I begin? — Oh yes, look here — (*Handing one over*) — that's a picture of our cove — we used to call it our cove because it practically *was* our cove — I'm afraid it was rather late in the day when I took that one.
He. I see. What's this white streak?
She. Oh, you needn't worry about that. That's in all of them. (*Passing another.*) Look — this is our cove looking the *other* way; do you see?
He. I see.
She (pointing). You can tell it joins on, because that rock in that picture's the same as that rock in *that* picture. (*Sighing.*) Oh dear, it *was* heavenly!
He. It must have been.
She (another). Well now, that's a bit of the cliff farther along, looking due west — no, no, no, looking due east — I think — (*Another*) — and that's a bit of the cliff farther along still — somebody committed suicide there — isn't it lovely?
He (puzzled). Is that the sea?
She. I think it must be. (*Another.*) Oh, look, look — you'll never, *never* guess what that is!
He. What on earth . . . ?
She (giggling). It's a man called George making a moustache out of a banana. He could do almost everything. He *was* so funny. (*Another.*) Er — that's just an awfully nice donkey. It was in a field. (*Another.*) That's the same donkey a bit blurred.
He. It's a pity about these white streaks.
She. Yes, aren't they a nuisance!
He. It looks like a white mist or something.
She. Oh, we didn't have any mist — unless it got into the camera. Come on, do let's get on. What fun this is! (*Another.*) That's a man I got to know — you wouldn't know him —
He. What, a black man?
She. Oh no, he was quite fair really. (*Another.*) That's another man with the sun in his eyes — you wouldn't know him either. (*Another.*) That's a better one of the first man — (*Another*) — and that's not *quite* such a good one of the second man — (*Another*) — oh, that's George blowing out his cheeks — I can't *describe* how funny he was — (*She giggles again.*)
He. Was he?
She (seriously). I say, you *do* like looking at these don't you? You *would* say if you didn't, wouldn't you?
He. Of course.

She (*jumping up*). I'll tell you what — I'll get a magnifying-glass — (*She gets it from a lower shelf in the tea-table*) — then you'll be able to see them better, won't you? (*She hands it to him.*)

He. Okitoke. (He *is holding the photographs already submitted and is trying to cope with his tea at the same time.*)

She (*sitting again*). Now, where were we? Oh yes. (*Another.*) That's the window of the room *next* to the one I slept in — ready? — (*Another.*) — that's my bathing things hanging out to dry — ready? — (*Another*) — that's the post office — (*Another*) — that's just a wall — oh, look, look — (*Another*) — that's a chicken I got rather fond of. I do wish I was back, don't you?

He. Rather!

She. I wonder what that chicken's doing now?

He. Perhaps someone else is taking a snap of it.

She. I wonder! Well, we can't waste time. (*Another.*) That's a place we had tea — (*Another*) — that's a bull, only it moved — (*Another*) — that's one of the chicken again — (*Another*) — oh, this is the *best* one of the chicken — or do you prefer the first one?

He (*holding them both up*). I think I like them about equal.

She. Do you really? (*Pointing.*) I like this one ever so much best. Ready? — (*Another*) — that's a deck-chair blown over by the wind — (*Another*) — that's the chicken again — (*Another*) — that's George's dog — (*Another*) — that's George's aunt with her hair all down after bathing. (*About to pass it over.*) That's — (*Pulling it in to her*). Oh, I really don't think I'll show you that one.

He (*alert*). Aha! but that's the one I want to see!

She (*leaning away from him*). No, really — you wouldn't understand — honestly, I'd rather not.

He. I believe it's one of you without — is it? (*Leaning across.*) I say, I must see.

She. I don't know what you'll think of me!

He. Come on, hand it over!

She (*bashful*). No I won't. No, no, no!

He. Yes, yes, yes! (*There is a little struggle. He wrests the snapshot from her.*) Aha! (*He looks at it.*) Good God! It's that blasted chicken again!

Black Out.

* * *

Reginald Beckwith wrote a number of highly successful and memorable sketches for little revue. The following is one of these and a classic of its kind.

It is, I think, the perfect little revue sketch: a stunningly original and funny idea, a joy for the actors to perform, brief and not a word could be changed to improve it.

MOMENT ROMANTIQUE

by Reginald Beckwith

A seaside bench. A refuse can beside it, inscribed 'MARGATE ON SEA – REFUSE.' *Two Lovers seated. He wears a suedette zip jacket, very long plus fours, and striped cycling stockings.* She, *a fussy afternoon dress and pearls. In the distance, on the pier, a band is heard playing a treacly waltz. They kiss, then slowly their faces slide round until they are gazing out at the audience cheek to cheek.*

She (*no feeling or emphasis*) . . . and I said to her, mind you I do like Tapioca Mrs Burterwhistle, but I like my Tapioca to taste of Tapioca Mrs Burterwhistle, I said . . .

(*Another prolonged kiss.*)

. . . which is more than you can say of this Tapioca Mrs Burterwhistle, I said, for if this Tapioca tastes of anything, I said, it tastes of washing up water, I said . . .

(*A quick kiss.*)

. . . and what's more Mrs Burterwhistle, it hangs on my stomach like lead, I said . . .

(*Her head slides down into his lap and she pulls him down into a Garboesque embrace.*)

. . . and it isn't only me what has complained of the Tapioca Mrs Burterwhistle, I said. There are others I could name, I said . . .

(*He now pulls her up into an even more passionate embrace.*)

. . . as have been made iller than me, I said, and it's not that I've got anything against . . . (*Their lips meet.*) . . . Tapioca. It's just that I don't like it with lumps in . . .

(She *has now achieved a picturesque position at rest upon the bench.* He *leans over her in an impassioned attitude, his face perhaps an inch from hers.*)

He. And what did she say?
She. Mrs Burterwhistle?
He. Ay.
She. Oh, she said it was Sago.
He. Oh! Sago!!

(*Ultimate kiss.*)

Black Out.

* * *

The success of intimate revue played in a small theatre encouraged the development of much shorter sketches. The shortest of these was the 'blackout'. A 'blackout' could be played with scenery and props or with the performers isolated by spotlights. It was really a brief joke whose point was revealed in the last line. The sudden shock of then plunging the stage into darkness accented the joke and encouraged the audience to laugh.

Here are three fairly typical little revue 'blackouts'.

THE MOTHER

by George Arthurs

She *is discovered bending over baby in cot.* He *enters hurriedly.*

He (*Passionately*). Mabel, I can't keep it back any longer. I love you madly. I adore you.

She (*Indignantly*). You coward! You cad, to say such a thing to me – a married woman. And in the presence of my child, too.

(*She rings a bell.*)

He. Mabel, what are you doing?

She. Have you no sense of honour? You dare to tell me, another man's wife, that you love me! And in the presence of my poor innocent child!

(*Enter* Butler.)

Butler. You rang, Madam?

She (*Angrily*). Yes, James, take –

He. Mabel, spare me!

She. James! Take the child away!

Black Out.

*　　*　　*

THE CAREFUL WIFE

by George Arthurs

Man *and* Friend *at table, on which is a large money box.*

Man. A little idea of mine for saving money, old chap. Every time I kiss my wife I give her a shilling and she puts it in this box.

Friend. Only a shilling?

Man. Yes, but it's surprising how the shillings mount up, especially if you're very affectionate. Now, I'm just going to open this box and show you what a loving husband I've been.

(*He opens box, and out come coins, notes, etc. He looks surprised.*)

(*Enter* Wife.)

Man. (*to* Wife). I say, Alice. What's the idea of all these notes? I only gave you a shilling each time I kissed you.
Wife. Yes, but other men are not so stingy as you.

Picture and Black Out.

*   *   *

THE PRIZE
by George Arthurs

Wife *is seated, sewing. Enter* Husband, *laughing uproariously.*

Wife. What's the matter, dear?
Husband. The funniest thing you ever heard. We were all having a drink with Tomkins, the hatter, when he said he'd give a new hat to any married man who had never been untrue to his wife.
Wife. Well?
Husband. The prize was won by young Harris. He swore on oath that he'd always been true to his wife. Tomkins gave him his new hat and then asked him how long he'd been married. Harris said, 'Two days!'

(*He laughs again, then catches her eye, as she looks at him.*)

What's the matter, dear?

(*She rises and points at him, accusingly.*)

Wife. Where's *your* new hat?

Black Out.

*   *   *

Writers of sketches for little revues were encouraged by the versatility of their performers — who were, in the main, highly talented if not yet 'stars' — to provide sketches which gave the actor a chance to act; to build up a character.

The following short sketch has a good, strong central idea — which has been used many times since — but leaves the actor or actress plenty of elbow room to make the character believable and so strengthen the payoff.

DIRECTORY ENQUIRIES
by Julian Elliston

Hullo! Operator! . . . Oh, there you are. I want Directory Enquiries, please . . . Thank you. Is that Directory Enquiries? Can you tell me if you have a subscriber called Miss Katie Prawle? — Katie Prawle. — Katie — K for knapsack, A for Ah — no, not R—A—Ah ah-ha, not R r-r-r-r. That's right. T for tse-tse — no! T! What you have for breakfast — That's right. I for inn — no, *not* N, I — I for impetigo — Yes. E for eisteddfod. — Katie, yes. Katie Prawle. Prawle. P for pneumonia, R for ray — no, it *is* R this time. R for ray, X-ray, you know — *no.* Not X, R. — That's right. A for axe — no, no, no! *Not* X — A! A for am — no, not M, *am* — A.M. — no, no, no. Not A M, just A. — Yes. W for wren — no, wren. What they have on the new farthings — no, it's *not* a sparrow. — L for leather. E for éclair. Prawle. Have you got that? P-R-A-W-L-E. — That's right. — What's that? — Oh! the address, yes. Five-twenty-two — I'm sorry, fife-double-tew Dymen Street, West One. — Dymen — *Dymen* — D for deaf, Y for you — no, not U, you — Y — Y for yell. — That's right. M for — M for — yes, if you like, M for mental. Thank you. E for exasperating, N for nuisance. Dymen. That's right. S for — oh, you can spell Street, can you? W. one. That's right. — Yes, I'll hold on. I'm in no hurry. — Well, you needn't be rude about it. I was only trying to help. — Hullo? Oh? *No* street of that name? Well, I may have got the address wrong. Could you find if there is a Katie Prawle anywhere else? Thank you. — Hullo? No Katie Prawle? Well, of course, I'm not absolutely sure of the Christian name. Are there any Prawles at all? — No Prawles? You're quite sure? — Oh, you needn't apologize. I'm very pleased. You see, I'm writing a book and you have to be so careful about names with our laws of libel. People are so touchy. — What? — *Well,* people *are* touchy.

* * *

Although the cast of a little revue was usually made up of performers of roughly equal status — unlike the big revues which had stars and a supporting cast — stars did emerge from the ranks. One such was Hermione Gingold. During the long runs of Alan Melville's wartime revues *Sweet and Low* and *Sweeter and Lower* the extravagant eccentricity of Hermione Gingold's characterizations became so popular that she was given the stage to herself from time to time to present a solo character sketch.

Bicycling was written by Hermione Gingold and, like the Harry Tate sketch, it is material which is only really funny when performed by the actor or actress whose idiosyncratic style it is carefully designed to exploit.

BICYCLING
by Hermione Gingold

Have you thought how you are going to get to work if transport becomes more difficult? I bet you haven't thought of a bicycle. And why not? A horse may be the friend of man. The bicycle is everybody's pal.

(*She produces a postcard from her pocket.*)

Look at this picture of one. Isn't it pretty? Why, it is as pretty as a picture.

(*She puts the card back.*)

Look at my blazer. Is not that pretty too? And I am proud to say that I am a bicycling blue and race for my college of shorthand.

Now I want you to try and make up your minds as to whether you would like the single-seater roadster or the tandem model. The single-seater roadster has one saddle and two pedals attached to a crank. The tandem model has two saddles and two cranks, usually attached to each other. On the tandem model the rider in front faces the same way as the rider behind, which is gay. The rider behind faces the behind of the rider in front, which is not so gay. But to business.

Of course you will find it difficult to buy a bicycle in war-time, but if you follow my instructions you will be able to make one for yourself.

First of all you will want some wire for the wheels. Any sort of strong wire will do, but I advise you not to get touching the telegraph wire or you will get into trouble.

Next you will want a bell and a lamp, but I advise you to get these ready made.

Now remove some wheels off an old pram, or it will save you trouble if you remove some wheels off an old bike; and why not remove the handles off it at the same time? You will be silly if you don't.

Now perhaps some of you young ladies have a boy friend. Don't be too shy to ask him to come round some night and help you to adjust your mudguard. And perhaps he will put a spoke in your wheel at the same time.

The peddler can supply you with pedals. Or you can wrench some off an old piano. Won't someone be surprised the next time they sit down? And if they're cross at first never you mind. Just laugh and tell them that they can play the piano without pedals but you can't ride a bicycle without, and then they will laugh too — I hope. Be unconventional, don't bother about brakes.

And now for the chain, which is to the bicycle what the engine is to the motor. You can either pull one off of something — (*she makes a gesture of pulling down the chain with her hand*) — or you can crochet one for yourself. Use a chain-stitch, and if you find it hurts you casting on cast-iron, cast off and cast round for something else.

The bicycle as we know it to-day was invented in 1840 by a Scotchman who was attracted by the idea of a free-wheel. And the free-wheel gives you this great advantage — you can ride downhill without pedalling. You can also ride uphill without pedalling, by simply getting off and pushing. And that is why the bicycle is sometimes known as the push-bike.

Oh yes, you thought I had forgotten the seat or saddle as we bicyclers call it. Well, I had not. And I advise you to get a good one, for, as Hamlet says, 'Aye, there's the rub.' And oh, how I wish I could show you my seat, for I think it is the only one in the world that is stuffed with feathers and covered with chintz.

Well, now your machine is almost finished and you are nearly ready to go on the streets. I hope you will all go home to-night determined to make yourselves bicycles, and maybe we shall bump into each other one fine day soon. I hope so. Ta-ta!

*   *   *

A whole new field of sketch writing was opened up when, during the war, the wireless became the nation's main source of news and entertainment.

To begin with, comedy on the wireless was mainly a matter of standing a comedian from a concert-party or a Music Hall in front of a microphone and letting him get on with his act. Here is a typical fast crosstalk patter act which was performed by Scott and Whaley in the long-running programme *The Kentucky Minstrels.*

THE NEVER-IDLE APPRENTICE

by Scott and Whaley

A. Hullo! Why what's the matter?
B. It isn't cricket!
A. What isn't cricket?
B. My brother's been arrested for making a *stump* speech.
A. On what grounds?
B. Outside Lords. And the magistrate refused to allow *bail.*
A. Never mind that. I heard you had started in business.
B. Quite true. I opened a large ice factory.
A. How did you get on with your ice factory?
B. Our creditors got so hot, it went into liquidation.
A. Well, it's very lucky we met.
B. We wouldn't have done if I hadn't been so short-sighted.
A. I think I can put you on the road to fortune.
B. I'd sooner you put me on a bus to Tooting.
A. Why Tooting?
B. I know you don't live there.
A. Now listen. I've just taken a small hotel.
B. And I've taken bicarbonate of soda.
A. Now how would you like to be my right hand man?
B. You want me to pick pockets?
A. No, no! I mean work in my hotel and be a sort of general factotum.
B. General factotum? You mean do the *major* portion of work?
A. Well, you see I want to cut down expenses at the start. So I shan't have a very large staff.
B. The doctor said I was only to do light work.
A. Oh, you'll find this work quite easy.
B. I know I'll *find* it easy, but will it be easy to do?
A. Yes. You will of course sleep on the premises.
B. And do I have a nice bedroom to myself?

A. Oh, no! I anticipate all the bedrooms will be occupied. You will have to sleep in the billiard room.
B. Huh! Why I might wake up and find myself snookered!
A. You will be quite comfortable on one of the tables.
B. And what will be my *cue* to rise?
A. Oh, you needn't get up — er — before five.
B. Fine — just in time for tea.
A. No, no! Five o'clock in the morning. You'll rise at dawn.
B. No fear. They shoot people who rise at dawn!
A. That's neither here nor there.
B. As the man said when he lost his collar stud.
A. As soon as you rise, you will wash yourself.
B. In the bathroom?
A. No, no! the bathrooms will be wanted by the guests.
B. I suppose I get myself dry-cleaned or go behind my ears with a vacuum cleaner?
A. You will then collect all the boots and shoes and clean them.
B. That's funny — my father's a farmer.
A. What has that to do with it?
B. He will be making hay while the son shines.
A. When you've finished the boots, you will then sweep all the carpets, polish the lino, shake the mats and clean the brass.
B. All in one week?
A. One week — this is before breakfast.
B. Huh!
A. After you've done all that, you will make tea.
B. Ah, I could do with a cup of tea by then.
A. Not for yourself. You will take up the early morning cups of tea to the visitors who have ordered them.
B. And can I have what I spill in the saucers?
A. Certainly not. You will then call the other visitors.
B. Is it left to my discretion what I call them?
A. No, no! I mean wake them up.
B. Ah, that's the part I shall enjoy. Can I use force?
A. Certainly not. You will then change into your waiter's suit and serve breakfast.
B. You mean help the other waiters?
A. Oh, there won't be any other waiters.
B. Huh!
A. They would only get in your way. You'll be much better on your own.
B. At any rate I'll be able to have all the tips for myself.
A. Oh, no! In my hotel there will be no tipping. Any employee caught accepting a tip will be instantly dismissed.
B. I see. If I catch myself taking a tip, I'll sack myself.
A. Now, after you've served all the guests' breakfasts —
B. I have my own.
A. No! You will then make all the beds.
B. What! But that's woman's work. The chambermaid will do that.
A. *You* will be the chambermaid.

B. I shall — huh! But how can I be in two places at once?
A. Oh, you'll manage.
B. I can see I shall be beside myself.
A. Of course — whilst you are making the beds —
B. Etcetera.
A. Should you hear the lift bell ring —
B. I take no notice.
A. You certainly do. You fly to the lift —
B. Fly? Have I got to grow wings for this job?
A. Well, when anyone wants the lift you work it.
B. Mere child's play. As well as being beside myself, I shall lead an up-and-down life.
A. If anyone rings from the basement, be sure you don't go down in my estimation.
B. Don't worry. If anyone rings from the top floor, I'll rise to the occasion.
A. Now all this should keep you pretty busy until ten o'clock.
B. At night.
A. No, no! Ten a.m.
B. A.m.?
A. You know what a.m. stands for?
B. 'Cos there's no room for it to sit down.
A. No, no! It means Ante Meridian.
B. I've never met her.
A. Never met whom?
B. Aunty Meridian.
A. Anyway, tell me — can you cook?
B. Boy, and how!
A. Is your cooking Oriental or Continental?
B. Neither — experimental.
A. Well, I shall want a chef, so will you give me your idea of a menu for lunch.
B. With the greatest of meningitis. Now first I'll give them gold soup.
A. Gold soup? How on earth do you make gold soup?
B. With fourteen carrots.
A. I see. And what to follow?
B. Herring à la Maître d'hôtel.
A. How's that?
B. Soused!
A. And the next course?
B. Frog-in-the-well.
A. What?
B. I mean toad-in-the-hole.
A. And what sweets would you give them?
B. Humbugs.
A. No, no! I mean what sort of pudding?
B. Oh, I'd give them hop-it pudding.
A. What on earth's hop-it pudding?
B. Sometimes called buzz-off pudding.
A. Buzz-off pudding?
B. Sago!

A. Then you will give them coffee.
B. Yes, and my coffee will be like 'the quality of mercy' — not strained.
A. Of course some of the guests may want a quick lunch.
B. Then I shall give them a lighted candle.
A. Why?
B. So they can have a quick blow out.
A. Anyway, I'll give you a trial.
B. Just a minute. What about wages?
A. Wages? Oh, you really can't expect any wages. Think of the experience you'll be gaining. You're an apprentice.
B. You mean I've got to go about with a large L on my back?
A. After a few years, I may be able to pay you. But first I must get the hotel on a firm footing.
B. Till then, I keep on my feet — infirm.
A. Oh, you'll be on your hands and knees sometimes.
B. No, I'm sorry, but my union won't let me.
A. Now, don't be silly, this is the chance of a lifetime. You take this job, and as regards wages — just forget them.
B. Forget them?
A. You'll of course get your board.
B. What to sleep on?
A. No, no! Board is what you eat.
B. Oh, it is, eh? It may be all right for a golliwog to have a sawdust tummy, but I don't want one.
A. Of course, you'll be far too busy to stop for meals. You'll just have to snatch a snack.
B. Snatch a which?
A. I said — smack a snitch — I mean catch a witch — hatch a snack —
B. Sack a match!
A. Oh — anyway — as regards your meals — just forget them.
B. And you know all these jobs you want me to do?
A. Yes.
B. I've forgotten them already. Goodnight.

* * *

Radio variety programmes like *Music Hall* were immensely popular throughout the war and the crackers-of-jokes and the patter acts were a welcome part. But there was another kind of Music Hall act which proved to be even more effective on radio: the character comedian.

One of the finest of these was Robb Wilton. His character was that of a kindly, bumbling, simple soul, who recounted his problems to you as though he was talking across the table of a pub. His most famous sketch was called *The Home Guard.* So famous was it that there can be few people in Britain over the age of fifty now whose memories are not stirred by the words 'The day war broke out. . .'

THE HOME GUARD

by Robb Wilton

The day war broke out, my Missus looked at me, and she said, What good are you? I said, What d'ya mean, what good am I? Well, she said, you're too old for the Army, you couldn't get into the Navy, and they wouldn't 'ave you in the Air Force, so what good are you?

I said, I'll do something. She said What? I said 'Ow do I know, I'll have to think. She said, I don't know 'ow that's goin' to help yer, you've never done it before, so what good are you? I said, Don't keep saying what good am I, I said. There'll, there'll be Munitions . . . She said, Now 'ow can you go on Muni — I said, I never said anything about goin' on — I said, There'll *be* some. Well, she said, all the young fellas'll be gettin' called up and she said, You'll 'ave to go back to work. . . . . Ooh, she's got a cruel tongue . . . Anyhow, I haven't had to go back to work; I'm a lamplighter.

Then she said, Now, she said, Our 'Arry, she said, Our 'Arry's sure to be getting called up, and she said, When 'e's gone there'll only be 'is Army allowance, and she said, What're yer goin' to do then? I said, I'll 'ave to try and manage on it. She said, *You'll* 'ave to try and manage — she said, What about me? I said, There'll be my insurance. She said I can't get that till you're dead; I said, Well then you'll 'ave to wait. She said, Suppose I die first? I said, Well then you won't want it. But y' can't reas — she's no brains — any'ow I got fed up, and I put me 'at on and I went down to the local. Ooh, the times that woman 'as driven me into the local.

Now when I got in there, there was a fella there, ooh 'e was as tight as a — I've never — and there was another fella with him, just as tight; and one of them was sitting at a table, trying to fill in a form. An' he said to his pal, he said, Herbert, he said — What's the name of this street, outside the pub here, he said, I've got to fill it in this — what's the name? The other fella, just as tight, says, The name, the name of what? 'E said, The name of this street, 'ere, outside the pub, 'ere; what's the name of it? 'E said, Oh, 'ow the 'ell do I know, I've never bin outside the pub.

Now, but the first day I got me 'Ome Guard uniform — I'm gettin' the trousers next year — but the first day I got it I went home and I slipped upstairs and I put it on, and I came down into the kitchen and the Missus looked at me, and she said, What are yer supposed to be? I said, Supposed to — I'm one of the Home Guards. She said, One of the Home — she said, What're the others like? And then, the Missus said, she said, Well, what d'yer *do* in the Home Guards? I said, I've got to stop Hitler's army landing. She said, What — you? I said, No . . . there's Harry Bates, and Charlie Evans and . . . I said, there's seven or eight of us altogether. I said, we're in a group. I said, we're on guard in a little hut behind the Dog and Pullet. She said, Now what's the good of being on guard in a little hut behind the Dog and Pullet? She said, I suppose that was *your* idea? I said, Aye, and that Charlie Evans wants to claim it as 'is. And then she looked at me and she said, Well, what're yer doin' with one stripe?, she said, You've only just got the uniform — 'ow can you 'ave one — I said, Wait a minute an' I'll explain the whole position. I said, as a matter of fact, Charlie Evans, Harry Bates an' meself 'ave got one each. She said, Well, 'ow did yer come by them, and 'ow did they, they've only just joi — I said, Wait a minute an' I'll explain it, I said. Tom Brierley, the Sergeant, got all browned off, fed to the teeth, chucked it, and 'e gave us one each. Ooh, aye, oh, we've all joined for the duration. Unless it finishes before then, we don't know, y'see . . . but — my Missus, she gets on my ner — she asks such daft questions.

She said, 'Ere, she said — only this morning, she said, What are you supposed to be guarding? I said, Oh don't start all that ag —, I said, we're guarding the British Isles. I said, we're guarding all the millions of men, women and children! Millions of them! *And* you . . . She said, Oh . . . then you're on our side. I said, Well of *course* I'm on our — Well, she said, I think we'd be a damn' sight better off if you were on the other side. She said, D'you know this 'Itler? 'Ave you ever — ? Do I know — I said, Now don't talk rubbish, Rita; do I know Hitler, 'ow would I . . . ? Not even in the paint business or anything, 'ow would — Well, she said, 'Ow're yer goin' to know which is 'im if they *do* land? I said, I've got a tongue in my 'ead, 'aven't I? But it's no good trying to reason, she doesn't seem to concentrate — only the other mor — Oh, good gracious me, look at the time, I should have been on guard two hours ago, they'll be, they'll be lookin' for me everywhere, no, I've left the whole of the coast exposed. You'll have to forgive me, I'll really have to go . . .

* * *

Most of the wartime and post-war radio comedy series were shows built round well-known performers. They tended to be fixed in a simple location, e.g., Much-Binding-in-the-Marsh. The shows usually had some kind of theme which was developed through interruptions from a gallery of resident characters, each with a stock-phrase and a comic characteristic or two.

One of the few shows to feature complete, self-contained sketches was *Take It From Here,* which I wrote with Denis Norden, and which ran from 1947 to 1958. In the early years of its run the show was divided into three parts, separated by musical interludes. The first segment was dialogue of topical comment between the three principals, Jimmy Edwards, Dick Bentley and Joy Nichols. The middle section was made up of one or more sketches and the final section was a pastiche of a well-known film, play or book.

Here are four 'idea' sketches from *Take It From Here.* The first two also include Alan Dean, one of the show's resident vocal group, the Keynotes. Alan was occasionally used in the character of a young, naive member of the cast.

TAKE IT FROM HERE

by Frank Muir and Denis Norden

Alan: Miss Nichols, excuse me. Before you finish the Focus on Entertainment I've written a very funny play. It's a light comedy — sort of Noel Coward.

Joy: Well, Alan, we'll be pleased to try it out for you.
Alan: Gosh, thanks. Here are the parts. Professor Edwards, you're the jealous husband, Cedric. Miss Nichols, you're the wife, Amanda, and Mr Bentley — you'll have the Noel Coward part. Can you tackle it?
Dick: But of course. When they revived 'Private Lives' I played the lead. What a sensation there was when the curtain came down.
Jim: They had to revive Noel Coward.
Joy: If you're all set, boys — let's go.
'Design for Bitter' or 'Sweet Lives'.

(*Orchestra plays* 'I'll See You Again')

Dick (*as Noel Coward*): Amanda, my sweet, these rock buns are delicious. Is this the last one?
Joy: Oh no, I have another dozen I'm keeping warm in the oven.
Jim: Never mind that now. Amanda, I must know — is this man your only lover?
Dick: Try not to be so crude, Cedric. I feel quite, quite faint. Shall I take a nip of something?
Jim: Yes, senna pods.
Joy: Oh dear, it must have been something you ate. Can you remember what the Aga Khan gave you for supper?
Jim: Don't change the subject. You thought I didn't know, but this evening I got wind.
Dick: But Cedric. When you look at Amanda, can you blame me?
Jim: It's the deception I hate. Every time you came to make love to Amanda you wore those thick dark glasses.
Dick: It is my . . . (*back to self*) Oh, Alan, this is the heaviest light comedy I ever read. Where's all the laughs?
Alan: Well, it makes *me* laugh, and gosh, I know it backwards.
Jim: Well, perhaps it's funnier backwards.
Joy: Yes, let's try it backwards, Jim. You start at your last line and we'll work in reverse through to the beginning.
Jim: Right. (*character*) Every time you came to make love to Amanda you wore those thick dark glasses.
Dick: But, Cedric, when you look at Amanda can you blame me?
Jim: Don't change the subject. You thought I didn't know, but this evening I got wind.
Joy: Oh dear, it must have been something you ate. Can you remember what the Aga Khan gave you for supper?
Jim: Yes, senna pods.
Dick: Try not to be so crude, Cedric. I feel quite, quite faint. Shall I take a nip of something?
Jim: Never mind that now. Amanda, I must know — is this man your only lover?
Joy: Oh no — I have another dozen I'm keeping warm in the oven.

* * *

Joy: We conclude our survey of nightlife with a thought for those creative artists who burn the midnight oil while the rest of the world is sleeping. To encourage these, TIFE held a playwriting competition with a large prize. The judges were Professor

Jimmy Edwards, M.A. (Cantab.) and Dick Bentley (Failed Matric). And here are the judges with their verdict.

Jimmy: I think we are unanimous, eh, Bentley?

Dick: Absolutely. Here are the winners, Joy.

Joy: Let's see the names. The winners are — James Edwards and D. Bentley. D. Bentley?

Dick: That's me.

Joy: Oh, you, Dick. You just put the initial — I was puzzled whether it was a man or a woman.

Dick: Well, now you know it's me.

Jimmy: She's still puzzled. Let me read you a scene from my play first, Joy. It's a drama of the North Country coalmines. Alan, just read the part of my son, will you?

Alan: Oh, yes, Professor.

Jimmy: Thank you, Alan. Listen now to the big scene.

Alan (*North country*): Here goes! Things are different down int' pit since National Coal Board took over. There's been a lot of improvements.

Jimmy (*North country*): Ay, but we are goint to strip the 'ole lot down and send 'em overseas for scrap. Trouble is, the air in the rain shaft is foul.

Alan: Might be because she's been bolstered up with old pit-props. It's my belief something's bound to slip sooner or later.

Jimmy: We'll have to blast to find out. I'd like to do t' job meself but I'm nigh on sixty-five . . .

Dick: Oh, stop it — Jimmy, that's terrible! Nobody wants to hear that heavy stuff nowadays.

Jimmy: No?

Dick: No. Now my play has that light, Noel Coward touch. The final curtain — you just gotta see it. Heavy velvet with big gold tassels and advertisements —

Joy: OK, Dick. Let's hear *your* play now.

Dick: Right. You read the part of my girl friend. I've just asked you out to supper as part of my plan to win your heart. Read from *there.*

Joy: I hear champagne is served every half hour by little page-boys. Do let's go along. All the most beautiful women go there.

Dick: Probably because *I* was there recently. Amanda, you look divine tonight in that off-the-shoulder gown. Only *you* can wear such daring creations.

Joy: You frighten me when you say things like that, Quentin. Your eyes have a strange look. What is going on inside that sleek head of yours?

Dick: Think nothing of it, little one. *I* am old enough to be your *father*!

Jimmy: No, no, no, Bentley, it misses by a mile. No depth, no bravura, no — what shall I say? — no darned good.

Joy: I'll tell you what's wrong, boys. Jimmy's play is too heavy. Dick's is too light. If you could combine the two you'd have something. Nothing you'd *want*, mind you . . .

Jimmy: An excellent scheme, Joy. We'll read one line of each play alternately.

Dick: That's it! Start with your play, Jimmy. Alan speaks first.

Alan: Things are different down int' pit since National Coal Board took over. There's been lots of improvements.

Joy: I hear champagne is served every half hour by little page-boys. Do let's go along. All the most beautiful women go there.

Jimmy: Ay, but we're going to strip the 'ole lot down and send them overseas for scrap. Trouble is, the air in the main shaft is foul.
Dick: Probably because *I* was there recently. Amanda, you look divine tonight in that off-the-shoulder gown. Only *you* can wear such daring creations.
Alan: Might be because she's been bolstered up with old pit-props. It's my belief something's bound to slip sooner or later.
Joy: You frighten me when you say things like that, Quentin, your eyes have a strange look. What is going on inside that sleek head of yours?
Jimmy: We'll have to blast it to find out. I'd like to do the job meself, but I'm nigh on sixty-five.
Dick: Think nothing of it, little one, *I* am old enough to be your *father*!

* * *

Jimmy: Mr Eric Johnstone of Hollywood says that Americans won't take British films because they find difficulty in understanding our language.
Dick: We think we should translate our English dialogue into good Hollywood American with the aid of sub-titles as we've just shown you.
Jimmy: After each Englishman speaks the American translation should follow.
Joy: To demonstrate this we have taken authentic lines from the great British picture of 'Hamlet' and added suitable Hollywood sub-titles. TIFE now brings you 'Hamlet in Hollywood' or 'Look you upon this picture and on this'.

(*Orchestra plays short imposing mood theme*)

Joy: Good my lord Hamlet, how does your Honour for this many a day?
Dick: How ya bin, Mac?
Jimmy: Oh, dear Ophelia, I have not art to reckon my groans but that I love thee best, most best, believe it.
Dick: Don't fight this thing, kid, it's bigger than both of us.
Joy: Oh, what a noble mind is here o'erthrown.
Dick: The guy's nuts.
Clarry: *I* like him not. Nor stands it safe with us to let his madness rage.
Dick: We gotta rub him out.
Jimmy: Thou wretched, rash intruding fool.
Thy natural magic and dire property
On wholesome life usurp immediately.
Dick: Drop dead!
Clarry: My Lord, I'll hit him now!
Jimmy: Though I am not splenitive or rash
Yet have I something in me dangerous
Which let thy wisdom fear.
Dick: Better lay off — I'll mow ya down.
Clarry: Come on, I pray you
Pass with your best violence!
Dick: Get in there and come out punching.
Jimmy: A hit, a very palpable hit!
Oh, Horatio, what a wounded name
Things standing thus unknown shall leave behind me.

Dick: They got me, kid — it's coitans!
Joy: Now cracks a noble heart.
He was most likely, had he been put on
To have proved most royally.
Dick: There goes a swell guy.
Clarry: I could a tale unfold whose lightest word
Would harrow up thy soul, freeze thy young blood,
Make thy two eyes like stars start from their spheres,
Thy knotted and combined locks to part.
Dick: What a story — get me the city desk!
Jimmy: The rest is — silence.
Dick: That's all, folks.

* * *

Adrian: Thank you, Keynotes. And now, TIFE Topic of the Week. This week we consider television's 'Toddlers' Truce'.

Wall: This is an agreement that all television channels will close down between six and seven in the evening in order that children will not be distracted from doing their homework.

Adrian: However, the latest news is that the Truce is likely to be broken, and parents are worried. How can the children concentrate on homework when there are cowboys shooting each other on the telly?

Wall: Well, we've got a suggestion. Why not include the homework in the actual cowboy programmes! Like this . . . (*Sounds of gun shots — 'cowboy type'*) Wild Bill Brady, M.A., B.Sc.!

(*Sounds of a bar room and piano*)

June: Sit down, Marshall Brady, have a beer. You look worried.

Dick: I am worried, Kitty. The Wyoming Kid just shot old Luke. I found the body in the creek.

June: What was it doing there?

Dick: Displacing its own weight of water.

June: Gee, that's tough. Have a beer, Marshall.

Dick: Thanks, Kitty. Say, why does a swell girl like you have to work in a saloon like this?

June: It's the money, Marshall. They pay me commission on every glass of beer I can persuade drunk prospectors to drink. If a drunk prospector and a half drinks a glass and a half every minute and a half, in a seven hour day, how much can I earn, working six days a week at thirty-seven cents per glass?

Dick: Well, now, let X equal a drunk prospector . . .

June: Hey, hold it, Marshall! Look who's just come in — Frenchy Larue! He's mighty excited.

Wall (*coming in*): Marshall! Marshall!

June: What is it, Frenchy?

Wall (*slowly*): *Le chat est sous la table.*

Dick: Gee! The cat is under the table.

June: Pourquoi le chat est-il sous la table?
Wall: Le chat est sous la table par ce que the Wyoming Kid has just hit town!
Dick: The Wyoming Kid!

(*Revolver shots*)

Jim: Okay everybody! Reach for the sky. Higher than that. As far up as the Heaviside or Appleton Layer. One move and I'll plug you full of $2PbCO_3$ $PbOH_2$ (Lead).
Dick: Drop that rod, Wyoming. You're the rat I'm gunning for.
Jim: I don't like the sound of that talk, Marshall.
Dick: No?
Jim: No. It should be 'for whom I am gunning'.
Dick: Get out of Dodge.
June: Careful, Marshall. He's drawn a bead on you.
Jim: Yeah, and it ain't the Venerable Bede, whose great *Ecclesiastical History of England* was finally concluded in the year A.D.731.
June: No, Wyoming, no! You can't shoot without giving him a chance to draw.
Jim: Can't I? I've only got to press the trigger and a bullet will emerge from the barrel, owing to the fact that in a given quantity of gas at a given temperature and pressure, pressure is invariably proportionate to volume.
June: But that ain't gun-law.
Jim: Nope. That's Boyle's law.
Dick: So why *don't* you shoot, Wyoming? 'Cos you can't, that's why.
Jim: Get back, I say. I'll shoot.
Dick: Oh no, you won't. A revolver only holds six shots. By taking the number of shots you fired coming in and adding the shots you fired into old Luke, I calculate you have *no bullets left in your gun!*
Jim: No?

(*Pistol shot.* Dick *groans and falls to the ground*)

Jim: Well, pards, that's what happens when you don't do your homework.

* * *

Balham has had an unusually long life for a sketch. In 1948 the BBC asked Denis Norden and me whether we would have a got at writing a comedy series for their cultural channel, the Third Programme. We came up with a monthly series which we called 'Third Division' and one of the items was *Balham.*

A year or so later one of the cast, Peter Sellers, searching for material for a comedy L.P., remembered the sketch and, with a few minor alterations, it was recorded as part of *The Best of Sellers,* which is still on sale in record shops.

It is interesting to note the cast of young hopefuls who played *Balham* in the original radio production of 1948. They were: Robert Beatty, Benny Lee, Harry Secombe, Benny Hill, Peter Sellers, Michael Bentine and Patricia Hayes.

The sketch itself, mocking Hollywood travelogues which were then still a part of almost every cinema programme, indicates how radio comedy was beginning to find its own sense of humour and was using techniques which could not be used in any other medium.

BALHAM – GATEWAY TO THE SOUTH

by Frank Muir and Denis Norden

Peter: Balham – Gateway to the South!

(*Music*)

Peter: We enter Balham through the verdant grasslands of Battersea Park and at once we are aware that here is a land of happy contented people who go about their tasks in truly democratic spirit.

(*Music*)

Peter: This is busy High Street, focal point of the Town's activities. Note the quaint old stores whose frontage is covered with handpainted inscriptions, every one a rare example of native Balham art. Let us read some of them as our camera travels past.

Harry: Cooking apples – choice eaters – green ration books only.

Michael: A Song to Remember at the Tantamount Cinema –

Benny Lee: A Suit to Remember at Montague Moss.

Benny H: Cremations Conducted With Decorum and Taste.

Michael: Frying tonight. Bring your own paper.

Harry: Rally Thursday. Berkeley Square – Bev Baxter and Quinny Hogg – Up the ruling classes.

Peter: This shows the manifold activities of Balham's thriving community. Yet Balham is also the home of a craftmanship which is slowly dying amid the industrialization of the modern world, and in quiet corners we still find examples of the exquisite workmanship that Balham craftsmen have made world famous.

Harry: Toothbrush holesmanship.

Benny H: On my forge I carve these little holes in the top of toothbrushes. It is exciting work, and my forefathers have been engaged on it since 1957.

Michael: I am a hair-pin corrugator. The bent bits in the middle of a hairpin – or, as we say in the trade, hairpin bends – are put in manually, or, in other words, once a year. I recently had the honour of demonstrating my craft before the Oni of Ife. He stopped by one day for a couple of words. I did not understand either of them.

Peter: Needless to say many of Balham's craftsmen today are engaged upon work which brings in much-needed dollars. An example is manufacture of spelkin binders. This is a fascinating process, a secret that is handed down from father to son.

Michael: My boy, I'm going to hand it down to you. Guard it carefully. It is a priceless heritage. Here – take it.

(*Sound of crash*)

Michael: Butterfingers!

Harry: Let us watch the last stages in the process of the manufacture of a typical spelkin binder in Balham's model factory.

Benny H (*Australian*): I am the factory manager. The boiling lead has just been poured from the graving crucible into a well-greased pan. The rubber slats are buckled in two at a time . . .

(*Sound of slats being buckled in*)

Benny H: Next the galvanators . . .

(*Sound of galvanators*)

Benny H: Followed by the trumble casing . . .

(*Sound of trumble casing*)

Benny H: and the meshed articulators. Next comes the prime grafter gudgeon pin . . .

(*Sound of gudgeon pin*)

Benny H: then the doofah . . .

(*Sound of doofah*)

Benny H: then the watchamacallit . . .

(*Sound of watchamacallit*)

Benny H: and the thingummybob . . .

(*Sound of thingummybob*)

Benny H: then that queer thing . . .

(*Sound of queer thing*)

Benny H: and the er . . . howd'yedo.

(*Sound of howd'yedo*)

Benny (*surprised*): then the – oh it's all over!

Harry: The completed assembly is wheeled into the paint shop for a coat of green enamel from whence it is taken on huge lorries to all parts of the world where it will find its way on to the breakfast table of a million homes.

Peter: So much for Balham's industries. Let us see a little more of the town. Here is the Great Park, covering nearly half an acre.

(*Music*)

Peter: This is where the children traditionally meet by the limpid waters of the old drinking fountain, a drinking fountain that has for countless years across the vast aeons of time, given untold pleasure to man, woman and child – all three of them. Beside this fountain – donated by able Councillor Stephen Colgate as long ago as 1928 – the little ones sit round a trim nursemaid and listen spellbound and enchanted as she reads them a story.

Pat: With one bound he was by her side. She felt his hot breath on her cheek as he ripped the thin silk from –

(*Music*)

Peter: We are now entering Old Balham. Time has passed by this remote corner. So shall we. But first let us take a peep at the inhabitants who carry about them the aura of a bygone era. This is Mrs Brisket, who as she chats to her neighbour still wears the colourful costume of long ago.

Carole: I said to my daughter, hem line or no hem line this skirt cost me six coupons and its good enough for knocking about the house in.

Peter: But Balham does not live in the past; it looks to the future.

Michael: Of course, the figures aren't available at the moment but the Housing Committee are considering plans for a new station waiting room and a creche.

Benny H: Councillor Colgate, my paper wants to know – what exactly *is* a creche.

Michael: Well, it's a – let's examine housing. By cutting red tape to the minimum we have housed (*Cough*) families, requisitioned (*Cough*) buildings and hope by the end of 1949 to have completed a further (*Cough*).

Peter: But Balham is not neglecting the cultural side. Balham has more bookshops and art museums than any other borough of the same name. This is Eugene Colgate whose weekly recitals are attended by a vast concord of people. He has never had a lesson in his life.

(*Piano played very badly*)

Peter: Such is the enthusiasm of Balham's music lovers that they are subscribing to send Eugene to Italy. Or Vienna. Or anywhere. Paintings are on view in the Great Park during the summer and all the town's younger folk flock there in the evening for those primitive exhibitions.

(*Music*)

Peter: Night falls on Balham.

(*Music*)

Peter: From Colgate's Folly, Balham's famous beauty spot, which stands nearly two feet above sea level, the town is spread below us in a fairyland of glittering lights, changing all the time. Green, amber, red, red and amber, and back to green. The nightlife is awakening.

(*Music*)

Peter: The El Morocco Tea Rooms.
Harry: Hey, miss.
Pat: Yes? Watcha want?
Harry: Pilchards.
Pat: They're off.
Harry: Ah! Baked beans?
Pat: Off.
Harry: Meat loaf salad?
Pat: Off.

Harry: Pot of tea?
Pat: No tea.
Harry: Well, just milk.
Pat: Milk's off.
Harry: A roll and butter, then.
Pat: No butter.
Harry: Just a roll.
Pat: Only bread.
Harry: I might just as well've stayed at 'ome.
Pat: Ooh — I dunno — does you good to 'ave a fling occasionally.

(*Music*)

Peter: And so the long night draws on. The last stragglers make their way home and the lights go out one by one as dawn approaches and the bell of St. Colgate's parish church tolls ten o'clock. Balham sleeps, and so we say farewell to the historic borough with many pleasant memories and the words of G. Colgate Smith, Balham's own bard, burning in our ears.

Michael: Broadbosomed, bold, becalm'd, benign
Lies Balham foursquare on the Northern Line.
Matched by no marvel save in Eastern scene,
A rose-red city half as gold as green.
By country churchyard, ferny fen and mere
What Colgate mute, inglorious, lies buried here.
Oh stands the church clock at ten to three
And is there honey still for tea?

Pat: Honey's off.

(*Music*)

*   *   *

Here are four more sketches from the Peter Sellers records. They show how his superb comic talent and versatility made it possible to present sketches of warmth and sublety as well as conventionally comic pieces like *Common Entrance.*

COMMON ENTRANCE

by Frank Muir and Denis Norden

Father. I have been trying to get my son into a good school. After trying Winchester, Marlborough and Charterhouse, I was recommended to send him to that great

British public school, Cretinby. Some of you may not have heard of Cretinby, in the heart of the swamp country; a difficult place to get into, and harder still to get out of. I motored down there the following day. (*Sounds of ancient motor horn and engine.*) I was shown into the headmaster's study.

Servant. Come into the headmaster's study, sir, would you. 'E'll be down in a minute.

(*Sound of keys.*)

Headmaster. Good afternoon. I am the headmaster. Are you a parent?

Father. Well, I . . . er . . . I have a small son.

Headmaster. I detest evasiveness. What age is he?

Father. He's eight.

Headmaster. Eight. Only eight? The awkward age — too old for Mother Goose and too young for Lolita. Here is my brochure. Just glance through it for a few moments, would you.

Father. That's very interesting; there's a photograph of the school. I say, the fire escape doesn't look very safe in this picture.

Headmaster. It's a lot safer in the picture than it is on the building.

Father. Is it examined every week?

Headmaster. It's used every week.

Father. Hm. Tell me, is this school co-educational?

Headmaster. You can't baffle me with long words.

Father. I mean, er, do the boys and girls share the same curricula?

Headmaster. No, we had separate ones built.

Father. Well, how do you segregate the sexes?

Headmaster. If you must know, I go round at night with a crowbar and prise them apart.

Father. Oh dear, I don't think this will suit my Basil. You see, he's very sensitive and he's never been separated from his mother.

Headmaster. He hasn't? Have you heard what Havelock Ellis has to say about that?

Father. No?

Headmaster. Then I'll show you. It's disgusting.

Father. Er, well, I don't think I'll see it now.

Headmaster. Then I'll send you a copy under plain wrappers. No one would know.

Father. I must tell you that my boy is very delicate, and there is something I would like to know: are your dormitories dry?

Headmaster. They are after 11 p.m. then they get drinks if they buy sandwiches.

Father. Hm. I see. Tell me, what types of pupil do you have here?

Headmaster. We have two types of pupil — Class A and Class B. At mealtimes the Class B boys get priority.

Father. And the Class A boys?

Headmaster. They get food.

Father. You mean to tell me that the Class B boys don't eat?

Headmaster. I never pry into their private lives. Perhaps you'd like to see one of our typical pupils? Farnsworth! *Fa-arnsworth*!

Boy. Coming sir!

Headmaster. This is Farnsworth, one of our better eight-year-olds. He is 29. You may go, Farnsworth.

Boy. Thank you, sir.
Headmaster. Hurry along.
Father. Tell me, the teaching, the books — is it on the Montessori system?
Headmaster. Sometimes, but I find that most people prefer to pay cash.
Father. Oh. Then you have no syllabus of your own?
Headmaster. I don't think it concerns you how I choose to spend my leisure. As it happens, we are just good friends.
Father. Mm, hm, it's very confusing. Your answers aren't a bit like the ones I received from the headmaster at Winchester.
Headmaster. Oh! You've been hawking your brat around, have you?
Father. Oh, no, it's not that, it's just that I want something to suit his personality. I'm looking for something progressive.
Headmaster. We encourage children to be children. You may not realize this, but some of our greatest men started life as children. (*Clanging bell.*) Ah — there goes the bell for prep.; one of the subjects we specialize in. Some of our boys speak it like a native.
Father. Er. Mr Headmaster, I'm going to be brutally frank with you. Have you got a record of juvenile delinquency?
Headmaster. Singing what?
Father. No, no, I mean, I want something to prove to me that the boys here have strengthened their personalities.
Headmaster. Well, ah, perhaps you would like to hear the school choir. Miss Pringle, I wonder if you would oblige.

(*Sounds of piano. Boys* (Peter Sellers) *singing 'Nymphs and Shepherds, come away' atrociously.*)

* * *

PARTY POLITICAL SPEECH
by Max Schreiner

(*Applause*)

Speaker: My friends, in the light of present-day developments, let me say right away that I do not regard existing conditions likely. On the contrary, I have always regarded them as subjects of the gravest responsibility, and shall ever continue to do so. Indeed, I will even go further and state quite categorically that I am more than sensible of the definition of the precise issues which are at this moment concerning us all. We must build, but we must build surely. (*'Hear, hear'; applause*) Let me say just this. If any part of what I say is challenged, then I am more than ready to meet that challenge, for I have no doubt whatsoever that whatever I have said in the past, or what I am saying now is the exact, literal and absolute truth as to the state of the case. (*Applause*) I put it to you that this is not a time for vague promises of better things to come, for if I were to convey to you a spirit of false optimism then I should be neither fair to you nor true to myself. But does this mean, I hear you cry, that we can no longer look forward to the future that it is come? Certainly not!

Voice. What about the workers?

Speaker. What about the workers indeed, sir! Grasp, I beseech you, with both hands — oh, I'm sorry, I beg your pardon, Madam — the opportunities that are offered. Let us assume a bold front and go forward together. Let us carry the fight against ignorance to the four corners of the earth, because it is a fight which concerns us all. And now finally, my friends, in conclusion, let me say just this . . .

* * *

SHADOWS ON THE GRASS

by Irene Handl

(*A middle-aged lady meets a young Frenchman in the park.*)

She. Hullo. I've been watching you, I say I've been watching you feedin' the birds. I think you're marvellous. Aren't they sweet? I don't know how anyone can be cruel to dumb animals, do you? I think it's worse than murder, because they can't speak. Excuse this somewhat crude attire, won't you? I was catchin' up with my sunbathin', hasn't it been gorgeous.

He (*French*). Beautifool weather we are having.

She. Yes, course I tan a lot faster in a bikini, you know — but where's the use of frightening everybody to death? (*Nervous laugh.*)

He. My goodness, you would not frighten me, because, when I saw you first, I say to myself, my goodness, what a beautifool woman, I would so very much like to know such a woman of beauty.

She. Ooh, now I call that truly gallant. Shall I get up and take a bow? (*Giggle.*)

He (*Laugh*). Please take one, by all means.

She. You come 'ere often, do you?

He. Well, I come here quite often, as I say, to feed these birds, because I love the open air, and . . .

She. Well, it's very nice, isn't it? I mean, it's private without being insulated, if you know what I mean. I can see you're like me, I will not go into a public park and mingle with the hoi polloi.

He. I quite agree. I like to keep myself to myself.

She. Ooh — aren't there some shockin' people about, I mean, even here — well, there's one woman at our hotel, well she's more of a person really — she *fas*cinates me (*laughs*). D'you know, anythink in trousers she gradiates to —

He. Really?

She. I think, You scum, how prurile can you get. And then they wonder, you know, that they end up as Exhibit A.

He. I'm so lonely, you know, that I want to have conversation with you, or someone.

She. Ah, well, you've only yourself to blame, you know, because I can never resist a true gentleman. My Jove, are they hard to come by nowadays. I should know; I was married straight out of the schoolroom, you know, to the most perfect gentleman that ever trod the earth.

He. Really?

She. I can see him now, on our wedding day. The tears was rollin' down his face. He was so conscious of his trust. He'd promised Pops and Mama — of course, they thought the world of me, y'know — 'e'd promised Pops and Mama that I should never want, and my Jove, I never did. 'E gave me the most smashin' home in Avalon Avenue — do you know Dalston at all?

He. Er, no, no, I don't.

She. Oh, well. They call it the Frinton of East Eight, so that'll give you some idea. Everythink a woman's heart could yearn for, oh . . .

He. He has obviously left you very well . . . er . . . off . . . er, like that, with money . . .

She. Well, yes he did, but mind you, I've got the ample means to buy a splendid home any time I wish. It was Tufnell's one prayer to leave me comfortably off . . .

He (*Murmuring*). That's very good to hear that . . .

She. I mean, they do me very well, you know, at my hotel — do you know the Royalston at all? It's very, very select, and the manager is a charming chap, Bill Oakshot, you know, ex-naval type, and the staff's charming too — I'm afraid they spoil me thoroughly, you know, they've given me a huge double-room on the first floor with a private bath attached. Oh, well, it's almost equally as good as private because all the others at the Royalston are business types, you know. They're almost always gone before Yours Truly has even opened 'er eyes.

He. Oh? (*Laughs.*)

She. I'm afraid I'm a bit of a naughty girl like that . . . I love to lay in my beddybyes dreaming my dreams.

He. I wish that I could — share your dreams — with you.

She. Now, that I did not hear. That I have decided completely to ignore! You're not nice to know, y'know. (*Nervous giggles*).

He. I'm so full of enthusiasm to have your friendship, to receive great pleasure from knowing you, that I said a stupid thing like that . . . Forgive me . . . I'm sorry . . . very sorry.

She. Oh, well, you're forgiven — I was just goin' to ask you back to din-dins with me. (*Giggle*).

He. Well, I would love to come, please, I . . .

She. They keep a smashin' table at the Royalston, you know, we nearly always have a second vegetable, and always croutons with the soup. An' if you ever feel like havin' half a bottle of Borjulais, they practically fall over themselves backwards bringing it in for you. I always say, as long as there's enough to see me out, what happens afterwards is sanny fairyanne.

He. Oh, you speak French?

She. Oon petit peu.
He. But you have got a very fine accent, you know.
She. Oh, you and your blue eyes . . . (*Giggle*).
He. No, no, I mean it. Listen, say thees with me, say thees with me, we'll speak French together . . . Are you ready?
She. Yes?
He. Voulez-vous . . .
She. Voulay-vous . . .
He. . . . coucher avec moi ce soir.
She. Ooh! Ooh, you rotten egg! (*Laughter.*) I'll set Bill Oakshot on to you.
He. You know what it means, you know what it means, you are a woman of the world.
She. Oh come on, let's go to my hotel and have a talk.
He. I like to come and sit closer to you.
She. Oh, what are you doing? (*Laughter.*)
He. Nothing. Listen, I don't even know your name, you know?
She. Well, shall I tell you the very private name that Tufnell kept for me?
He. Please, please.
She. 'E used to call me Squidgy. (*Laughter.*)
He. Oh no . . . (*Laughter.*) . . . Squeedgy . . .
She. Don't you think that's sweet?
He. It's beautifool for you, it fits you so perfectly.
She. D'you like this shade of blue?
He. Yes, er, what ees, er?
She. It's called Blue Toast.
He. Oh.
She. Tufnell used to go crackers about me in anythink blue. He used to say, 'Squidgy buy herself a blue nightie, make her eyes look like stars'.
He. Ah — that is so sad, so beautiful.
She. I believe you're jealous!
He. Oh — (*General giggles.*) — come along, come along —
She. What *are* you doing? (*Giggling.*)
He. Nothing — I'm just helping you from your deckchair.
She. Well, pick my bag up then.
He. All right. Come, let us go to your hotel . . .

Exeunt, giggling.

* * *

LORD BADMINTON'S MEMOIRS

by Max Schreiner

Nowadays, it is the custom to think of the aristocracy and leisured classes as being devoted to little else besides selfish pleasures and amusements. This simply was not the case, and I would like in the next few minutes to destroy this fallacy.

As a very young boy, some of my earliest recollections are of being taken by my father, in those days Chancellor of the Exchequer, on his occasional tours of the estate at Charters. In the course of these expeditions it was his practice to visit those among his poorer tenants and employees who, by reason of accident, old age or sheer carelessness, happened to be destitute and nearly starving. Dear faithful Eliot, the coachman, would invariably accompany us, carrying an enormous wicker basket, which was covered with a dazzling white cloth, and contained bowls of chicken and cold stock, ah, cabbage stalks, potato peelings and other nutritious kitchen scraps.

As well as these material comforts, my father also distributed tracts of an improving and uplifting nature which he wrote himself and had printed at his own expense.

I very well remember one occasion when my father and I visited the sickbed of an ancient and decrepit waggoner, who had somehow managed to get himself badly trampled underfoot while attempting to stop a runaway horse and cart. Although the poor old fellow could hardly move, he made a pathetic effort to sit up in bed and tug at his forelock as we entered the wretched bedroom. You see, our sudden appearance induced in him what psychologists now call a conditioned reflex, and this honest rustic could no more have prevented himself from trying to show his respect than a dog can prevent its tail from wagging at the sight of its master.

My father, who I think I may have mentioned before was at this time First Lord of the Admiralty — he began to tell the invalid that such formalities could be dispensed with, under the circumstances. But, too late. With a sickening thud, that I can hear to this very day, the grizzled pate came into smart contact with an oak beam, which curved down just above the bed, and with a low moan the unhappy man fell back stunned on to his pillow. He never regained consciousness.

Distressed as we were at this incident, my father and I offered a word of cheer to the waggoner's wife, and we pressed upon her a basketful of rotten apples and a bundle of tracts before proceeding on our philanthropic way.

'A most merciful release,' observed my father, after the waggoner's funeral. 'Why, he might have lingered on, in a bedridden condition, for many years, a misery to himself and a burden to others. Providence works in many strange ways.'

As a footnote, I would like to add that there is no doubt in my mind at all that my father, who was then, I fancy, President of the Board of Trade, would actually have attended the funeral of his late employee, had it not been for a sudden attack of gout, which kept him indoors on the day.

I hope, in relating this anecdote, that I have indicated something of the wonderful sort of relationship which used to exist between the family at the hall and the peasantry on the estate — a relationship, alas, which is nowhere to be found nowadays. It is not everything, I fear, that has changed for the best.

* * *

Little revue, or intimate revue as it was also called, continued to flourish through the 40s and to attract bright young minds to write its sketches. The next two were products of Cambridge University, always a fertile source of revue material.

LA PLUME DE MA TANTE

by Simon Phipps

Scene: A hotel lobby. All the characters read from phrase books.

When the Curtain *rises the* Hotel Manager *is arranging a table. The* Stranger *enters.*

Stranger. Good morning, good afternoon, good evening, good night. I will pay for what the coachman eats. Have you a room on the first, second, third, fourth floor?

Hotel Manager. We have one facing east, west, north, south, overlooking the courtyard, garden, street, canal, gas-works, sewer, municipal museum, cemetery, Corporation refuse dump.

Stranger. I will take a double-bedded room. Send me the chambermaid. I am going to be sick. I am not going to be sick. Are the beds well aired? Can I have a warm bath?

Hotel Manager. Yes, sir.

Stranger. I would like a cold bath, turkish bath, a swimming-bath, a bathing-dress. Give me a candle please. Where is the W.C.?

(*He exits. Enter* Mum *and* Dad.)

Dad. This town is the Capital of the Department, it has a population of ten thousand persons.

Mum. The Public Park is twenty-five acres and in the opinion of many is the finest of the city's pleasure-grounds.

Dad. The clock-tower, overlooking the bridge, is three hundred and sixteen feet high and forty feet square.

Mum. There is a draught here. Waiter, please shut the window.

Dad. I will order lunch, afternoon tea, high tea, dinner. Waiter, please to hand me the menu.

Mum. I will take clear soup, pea soup, soup with vegetables, Scotch broth, soup.

Dad. I shall prefer salmon, with sauce hollandaise, fried soles, eels, grated cheese, fresh herrings, mackerel, fish and chips. Waiter, bring me also a newspaper.

(*Enter the* Stranger.)

Stranger. I want another blanket. Give me a brush down. Cut my hair. I shall be leaving tomorrow. Is there a W.C. on the train? I want a seat from here to Naples.

Dad. This town is the Capital of the Department.

Mum. The public park has twenty-five acres and the clock tower three hundred and sixteen feet.

Stranger. Assuming that I am a bird of passage to or from the province how shall I employ the time at my disposal to the best advantage?

Mum. The following are a few attractive modes of spending what must perforce be a very hurried day, the proportion of time given in each place depending, of course, on whether the pilgrim's bent is in the direction of art, architecture, historical associations or shops and the life of the street.

Dad (clearing his throat). It is very oppressive in here. Waiter, please to open the window.

Mum. This plant wants watering.

Stranger. Kindly give me a drink. Have you a pencil? I wish to do some sketching.

Dad. Here is the pen of my aunt.

Mum. I hope you secure some fine views.

Stranger. Where is a point of vantage?

Mum. The clock tower is three hundred and sixteen feet high.

All. And forty feet square.

Stranger. Is there an English church here?

Dad. Visitors are welcome at San Salvolatili. Services are held daily at eight, nine, ten, eleven, twelve, thirteen, fourteen . . .

Stranger. Lend me a hymn-book please.

Mum. There is a strong choir.

Dad. The seats are free.

Stranger. Is there a collection?

Mum. An offertory is taken.

Stranger (pulling some money from his pocket). For shame! The chambermaid has robbed me of five sovereigns.

Dad. Call the police!

Mum. Help! (*She faints into the arms of a* Waiter.)

Stranger. Where is the British Embassy? Does the Judge speak English? I shall attend upon him.

Dad. How much is the doctor's fee for a visit?

Hotel Manager. Two hundred francs.

Dad (after totting up his money). Send for the doctor, my wife has vapours.

Mum. I feel better.

Dad. Do not send for the doctor. How are you?

Mum. I am in pretty good health, with many thanks.

Dad. Then let us go home. We shall return this year, next year, sometime — never!

Black Out.

* * *

TIE UP

by Ben Gradwell

Scene. *The Smoking-Room of a club. Two deep leather armchairs are set C. In one of them is slumped a figure —* Snod *— asleep, but quite obscured by 'The Times'.*

When the Curtain *rises* Higgins *enters carrying a drink and a newspaper, crosses down in front of* Snod *and trips over his feet in making for the vacant chair.* Snod *drops his paper and* Higgins *glares aggressively at him and then sits. He is just becoming immersed in his paper when he notices* Snod's *tie, which is identical with his own.*

Higgins. I say, I say.
Snod. Uh?
Higgins. I say, aren't you wearing the O.B. tie?
Snod. Uh?
Higgins. I said isn't that the O.B. tie you're wearing?
Snod. Yes, as a matter of fact it is.
Higgins. Well, Well. When were you there?
Snod. 'Sixteen.
Higgins. Jove, were you? So was I.
Snod. Jove, were you?
Higgins. Jove, yes.
Snod. Jove.

(*There is a retrospective pause.*)

Higgins. My name's Higgins. George Higgins.
Snod (pensively). Ye-es, I *think* I remember you. I'm Snod — Cyril Snod.
Higgins. Ye-es, I think I remember you too. What house were you in?
Snod. The Rockery.
Higgins. Jove, were you? So was I.
Snod. Jove, were you?
Higgins. Jove, yes.
Snod. Jove.
Higgins. Old Belcher Clayton was Head of the house.
Snod. Yes, that's right. (*Tentatively.*) Bit of a B.F.
Higgins. Oh, the complete B.F. But George, he could belch!
Snod. Yes, you've got to admit, he could belch.

(*There is a pause for further reflection.*)

Higgins. Well, here's to it. Cheers.

(*They raise their glasses.*)

Snod. Cheers.
Higgins. Yes, old Belcher Clayton — you remember he used to have a spotty face. Sort of dry skin — at least, I *think* it was dry skin.
Snod. Yes, it *was* dry skin and I think he had it all over too. Don't you remember he used to walk like this? (*He walks like a man with dry skin all over.*)
Higgins. Yes, perhaps he did have it all over. Come to think of it he *did*. I was in the same dormitory as he was and he used to scratch himself all over before he got into bed.
Snod. Cheers.
Higgins. Cheers.
Snod. What a coincidence. Wonder what old Belcher's doing now.
Higgins. Oh, of course, after his illness — overdosed himself with bromide, you know.
Snod. Why?

Higgins (emphatically). Hormones.
Snod. Don't remember him. Was he in my time?
Higgins. No, *hormones.*
Snod. Oh. Cheers.
Higgins. Cheers. Anyway he went up to Cambridge and took a Double First in English. Brilliant chap, you know.
Snod. What's he doing now?
Higgins. Working in a potted meat factory in South Shields.
Snod. Do you remember that time he was caught having an affair with one of the housemaids?

Higgins *is just about to reply when there is a resounding belch from behind the armchairs (the belch is optional) and a man, who has been invisible throughout to the audience, rises from behind. He has an air of ill-suppressed rage, he is wearing the O.B. tie and he walks like a man who, manifestly, is suffering from dry skin all over.* Higgins *and* Snod *watch him depart; they turn to one another, their mouths fall open and —*

Black Out.

* * *

For many years the doyen of revue writers was Alan Melville, whose *Sweet and Low* and *Sweeter and Lower* were hugely successful during the war. He continued to turn out a stream of first-class material until the public taste for this kind of theatre changed. He is probably the wittiest and most 'West End' of all the writers of West End revues. His work is always highly professional; the sketches have a strong basic idea, plenty of laughs along the way and a good finish.

THE TROUBLE WITH MISS MANDERSON

by Alan Melville

There is a rostrum C, with a wall backing which includes a french window. The window is open, and looks out on a low balcony with a view of rooftops and sky. On the rostrum the Psychiatrist *is staring down at his patient,* Miss Manderson, *who is lying prone on a couch.*

He. Just lie back, Miss Manderson. I want you to feel completely relaxed. That's the idea. Now: can you tell me when this — started?
She. I was four.
He. I beg your pardon?
She. Well, I was a bit more than that, really. It was just after my fourth birthday. I was four years, three weeks, as a matter of fact, and Mum and Dad took us to Worthing for our summer holidays, you see: me and my little brother Arnold: he was two. And I pushed him over.

He. You did what?

She. Well, we were on the pier one morning, you see: it was a Tuesday: I remember, because there was a matinée of 'Worthing Follies of 1939' in the Pier Pavilion in the afternoon, and me and my little brother Arnold wanted to go and see it, you see, and Mum said no because she and Dad had seen it on the Monday night and they said some of the things the comic said weren't fit for children: and I pushed him over.

He. You pushed your little brother over?

She. That's right. Who did you think — the comic?

He. You mean — over the edge of the pier, into the sea?

She. That's right. He was standing near the edge, you see. As a matter of fact, he was looking down to see if he could see any fish. And I just gave him a push.

He. Didn't your parents see you?

She. Well, no. I was looking after Arnold at the time, you see, because as a matter of fact Dad was buying jellied eels from a stall — he was mad keen on jellied eels, my Dad was: always had been — and Mum was having her hand read by Madame Zenobia. I remember, because when she came out of Madame Zenobia's she was looking as white as a sheet and I asked her if there was anything the matter and she said Madame Zenobia had told her she was going to hear of an unexpected family bereavement within a seven: and she said she didn't think it was right people saying things like that in the middle of other people's holidays.

He. But your little brother — he got out all right, did he?

She. Oh, yes.

He. Thank God for that.

She. He was washed up near Folkestone.

He. *Folkestone?* But that's seventy miles away.

She. I know. And it was seven weeks later he was washed up. That's what gave us all a bit of a turn. I don't care what you say: it shows there's something in it.

He. In what?

She. People like Madame Zenobia.

He. Oh — yes. Is there — anything else, Miss Manderson?

She. Well, yes, there is, as a matter of fact. I was at school, you see: and I had a crush on a girl in the hockey team called Edith Rosebury; and in the Christmas holidays I asked Mum and Dad if I could have Edith to our place to spend the day, you see; and Dad bought us seats for the panto. It was 'Jack and the Beanstalk' at Kingston Empire, with Dorothy Ward and Shaun Glenville. I'm not boring you, am I?

He. Not at all. Go on.

She. Well, we had seats in the front row of the upper circle, you see, and in the scene just before the interval Dorothy Ward started climbing the beanstalk, and my friend Edith got so excited she stood up on her chair and started cheering: and I pushed her over.

He. Over the edge of the circle?

She. That's right. Mind you, I didn't have to push her hard, because she was sort of off her balance in any case. She landed in the stalls, in Row K.

He. And what — er — happened?

She. Well, I had a choc ice in the interval, and then in the scene after the interval Dorothy Ward managed to get to the top of this beanstalk, you see, and she sang

'There'll Always Be an England' — and all the audience joined in. Oh, it was lovely: I'll never forget it.

He. Anything — er — else, Miss Manderson?

She. Well, yes, there is, as a matter of fact. I had a boy friend, you see: and I'd saved up to go to Paris for a week's holiday — fourteen pounds ten all-in on the Polytechnic, including tours of the Louvre and saucy Montmartre: and my boy friend said he'd come over at the same time, you see, and one afternoon he took me right up as far as you can go up that Eiffel Tower . . .

He. Please. Don't tell me.

She. No, that was the funny thing: I didn't. I remember we were walking home to the hotel, crossing one of those bridges over the Seine, and I kept wondering why I hadn't, and then I did.

He. Did what?

She. Pushed him over.

He. Did *he* get out all right?

She. Well, I never saw anything about it in the papers at the time, but then, you see, I don't speak French.

He. Miss Manderson: have these — er — phenomena persisted in more recent years?

She. Well, not regularly. Just every now and then, really. Nothing serious. I was a Sunday School teacher, you see, and one year I took my whole Sunday School class for its annual outing. There were forty-two in the class: we hired a bus from London Transport.

He. Where did you take them?

She. Beachy Head. I must say I did feel a fool coming back all by myself in a double-decker.

He. Tell me, Miss Manderson: are your parents still alive?

She. Well, no. You see, Dad and I went on a mountaineering holiday in Switzerland.

He. And your mother?

She. Well, after I got back from Switzerland, she was a bit depressed, you see, and I thought I'd like to cheer her up, so I took her to tea at Derry and Tom's roof garden.

He (*rising*). Miss Manderson: your is a very simple case of self-induced pathogenic hallucination. Your psychopathic complexes, increased no doubt by strong retrogressive inhibitions, have caused your libido to become a little repressed, that is all. Your subconscious mind has become so obsessed with this ridiculous notion of pushing people off piers and bridges and precipices and so on that — in a mental process which we psychiatrists know as 'repetition-compulsion' — you have persuaded yourself that you have in fact done these things.

She. You mean — I just imagined it?

He. Of course.

She (getting off the couch and going to him) Well, that is a relief, I must say. D'you know, every now and then I've been quite worried about it. I'm ever so grateful, Doctor. How much is the fee?

He. Fifty guineas.

She. Oh.

(*She pushes him over the balcony. He disappears out of sight with a scream.*)

She. Well, thank goodness it's only my imagination.

Black Out

* * *

RESTORATION PIECE

by Alan Melville

The Compere *comes out in front of the tabs.*

Compere: Ladies and gentlemen . . . if distinguished revue artists like Mr Cyril Ritchards and Miss Madge Elliot can get away with Restoration Comedy, we see no reason why we shouldn't do the same: and we are presenting now one of the lesser-known works of Mr Congreve entitled 'Virtue in Labour' or ''Tis Pity He's a Coxcomb.'

This is the first time that this company has played Restoration Comedy, and there is one thing which we feel ought to be explained. The Company rehearsed from the original 18th-century copies of the play, in which — as you know — the letter 's' very often appears looking rather like the letter 'f'. There has been a certain amount of confusion over this . . . however:

The characters are: Sir Militant Malpractice, a sop — I beg your pardon, a *fop*: Sir Solemnity Sourpuss, a cuckold: Lady Wanton Malpractice, wife to Sir Militant: and Simple, a maid.

(*He exits. The tabs open on a Restoration boudoir.* Lady Wanton Malpractice *is restoring herself in front of a Restoration mirror. She calls off R.*)

Lady Malpractice. Fimple! . . . *Fimple!* . . .

(*There is no reply.*)

A pox on all fervants! . . . (*She calls again.*) *FIMPLE!* . . .

(Simple *enters R.*)

Simple. My Lady fummoned me?

Lady Malpractice. Fummoned thee, i' faith? I ha' fummoned thee, wench, fince a quarter past fix.

Simple. La, ma'am, you flander me!

Lady Malpractice. Flander thee, by my troth! Here I fit — fad and forlorn — while you, perfidious jade, are gone to a cockfight with that tatterdemalion of a foldier! (*Aside, she comes right down to the footlights.*) Flap my vitals if the bawd is not in labour wi' the fauciest foldier that ever ferved as a fentry! . . . (*She goes back to her seat.*)

Simple. He is not a foldier, ma'am. He is a failor.

Lady Malpractice. Foldier or failor, what matter? And I left here, fitting on the fofa like a midwife wi' the vapours! (*Accusingly.*) I faw you, Fimple — behind the fummer-houfe. *Kiffing.*

Simple. La, ma'am, 'tis not a fin to kiff.
Lady Malpractice. Nay, good Fimple, 'tis a most fatisfying fenfation.

(Simple *and* Malpractice *come right down stage to hold a carefully-posed picture and sing:*)

Both: Passion's a teafing, fickle jade
Coming to mifftress as to maid.
Love is a trollop, fo, 'tis faid,
Fex is a whore that lies abed.
Fa-la-la-la-la-la! . . .
La-la-la! . . .
Fa-la-la-la-la-la-la! . . .
La! . . .

(*They scuttle back to their former positions.*)

Lady Malpractice. What's his name, this coxcomb of yours?
Simple. Fam.
Lady Malpractice. Fam? (*Aside.*) Vouchsafe my virtue, I'll warrant they'll be married and bedded by fummer.
Simple. Before fummer, ma'am. 'Tis fixed for the fecond Funday after Feptuagefima.
Lady Malpractice. La, my fine flut! . . . 'tis plain what is the matter with you. Thou'rt over-fexed! . . .

(*They run down again to hold another attractive picture and sing gaily:*)

Both: If a bawd wi' the vapours
Starts cutting her capers,
A fig for the fate of the strumpet
She'll take tea with a cuckold
And very soon look old
Demanding a helping of crumpet!
Fol-de-rol-lol-de-lol-lol-de-lol-lay! . . .
The Lord help a bawd i' the family way!

(*They scamper back to their former positions. There is a knock off.*)

Lady Malpractice. But foft! . . . fomeone comef! Fee who it is, Fimple.

(Simple *looks off L.*)

Simple. 'Tis Fir Folemnity Fourpuff, my Lady.
Lady Malpractice (rising and over-acting a good deal.) Folemnity! . . . oh, a fleek, flimy, flippery fellow if ever I new one! A beperiwigged cuckold wi' the face of a faint and the foul of a finner! (*Aside, she goes right downstage.*) Flap my fide-faddle, 'tis a forry fituation! He lies on my stomach as heavy as a fuet dumpling! And yet I'll warrant that this very night — and on that very fofa — he'll feduce me! (*She goes upstage.*) Fimple, my ratafia! . . . (*She looks in the mirror.*) La, my face is a fight! . . . (*She powders herself.*) Bid him enter, Fimple.

(Simple *goes to the door L., and then announces:*)

Simple. Fir Folemnity Fourpuff! . . .

(Sir Solemnity *enters, beperiwigged and bedizened.*)

Lady Malpractice. Folemnity! . . .
Sir Solemnity. Lady Fufan! . . . (*Aside, going down to the footlights.*) Burst my britches, I ha' feldom feen her looking more faucy! These filks and fatins become her well, methinks, and yet I'll warrant if I do not have them off by fundown my name is not Fourpuff!
Lady Malpractice. Leave us, Fimple.
Simple (*curtseying*). Your fervice, ma'am.

(Simple *exits, banging the door.*)

Lady Malpractice (*calling after her*). Fimple! . . .
Simple (*reappearing*). Yef? . . .
Lady Malpractice. Don't flam the door.
Simple. Forry.

(*She exits.*)

Lady Malpractice. Folemnity! . . .
Sir Solemnity. Fufan! . . .

(*They embrace, then tear down stage to sing:*)

Sir Solemnity: When a man meets a bawd who is willing,
Who is flighty and flender and flim,
Then i' faith, you can wager a shilling
That the flut will be fleeping with him.
Lady Malpractice: When a maid meets a cuckold who's eager,
Who adores her and presses his fuit,
Her virginity may have been meagre:
'Tis now, stap my vitals, caput!
Sir Solemnity: He may say many things to incense her,
Make improper suggestions all day –
Lady Malpractice: But you get all the lines past the censor
Because it's a classical play.
Both: Sing la! for the trollop
Who likes a good dollop
Of Congreve and similar chaps!
Sing folderol-dirral!
For Madge and for Cyril
When romping around in 'Relapse'!

(*She goes upstage.*)

Sir Solemnity (*aside*). And now – to feduce her! (*He joins her.*) Fufan –
Lady Malpractice. Not fo fast! Fomeone might fee.
Sir Solemnity. 'Tis perfectly fafe.
Lady Malpractice. Then pray be feated.
Sir Solemnity (*sitting*). I come to your clofet as a humble fuitor.

Lady Malpractice. I beg your pardon?
Sir Solemnity. A fuitor. Fomeone who fain would folace you.
Lady Malpractice. Folace me? Fire, are you fuggesting — ?
Sir Solemnity. Come, don't be filly — fubmit! . . .
Lady Malpractice. Oh, this is fo fudden! My falts! . . . my falts! . . .
Sir Solemnity. I know all about them.
Lady Malpractice. No, no. (*She points to some smelling salts.*) My *falts!* . . .
Sir Solemnity (*handing them to her*). Oh. Forry.
Lady Malpractice. Oh, I feel fick.
Sir Solemnity. My Lady should fee a furgeon.
Lady Malpractice. Nay, fir — 'tis not a fickness that can be cured by a furgeon. By my troth, 'tis not my body that is fick. 'Tis my foul. Fick and fad with forrow. (*She sees him bringing out a snuff-box.*) What's that?
Sir Solemnity. Fnuff. (*Aside.*) If I can but lure the bawd to yonder inner fanctum, i' faith I shall make her mine more quickly than an apothecary mixes a potion for the gall-bladder — powder my periwig! . . .
Lady Malpractice (*aside*). Ods my life, 'tis a ferious fituation to be faddled with a coxcomb with one eye on a maiden's virtue and the other on her purfe-strings — bedizen my bloomers! . . .
Sir Solemnity (*aside*). Marry, if I could but fample her kiffes I warrant I should belch with content — freeze my assets! . . .
Lady Malpractice (*aside*). I' faith, I would as soon to bed with the philanderer as take coach to Colchester for the cock-fighting — rot my ratafia! . . .

(*After these four asides, they turn to face each other again on the sofa and shake hands solemnly.*)

Lady Malpractice. How d'you do?
Sir Solemnity. How d'you do?

(*There is a knock off.*)

Lady Malpractice. Lift! . . .
Sir Solemnity. Lift what?
Lady Malpractice. No, no. Methought I heard a found.

(Sir Militant Malpractice *is heard off.*)

Sir Militant. Fufan! . . .
Lady Malpractice. My hufband! He must not fee us! Quick — fecrete yourfelf!
Sir Solemnity. In the fitting-room?
Lady Malpractice. No, no — behind the fettee! . . .

(*But it is too late.* Sir Militant *enters.*)

Sir Militant. Fo! . . . thif if a forry fight I fee! . . .
Lady Malpractice. Oh, that I should fuffer fo! . . .
Sir Militant. Out of my houfe, you finful flut! . . .

(Simple *makes a dramatic entrance.*)

Simple. Ftop! . . . I have fomething to fay. 'Twas not Lady Fufan that Fir Folemnity came to fee. 'Twas I — Fimple! . . .

Sir Solemnity. Fimple! . . .
Simple. Folemnity! . . .

(Simple *and* Sir Solemnity *embrace.*)

Sir Militant. Fufan! . . .
Lady Malpractice. Fefil — damn! *Cecil!* . . .

(Sir Militant *and* Lady Malpractice *embrace.*)

Lady Malpractice (*coming down to address audience*).
  Fo ends our flight and flender faga, and — thank God! —
  Fo alfo ends my hufband's foul fufpicions — filly fod!

(*The* Quartet *takes positions for the final song and dance:*)

All: Virtue's a vessel that easily cracks:
  La! for a lecherous life!
  Lust is a fatal disease which attacks
  Husband and mistress and wife!
  Passion can pierce through virginity's crust:
  La! for a life that is gaudy!
  Plays you might think would be drier than dust
  Run for a year if they're bawdy!
  Fol-de-rol-lol-de-rol-lol-de-lol-lay!
  La! for the Restoration Play!
  Fol-de-rol-lol-de-rol-lol-de-lol-lay!
  With plenty of smut
  And not a line cut
  And no Entertainment Tax to pay!

They curtsey and bow to each other.

Black Out.

* * *

The famous Windmill Theatre ('We Never Closed') put on revues but few if any of the patrons went there to see sketches performed. The house-style was musical scenas with girls in ingeniously minimal costumes leaping about, fan dancers, balloon dancers, nudes decorously and rigidly posing on plinths, and young comedians starting out on their careers. (Comedians who began their working life at the Windmill include Jimmy Edwards, Alfred Marks, Harry Secombe, Peter Sellers and Michael Bentine. Kenneth More also began his career there, but he was a song and dance man.)

Yet the Windmill did include sketches from time to time. The most beguiling of these were played by two very old comedians who were part of the theatre's permanent company. One was Gus Chevalier, brother of the more famous Albert

Chevalier; the other, who was a tiny, frail figure like the painter Stanley Spencer, was Stanley West. Together they would wander on to the stage (while behind the curtain the Cathedral scene was struck and the Artist's Garret, Montmartre, was erected) dressed as two old ladies, Biddy and Fanny.

Biddy and Fanny in FANNY WRITES A BOOK

by Stanley C. West

(Biddy *and* Fanny *meet.* Fanny *is holding a small book.*)

Biddy. Why bless me 'eart and soul! I-it *is* you ain't it Fanny?

Fanny. 'Course 'tis. 'Oo did you think it was — Mae West?

Biddy. You give me quite a turn. I read in the paper this mornin' that you was dead.

Fanny. Ah yes — I read it too, and I'm very upset about it. I'm walkin' about the town lookin' like a liar.

Biddy. Wot are you goin' to do about it, Fanny?

Fanny. Well I've been round to the Egitor of the paper about it and 'e was very kind and obligatory about it. And 'e's promised to put me among the Births tomorrow mornin'.

Biddy. So 'e ought to. Raisin' people's 'opes like that. Wot 'ave you got there, Fanny? Yer national call-up papers?

Fanny. No, Biddy. Listen — I've took up with writin' a book.

Biddy. 'Eavens preserve us! At your age.

Fanny. Well, I'm told there's a lot of money to be made writin' books and sech — so I thought I'd 'ave a try.

Biddy. Wot to goodness do you write about?

Fanny. Love. Dollops of it. You can't give the public too much love, you know.

Biddy. And wot do you know about love? You never learnt it from that cold fish of a 'usband of yours.

Fanny. Just where you're wrong. Two stouts and a plate of whelks and 'Arry is a menace to our sex.

Biddy. Well wot's the title of your book?

Fanny. I'm going to call it 'Love-lies-bleedin'' in three parts.

Biddy. A bit anaemic by the last chapter I should say.

Fanny. Like to 'ear as far as I've writ, Biddy?

Biddy. No, I would not, Fanny.

Fanny. Right then. Off we go. (*Reads.*) 'The young Moon swam over the Pyramids like a ripe banana in the blue gravy of the 'eavens.'

Biddy. That's enough thank you —

Fanny. Wot's wrong with that, Biddy?

Biddy. I never 'eard sech dribble. Ripe bananas and blue gravy —

Fanny. That's poetical. Listen. (*Reads on.*) 'Thro' the velvet night come the soft tinkle of camel bells. Let us step into the darkness and see 'oo the h— who it is. It is a tall dark man ridin' a camel with a stiff waxed moustache.'

Biddy. A military camel, I s'pose.

Fanny. No dear. The man 'ad the moustache — not the camel. 'It is none h'other than the Sheik Abdul Binshama who is 'urrying thro' the dessert.'
Biddy. Scattering the nuts and oranges all over the place.
Fanny. Ah — no. That should be *desert.* Only one Z. 'Suddenly 'is camel shies and a dark contralto voice cried "Elp save me!"'
Biddy. I echo that cry.
Fanny. Don't make fun Biddy. This book is goin' to be in the thousand best sellers.
Biddy. Depends 'ow you spell sellers.
Fanny. 'The Sheik's proud heyes snapped violent. 'Is well manicured teeth was set in a vice, as leapin' from 'is saddle 'e tied 'is camel to the nearest oak.'
Biddy. That 'ud be about two thousand miles away.
Fanny. Ah — not oak — oasis. Tied 'is camel to an oasis. That's a tall Egyptian tree.
Biddy. I know. I'm not iggerant.
Fanny (*reads on*). 'Surveyin' the beautiful maid wot was standin' in the bath — no path not bath — tremblin' like a h'asperin 'e h'asked "Wot doest thou 'ere?"'
Biddy. '"I dust the pyramids" said she, spittin' on 'er duster.'
Fanny. Don't interrupt Biddy. We don't want your injections. 'The girl turned a vivid mauve and 'er breast rose and fell with ammunition.'
Biddy. Got a blouse full of cartridges, I s'pose.
Fanny. Ah — not ammunition — emotion. '"I h'am a flower-girl" she said. 'Men called me Moo-Moo."'
Biddy. Moo-Moo! I could give 'er a better name than that.
Fanny. '"A pretty name with all" said the Sheik, lighting a cigar on which the band said ninepence. For 'e was a man wot lived well.'
Biddy. Reckless dog.
Fanny. '"Who dost fear" he h'asked, flickin' a bit of dust from 'is howdah.'
Biddy. Howdah? Wot's howdah?
Fanny. It's an Egyptian dicky. 'The girl tossed 'er 'ed and threw frightened eye-balls over 'er shoulder.'
Biddy. Bit of a jugglist.
Fanny. '"It is a man," she said, 'angin' 'er 'ead on 'er bosom.'
Biddy. Blimee! First she throws 'er eyes over 'er shoulder then she 'angs 'er 'ead on 'er bosom. Wot's she do for an encore?
Fanny. Biddy, I shall stop readin' altogether if —
Biddy. No, no — go on to the part where 'e drags 'er into the tent.
Fanny. There's no sech bit. Listen — 'With that the poor girl burst . . .'

(*Turns over page.*)

Biddy. That's the ammunition goin' off.
Fanny. '. . . into tears. Burst into tears.' Now that's as far as I've writ up to the now. But I got the whole plot in me 'ead.
Biddy. Well you keep it up there or you'll 'ave the Lord Chambermaid after you.
Fanny. You see the man wot she's running away from is an oboe.
Biddy. Oh, American tramp.
Fanny. No no — a musical instrument. It's an ill wood-wind that nobuddy blows good. Now this oboe's name is Boo-Boo.
Biddy. Boo-Boo.

Fanny. But Moo-Moo's in love with a man named Ba-Ba.
Biddy. Boo-Boo — Boo-Boo — Ba-Ba —, it's a ruddy farmyard!
Fanny. Now Moo-Moo has a camel named Oui Oui.
Biddy. French camel.
Fanny. And one day Oui Oui bites a large piece out of Moo-Moo's Ba-Ba.
Biddy. I don't like the sound of it.
Fanny. Ba-Ba is the man I was tellin' you about. So Moo-Moo runs off to the Sheik and they're about to be married with great pump and ceminory, when it turns out that the Sheik is none hother than the grand-uncle of — who do you think?
Biddy. Oui Oui the camel!
Fanny. No, no. Boo-Boo the oboe! *Now* then — Moo-Moo has a crocodile named Ha Ha —
Biddy (*Jumping up*). That's quite enough Fanny. Now if you must write I'll tell you wot to write about.
Fanny. Well wot?
Biddy. Right about turn — quick march. I'm thirsty.

(*Exeunt both.*)

* * *

Peter Myers, Alec Grahame and David Climie were a youngish group of writers who managed to steer 'little' revue away from its parochial 'West-End' style and into fresh areas during the 50s. Their shows were swift and lively; they were masters of the 'quickie' sketch and the 'black-out'. They also tended to look for topical targets. Here is one of their sketches based upon the hugely popular *Archers* radio series.

WE COME UP FROM MUMMERSET

by Peter Myers, Alec Grahame and David Climie

In front of the tabs are several tubular steel chairs. On the stage are Dymphna, Angus, Gwladys *and* Mr Croot. Dymphna *is sitting cross-legged in front of the chairs, her face buried in an enormous book. She is obviously an intellectual type. She wears an immense black page-boy wig, with a fringe that comes well down over her eyes, huge spectacles, tartan or leopard skin drain-pipe slacks, a huge thick woollen sweater that comes down almost to her knees, and ballet shoes. She is surrounded by other books, spare shoes, knitting, oddly shaped parcels and a radio script.* Mr Croot *is sitting in one of the chairs. He is incredibly old, with a long, long white beard, no hair, blue spectacles, an ear trumpet and very archaic clothes. A script droops from his palsied hand.* Angus *is leaning against the proscenium arch, studying his script. He is also an earnest intellectual type, with a neat dark suit, woollen tie, hair parted in the middle and plastered down each side of his face, a pale complexion, a pipe drooping permanently from his mouth, a monocle and a*

Van Dyke beard. Gwladys *is a very chic and stately matron, dressed very smartly in a beautiful silk dress, enormous sables dripping from her shoulders, more jewels than a Christmas tree, a carefully arranged blue-rinse wig, with a very smart hat on it, lorgnettes, an umbrella five feet long and as thin as a pencil, and a script bound in a red morocco folder. The scene opens in silence, except for the heavy breathing of* Mr Croot *who is asleep, and the tuneless, abstracted and basso profundo humming of* Dymphna. *After a moment* Angus *consults his watch, produces a small bottle of pills and takes one. This he does at intervals throughout the sketch.* Gwladys *looks impatiently at* Dymphna *but before she can speak* Hilary *hurries on to the stage. He is an extremely affected young man. He has brassy golden hair arranged in steppes up to the top of his head. He wears a brick red pair of slacks, a bright tartan shirt, a huge flowing neckerchief and a very long jade cigarette holder with a pink cigarette in it. He also carries a script. He rushes in and clutches* Angus's *arm contritely.*

Hilary. My dears! I'm so sorry I'm late! I had such trouble parking my little Corgi you wouldn't *believe*! That beastly commissionaire was quite abusive! Angus, you old trollop, how *are* you?

Angus (*moving away from him nervously*). Not very well, thank you, Hilary.

(*He takes another pill.*)

Hilary (*discovering* Dymphna). And whatever is *this*? (*He bends down and parts her fringe.*) Dymphna! Darling — why are you *hiding*?

Dymphna (*vaguely*). Hmmm?

Hilary. Let it pass, dear, let it pass. Good afternoon, Mr Croot!

(*There is no visible reaction from* Mr Croot.)

(*He yells.*) Good afternoon Mr Croot!

(*There is still no reaction*)

(*To Angus*) Dead?

Gwladys. No more than usual.

Hilary (*turning to her*). Ah, Gladys, darling. How are we?

Gwladys (*speaking with a very languid, drawling Kensington accent*). Very well, thank you. But I've told you before, Hilary, my name is pronounced Glay-dis — not Gladdis!

Hilary. Sorry, I'm sure.

(*They are interrupted by the arrival of* Rhona, *who is overdressed, over-made-up, over-developed, and over the age of consent — a consent evidently not too jealously withheld. She has a black bubble cut, chunky jewellery and the most horrible ensemble you ever saw — something like bright yellow slacks, diamanté slippers, a Regency-striped satin blouse, elbow length gloves and a tartan tam-o-shanter. She chews gum incessantly and talks American with a Cockney accent. She carries a patent leather sling bag and a script.*)

Rhona (*flicking a salute at everyone*). Greetin's gates! What's noo?

Angus. Ah, Rhona, my dear. Are you still with us?

Rhona. Yup. So far. But don't take no bets. They got to write me out again next week. I'm going away for the weekend.
Hilary. Brighton again?
Rhona. As a matter of fact yes!
Gwladys. Disgusting!
Rhona. Now, look here, Gladys —
Gwladys. Glaydis!
Hilary. Such affectation!
Gwladys. It's nothing of the sort. Just because you were brought up badly it's . . .
Angus. Oh, I say, we don't want to bring the chap's antecedents into this, do we? I mean, sociologically speaking surely . . .
Gwladys. Oh, shut up, you drivelling old idiot!
Rhona. Why don't *you* shut up for a change?
Gwladys. Why, you little . . .

(*As they are screaming at one another, a bell suddenly rings. They stop immediately.*)

Angus. Come on — we're on!

(*The tabs open, to reveal a stand microphone, with a little red bulb attached to it, in the middle of the stage. Everyone, except* Mr Croot, *rushes over and forms a group round it, clutching their scripts.* Mr Croot *sleeps peacefully on his chair.*)

Hilary (*as they go to the mike*). Oh, well, back to the factory!

(*The little red light flickers on and off and* Angus *holds up a warning finger. They wait motionless except for* Rhona's *jaw, still chewing.*)

(*An* Announcer's *voice is heard speaking through a mike back stage.*)

Announcer. Good afternoon, ladies and gentlemen. Once again we present 'The Starchers — the story of just an ordinary farmer's family'!

(Angus *still keeps his finger poised and then, as the red light comes on steady, brings it down.* Gwladys *nods regally and begins to read from her script. She has to hold it arms-length and read it through her lorgnettes.*)

Gwladys (*but now in the broadest country accent she can muster*). Ah, well, Dan'l, I've always said we're just a great big 'appy family 'ere at Meadowsweet Farm.
Angus (*holding his script as close to his face as he can and using his monocle like a magnifying glass*). Ar! (*He hastily produces a throat spray and uses it on himself*)
Gwladys. But I'm warnin' you, Dan'l Starcher, there'll be trouble if I don't get a new overall in place of this ragged filthy ole thing! (*She twitches her sables contemptuously*) I'm ashamed to wear it.
Angus (*having lost his place in the script, finds it again*). Ar!
Gwladys. Dan'l — you ain't payin' no 'eed to me. What're you doin'?
Angus (*also broad Mummerset*) Tryin' to piece out there 'ere forms from the Government. As you know, Doris, I never 'ad no book-larnin' like, an' I'm proper foxed by readin' matter. Look — what's this word — C.O.W. — what does that spell to you?

(Gwladys *looks hard at* Rhona *who scowls back.*)

Gwladys. Grace!
Angus. Eh?
Gwladys. It's Grace, Dan'l. Young Grace Freebody, come to see us.
Rhona (*in the most timidly genteel accent*). Hullo, Mr Starcher, how are you?
Angus. Ooo, same as usual, thank'ee, Grace. Fit as a fiddle! (*He takes a hasty pill.*) Never 'ad a day's illness in me life. (*He takes a stethoscope out and listens anxiously to his chest.*)
Rhona. That's a very nice dress you're wearing, Mrs Starcher.
Gwladys (*exposing her fabulous dress*). What — this ole rag? Why, I run this up out of a flour sack twenty-five years ago.
Rhona. Well, if you like, *I* could make a dress for you. My friends say I have very good taste in clothes.

(Gwladys *raises very disdainful eyebrows at* Rhona's *outfit.*)

Angus. Ar, well, that'd depend 'ow much you charge, Grace.

(*In a flash,* Rhona *opens her bag and distributes cards to the men.*)

Rhona (*coyly*). 'Course there'd be no charge to *you,* Mr Starcher.
Angus. Ar, well, we'll talk about that later. I jest want to 'ave a word with ole Walter Gamaliel first — hoy, Walter!
Hilary (*in deep hoarse Mummerset*). Oo-ar-ee-oo — how do, Mester Starcher! (*He draws languidly on his jade holder.*)
Gwladys. Walter — I wish you wouldn't smoke in here. I can't stand that 'orrible shag o' yourn.
Hilary. Well, you know what they say, Mrs Starcher. Strong baccy for strong men.
Angus (*laughing merrily*). That's you all right, Walter. Proper ole son o' the sod you are and no mistake. 'Ere — by the way. 'Ow's your King Edwards?
Hilary. Oo-ar-ee-oo, they're a rare ole size this year, Mr Starcher. It ain't them I'm frettin' about. It's Daisy.
Angus. Daisy? Why? What's wrong with the old gal?
Hilary. Well, look at 'er — she's just comin' — look . . . 'Ullo, Daisy.

(*Everyone moves away from the mike as* Dymphna *steps up and solemnly intones into it.*)

Dymphna. Mmmmmoooo-ooo!

(*After which, she folds her script neatly, leaves the mike, goes over and collects all her belongings and walks sedately off the stage.*)

Gwladys. Ar — I don't like the look of her fetlocks.
Rhona. I doubt if *she'll* yield any more.
Angus. Never mind 'er, Walter — 'ave you done that muck-spreading over by the pigsty yet?
Hilary (*shuddering in horror*). Oo-ar-ee-oo. No, I ain't, Mr Starcher.
Gwladys. You can do it when you take the swill over, Walter. There's a nice ole bucket of mouldy bread and cold gravy I mixed for you in the scullery.
Hilary (*looking very ill and passing a shaking hand over his forehead*). Oo-ar.
Angus. An' when you done that you can worm ole Rover. An' if you got time, clean

out that slaughter 'ouse. It's a proper mess with all them ole tripes 'anging around.

Hilary (*who has been getting steadily sicker throughout this — very faintly*). Oo-ar-ee-oo!

(Hilary *pulls out a bright silk handkerchief, claps it over his mouth, and with a final heartfelt* 'Ooh' *he exits hurriedly.*)

Angus (*comfortably*). Ar, it's a good job we got ole Walter for the rough stuff. 'E's good enough for *ten* men, 'e is. Why . . .

Gwladys. 'Ere — 'oo's that coming over the ten acre field? (*She holds her script even further away to get it in focus*) You 'ave a look, Dan'l — you got better eyes 'n what I have.

Angus (*with his script even closer to his face*). Well, 'e's about five mile away, but it looks to me like young Phil — yes, it is. 'E's 'ad an 'aircut I see.

Gwladys. Ar, so that's why you're 'ere, Grace. Waitin' for your young man.

Angus. Ar! 'E's coming this way too. (*He suddenly realizes that Mr Croot is still asleep. He yells.*) *I said 'e's coming this way!*

(Rhona *and* Gwladys *dash over and rouse* Mr Croot *who comes to, and totters mumbling towards the mike, supported by the ladies.*)

(*Frantically ad libbing and swallowing nerve tonic*) Oo, ar, 'e's comin' this way all right. 'E ain't 'arf in an 'urry too. 'E's runnin' all the way. Coo — did you see 'im jump that 'edge down by the sheep dip? Ar, 'ere 'e is. Come on in, Phil!

(*But* Mr Croot *is too exhausted by his journey to do more than croak feebly at the mike.*)

Ar, I reckon you're a bit puffed after your run, aincher?

(Mr Croot *who is being fanned by* Rhona *nods feebly.*)

Well, runnin' won't do you no 'arm — a well set-up young feller like you — especially when there's a pretty gal at the end of it, eh, Phil?

(*He pokes* Mr Croot *jocularly in the ribs. This is a mistake, since* Mr Croot *immediately collapses. The ladies try to bring him round without success.*)

Angus. Well, come along, Phil — aincher you got anything to say for yourself?

(*The two ladies shake their heads sadly at* Angus *who looks frantically at the mike and then beckons feverishly to the wings. And from the wings comes the most countryfied yokel you ever saw. Smock, gaiters, leggings, shock of hair hanging down from a ragged old slouch hat, straw in the mouth, idiot grin revealing several blacked-out teeth, and large, round apple-red cheeks. He walks up to the mike and speaks.*)

Yokel (*in the most cultured Oxford accent possible*) Ladies and gentlemen, you have just heard the one millionth episode of 'The Starchers'!

Black Out

* * *

Revue writers in the 50s continued to move away from the conventional 'little revue' sketch ideas and explore new subjects and new treatments.

The first of the following four sketches is the most conventional but the dialogue and the payoff have a strong whiff of the changing times.

Traveller's Tale by Myles Rudge is a little exercise in the bizarre which is held tightly under control and is an example of really imaginative sketch-writing.

Gladly Otherwise is a work of peculiar genius by N. F. Simpson. He wrote several other sketches, some plays and a series for BBC Television, all in his wholly individual style which might be called Comic Kafka.

Trouble in the Works represents another totally individual approach, that of Harold Pinter.

NO BALL

by Arthur Macrae

Scene: A kitchen

When the Curtain *rises* Cinderella, *in jeans, her hair drawn back in a pony-tail, is abstractedly sweeping the floor with the traditional type of broom made of twigs. Sitting in a chair, and looking a little bemused, is a traditional* Fairy Godmother. Cinderella, *who is frowning heavily speaks in a very down-to-earth tone of voice.*

Cinderella (*stopping her work for a moment*). Look! I may as well be frank. I don't know that I want to *go* to the Ball.

Fairy Godmother (*very sweetly*). Cinderella! What are you saying? Every girl wants to go to a Ball.

Cinderella. Not nowadays! Frankly — not nowadays. (*She goes on sweeping*).

Fairy Godmother. You'll love it. You'll be the prettiest one there, and everyone will smile to see how you're enjoying yourself.

(Cinderella *stops work, and stares at her hard.*)

Cinderella. I'm going to enjoy myself in public and *show* it? What d'you think I am? Dated?

Fairy Godmother (*undaunted*). One wave of my wand, and you'll find yourself dressed from head to foot in white satin with sequins everywhere . . .

Cinderella. White satin, with sequins everywhere?

Fairy Godmother (*blithely*). And when you arrive at the Ball, everyone will look at you, and do you know what they'll think?

Cinderella. Yes. They'll think I'm Lady Docker.

Fairy Godmother. What?

Cinderella. I'm going to no Ball in white satin and sequins, and that's flat.

Fairy Godmother. But you can't go like that.

Cinderella. Why not? Everyone else does. (*She looks at her feet.*) I might wash my feet.

Fairy Godmother. Put away your broom.

Cinderella. The Ugly Sisters said I was to do this floor.

Fairy Godmother (*with infinite sympathy*). Are they cruel to you, the Ugly Sisters?
Cinderella. Sometimes.
Fairy Godmother. That's dreadful.
Cinderella. Not really. I rather enjoy it.
Fairy Godmother. Fetch me a pumpkin!
Cinderella. What for?
Fairy Godmother. I'm going to turn it into a fairy coach.
Cinderella. What's he going to teach me?
Fairy Godmother. Who?
Cinderella. I did my eleven-plus years ago.
Fairy Godmother. You don't understand. A fairy coach on wheels, to take you to the Ball. Quickly — a pumpkin and six mice.
Cinderella. Mice? Where d'you think I'm going to get mice, at this time of night?
Fairy Godmother. Run quickly to do my bidding.
Cinderella. Look! I'll tell you something straight. If I wanted to go to the Ball — which I don't — I couldn't go by myself, without an escort.
Fairy Godmother. I'll provide one.
Cinderella (*suddenly brightening*). You will?
Fairy Godmother. A handsome young man.
Cinderella. Really?
Fairy Godmother. Tall, dark, glamorous.
Cindrella (*delighted*). Oh, well! That's different. Now you're talking.

(*The* Fairy Godmother *is about to wave her wand over the sleeping cat on the hearth.*)

What are you doing?
Fairy Godmother. I'm going to turn him into a young man.
Cinderella. Him? (*She bursts into tears.*)
Fairy Godmother. Don't cry, Cinderella. Everything will be arranged.
Cinderella. Will be? He has been.

Curtain.

* * *

TRAVELLER'S TALE

by Myles Rudge

(*Single spot comes up on* Storyteller. *He is sitting D.L. in an armchair, reading 'Country Life'. He wears glasses. He looks up, smiles, and puts down his magazine.*)

Storyteller. This is a true story. (*Takes off glasses.*) I mean it actually happened, though not to me. A friend of mine was sitting on top of a bus —

(*Spot comes up on* Young Man *sitting on chair, C. He wears a tweed hat.*)

— minding his own business —

(Young Man *gazes out of window.*)

— when a woman sat down beside him —

(*Plump, Mum-type* Woman *sits on chair next to* Young Man.)

— and tried to start a conversation.

Woman. Warmer today, isn't it?
Storyteller. She said. My friend, who is rather shy —

(Young Man *squirms awkwardly.*)

— nodded and smiled —

(Young Man *does this.*)

— and went on minding his own business —

(Young Man *gazes fixedly out of the window.*)

— but the woman wasn't going to be put off that easily.
Woman. The wireless said cooler, but I think it's warmer.
Storyteller. She said.
Woman. Much warmer, and between you and me I've got far too many clothes on. Fairly baked, I am.
Storyteller. Then she stood up and took off her coat.

(Woman *does this.*)

So my friend, who though he is shy is very well-mannered, said —
Young Man. Would you like me to open the window?
Woman. Oh no, dear —
Storyteller. The woman said.
Woman. I don't want to be a trouble, I can always take something off.
Storyteller. And then she took off her shoes.

(Woman *sits down and does this.*)

Woman. And there's nothing so hot as a hat, is there?
Storyteller. She said.
Woman. Especially one with feathers.
Storyteller. And then she took her hat off.

(Woman *takes off hat.*)

Woman. Except wool.
Storyteller. She added.
Woman. And even more so when it shrinks.
Storyteller. She said.
Woman. But you wouldn't know that, would you? Being a man.
Storyteller. And then she laughed.

(Woman *nudges* Young Man *while doing this.*)

Woman. Oh, I knew that's what you were the minute I sat down.

(Woman *winks.* Young Man *looks nervous.*)

Woman. All the same –
Storyteller. She said.
Woman. I must take it off. I'm baked.
Storyteller. And she took off her cardigan.

(Woman *does.*)

Woman. That's better, isn't it?
Storyteller. She said.
Woman. Don't you want to take something off? You'll feel much cooler.
Young Man. I'm not hot.
Storyteller. Said my friend.
Woman. Isn't that just like a man?
Storyteller. She replied.
Woman. Bowler hats, treacle pudding, rolled umbrellas, I don't know how you put up with it. My husband's just the same. He's an interior decorator, you know. Brings home good money, though.
Storyteller. And then she took off her skirt.

(Woman *stands up and removes skirt.*)

Woman. But it's seasonal.
Storyteller. She said. By this time my friend was getting worried.

(Young Man *stands up.*)

He wondered whether to get off the bus. But the woman said –
Woman. Where are you going?
Storyteller. And he said –
Young Man. The Aldwych.
Storyteller. And she said –
Woman. We're not at Oxford Circus yet. I'll tell you, don't you worry.
Storyteller. So he sat down again.

(Young Man *sits, so does* Woman *with skirt across her knees.*)

My friend isn't sure what happened next, but he thinks she said –
Woman. I got this skirt in a sale, you know. A real bargain. I've never liked it, though I will say it's warm – and very hard-wearing.
Young Man. Oh, yes.
Storyteller. Said my friend. And then she said –
Woman. Warm? I should say it is. I'm baked.
Storyteller. And then she took off her necklace and her earrings, and put them in her handbag.

(Woman *does this.*)

Woman. There!
Storyteller. She said.

(Young Man *gives a frozen smile and stares desperately out of the window.* Woman *does too.*)

Woman. Oh, look!
Storyteller. She said suddenly.
Woman. Selfridges. They're having an International Fur Event. I ask you — who would want to buy an International Fur this weather? It must be the warmest day in living memory.
Storyteller. And then she started unbuttoning her blouse.

(Woman *does this.*)

Storyteller. So my friend thought the only thing to do was to open the window. Which he did.

(Young Man *frantically winds down window.*)

And she said —
Woman. We aren't at the Aldwych yet, you know. I'll tell you, don't you worry.
Storyteller. And my friend, who although he's shy is very well-mannered, raised his hat —

(Young Man *does.*)

— said —
Young Man. Good afternoon.
Storyteller. — and climbed out of the window.

(Young Man *starts doing this, during which his spot fades. He gives a loud yell as though falling.*)

Storyteller. My friend still travels by bus —

(*He puts on his glasses.*)

— but now he always sits downstairs . . .

(*He goes back to 'Country Life'. His spot fades.*)

*　　*　　*

GLADLY OTHERWISE

by N. F. Simpson

Scene: An ordinary living-room.

Mr Brandywine *sits on a backless chair at one side of the stage with his back to the other characters. He is probably over forty but otherwise of indeterminate age; he is wearing a dark jacket from one suit and trousers which more or less match it from another. A wig conceals a completely bald head. He can be reading a small paper-backed book, but is quite motionless throughout — more like a human doorstop than anything else.* Mrs Brandywine *is a woman in her early forties, whose manner has a sort of surface equanimity which may well conceal hidden depths of neurosis. She has on a good plain grey dress. She sits with her back to both her husband and the door; she is sorting through a number of what appear to be quarto size photographs until she holds up one for inspection at arm's length and it is seen to be a full-sized hand print, such as a palmist might find useful. She starts up at the sound of a voice off. It is full of booming resonance. It belongs to a* Man *with a briefcase, who, when he appears, is large and dominant and may well be a salesman. If not, then he is in all probability either a practitioner of psychiatric hypnotism or a trade unionist turned marriage guidance counsellor. Failing this, he can only be a rent collector without portfolio. At all events he is brisk and in control throughout, and at his most disquieting when least emphatic. He catches* Mrs Brandywine *on the wrong foot at the outset and thwarts every attempt she makes to regain her balance by tilting the ground under her whenever she seems to have steadied herself.*

Man (*off*). Mrs Brandywine?

(Mrs Brandywine *starts up. The* Man *enters.*)

In here, is it? Ah — there you are, Mrs Brandywine.

Mrs Brandywine (*at a loss*). Good morning.

Man (*tapping the door-handle*). How are your handles? Fit the hand, do they? More or less?

Mrs Brandywine (*hesitant*). Yes. Yes — I should say they do. On the whole.

Man. Good. (*He stands back a pace or two from the door and casts a professional eye at the handle*). What are they like to look at?

Mrs Brandywine. To what?

Man (*glancing up at her*). When you look at them — do they give you any particular feeling? Revulsion? Contempt? Anything of that sort? Nausea?

Mrs Brandywine. Not in the ordinary way. No. I can't say they do.

(*The* Man *turns abruptly and crosses to the table uninvited, where he sets down his briefcase and begins to open it.*)

Man. You see, handles are funny things, Mrs Brandywine. You don't mind if I come in a moment — these aren't my outdoor shoes and the sooner I get inside . . .

Mrs Brandywine. Of course not. Come in.

Man. Thank you very much, Mrs Brandywine. A cup of tea would be very welcome if you could manage it.

Mrs Brandywine (*flustered still*). Yes. I've got one outside.

(Mrs Brandywine *exits.*)

Man. It's nearly four hours since I had anything.

(Mrs Brandywine *reappears.*)

Mrs Brandywine. Hot or cold?

Man (*taking papers out of his briefcase and closing it; without looking up*) Depends entirely on the temperature, Mrs Brandywine.

(Mrs Brandywine *goes out again. The* Man *surveys the room, examining handles.* Mrs Brandywine *returns with a cup of tea.*)

I've been looking at your handles, Mrs Brandywine.

Mrs Brandywine (*setting down a tea-cup and saucer, and beginning to recover her composure*). Do you like them?

Man. Very nice. A present from someone, I expect.

Mrs Brandywine. No, not really.

Man. Keepsake, perhaps — eh? Former lover? Childhood sweetheart?

Mrs Brandywine. Good gracious, no. There's no secret about those.

Man. Oh?

Mrs Brandywine. They were there when we came.

Man. But how did they get there, Mrs Brandywine?

(Mrs Brandywine *is brought up short by this question, and keeps a very precarious hold on her poise during the following colloquy.*)

Two handles on each door — one on either side. They didn't come there by accident.

Mrs Brandywine. I've never really thought about it to tell you the truth.

Man. I'm asking you to think about it now, Mrs Brandywine.

Mrs Brandywine. Unless the builder put them there.

Man. I see.

Mrs Brandywine. For some reason.

Man. What else was he responsible for?

Mrs Brandywine. What else?

Man. The builder. Besides the handles.

Mrs Brandywine. Oh. Well, everything really. Oh, yes — he was very good.

Man (*looking at her*). I see.

Mrs Brandywine. Made all the arrangements. I didn't have to do a thing. Doors, windows, ceilings.

Man. Took complete charge in other words.

Mrs Brandywine. Yes, I left it entirely to him, I'm afraid.

Man. Chimneys?

Mrs Brandywine. Chimneys. Roof. Drains. *I* wouldn't have known where to start. But he seemed to have it all organized.

Man. You were reasonably satisfied, were you? On the whole?

Mrs Brandywine. Very much so.

Man. Plumbing?

Mrs Brandywine. Oh, yes.

Man. No snags there?

Mrs Brandywine. Not that I could see. We had pipes, and outlets for the water. Bath upstairs. Everything — even down to the washers on the taps. And plugs, for the washbasins.

Man. He seems to have thought of everything.

Mrs Brandywine. Quite honestly we should have been lost without him.

Man. What did he charge you?
Mrs Brandywine. I really can't remember now. I expect he put a bit on the bill — but whatever it was I didn't begrudge a penny.
Man. I'm sure you didn't. (*He peers out through a window.*) How far can you see through these windows?
Mrs Brandywine. It depends, really.
Man. What are these? Shelves?
Mrs Brandywine. Some are shelves. Some are ledges.
Man. Getting proper support from them?
Mrs Brandywine. Oh, yes. I can't complain.
Man. I'm not asking you to complain, Mrs Brandywine.
Mrs Brandywine. I'm more than satisfied with them, actually.
Man. Recesses go back far enough?
Mrs Brandywine. Just right, really.
Man. Not too deep?
Mrs Brandywine. Oh, no.
Man. Nice upright walls.
Mrs Brandywine. Oh, yes. They're very vertical.
Man (*looking round the room*). I don't see the floor anywhere.
Mrs Brandywine. It's under the carpet.
Man. Making full use of it, I hope.
Mrs Brandywine. It's just so that we've got something to walk about on really.
Man. What length are your floor-boards?
Mrs Brandywine. I'll get a tape-measure. (*She finds one in a drawer but never gets round to using it.*)
Man. Wall-paper? That seems to be missing.
Mrs Brandywine. We've had it all pushed back against the wall.
Man (*looking first at the wall, then significantly at Mrs Brandywine*). Why have you done that, Mrs Brandywine?
Mrs Brandywine. It gives us more space. In the middle.
Man. Space?
Mrs Brandywine. In case we have people in.
Man. What sort of people?
Mrs Brandywine. I can tell you better when they've been, really.
Man. I'd rather you told me now, Mrs Brandywine.
Mrs Brandywine. People vary so.
Man. You could give me a rough idea.
Mrs Brandywine. Well . . .
Man. Total strangers? Friends of the family? Horsemen of the Apocalypse?
Mrs Brandywine. It's hard to say. I suppose some of them might be.
Man. And the others?
Mrs Brandywine. I'd only be guessing.
Man. Laundry workers, perhaps.
Mrs Brandywine. I just couldn't say till I've seen them.

(*The* Man *goes dubiously back to the table where he sits down to fill in the questionnaire he earlier took out of his briefcase.*)

Man (*looking up in a disenchanted way*). Where are your colanders?
Mrs Brandywine (*a little anxious to make amends*). There's one in the kitchen. (*She makes tentatively for the door.*)
Man. Plenty of holes?
Mrs Brandywine. Oh, yes. Any amount.
Man (*stopping short*). *Any* amount?
Mrs Brandywine. It's choc-a-bloc with holes.

(*The* Man *continues looking at her.*)

I don't know what to do with them sometimes. (*A little wildly.*) I'm falling over them. There's just too many. You don't need all that many. There's no room for anything else.
Man. You don't know the exact number?
Mrs Brandywine. Not offhand. I'm afraid I don't.
Man (returning to the form) Sieves all letting the small stuff through?
Mrs Brandywine. So far, touch wood.

(*The* Man *makes one or two jottings, puts the paper back in his briefcase and seems to relax. His eye as he does this is caught by a tea-cosy knitted in bright colours. He momentarily interrupts himself to pick it up, comment, and put it down again.*)

Man. Pretty.
Mrs Brandywine. Do you like it?
Man. Attractive colours.
Mrs Brandywine. It's a tea-cosy.
Man. Did you knit it, Mrs Brandywine?
Mrs Brandywine. I did and I didn't, really.
Man. Had an accomplice very likely.
Mrs Brandywine. I wouldn't call it that exactly.
Man. Why not, Mrs Brandywine?
Mrs Brandywine. Unless you call Mrs Prebabel an accomplice.
Man. What's wrong with calling her Mrs Prebabel?
Mrs Brandywine. Oh, nothing at all.
Man. It's her name presumably?
Mrs Brandywine. Oh, yes.
Man. Not an alias, or anything of that sort?
Mrs Brandywine. Oh, no. It's her proper name. She married a Mr Prebabel.
Man. Then why are you asking me to call her an accomplice, Mrs Brandywine?
Mrs Brandywine. It's just that she helped me with the tea-cosy.
Man. Oh?
Mrs Brandywine (becoming a little wild again) She held the needles. I looked after the wool.
Man. I see.
Mrs Brandywine. We were in it together, as you might say.
Man. In other words you were just as much an accomplice as Mrs Prebabel was?
Mrs Brandywine. If you put it like that, I suppose I was.

(*Pause, during which the* Man *looks intently at* Mrs Brandywine *before changing course. He closes his briefcase with a snap, takes it up and makes for the door.*)

Man (speaking without looking at her) Not always very sure of yourself, are you, Mrs Brandywine?

Mrs Brandywine. Oh . . .

Man. Some of your answers could come a little more pat. (*He checks on seeing Mr Brandywine for the first time and goes towards him inquisitively.*) You should try to get a lot more glibness into your whole approach. (*Looking back at her.*) This is new.

Mrs Brandywine. It's my husband.

Man (looking him over from various angles) Everything functioning?

Mrs Brandywine. Oh, yes.

Man (lifting his wig to reveal a totally bald head; accusingly) Except his hormones.

Mrs Brandywine. I've tried everything.

Man. What does he weigh?

Mrs Brandywine. Naked?

Man. Dressed.

Mrs Brandywine. Eleven stone twelve.

Man (trying the chair with his foot) The chair's taking most of that.

Mrs Brandywine. He manages on what's left.

Man (about to go) Is he serving any purpose? Sitting there?

Mrs Brandywine (wildly trying to be more glib) Only to keep the floor-boards in position.

Man (in a tone of grave reproof) There are nails for that, Mrs Brandywine.

(Mrs Brandywine *is at a loss.*)

(*Going*) You could dispense with one or the other. You don't need both. (*Checking.*) What are his kidneys like?

Mrs Brandywine (as before) He never lets me see them.

Man. You could wait till he's gone out.

Mrs Brandywine. I don't like to rummage behind his back.

Man. It's in his own interests, Mrs Brandywine.

(*The* Man *goes out.*
Mrs Brandywine *turns away bemused and notices the full cup of tea.*)

Mrs Brandywine (calling) You haven't drunk your tea.

Man (off) I prefer to see it in the cup. *(More distant.)* I'll be in touch with you, Mrs Brandywine. As soon as anything comes through.

(Mrs Brandywine *sits down. She shrugs off the episode and is herself again. All the same she is too preoccupied to return to the album.* Mr Brandywine *looks up from his reading and turns his head to look at* Mrs Brandywine, *who has her back to him. He turns back and half turns his head and speaks without looking at her.*)

Mr Brandywine (nodding slightly towards the door) Relative?

Mrs Brandywine (returning sharply to the album as she answers with unemphatic asperity.) He didn't say.

Mr Brandywine *returns to his book. The scene is exactly as at the beginning. There is a tableau for less than a second.*

Fade Out

*   *   *

TROUBLE IN THE WORKS

by Harold Pinter

Scene: *An office in a factory.*

When the Curtain *rises* Mr Fibbs *is at his desk. There is a knock at the door.* Mr Wills *enters.*

Fibbs. Ah, Wills. Good. Come in. Sit down, will you?
Wills. Thanks, Mr Fibbs.
Fibbs. You got my message?
Wills. I just got it.
Fibbs. Good. Good.

(*Pause.*)

Good. Well now . . . Have a cigar?
Wills. No, thanks, not for me, Mr Fibbs.
Fibbs. Well, now, Wills, I hear there's been a little trouble in the factory.
Wills. Yes, I . . . I suppose you could call it that, Mr Fibbs.
Fibbs. Well, what in heaven's name is it all about?
Wills. Well, I don't exactly know how to put it, Mr Fibbs.
Fibbs. Now come on, Wills, I've got to know what it is, before I can do anything about it.
Wills. Well, Mr Fibbs, it's simply a matter that the men have — well, they seem to have taken a turn against some of the products.
Fibbs. Taken a turn?
Wills. They just don't seem to like them much any more.
Fibbs. Don't like them? But we've got the reputation of having the finest machine part turnover in the country. They're the best-paid men in the industry. We've got the cheapest canteen in Yorkshire. No two menus are alike. We've got a billiard hall, haven't we, on the premises, we've got a swimming pool for use of staff. And what about the long-playing record room? And you tell me they're dissatisfied?
Wills. Oh, the men are very grateful for all the amenities, sir. They just don't like the products. At least, some of them.
Fibbs. But they're beautiful products. I've been in the business a lifetime. I've never seen such beautiful products.
Wills. There it is, sir.
Fibbs. Which ones don't they like?
Wills. Well, there's the brass pet cock, for instance.
Fibbs. The brass pet cock? What's the matter with the brass pet cock?
Wills. They just don't seem to like it any more.
Fibbs. But what exactly don't they like about it?
Wills. Perhaps it's just the look of it.

Fibbs. That brass pet cock? But I tell you it's perfection. Nothing short of perfection.
Wills. They've just gone right off it.
Fibbs. Well, I'm flabbergasted.
Wills. It's not only the brass pet cock, Mr Fibbs.
Fibbs. What else?
Wills. There's the hemi unibal spherical rod end.
Fibbs. The hemi unibal spherical rod end? Where could you find a finer rod end?
Wills. There are rod ends and rod ends, Mr Fibbs.
Fibbs. I know there are rod ends and rod ends. But where could you find a finer hemi unibal spherical rod end?
Wills. They just don't want to have anything more to do with it.
Fibbs. This is shattering. Shattering. What else? Come on, Wills. There's no point in hiding anything from me.
Wills. Well, I hate to say it, but they've gone very vicious about the high speed taper shank spiral flute reamers!
Fibbs. The high speed taper shank spiral flute reamers! But that's absolutely ridiculous! What could they possible have against the high speed taper shank spiral flute reamers?
Wills. All I can say is they're in a state of very bad agitation about them. And then there's the gun-metal side outlet relief with handwheel.
Fibbs. What!
Wills. There's the nippled connector and the nippled adaptor and the vertical mechanical comparator.
Fibbs. No!
Wills. And the one they can't speak about without trembling is the jaw for Jacob's chuck for use on portable drill.
Fibbs. My own Jacob's chuck? Not my very own Jacob's chuck.
Wills. They've just taken a turn against the whole lot of them I tell you. Male elbow adaptors, tubing nuts, grub screws, internal fan washers, dog points, half dog points, white metal bushes . . .
Fibbs. But not, surely not, my lovely parallel male stud couplings?
Wills. They hate and detest your lovely parallel male stud couplings, and the straight flange pump connectors, and back nuts, and front nuts, *and* the bronze draw off cock with handwheel and the bronze draw off cock without handwheel!
Fibbs. Not the bronze draw off cock with handwheel?
Wills. And without handwheel.
Fibbs. Without handwheel?
Wills. And with handwheel.
Fibbs. Not with handwheel?
Wills. And without handwheel.
Fibbs. Without handwheel?
Wills. With handwheel *and* without handwheel.
Fibbs. With handwheel *and* without handwheel?
Wills. With or without!

(*Pause.*)

Fibbs (broken) Tell me. What do they want to make in its place?
Wills. Brandy balls.

Black Out

* * *

Towards the end of the 1950s humour in the theatre and on radio and television received a shot in the arm from the arrival of what might be termed the University Wave. The writing and performing of comedy had traditionally been a province of the middle-aged. In the early days it took time for a performer or writer to make his or her mark and gain a reputation high enough to be sought by West End managements, and it was widely thought that comedy came best from people who had 'lived' a little. This point of view evaporated when a number of young graduates, fresh from successful amateur work with the Cambridge Footlights Club and similar university theatre groups, had a go at becoming professional writers and performers.

Perhaps the most brilliant of these young writer/performers was Peter Cook. In the late 50s, while he was still at Cambridge, he wrote for two successful revues, *Pieces of Eight* and *One Over the Eight*. Here are four of those sketches which indicate something of his originality, and his relish for odd human behaviour which is more than mere eccentricity.

NOT AN ASP

by Peter Cook

(A *and* B *are sitting on a bench.* B *is reading a newspaper.* A *has a box on his lap.*)

A. I've got a viper in this box, you know.
B. Really? Good gracious me.
A. Oh yes, not an asp.
B. Oh good.
A. Looks rather like one, but it's not one. Ooh no, I wouldn't have an asp.
B. No, I suppose not.
A. Some people can't tell the difference between a viper and an asp. More fool them, I say.
B. Yes.
A. Cleopatra had an asp. *I* haven't.
B. Yes, well, I'm glad of that.
A. I don't want one either. No, I'd rather have a viper myself.
B. Yes, well, that's all right then, isn't it?
A. Oh, it's not that they're cheaper to run, because if anything a viper is more voracious than the asp. My viper eats like a horse.
B. Like a horse, eh?

A. Yes, I'd like a horse. I could do with a horse, nothing against horses. But mind you, I could never get a horse into a little box like this.

B. Yes, that would be a bit difficult.

A. Ooh, no, couldn't cram a horse into a little box like that. It's not a horse box. A viper, yes, but a horse, no.

B. I realize that.

A. It's just about right for a viper, this box. Or an asp.

B. Yes, yes, quite.

A. No good for a fish, 'cause you'd get all the water seeping through in no time. It's only cardboard, you see, it's not waterproof.

B. Yes, I see.

A. Oh no, they haven't waterproofed cardboard yet. Or if they have, they haven't told me. Or if they have told me I've forgotten, one of the two. No, it's no good for fish. I wish it was, but it isn't, so there it is. No good for fish. I haven't got a toad in here, if that's what you're thinking — you wouldn't catch me with a toad. I can't *abide* toads. Ugh. Vipers devour toads, I'm glad to say. Serpents hear through their jaws, you know. It's the bone structure that does it. Oh yes, there's no doubt about that. Oh good gracious yes, it's the bone structure.

B. Yes, yes, I suppose it would be.

A. I haven't got a bee in here. I don't know why you should think I'd got a bee in here. There's no bee in my box. You have a listen. You'd soon hear it buzzing if there were. Can't hear no bee, can you?

B. I . . . I quite believe you. No, thanks.

A. No fangs? There are no fangs on a bee, if that's what you mean. I've never seen a bee with fangs. Vipers have fangs. They're very fangy creatures — so are asps.

B. I said no thanks, not fangs.

A. Not fangs, no, not fangs, no, no, not fangs, no, bees never have fangs. You find they sting, but they never bite. No, serpents bite, bees sting. That's the way you tell the difference between a bee and a serpent.

B. Yes, yes, yes.

A. I haven't got a stoat in here, if that's what you're thinking. Some people think I've got a stoat in here but they are completely wrong. I haven't got a stoat in here, not by a long chalk. I can't say I fancy stoats, no, no, I'd rather have a viper, they're easier to rear. Oh yes, they're easier to rear all right — need you ask?

B. I'm trying to read the paper. Would you please be quiet.

A. Bees aren't quiet. Bees buzz. But vipers are quiet. Listen, there's no noise from my viper, is there, eh? You can't hear any noise from my viper, can you?

B. I wish you would shut up.

A. Oh yes, he's shut up all right, don't worry. You wouldn't catch me letting a viper loose. Oh no. (B *stands up*) Where are you going?

B. I'm moving, if you don't mind.

A. Why, I don't see why you want to go, there's plenty of room in here. It's not as though it's an asp.

B. If you must know, I'm finding your conversation a bit of a bore.

A. Boar, was that? Boar, you said?

B. Yes, bore. B.O.R.E. Bore.

A. There's no boar in my box. I don't know why you should think I got a boar in here. I haven't got a boar in this box. Gracious no! I can't abide boars. It's a viper all right. It's not an asp.

*　　*　　*

HAND UP YOUR STICKS
by Peter Cook

Thief (practising). Hands up, this is a hold-up. This is a hold-up, hands up. Hold up your hands, this is a stick-up. Stick up your hands, this is a hold-up. Give me the money. Oh, I must get that right. Give me the money. Hands up, this is a stick-up, give me the money. Hands up, this is a stick-up, give me the money. Hands up, this is a stick-up, give me the money. Oh yes, that's it, hands, up this is a stick-up, give me the money. Hands up, this is a stick-up, give me the money. Hands up, this is a stick-up, give me the money. (*Runs into bank.*) Hold hands, this is an up stick, I mean, up sticks this is a handle.
Cashier. I beg your pardon?
Thief. I mean this is a stick-up, a hold-stick.
Cashier. A hold-stick?
Thief. I mean a hand-stick.
Cashier. Oh, I see, you mean this is a hold-up.
Thief. Yes, that's right, this is a hold-up, yes. Up with your hands and give me the money.
Cashier. How?
Thief. What do you mean, how?
Cashier. How do I give you the money with my hands up?
Thief. Well you put your hands up and give me the money. No, you give me the money and then put your hands — oh, I don't know. Work it out for yourself, but give me the money.
Cashier. No, I don't think I will.
Thief. Come on.
Cashier. Why should I?
Thief. I've got a gun, stupid . . .
Cashier. Yes.
Thief. . . . and it's loaded . . .
Cashier. Yes.
Thief. . . . with real bullets, and if I fire, you'll be dead, all sprawled on the floor, dead.
Cashier. Well, go on, then, shoot me.
Thief. Do you mean that?
Cashier. Yes.
Thief. What, cross your heart and hope to die?
Cashier. Cross my heart and hope to die.
Thief. Oh, stop messing about. Give me the money.

Cashier. No.
Thief. But you don't understand. I don't want to shoot you.
Cashier. No, I know that.
Thief. You see, you're supposed to be terrified by my threat . . . .
Cashier. I see.
Thief. . . . I waggle the gun . . .
Cashier. Uh-huh.
Thief. . . . . . you give me the money . . .
Cashier. Hm.
Thief. . . . and then I run out with the bag.
Cashier. Of course.
Thief. But if I take the wrong one, you call me back and give me the right one.
Cashier. Yes.
Thief. All right then, shall we do it again?
Cashier. Right.
Thief. Close your eyes. I won't go all the way out. I'll just go a little way. (*Goes out and comes back.*) Hold up your hands and give me your money. (*A bell sounds.*) Oh, what did you do that for — that's the alarm bell.
Cashier. I know.
Thief. The police'll be round here any minute.
Cashier. Well, you'd better be quick.
Thief. They'll take me away and put me in prison.
Cashier. Well, hurry up and go away, then.
Thief. What, without the money?
Cashier. Yes, hurry. They'll be here any moment.
Thief. No, I won't go.
Cashier. Get out, you idiot, I don't want you to go to prison.
Thief. I know you don't.
Cashier. Well go away then.
Thief. But I'm not going.
Cashier. Go *on.*
Thief. No.
Cashier. Go on.
Thief. No.
Cashier. Go on.
Thief. Shan't.
Cashier. All right then, take the money.
Thief. Thanks. (*Runs off.*)

* * *

CRITICS' CHOICE

by Peter Cook

Scene: A television studio.

Presenter. Good evening, and welcome once again to *Theatre Spotlight.* Now last week, *The Heron Dies,* a new play by David Frost, opened in London. The author is in the studio this evening to talk about it. Mr Frost, how would you say your play has been received?

David. The Heron has had a very mixed critical reception, ranging right from disastrous all the way up to abysmal. The *Telegraph* found it tedious, the *Mail* found it insufferable and the *Express* didn't find it at all, or rather they found it and left after only seven minutes playing time. My writing has been variously described as trite — that's the *Telegraph* again — trivial — that was Mr Tynan's word for it — and effete in the *Evening News* was the nearest I got to a compliment — effete.

Presenter. Effete?

David. Yes. The directing of the play, also by myself, was generally thought to be either loose, weak or non-existent, and the playing of the leading role by my wife has been universally dismissed as ludicrous. So I think you can say we have had a pretty mixed bag.

Presenter. Hm. And are you very disappointed at this reception?

David. No, no, I am *not* disappointed. Or rather, let me put it another way, I *am* disappointed, but it *is* a very difficult play to enjoy and I am not at all surprised that once again the critics have proved themselves incapable of appreciating my work.

Presenter. And how have the public reacted to the piece?

David. The reaction of the general public has been extremely favourable. Those we have had in have sat very quietly and the bar sales have been out of this world.

Presenter. Hm. Now, Mr Frost, when I passed the theatre this morning I noticed a great deal of activity going on outside.

David. Oh yes, that would be management — they were very busy plastering up all the favourable notices which the play has received.

Presenter. But I thought you said it has been universally condemned.

David. Well, that is true, but however we have managed to salvage one or two excerpts from reviews that we felt would take the public — *draw* the public in. Yes, you may have noted that one that says, 'This play lasts three hours' in the *Evening Standard.* That'll appeal, you see, to people who like to get their money's worth. And then there's 'What an evening at the theatre' — *Daily Herald.*

Presenter. Oh yes.

David. What an evening at the theatre, yes. We had to cut out the word 'atrocious', we didn't feel it was fulfilling any useful purpose, and we put a few exclamation marks in instead. And then there was 'Mr Frost has a hit' — *Daily Telegraph.*

Presenter. Oh, the *Daily Telegraph* thought it was a hit?

David. No, that's an extract from a longer sentence Mr Darlington wrote: 'Mr Frost has a hit and miss approach to the theatre which I find utterly exasperating.'

Presenter. Oh.

David. Then there was 'A feast of impeccable acting' — *News Chronicle.*

Presenter. But surely the *News Chronicle* has gone out of existence?

David. Exactly. That's merely a reconstruction of what we feel Mr Alan Dent *would* have written had the paper been alive.

Presenter. Hm. Now Mr Frost, there was one other notice which attracted my attention this morning — the one by Harold Hobson?

David. Oh, yes, I'm very glad you mentioned that — one of our better efforts, yes. 'An evening of incomparable theatrical splendour. Lovely performance by Stella Frost, haunting, human, hilarious. I will go again and again and again.' Oh yes, we were very proud of that one.

Presenter. Mr Frost, I read the *Sunday Times* review and as far as I can remember he said it was one of the most distressing evenings he'd ever spent in the theatre.

David. That is true. Mr Hobson didn't appear to enjoy the play at all. But as you know these critics have to write their pieces in a great hurry, they have to work to a deadline, you know, and quite often I think they say things they don't really mean at all. That's the charitable view of it, anyway. So here we've taken the liberty of extracting individual letters from Mr Hobson's original review and putting them together more carefully than he would have had time to do.

Presenter. But surely that is a gigantic distortion of the truth?

David. That is correct, it is gigantic.

Presenter. You mean to say you are quite deliberately setting out to deceive the public by twisting the critics' words to suit your own purposes?

David. That is the plan.

Presenter. Well, Mr Frost, I can only say that I am utterly disgusted at your behaviour and *I* think your play is the most boring rubbish ever to reach London.

David. Thank you. May I quote you on that?

* * *

ONE LEG TOO FEW

by Peter Cook

Peter. Miss Rigby! Stella, my love! Would you send in the next auditioner, please Mr Spiggott, I believe it is. (*Enter* Dudley.) Mr Spiggott, I believe?

Dudley. Yes — Spiggott by name, Spiggott by nature.

(Dudley *follows* Peter *around chair.*)

Peter. Yes . . . there's no need to follow me, Mr Spiggott. Please be stood. Now, Mr Spiggott, you are, I believe, auditioning for the part of Tarzan.

Dudley. Right.

Peter. Now, Mr Spiggott, I couldn't help noticing almost at once that you are a one-legged person.

Dudley. You noticed that?

Peter. I noticed that, Mr Spiggott. When you have been in the business as long as I have you get to notice these little things almost instinctively. Now, Mr Spiggott, you, a one-legged man, are applying for the role of Tarzan — a role which traditionally involves the use of a two-legged actor.

Dudley. Correct.

Peter. And yet, you a unidexter, are applying for the role.

Dudley. Right.

Peter. A role for which two legs would seem to be the minimum requirement.

Dudley. Very true.

Peter. Well, Mr Spiggott, need I point out to you where your deficiency lies as regards landing the role?

Dudley. Yes, I think you ought to.

Peter. Need I say with over much emphasis that it is in the leg division that you are deficient.

Dudley. The leg division?

Peter. Yes, the leg division, Mr Spiggott. You are deficient in it — to the tune of one. Your right leg I like. I like your right leg. A lovely leg for the role. That's what I said when I saw it come in. I said, 'A lovely leg for the role.' I've got nothing against your right leg. The trouble is — neither have you. You fall down on your left.

Dudley. You mean it's inadequate?

Peter. Yes, it's inadequate, Mr Spiggott. And to my mind, the British public is just not ready for the sight of a one-legged ape man swinging through the jungly tendrils.

Dudley. I see.

Peter. However, don't despair. After all, you score over a man with no legs at all. Should a legless man come in here demanding the role, I should have no hesitation in saying, 'Get out, run away.'

Dudley. So there's still a chance?

Peter. There is still a very good chance. If we get no two-legged character actors in here within the next two months, there is still a very good chance that you'll land this vital role. Failing two-legged actors, you, a unidexter are just the sort of person we shall be attempting to contact telephonicly.

Dudley. Well . . . thank you very much.

Peter. So my advice is: to hop on a bus, go home, and sit by your telephone in the hope that we will be getting in touch with you. I'm really sorry I can't be more definite, but as you realize, it's really a two-legged man we're after. Good morning, Mr Spiggott.

(Dudley *exits.*)

Fade Out

* * *

The little intimate revue, of wit and charm, became less and less attractive to audiences as the 1950s progressed. Some said that its decline was due to the sketches and the humour generally being too 'West-Endy' and parochial in an era when television comedy was offering a much wider choice.

What is probably true is that public taste was changing fairly rapidly. The revue which reflected this change, and indeed by its success accelerated the change, was a modest little affair brought into London in 1959 after a run at the Edinburgh Festival Fringe. It was called *Beyond the Fringe*, and was written and performed by four young men, Peter Cook, Dudley Moore, Alan Bennett and Jonathan Miller. Gone were the clever point-numbers, the costumes, scenery, the sentimental mini-ballet. The scenery consisted of a few useful geometric blocks and the actors were dressed in slacks and sweaters. The form of the revue was irrelevant; the content was everything. Here are three of the sketches: Peter Cook's solo as Prime Minister Harold Macmillan talking to the nation on television, Alan Bennett's sermon, and a police sketch which was added when *Beyond the Fringe* played on Broadway.

T.V.P.M.

by Peter Cook, Alan Bennett, Jonathan Miller and Dudley Moore

Good evening. I have recently been travelling round the world, on your behalf and at your expense, visiting some of the chaps with whom I hope to be shaping your future. I went first to Germany, and there I spoke with the German Foreign Minister, Herr . . . Herr and there. And we exchanged many frank words in our respective languages —

From thence I flew by Boeing to the Bahamas, where I was having talks with the American President, Mr Kennedy, and I must say I was very struck by his youth and vigour. The talks we had were of a very friendly nature and at one time we even exchanged photographs of our respective families, and I was very touched, very touched indeed, to discover that here was yet another great world leader who regarded the business of Government as being a family affair.

Our talks ranged over a wide variety of subjects including that of the Skybolt Missile programme. And after a great deal of good-natured give and take I decided on behalf of Great Britain to accept the Polaris in the place of the Skybolt. This is a good solution — as far as I can see, the Polaris starts where the Skybolt left off. In the sea.

I was privileged to see some actual photographs of this weapon. The President was kind enough to show me actual photographs of this missile, beautiful photographs taken by Karsch of Ottawa. A very handsome weapon, we shall be very proud to have them, the photographs, that is, we don't get the missile till round about 1970 — in the meantime we shall just have to keep our fingers crossed, sit very quietly and try not to alienate anyone.

This is not to say that we do not have our own Nuclear Striking Force — we do, we have the Blue Steel, a very effective missile, as it has a range of one hundred and fifty miles, which means we can just about get Paris — and by God we will.

While I was abroad I was very moved to receive letters from people in acute distress all over the country. And one in particular from an old-age pensioner in Fife is indelibly printed on my memory. Let me read it to you. It reads, 'Dear Prime Minister, I am an old-age pensioner in Fife, living on a fixed income of some two pounds, seven shillings a week. This is not enough. What do you of the Conservative Party propose to do about it?'

(*He tears up the letter.*)

Well, let me say right away, Mrs MacFarlane — as one Scottish old-age pensioner to another — be of good cheer. There are many people in this country today who are far worse off than yourself. And it is the policy of the Conservative Party to see that this position is maintained.

And now I see the sands of time are alas drawing all too rapidly to a close, so I leave you all with that grand old Celtic saying that is so popular up there: good night, and may God be wi' ye!

Black Out

* * *

TAKE A PEW

by Peter Cook, Alan Bennett, Jonathan Miller and Dudley Moore

The eleventh verse of the twenty-seventh chapter of the book of Genesis, 'But my brother Esau is an hairy man, but I am a smooth man' — 'my brother Esau is an hairy man, but I am a smooth man.' Perhaps I can paraphrase this, say the same thing in a different way by quoting you some words from the grand old prophet, Nehemiah, Nehemiah seven, sixteen.

And he said unto me, what seest thou?
And I said unto him, lo

(*He reads the next four lines twice.*)

I see the children of Bebai,
Numbering six hundred and seventy-three,
And I see the children of Asgad
Numbering one thousand, four hundred and seventy-four.

There come times in the lives of each and every one of us when we turn aside from our fellows and seek the solitude and tranquillity of our own firesides. When we put up our feet and put on our slippers, and sit and stare into the fire. I wonder at such times whether your thoughts turn, as mine do, to those words I've just read you now.

They are very unique and very special words, words that express as so very few words do that sense of lack that lies at the very heart of modern existence. That — don't — quite — know — what — it — is — but — I'm — not — getting — everything — out — of — life — that — I — should — be — getting sort of feeling. But they are more than this, these words, much, much more — they are in a very real sense a challenge to each and every one of us here tonight. What is that challenge?

As I was on my way here tonight, I arrived at the station, and by an oversight I happened to come out by the way one is supposed to go in, and as I was coming out an employee of the railway company hailed me. 'Hey, mate,' he shouted, 'where do you think you are going?' That at any rate was the gist of what he said. You know, I was grateful to him, because, you see, he put me in mind of the kind of question I felt

I ought to be asking you here tonight. Where do you think you're going?

Very many years ago when I was about as old as some of you are now, I went mountain climbing in Scotland with a very dear friend of mine. And there was this mountain, you see, and we decided to climb it. And so, very early one morning, we arose and began to climb. All day we climbed. Up and up and up. Higher and higher and higher. Till the valley lay very small below us, and the mists of the evening began to come down, and the sun to set. And when we reached the summit we sat down to watch this most magnificent sight of the sun going down behind the mountain. And as he watched, my friend very suddenly and violently vomited.

Some of us think Life's a bit like that, don't we? But it isn't. You know, Life — Life, it's rather like opening a tin of sardines. We are all of us looking for the key. Some of us — some of us think we've found the key, don't we? We roll back the lid of the sardine tin of Life, we reveal the sardines, the riches of Life, therein and we get them out, we enjoy them. But, you know, there's always a little piece in the corner you can't get out. I wonder — I wonder, is there a little piece in the corner of your life? I know there is in mine.

So now I draw to a close. I want you when you go out into the world, in times of trouble and sorrow and helplessness and despair amid the hurly-burly of modern life, if ever you're tempted to say, 'Oh, shove this!' I want you then to remember, for comfort, the words of my first text to you tonight . . .

'But my brother Esau is an hairy man,
but I am a smooth man.'

Black Out

* * *

THE GREAT TRAIN ROBBERY

by Peter Cook, and Alan Bennett

Alan. The great train robbery of over three million pounds continues to baffle the British Police.

Peter. Good evening.

Alan. However, we have here with us in the studio this evening . . .

Peter. Good evening.

Alan. Sir Arthur Gappy, the First Deputy Head of New Scotland Yard and I'm going to ask him a few questions about the train robbery.

Peter. Good evening.

Alan. Good evening. Sir Arthur, I'm going to ask you a few questions about the train robbery.

Peter. Good — the very thing we are investigating. In fact I would like to make one thing quite clear at the very outset and that is, when you speak of a train robbery, this involved no loss of train, merely, what I like to call, the contents of the train, which were pilfered. We haven't lost a train since 1946, I believe it was — the year of the great snows when we mislaid a small one. Trains are very bulky and cumbersome, making them extremely difficult to lose as compared with a small jewel for example or a small pearl which could easily fall off a lady's neck and disappear into the tall grass — whereas a huge train with steam coming out is very . . .

Alan. I think you have made that point rather well, Sir Arthur. Who do you think may have perpetrated this awful crime?

Peter. Well, we believe this to be the work of thieves, and I'll tell you why. The whole pattern is very reminiscent of past robberies where we have found thieves to have been involved. The tell tale loss of property — that's one of the signs we look for, the snatching away of the money substances — it all points to thieves.

Alan. So you feel that thieves are responsible?

Peter. Good heavens no! I feel that thieves are totally irresponsible. They're a ghastly group of people, snatching away your money, stealing from you . . .

Alan. I appreciate that, Sir Arthur, but . . .

Peter. You may appreciate it, but I don't. I'm sorry I can't agree with you. If you appreciate having your money snatched away from you I will have to consider you some sort of odd fish . . .

Alan. You misunderstand me, Sir Arthur, but who in your opinion is behind the criminals?

Peter. Well, we are — considerably. Months, days, even seconds . . .

Alan. No, I mean, who do you think is the organizing genius behind the crime?

Peter. Of course now, you're asking me who is the organizing genius behind the crime.

Alan. You are a man of very acute perception, Sir Arthur.

Peter. Yes. Through the wonderful equipment known as 'Identikit' — do you know about that?

Alan. Yes, I believe it's when you piece together the face of the criminal.

Peter. Not entirely, no — it's when you piece together the appearance of the face of the criminal. Unfortunately we're not able to piece together the face of the criminal — I wish we could. Once you have captured the criminal's face the other parts of the criminal's body are not too far behind, being situated immediately below the criminal's face . . . anyway through this wonderful equipment of 'Identikit', we have pieced together a remarkable likeness to the Archbishop of Canterbury.

Alan. So His Grace is your number one suspect?

Peter. Let me put it this way. His Grace is the man we are currently beating the living daylights out of down at the Yard.

Alan. And he is still your number one suspect?

Peter. No, I'm happy to say that the Archbishop, God Bless him, no longer resembles the picture we built up. A change I think for the better.

Alan. I see. I believe I'm right in saying that some of the stolen money has been recovered?

Peter. Yes, that's right.

Alan. And what is being done with this?

Peter. We're spending it as quickly as we can. It's a short life, but a merry one. Goodnight.

Fade Out.

*　　*　　*

The sixties came to be labelled 'the swinging sixties' and 'the age of the permissive society'. Humour with some bite to it, as so brilliantly provided by the *Beyond the Fringe* team, proved to be much to the taste of the times, and came to be labelled 'satire'. Very little indeed of it was satirical in the classical sense of 'a mockery of evil through the use of irony'. Most of it could be better described as 'malicious entertainment', and it came as a breath of fresh air. The barriers of taste were probed and it was found that the perimeters of how far you could go and what you could make fun of and what language was acceptable had been taken for granted for too long and needed to be adjusted. This led, quite properly, to new television programmes being devised to reflect this significant change in public taste. The most effective of these was *That Was The Week That Was,* a topical revue of the week's events. The sketches were mostly conventional in shape and technique but had a shock effect on viewers and critics because they had fun in areas which were previously considered to be sacrosanct, e.g., royalty, the church, the workings of politics. They also used swear words when they were called for and were more explicit in sexual themes. But perhaps the most interesting innovation was that the programme treated its viewers as intelligent adults rather than as a mindless mass.

That Was The Week That Was was produced by Ned Sherrin, who achieved the style he wanted by courageous and surprising casting and by attracting writers who did not normally write that kind of thing, e.g. university dons, film and television critics, novelists, playwrights, as well as the brightest of the professional sketch-writers.

Internal Combustion by David Nobbs, a highly able writer of sketches, shows the freedom with which writers could approach ideas based upon sex.

Nobel Prize and *Naked Films* were the work of Steven Vinaver, a novelist and critic.

But My Dear was written by Peter Shaffer, the distinguished playwright.

INTERNAL COMBUSTION

by David Nobbs

(*Reviewing the British film comedy 'The Fast Lady' — based on the idea that cars are funny — Penelope Gilliatt said in the* Observer *that English films seem to use cars instead of sex in a particularly British sort of symbolism that was worth exploring . . .) A man and his car are in conversation.*

She. I'm a nice car.
He. Yes. How many cylinders have you got?
She. Two.
He. Good. And you're only eighteen horsepower.
She. No. Please. Don't start.
He. What's wrong?

She. It's been so nice. Don't spoil everything.
He. Women!
She. I'm sorry. I can't help it.
He. Here. Have a sump oil.
She. You just want to get me tanked up, don't you? And then before I know where I am you'll be obtaining the power for automatic clutch operation by making use of the partial vacuum in the engine inlet manifold.
He. I just want to take you for a drive.
She. I'm sorry. But a girl's got so much to lose. She's never the same once she's been decarbonized.
He. Well, I'm off, then.
She. No, don't. Well, just a little ride. But not fast. (*He sets off*) Be gentle with me. I haven't got shock absorbers.
He. Change gear. (*She changes gear.*) Horn. (*She blows the horn.*)
She. I like that. (*She blows the horn again.*)
He. Double bend.
She. Do it again.
He. We'd be in the hedge. (*Pause.*) Let's double de-clutch, Mildred.
She. No — I — please. Be patient with me. I may later.
He. That's right. Keep yourself in a state of independent front-wheel suspension — a disadvantage of which is that the unsprung weight of the heavy beam axle is inconsistent with good road-holding.
She. I loved the way you said that.
He. You did? You know you wouldn't look bad if you used a bit more anti-freeze.
She. Do another double bend.
He. It's kinky.
She. It's not. I like other things.
He. Such as?
She. I don't like to say it.
He. Go on.
She (*coyly.*) I like it when you move the gear· lever and close the switch, thus energizing the solenoid and causing the left hand side of the piston to be exposed to the partial vacuum in the reservoir.
He. You've been driven by other men.
She. You've driven other women.
He. It's not the same thing.
She. Why are you stopping? I'm not going in a lay-by with a strange man.
He. I'm not stopping.
She. What are you doing?
He. Reversing.
She. Pervert.

*　　*　　*

NOBEL PRIZES

by Steven Vinaver

The announcement of the lucky winners on the Alfred Nobel Peace Pools is not an entirely happy occasion. For everyone who wins there are hundreds who lose.

He. I see where the Nobel Prizes are gone.
She. Oh yeh.
He. Nabbed, every last one of 'em.
She. Uh-huh.
He. Four British scientists got 'em.
She. Mmmmm.
He. Max Perutz got one.
She. Oh, did he? Max Perutz, eh?
He. Yes, for haemoglobin.
She. Oh.
He. John Kendrew's got one.
She. Is that so?
He. Protein Myoglobin. Composition of the atoms.
She. Fascinating.
He. Francis Crick and Maurice Wilkins both got 'em.
She. Uh-huh.
He. Study of chromosomes transmitting messages to living tissues.
She. You don't say.
He. All gone. All the Nobel Prizes. There's an American got one. (*Silence.*) I say there's an American got one.
She. Oh yes?
He. J. D. Watson.
She. Oh really? Little J. D. Watson. Who'd have thought he'd ever get the Nobel Prize? Makes you think, doesn't it.
He. All gone. Every flippin' Nobel Prize.
She. Uh-huh.
He. And I didn't get one. Not one. Not even a mention.
She. Just like last year.
He. That's right.
She. Well, it's not surprising, is it?
He. Not surprising?
She. Well, you're not a scientist, are you?
He. That's right. Rub salt in the wounds. You don't know what this means to me. Just look at this year, what a record I've got. I didn't win a gold medal at Perth.
She. Or a silver.
He. Or a bronze.
She. You weren't there, were you?
He. I was counting on that Nobel Prize. I thought that this year for sure. I had the feeling they were going to pick me. Why didn't they pick me? What made them change their minds?
She. Maybe they forgot.

He. They forgot last year. They can't just keep forgetting. There's something suspicious going on. I think they're avoiding me.
She. That must be it.
He. It wouldn't be so bad if no one in England had got it. But four British scientists, four!
She. Mmmmm.
He. I came so close!
She. You're gonna be late for work. (*Rising to get his jacket and lunchbox.*)
He. Work! All those people! All knowing I didn't get the prize.
She. That's life.
He (*Getting into jacket as she holds it.*) The jeers, the jibes . . .
She. Don't take it too hard.
He. And it's a whole year before I get another chance.
She (*Giving him box.*) Don't forget your lunch. 'Bye. (*They kiss.*) And cheer up. (*As he goes.*) There's always the Academy Award.

*   *   *

NAKED FILMS
by Steven Vinaver

She. You've been again.
He. I haven't.
She. You have. You've been again.
He. I don't know what you're talking about.
She. Oh no, of course you don't.
He. I haven't been.
She. I don't know why you do it. Sneaking in here with guilt written all over your face.
He. Nonsense.
She. Deny it if you can. You've been to naked films all afternoon.
He. What if I have?
She (*Consulting small notebook.*) Two-fifty-eight, entered Gala Royal to see 'Naked as Nature Intended'. Three-thirty, down to the Cameo Moulin for 'My Bare Lady'. Four-fifteen, out of the Cameo Moulin and a number 13 bus across town to catch 'Some Like it Naked'.
He. Nude.
She. What?
He. 'Some Like it Nude'.
She. Oh. (*Makes correction in her book.*) Right. Then back across town by taxi this time, (*conversationally*) that must have cost a pretty penny. My fare came to seven bob, (*back to notebook*) and once more into 'Naked as Nature Intended'. Out of 'Naked as Nature Intended', across into a Wimpy for a Whippsy, and back to 'My Bare Lady' at five-o-seven. Out again at five-o-nine.
He. The newsreel was on.

She. And over to 'Sun Lover's Paradise' at the Berkeley. Out at five-thirty and over to a Wimpy for a Whippsy and a Wimpy and back to 'Naked as Nature Intended'.
He. Well, you've spent a busy afternoon.
She. Aren't you ashamed of yourself? In and out of nude pictures all day.
He. Me? What about you then, flipping around after me in bleedin' taxis? Waitin' on the street corners eyein' the doors for my appearance. Following me at tremendous expense, I believe I heard the sum of . . .
She. Seven shillings.
He. For taxi alone. And Lord only knows what else in bribes to loose-tongued Wimpy waitresses anxious to reveal their sordid secrets.
She. Oh, come on.
He. I had a sausage, too.
She. When?
He. In the cinema. At the Cameo Moulin, second trip.
She. How often have you seen 'Naked as Nature Intended'?
He. I've lost count.
She. Is it good, then?
He. How do you mean?
She. You know. Well acted.
He. Oh it's reasonably well acted. For a nudist film. Performed more than acted, I'd say. I mean, your Ralph Richardsons aren't liable to show up in 'Naked as Nature Intended'. I mean your young Ralph Richardsons and Edith Evanses are not to be found in the nude films, you understand.
She. No?
He. Definitely not. I mean no budding Laurence Oliviers are liable to turn up in 'My Bare Lady'.
She. Well, is it well written?
He. Not bad, not bad. Again it's not your vintage Rattigan, now is it? But then that's not what you're goin' for, is it? It's quite pleasant in its own way, quite distinctive, but not gripping, if you follow me. (*Laughs.*) If you follow me. (*She doesn't get it. He tries to explain through his laughter that the joke is that she followed him all afternoon. She doesn't get it. He gives up.*)
She. Well what's the big attraction then?
He. Well, if pressed, I'd say the photography. Yes, the photography's definitely the main attraction.
She. Is it well photographed, then?
He. No, no, it's pretty rotten actually.
She. Well, how is it that you've been to see 'Naked as Nature Intended' in whole or in part, for a minimum of three and maximum of seven times each Sunday for the past eighteen weeks? November sixteen, five-seventeen, out at five-forty . . .
He. All right. Do you mean you've been following me for the past four months?
She. Every Sunday. During which I may add you have consumed a total of thirty-two Wimpyburgers with and without cheese, and unknown Whippsys of various flavours.
He. And you've got it all down in your little book?
She. Black on white.
He. Every Sunday for eighteen weeks?

She. That's right.
He. Well, you have made me ashamed. I feel small and little. The thought of you waiting on all those corners Sunday after Sunday, for me to go in.
She. And come out!
He. And come out. Tallying up the Wimpys.
She. As I fought against my own appetite.
He. Dashing from end to end of town, from one naked cinema to another.
She. The ticket ladies know my face.
He. Every week another . . .
She. 'Nudes Round the World'.
He. 'Mamzelle Striptease'.
She. 'The Fruit is Ripe'.
He. 'Nudes in the Snow'.
She. 'Potemkin'.
He. What?
She. An expensive mistake.
He. Well, I'm cured. From now on I'm not wasting my life any longer. I've seen my last nude film.
She. You mean it?
He. Absolutely. Never again will I step inside a naked cinema. The occasional Wimpy yes, but no more nudes.
She. You're sure?
He. Yes.
She (*Deflated.*) Oh. (*She tears up notebook.*)
He. What's the matter?
She. I was just wondering what I'd do on Sundays from now on.

*   *   *

BUT MY DEAR

by Peter Shaffer

(*Mr Galbraith declared that he will never again use the words 'Dear' or 'My dear' to begin a letter. In high places in Whitehall the language of all business letters is still being subjected to the most careful examination.*)

The scene is an office. A senior official is sitting at his desk; a junior official is quaking nervously as he hands a letter he has just composed to his pompous and bullying senior.

Senior Officer (*Taking the letter*). Give it here. (*Reading.*) 'To Mr Jenkins.' Good. None of that 'dear' nonsense. (*Reading.*) 'Pursuant to your letter . . .' *Pursuant?*
Junior Officer. It's the usual phrase, sir.
Senior Officer. I don't like it. The word has an erotic penumbra. Take it out.
Junior Officer. Yes, sir.
Senior Officer (*Reading*). 'I am hoping for the favour of an early reply.' *Favour?*

Junior Officer. The Oxford Dictionary defines the verb favour as 'to look kindly upon'.

Senior Officer (*Pouncing*). Exactly. I am amazed you can be so naïve. Looking kindly upon anyone who earns less than you do is a deeply treacherous procedure.

Junior Officer. I'm very sorry, sir.

Senior Officer. You need some basic training in modern manners, I can see that. If a man comes 300 miles to see you with papers, keep him waiting in the hall — or better still the drive, if you have one. If you offer him so much as a sandwich you will be suspected of improper relations; and a three-course lunch spells treason.

Junior Officer. Yes, sir.

Senior Officer. You really are an innocent, aren't you?

Junior Officer. I'm afraid I am, sir.

Senior Officer. Well we must change all that. (*Continuing to read.*) 'Hoping for the favour of an early reply . . . *Thanking you in anticipation.*' Are you doing this on purpose?

Junior Officer. What, sir?

Senior Officer. Thanking you in anticipation.

Junior Officer. Is that wrong, sir?

Senior Officer. Wrong? It's just about the most sexually provocative sentence I've ever read. It whinnies with suggestiveness.

Junior Officer. I hadn't intended it like that, sir.

Senior Officer. We're not concerned with your intentions, man — merely with the effect you create. And I can tell you that it's nauseating. You have the correspondence style of a lovesick *au pair* girl. In more honest days one would have said kitchen-maid.

Junior Officer. But, sir —

Senior Officer. Don't interrupt, or I may lose control. Now understand this: in the Civil Service you will never thank anybody for anything, especially in anticipation. You will simply end your letter without innuendo of any kind. Now let's see what you've done. (*Reading.*) 'Yours faithfully' . . . I don't believe it.

Junior Officer. That's normal, sir.

Senior Officer. Normal? In the context of a man writing to a man it's nothing less than disgusting. It implies you can be unfaithful!

Junior Officer. I never thought of that, sir.

Senior Officer. You think of very little, don't you? Even the word 'Yours' at the end of a letter is dangerous. It suggests a willingness for surrender.

Junior Officer. Then what can I say, sir?

Senior Officer. What do the Pensions Department use? They're about as unemotional as you can get, without actually being dead.

Junior Officer. 'Your obedient servant', I think.

Senior Officer. Are you mad?

Junior Officer. Sir?

Senior Officer. 'Your obedient servant' . . . That's just plain perverted. People who want to be other people's obedient servants are the sort who answer those advertisements: Miss Lash, ex-governess of striking appearance. To sign yourself an obedient servant is an *ipso facto* confession of sexual deviation. And *that*, as we all know, is an *ipso facto* confession of treason.

Junior Officer. Oh, I say, sir!

Senior Officer. What do you say? (*Looking at him narrowly.*) I believe you are one of those cranks who believe that there are loyal homosexuals! (*Accusingly.*) I think you secretly believe that the way to stop homosexuals being blackmailed into subversive acts is to change the law so they can't be.

Junior Officer. Well, it had crossed my mind, sir. Amend the law and the possibility of Vassalls is lessened.

Senior Officer. Sloppy, left-wing sentimentality! The only way to stop a homosexual being blackmailed is to stop him being a homosexual. And the only way you can do that is to lock him up in a building with five hundred other men. That way he can see how unattractive they really are. Now take this pornographic muck out of here and bring it back in an hour, clean enough to be read by a six-year-old girl, or John Gordon. And leave out everything at the end except your name: a bare signature, brusque and masculine. What is your name, by the way?

Junior Officer. Fairy, sir.

Senior Officer. I don't think somehow you are going to go very far in Her Majesty's Service. Good morning.

* * *

That Was The Week That Was was succeeded by *Not So Much A Programme, More A Way Of Life,* also produced by Ned Sherrin.

The sketches for the new series bit equally deeply. The cast of actors was perhaps a little broader in scope. Ned Sherrin had brought in Roy Hudd, a young comic who worked very much in traditional Music Hall style.

Educating Alec was written for Roy Hudd by the ever-reliable team of Marty Feldman and Barry Took. It shows how far the programme was prepared to go to seek laughs in the delicate areas of party politics and race relations.

(According to Roy Hudd, Ned Sherrin had been asking Feldman and Took to write for the show for some time, but they objected that they weren't satirists, that the only political thought they had ever had was how like a ventriloquist's dummy Sir Alec Douglas-Home looked. So it is that comic ideas develop . . .)

Boy Scouts was by Keith Waterhouse and Willis Hall, who were towers of strength during the run of all the television 'satire' shows. Humour is subjective and what one person greets with a guffaw is greeted by another with a cold, hard stare. For what it is worth, I have yet to read through to the end of this sketch without crying with laughter.

EDUCATING ALEC

by Marty Feldman and Barry Took

David. Here is a party political broadcast on behalf of the Conservative and Unionist Party –

(*Vocal group at mike.*)

Group (*sings*). We'll be Educating Alec
Oh what a job for anyone . . .

(*Hold last note under next speech.*)

Announcer. Yes, it's fun, music and laughter all the way with debonair Eddie Du Cann and that lovable little wooden rascal — Sir Alec. And so for the next five minutes we'll be . . .
Group. Educating — Alec.

(*Music up and segue into variety-type play-on music as played by provincial pit band. Roy enters carrying a suitcase set centre stage a table and chair. On the table stands a 'Senor Wences' type hinged wooden box: this contains another vent dummy head.*)

Roy. All right, stop the music, stop the music — Have no fear, Alec's here. (*Knocks on suitcase.*) Are you in there, Sir Alec?

(*Next few speeches in quick succession.*)

Alec (*muffled voice from inside suitcase*). Yes, I'm in here —
Roy. Are you coming out?
Alec (*muffled*). No, I'm shy.
Roy. You're coming out.
Alec. No, I'm not.
Roy. Yes, you are.
Alec. I'm not.
Roy. (*opening case*). You are.
Alec (*loud and clear*). I'm not. (*As Roy lifts dummy out and props him on his knee.*) Put me back in the case; I don't want to come out.
Roy. Now don't be shy, Alec my boy — say something nice to the voters.
Alec. Life is getter under the Conservatives.
Roy. Very good. Now what's the slogan I taught you today?
Alec. Keek Gritain white, keek Gritain white, keek Gritain white, and send the glack gleeders gack to Gargados.
Roy (*slaps hand over dummy's mouth*). Ha ha ha — that's not it at all —
Alec. Well it was last Octoger.
Roy. It isn't now. Now say after me — Our policy . . .
Alec. Our policy . . .
Roy. Is to integrate . . .
Alec. Is to integrate . . .
Roy. Our dusky skinned cousins . . .
Alec. Our dusky skinned cousins
Roy. Into the community . . .
Alec. Into the community . . .
Roy. Very good.

(*Pause*)

Alec. . . . and *then* send the glack gleeders gack to Gargados.
Roy (*slaps hand over dummy's mouth*). That's quite enough of that — Now tell the nice ladies and gentlemen all the nice things you're going to do for them when you're re-elected . . .
Alec. When I am re-elected.
Roy. Yes, yes . . .
Alec. I shall agolish sukertax, stagilize the galance of kayments, and lead Gritain gack to kroskerity.
Roy. You said that without moving your lips.
Alec. Yes, I know. I'm talking out of my gackside.
Roy. Now Alec, you little tinker, the Ladies and Gentlemen are waiting to hear — what's your position on UNO?
Alec. I geg your kardon?
Roy. I said how do you feel about UNO?
Alec. The Conservative karty has no objection to UNO providing it's getween consenting adults.
Roy. That's quite enough of that — but while we're on the subject, will you implement the recommendations of the Wolfenden Report?
Alec. The what?
Roy. The Wolfenden Report . . .
Alec (*swinging head round face to face with Roy*). Give us a kiss and I'll tell you.
Roy. Now, now, now — any more of that and I'll put you back in the case.
Alec. I don't want to go back in the case.
Roy. Well, behave yourself. Now — Capital Punishment.
Alec. Kakital Kunishment?
Roy. Yes. Capital Punishment. Tell the ladies and gentlemen our policy on hanging?
Alec. Well — gy and large, the Konservative Karty gelieves in freedom of choice . . .
Roy. Freedom of choice? Then you don't believe that all murderers should die by hanging?
Alec. Gless my soul no! All we advocate is that the hangman puts the rope round the murderer's neck . . .
Roy. Yes, yes
Alec. Pulls the lever. . . .
Roy. Yes, yes.
Alec. And after that, it's up to him.
Roy. That's Conservative Freedom, Ladies and Gentlemen.
Alec. Hear, hear — er — who's that in the cabinet? (*Gestures at box on table.*)
Roy. What? Why that's your little friend Mr Wilson. Let's see how he's getting on in there (*opens cabinet.*) All right?
Deep Gruff Voice from within. S'allright.

(*Roy closes box.*)

Roy. Right now, you little ragamuffin, what's your policy on foreign affairs?
Alec. I don't know. I've never had any. (*Awful laugh. Mouth sticks open.*) Hey — hey — you've jammed my mechanism! Oh, I haven't laughed so much since the Leyton Gy-Election. Gut seriously folks, when I am returned to a position of cower . . .

Roy. Cower? Surely you mean power?
Alec. I know what I mean. We shall re-establish ourselves with our friends in Europe. .
Roy. And who *are* our friends in Europe?
Alec. The Cortugese, The Scaniards and the Goche.
Roy. I see — the Portuguese, the Spaniards and the Boche. That's all very well, but what about the French? You're rather unpopular there, aren't you? And they say that fifty million Frenchmen can't be wrong.
Alec. Fifty million Frenchmen? That's a lot of Gauls.
Roy. I think we'd better sing. Maestro!

(*Piano arpeggio:* 'Little Man You've Had A Busy Day'.)

Roy (*Sings*). Little man you're crying
I know why you're blue . . .
Alec (*Sings*). Someone's stole my government away. . . .
Roy (*Singing as puts dummy back in case*).
Better go to sleep now
Little man you've had a busy . . .
(*Breaks off*) Goodnight Sir Alec. . . .
Alec (*Clearly at first then muffled as case is shut*). Goodnight, goodnight, goodnight.

(Roy *closes lid and makes shushing gesture to audience.*)

Roy (*sings quietly as tiptoes off*) . . . . You've had a busy day. . .

(*Exit. Orchestra plays 'Educating Archie'.*)

Fade

* * *

BOY SCOUTS

by Keith Waterhouse and Willis Hall

Scene: The officers' mess at Mafeking. Baden-Powell *and two fellow officers are sitting around, waiting to be relieved.* Baden-Powell *is working on a manuscript while the others talk.*

1st Officer. How long do you think the siege will go on?
2nd Officer. God knows. We'll hold out. Relief is bound to come.

(Baden-Powell *puts down his manuscript and looks up, a far-away look in his eyes.*)

Baden-Powell. Look, fellows do you know what I'm going to do, if I ever get out of this lot?
1st Officer. Get stinking, Baden-Powell?
Baden-Powell. Oh, no. I don't drink. It isn't such a wonderful thing to do, you know.
2nd Officer (*winding an imaginary gramophone handle*). He's off.

Baden-Powell. If I'm thirsty I have a drink of water, or if I can't have a drink of water I suck a pebble. Actually, alcohol's shown to be quite useless as a health-giving drink. No, I'm not going to get stinking. But I'm going to have a jolly fine time.
2nd Officer. What are you going to do?
Baden-Powell. I'm going to start taking a serious interest in young lads.

(*There is an awkward silence. The* 1st Officer *clears his throat.*)

1st Officer. I see . . .
2nd Officer. Lads.
Baden-Powell. That's it. Little chaps of about twelve or thirteen.
2nd Officer. School teacher? Choir master? That sort of thing?
Baden-Powell. No, no, no! Something quite new! I'm going to dress 'em up!

(*The two* Officers *nod their heads slowly.*)

1st Officer. Yes.
Baden-Powell. Little shorts, little shirts, little neckerchieves. (*Excitedly.*) Big hats! And they'll have garters with gay little green garter tabs. I'm going to be their leader. Dress up the same way meself. I'll shout 'Be Prepared'. And they'll all shout 'Zing a Zing! Bom! Bom!'
1st Officer. These boys.
Baden-Powell. Yes.
1st Officer (*politely*). In broad daylight?
Baden-Powell. We're going to camp.
2nd Officer. We got that.

(1st Officer *hands cigarettes round.* Baden-Powell *refuses.*)

Baden-Powell. I don't smoke. It isn't such a wonderful thing to do, you know. Smoking makes the heart feeble, and the heart is the most important organ in a man's body. Most chaps smoke because they're afraid of being chaffed by the other fellow. (*He picks up a pen.*) I'll put that down. (*He writes, and then looks up reflectively.*) There's a little island I know. Brownsea Island. Quite deserted. I'll take the little chaps over there. Two or three tents.
1st Officer. He'll get fifteen years.
Baden-Powell. I've written a book about it. 'Scouting for Boys.'

(*The* 2nd Officer *picks up the manuscript and reads.*)

2nd Officer. 'When you are wet, take the first opportunity of getting your wet clothes off and drying them, even though you may not have other clothes to put on. I have sat naked under a waggon while my one suit of clothes was drying.'
1st Officer. Fifteen years.
2nd Officer. Look, old chap, it's none of my business, but you've got to have a good story. What are you going to tell the magistrates, if it comes to it?
Baden-Powell. In a nutshell, I'm going to teach these lads to do their best and to help other people at all times.
1st Officer. I see . . . (*Returning to the manuscript.*) Camp fire yarn number eleven. It may happen to some of you that one day you will be the first to find the body of a dead man' . . . Yes . . .

(*He puts the manuscript down.*)

2nd Officer. It's the waiting, you see. That's what's done it. (Baden-Powell *has picked up the manuscript and is writing again*). Boys. Little boys. I could understand it if it were girls.

Baden-Powell. (*looking up*). What was that again?

2nd Officer. Nothing, old chap.

Baden-Powell. Spit it out, man. I heard a reference to girls. You know what you've just done, don't you? You've just invented the Brownies!

(*He begins to scribble furiously. The others look at him sympathetically.*)

1st Officer (*quietly*). Zing-zing.

Baden-Powell (*absently, still writing*). Bom bom.

* * *

The 'satire' shows were only part of television's comedy output, of course. Before, during, and after the 'satire' boom there were many other sketch programmes whose only intent was to amuse.

Perhaps the most inventive and prolific of the writer/performers was, and is, Michael Bentine. His original stage act was a lecture illustrated with appropriate manipulations of the back of a broken chair. He then moved to television and, often with John Law as co-writer, wrote and performed a great number of highly original sketches in his long-running series *It's a Square World.*

FRENCH FOR BEGINNERS

by Michael Bentine

Announcer. And now, Intermediate French for beginners. *Je suis ici à la maison de Monsieur et Madame Dubois.* I am here at the house of Mr and Mrs Wood. *Madame Dubois fait la ménage dans la cuisine.* Mrs Wood is washing up in the kitchen.

Madame Dubois (*singing*). *Frère Jacques, frère Jacques,*
Dormez-vous.
Sonnez les matines, ding, ding, dong.

Announcer. Brother Jack, brother Jack, sleep well, ring the bell and let's have a ding dong. *Ah, voilà Monsieur Dubois.* Ah, there's Mr Wood.

Madame Dubois. Ah, Henri.

Announcer. Ah, Henry.

Monsieur Dubois. Allo, Clothilde.

Announcer. Hallo, Clothilde.

Madame Dubois. Tu es à la bonne heure ce soir.

Announcer. You are early tonight.
Monsieur Dubois. Oui, j'ai fini à la bonne heure au bureau.
Announcer. Yes, I finished early at the office.
Monsieur Dubois. Quelles nouvelles aujourd'hui?
Announcer. What's been happening today?
Madame Dubois. Oh, rien.
Announcer. Nothing.
Monsieur Dubois. Eh, qui est-il?
Announcer. Who is he?
Madame Dubois. Qui?
Announcer. Who?
Monsieur Dubois. Cet imbecile au coin avec un micro.
Announcer. That imbecile in the corner with a microphone.
Madame Dubois (*hysterically*). *Je ne l'ai jamais pas vu, jamais, jamais, jamais!*
Announcer (*impassively*). I've never seen him, never.
Monsieur Dubois (*angrily*). *Tu crois que je suis un idiot. Je suis venu à la bonne heure du bureau et je te trouve avec ton amant au coin avec un micro. Salaud!*
Announcer (*as before*). You think I'm an idiot. I come back early from the office and I find your lover in the corner with a microphone. Um, salaud.
Madame Dubois. Ah, Henri, pas ton revolver, non!
Announcer. Ah, Henry, not your revolver, no.

(*Monsieur Dubois shoots announcer.*)

Madame Dubois. Oh mon Dieu, il est mort!
Monsieur Dubois. Oui, il est mort. Un moment, chérie. (Picks up microphone, clears his throat and speaks carefully into it.) He ees dead.

* * *

In the middle of the 1960s two of the old *Beyond the Fringe* team, Peter Cook and Dudley Moore, took part in a single television programme for BBC-2 designed to display their talents. It was a sketch show with a little music and it was called *Not Only . . . But Also* . . . It was successful and the BBC asked them to do a series. They eventually wrote and performed in four series from 1965-1971. From these programmes emerged Pete and Dud, the two thoughtful characters from Dagenham, besides a huge number of self-contained sketches.

They were both so creative when ad-libbing that their usual method of working was to form an idea, shape it and then get up and do it into a tape-recorder. The piece was then rehearsed, and finally transcribed on to paper.

THE RAVENS
by Peter Cook and Dudley Moore

Interviewer. We are very pleased to have in the studio tonight one of the very few people in the world, if not the only person in the world, who has spent the major part of his life under water attempting to teach ravens to fly.

Arthur. Good evening.

Interviewer. Good evening. We're very pleased to welcome to the studio Sir Arthur Grebe-Strebeling.

Arthur. Strebe-Grebeling.

Interviewer. I beg your pardon.

Arthur. You're confusing me with Sir Arthur Grebe-Strebeling. Strebe-Grebeling is my name. Good evening.

Interviewer. Yes.

Both. Good evening.

Interviewer. Thank you very much. Good evening.

Arthur. Good grebeling.

Interviewer. Good grebeling indeed.

Arthur. Good evening. Hello, fans.

Interviewer. Good evening. Shut up, Sir Arthur.

Arthur. Good evening.

Interviewer. Good evening. Sir Arthur, could you tell us what first led you to this way of life? Teaching ravens to fly under water.

Arthur. Yes. Well, it's always very difficult to say what prompts anyone to do anything, let alone getting under water and teaching ravens to fly but I think it probably all dates back to a very early age when I was quite a young fellow. My mother, Lady Beryl Strebe-Grebeling, you know, the wonderful dancer, 107 tomorrow and still dancing. She came up to me in the conservatory — I was pruning some walnuts — and she said 'Arthur' — I wasn't Sir Arthur in those days — 'Arthur, if you don't get under water and start teaching ravens to fly I'll smash your stupid face in.' And I think it was this that sort of first started my whole interest in the business of getting them under water.

Interviewer. Yes, how old were you then?

Arthur. I was 47. I'd just majored in 'O' level forestry and got through that and was looking for something to do.

Interviewer. Yes. And where did you stratt your work?

Arthur. I think it can be said of me that I have never ever stratted my work. That is one thing I have never done — I can lay my hand on my heart or indeed anybody else's heart and say I have never stratted my work. Never stratted at all. I think what you probably want to know is when I started my work.

Interviewer. Yes, I'm awfully sorry, I did make an error. When did you start your work?

Arthur. When did I start it? Well, I started almost immediately. My mother had given me this hint — she's a powerful woman, my mother — she can break a swan's wing with a blow of her nose.

Interviewer. Sir Arthur, is it difficult to get ravens to fly under water?

Arthur. Well, I think the word 'difficult' is an awfully good one here. It's well nigh impossible. The trouble is, you see, God in his infinite wisdom and mercy designed these creatures to fly in the air rather than through the watery substances of the deep – hence they experience enormous difficulties, as you said, difficulty, in beating their tiny wings against the water. It's a disastrous experience for them.

Interviewer. How do you manage to breathe?

Arthur. Through the mouth and the nose. The usual method, in fact. God gave us these orifices to breathe through and who am I to condemn him? I think you can't breathe through anything else. If you start breathing through your ears you can't hear yourself speak for the rushing of the wind – nose and mouth is what I use and I trust you do.

Interviewer. Yes, well, I most certainly do, of course, but what I was meaning was – how do you manage to breathe under water?

Arthur. Oh, that's completely impossible, nobody can breathe under water, that's what makes it so difficult, I have to keep bobbing to the surface every thirty seconds, makes it impossible to conduct a sustained training programme on the ravens. And they're no better – they can't even be taught to hold their beaks. There they are, sitting on my wrist, I say 'Fly, fly, you devils' and they inhale a face full of water and . . .

Interviewer. I suppose they drown do they?

Arthur. It's curtains, yes, they drown. Topple off my wrist, little black feathery figure topples off my wrist and spirals very slowly down to a watery grave. We're knee deep in feathers off that part of the coast.

Interviewer. Sir, Arthur, have you *ever* managed to get a raven to fly under water?

Arthur. No. I have never managed to get one to fly under water. Not at all, not a single success in the whole 40 years training.

Interviewer. Sounds rather a miserable failure then, your whole life.

Arthur. My life has been a miserable failure, yes.

Interviewer. How old are you, if that's not a personal question?

Arthur. It is a personal question, but I am 83. Remarkably well-preserved because of the water on the face.

Interviewer. I would say that your life has been a bit of a failure.

Arthur. It's a bit late, you see, in life, to turn to anything else. I've often thought of taking something else up, you know, something a bit more commercial, but it's very difficult when you go round to a firm and they say, 'What were you doing before this?' and you say, 'Well, I was hovering about about ten foot under water attempting, unsuccessfully, to get ravens to fly.' They tend to look down their noses at you.

Interviewer. What a miserable thing. Thank you very much, Sir Arthur, for telling us your absolute tale of woe. Thank you very much for coming along.

Arthur. Thank you and good evening.

Interviewer. Good evening.

Etc.

*   *   *

AT THE ART GALLERY

by Peter Cook and Dudley Moore

Dud. Pete! Pete! Peter! Oh look, there you are.

Pete. I'm looking at 'The Passing-out of the Money Lenders'.

Dud. I don't care about that. I've been looking for you for the last half hour. We said we'd rendez-vous in front of the Flemish Masters.

Pete. No we didn't, Dud, we never said anything of the sort.

Dud. When I last saw you you were in the Breugel, weren't you?

Pete. That's right. I said I'd whip through the Abstracts, go through the El Greco, up the Van Dyke and I'd see you in front of the bloody Rubens.

Dud. I said I was going to go round the Velasquez, through the Abstracts, up the Impressionists and meet you in front of the Flemish Masters.

Pete. No, you didn't, Dud. It doesn't matter anyway.

Dud. Here, have a sandwich. My feet are killing me.

Pete. What's that got to do with the sandwich?

Dud. Nothing, I just said it afterwards, that's all.

Pete. Well you shouldn't say things like that together, it could confuse a stupid person.

Dud. Y'know, Pete, I reckon there's a lot of rubbish in this gallery here.

Pete. Not only rubbish, Dud, there's a lot of muck about. I've been looking all over the place for something good.

Dud. I've been looking for that lovely green gipsy lady, you know the one with . . .

Pete. The one with the lovely shiny skin.

Dud. Where is she? Nowhere.

Pete. Nowhere.

Dud. So I went up to the commissionaire. I said 'Here'. I got him by the lapel. I said 'Here . . .'

Pete. 'Here . . .'

Dud. I said, 'Here . . .'

Pete. You didn't spit sandwich at him, did you?

Dud. Sorry, Pete. Sorry about that. I said. 'Where's that bloody Chinese flying horse then?'

Pete. What did he say?

Dud. He said, 'Get out.' So I had to run up the Impressionists for half an hour and hide out. But what I can't understand frankly, Pete, is that there's not a Vernon Ward gallery in here.

Pete. There's not a duck in the building, there's no Peter Scott, there's no Vernon Ward. Not a duck to be seen.

Dud. Nothing. The marvellous thing about Vernon Ward is that of course he's been doing ducks all his life.

Pete. Well, he's done more ducks than you've had hot breakfasts, Dud. If he's done anything he's done ducks.

Dud. He's done ducks in all positions.

Pete. Yer.

Dud. Ducks in the morning, ducks in the evening, ducks in the summertime. What's that song?

Both (*sing*). Ducks in the morning. Ducks in the evening. Ducks in the summertime.
Dud. Thought I recognized it.
Pete. The thing what makes you know that Vernon Ward is a good painter is if you look at his ducks, you see the eyes follow you round the room.
Dud. You noticed that?
Pete. Yer, when you see sixteen of his ducks, you see thirty two little eyes following you round the room.
Dud. No, you only see sixteen because they're flying sideways and you can't see the other eye on the other side. He never does a frontal duck.
Pete. No, but you get the impression, Dud, that the other eye is craning round the beak to look at you, don't you? That's a sign of a good painting, Dud. If the eyes follow you round the room, it's a good painting. If they don't, it isn't.
Dud. It's funny you say that, Pete, 'cause I was in the bathroom the other day.
Pete. Course you were, I remember that.
Dud. Course I was, Pete, and I had the feeling of somebody in the room with me. I thought – funny – you know, and I didn't see no one come in and I thought – funny. And I felt these eyes burning in the back of my head.
Pete. Funny.
Dud. So I whip round like a flash and I see the bloody Laughing Cavalier up there, having a giggle. I felt embarrassed, you know.
Pete. Of course you would, Dud.
Dud. So I went out of the bathroom and I went to Mrs Connolly's across the road and asked if I could use her toilet.
Pete. Of course. You feel a bit daft with someone looking at the back of you.
Dud. She's all right, though, 'cause she's only got a bowl of pansies in her toilet.
Pete. A real bowl of pansies or a painting, Dud?
Dud. A real painting.
Pete. Oh that's all right then. I tell you what's even worse, Dud, than the Laughing Cavalier.
Dud. What's that?
Pete. Can you think of anything worse?
Dud. No.
Pete. There is something worse than a Laughing Cavalier, what my Auntie Muriel has. She has the bloody Mona Lisa in her toilet.
Dud. That's dreadful.
Pete. That awful po-faced look about her, looking so superior, you know, peering down at you. She looks as if she'd never been to the lav in her life.
Dud. I mean that's the thing about the Laughing Cavalier, at least he has a giggle. He doesn't sit there all prissy.
Pete. No.
Dud. That's dreadful.
Pete. You been down the Rubens?
Dud. No.
Pete. You haven't seen the Rubens?
Dud. No.
Pete. There's one over there.
Dud. Is there?

Pete. Yer, he does all the fat ladies with nothing on. Great big fat ladies, naked except for a tiny little wisp of gauze that always lands on the appropriate place, if you know what I mean. Always the wind blows a little bit of gauze over you know where, Dud.

Dud. Course, it must be a million to one chance, Pete, that the gauze lands in the right place at the right time, you know.

Pete. Course it is.

Dud. I bet there's thousands of paintings that we're not allowed to see where the gauze hasn't landed in the right place — it's on their nose or something.

Pete. But I suppose if the gauze landed on the wrong place, Dud — you know, landed on the nose or the elbow or somewhere unimportant, what Rubens did was put down his painting and go off to have lunch or something.

Dud. Or have a good look. Course you don't get gauze floating around in the air these days, do you?

Pete. No, not like in the Renaissance time. There was always gauze in the air in those days.

Dud. Course, similarly, you don't get those lovely little Botticelli cherubs.

Pete. They died out, of course. They hunted them down for their silken skin, you know.

Dud. No, they didn't, they couldn't kill them, Pete, 'cause they were immortal.

Pete. No, they weren't, they shot them through with arrows through their tiny little bellies, and then their skin was turned into underwear for rich ladies and courtesans.

Dud. I reckon they went up to heaven like the angels.

Pete. No they didn't.

Dud. Course there's no call for angels now, is there?

Pete. No you don't see much of them these days, do you? Mrs Wisbey saw one actually the other day in the garden. She saw this angel. Actually it turned out to be a burglar. She went down on her knees praying to it and he was in the kitchen whipping away her silver.

Dud. Awful business.

Pete. Terrible. Have you seen that bloody Leonardo Da Vinci cartoon?

Dud. No.

Pete. I couldn't see the bloody joke. Went down there — nothing.

Dud. Well, of course, you know, Pete, people's sense of humour must have changed over the years.

Pete. Yes of course it has, that's why it's not funny any more.

Dud. I bet, when that Da Vinci cartoon first come out, I bet people were killing themselves. I bet old Da Vinci had an accident when he drew it.

Pete. Well, it's difficult to see the joke, just that lady sitting there with the children round her. It's not much of a joke as far as I'm concerned, Dud.

Dud. Well apart from that Pete, it's a different culture. It's Italian, you see.

Pete. It's Italianate.

Dud. We don't understand it. For instance, *The Mousetrap* did terribly in Pakistan.

Pete. Another thing we've wasted public money on is that bloody Cezanne — 'Grandes Baigneuses'. Have you seen that load of rubbish?

Dud. No.

Pete. It's over there — there it is. Those fat, nude ladies with their bottoms towards you. That's 'Les Grandes Baigneuses'. You know what that means, don't you?

Dud. No what does it mean?

Pete. 'Big Bathers'.

Dud. Is that all?

Pete. That's all. Big Bathers. £500,000 quid we paid for that. Those nude women come out of our pocket, Dud.

Dud. Well you could get the real nude ladies over here for that price. My Aunt Dolly would have done it for nothing.

Pete. She does anything for nothing, doesn't she? Dirty old cow.

Dud. And you can't tell whether it's a good painting or not, either, 'cause you can't see their eyes, whether they follow you round the room.

Pete. No, the sign of a good painting when it's people's backs towards you is if the bottoms follow you round the room.

Dud. If it's a good painting the bottoms will follow you round the room?

Pete. Right.

Dud. Shall I test it, then?

Pete. They won't bloody budge. I'll tell you that much.

Dud. I can't look directly at the painting or else they'll know I'm looking and get all cagey.

Pete. Are they moving, Dud?

Dud. I think they're following me, Pete.

Pete. I don't think they are, Dud.

Dud. I reckon they are, Pete.

Pete. No, those bottoms aren't following you around the room, your eyes are following the bottoms around the room.

Dud. The same thing, isn't it?

Pete. Course it isn't. There's a good deal of difference between being followed by a bottom and you following a bottom.

Dud. You come here, then, and see what I see.

Pete. I don't see anything at all — just a load of bottoms, extremely stationary.

Dud. Well, you go that way and I'll go this way and you see if your bottoms move the same as mine.

Pete. That's difficult for the bottoms, if we go in different directions.

Dud. Well, they can divide up amongst themselves.

Pete. See what happens.

Dud. Mine are moving, Pete.

Pete. My bottoms haven't budged yet.

Dud. Mine are going berserk.

Pete. Mine haven't moved at all. You've got a fevered imagination. You coming?

Dud. No, I'll hang on a bit.

Pete. All right. See you in the Pissaro.

* * *

SIX OF THE BEST

by Peter Cook and Dudley Moore

(*There is a knock on the door of the* Headmaster's *study.*)

Headmaster. Come in! (*A very tall sixth-former enters.*) . . . Ah, Rawlings.

Rawlings. You sent for me, sir?

Headmaster. Yes, I did indeed, Rawlings. Ahe-hem . . . Rawlings, I had a rather disappointing piece of news this morning.

Rawlings. Sir?

Headmaster. Ahe-em. As you know, three generations of Rawlings have brought distinction and credit to this school; your father, your grandfather and your great-grandfather have all, in their time, been Head Boy of the school . . .

Rawlings. Sir.

Headmaster. Ahem, you yourself are in line for this privilege when Witwell leaves the school this year and goes up to Oxford to study Forestry. However, Rawlings, I was very disappointed to hear from Mr Asprey, the Physical Training master, that a pair of very valuable gymnasium slippers disappeared from the staffroom Tuesday last, and reappeared in your desk next door to a *Spic'n'Span* Summer Extra Annual for 1958.

Rawlings. Yes, sir, and a copy of *Razzle,* sir.

Headmaster. And a copy of *Razzle,* Rawlings?

Rawlings. Sir.

Headmaster. Well, thank goodness you're man enough, and honest enough, to admit that. Some consolation in this sordid little affair, Rawlings . . . Rawlings, do you have any explanation for the appearance of these slippers in your desk – other than the one that immediately springs to mind?

Rawlings. No sir . . . I wanted the slippers, sir, and I took them.

Headmaster (*Noises of speechlessness*). You wanted the slippers, Rawlings, and you *took* them?

Rawlings. Sir.

Headmaster. Rawlings! Do you realize what would happen if in this world people took exactly what they wanted?

Rawlings. Sir?

Headmaster. We'd be living in a state of anarchy, and the whole moral fibre of society would fall apart! Do you feel you're in some way unique, and divorced from this basic moral law?

Rawlings. No sir.

Headmaster. Ah! Well, Rawlings, I'm afraid there's only one course open to me. I'm going to have to punish you very severely. I'm going to have to ask you to bend over, and take six of the best!

Rawlings. Yes, sir. Could I just say one thing, sir?

Headmaster. Well, come on, Rawlings, what is it?

Rawlings. Well, it's – Although I did take the slippers, sir, and although I deserve to be punished, sir, and you're quite right and you're much older and wiser than I am, sir –

Headmaster. Come on, Rawlings.

Rawlings. I'm much bigger than you are, sir, and if you lay a finger on me, I'll smash your stupid little face in.

Headmaster. Um, Rawlings, this puts a completely different complexion on things. I mean, my dear chap, my dear chap, why didn't you tell me all this before? I'd like you to accept, on behalf of the school, this packet of cigarettes, er, smoke them in the lavatory at your own convenience — also this five pound note, go down to the tuckshop and do what you will with it — also this rather beautifully bound book, *Razzle*, 1956, I don't think you've got that one. Well, you're a credit to the school, er, Rawlings, run along now, it's a privilege to work with you. Come along, old boy, yes . . .

Rawlings. Thank you, sir.

(*Exeunt.*)

* * *

ARE YOU SPOTTY?
by Peter Cook

(E. L. Wisty *philosophizes on a park bench.*)

I was, er, I was looking through the newspaper the other day, and I saw a little advertisement that was very rude. A very rude little advertisement. It said 'Are you spotty?' There was a nasty man, pointin' his finger out at you, and said, 'Are you spotty?' I don't think people should be allowed to say, 'Are you spotty?' just like that. You don't buy a newspaper to have people say 'Are you spotty?' to you. I mean, if you are spotty you know you're spotty, you don't want people tellin' you you're spotty or asking if you're spotty, and if you're not spotty, why should people imply you're spotty by saying 'Are you spotty?' I don't think people should be allowed to say 'Are you spotty?' just like that.

I've got a very spotty friend, he's called Arthur Muldoon, he's covered in spots. He's got spots all over him, he's a very spotty person. People call him Spotty Muldoon because of his spots. He wasn't christened Spotty, of course, he was christened Arthur, but people call him Spotty and when he goes out for a walk, people come up to him in the street and say, 'Hello, aren't you a spotty one then?' 'Course, it gets Arthur down being so spotty, and he saw an advertisement which said, 'Are you spotty? Are you very spotty? Are you unbelievably spotty? Tick in the right box, and enclose five shillings.' Well, poor old Arthur didn't know what he was, so he came round to me and asked which he was, spotty, very spotty or unbelievably spotty. And I told him he was somewhere between very spotty and unbelievably spotty. So he wrote in saying he was almost unbelievably spotty. He wrote in saying 'I am almost unbelievably spotty. I enclose five shillings.' And he got a letter back saying 'Bad luck.' That's all he had out of them.

I saw an advertisement the other day for the Secret of Life. It said 'The Secret of Life can be yours for twenty-five shillings. Send to Secret of Life Institute, Willesden.'

So I wrote away, it seemed a good bargain – Secret of Life, twenty-five shillings – and I got a letter back saying, 'If you think you can get the Secret of Life for twenty-five shillings, you don't deserve to have it. Send fifty shillings for the Secret of Life.' So I sent fifty shillings along, and got no reply. So I went along to the place, the Institute, and there was a little man there, and he said the Secret of Life people have gone out of business, but would you be interested in 'Dynamic Strength through your Glands? Gandhi's wonderful secret in tablet form at last.' I asked him if it would be any good for spots and they said well Gandhi never had any trouble with that at all. So I bought some for Arthur Muldoon and gave them to him. I don't know if they've done any good, I've not seen much of him recently. Pity about those Secret of Life people goin' out of business. I could do with the Secret of Life.

*　　*　　*

In 1966 another member of *Beyond the Fringe* appeared on BBC-2 screens, Alan Bennett.

His agent offered for consideration a script which Mr Bennett had written. Mr Bennett had in mind a series of eight revue programmes to be called *On The Margin.* The Man at the BBC (me) read the script and after due deliberation, for about a second and a half, rang the agent and said that he would dearly like to put the show on but how long would it take Mr Bennett to write the other seven shows? 'That's all right,' said the agent, 'he has already written them.'

Here are two of Alan Bennett's sketches from *On The Margin.*

THE TELEGRAM

by Alan Bennett

(*Man speaking into telephone*)

Hello, I want to send a telegram please . . . Yes my name is Pratt, Charles Pratt . . . Yes, 68 Chalfont Square . . . Yes and it's going to a Miss Edith Harness . . . Yes, 87 Fitzroy Road. Yes . . . Right, well the telegram, uh, right . . . no, 'right' is not the telegram, no. I will say uh, this is the telegram, and whatever comes after that is the telegram . . . Yes. This is the telegram . . . Are you still there? No sorry that's not it, no, no, well, um um, well it's, 'Bless your little', . . . yes . . . 'bless your little . . . bottibooes,' Ah, well I have never been called upon to spell it actually. Ah that is your job, yes, I will hazard a guess and say B-O-T-T-I-B-O-O-E-S. I don't think that the last E is statutory. No . . . well, it's a diminutive of bottom, isn't it? . . . No, she has not got a diminutive bottom. That's really the joke, yes, yes, so . . . 'Bless your little bottibooes' and I want to sign it 'Goody goody gum drops'. G. G. gum drops will be cheaper . . . yes, yes . . . sounds rather absurd, doesn't it. I don't want to save a shilling just to sound absurd, no no 'Goody goody gum drops' in full, yes. Then I want to end up 'Norwich', yes. Well it's an epigrammatic way of saying . . . Ah . . . 'Knickers off ready when I come home'. It's the initial letters of each word . . . Yes, um, I know knickers is spelt with a K, um I did go to Oxford, it was one of the first things they taught us. Yes, and in a perfect world I agree it would be Korwich, but ah, it doesn't have quite the same idiomatic force as Norwich, does it? . . . 'Burma'? no I haven't come across that. What's that? . . . 'Be upstairs ready my angel'. Well, it's very nice, I like it. But I think it would be rather inappropriate in this case, because Miss Harness lives in a basement flat and . . . if she was upstairs ready she would be in the flat of the Irish labourer who lives upstairs, and we don't want that do we? No, no, I don't think 'Norwich' is obscene, no, oh, surely not? But what about the Bishop of Norwich, I mean when he signs his letters Cyril Norwich, does he mean Cyril Norwich or 'Knickers off ready when I come home'? Exactly . . . We just don't know, no. . . . Twelve words of conventional greeting would be cheaper? Yes, but I don't think somehow that 'Keep your chin up, every cloud has a silver lining' quite mirrors my thought. No, but thank you all the same. Goodbye.

* * *

THE DEFENDING COUNSEL

by Alan Bennett

(*The* Counsel *enters the police cell, where* Golightly *sits.*)

Counsel. Good morning to you Mr Golightly. My name is Prevost Battersby. I am your counsel.

Golightly (*Irish*). Good morning to you, sir, and the top of the milk to you.

Counsel. Good morning. Now then I just want to ask you one or two questions. And I must emphasize that you must be completely frank with me.

Golightly. Oh yes.

Counsel. I must be in possession of all the facts if I am to get up in court to plead your innocence. You must be frank with me. Do you understand? . . . Now then I want to begin by asking you whether or not you in fact committed the crime of which you are accused?

Golightly. Oh yes sir, I did sir.

Counsel. Ah . . . um . . . I don't think you can have understood me quite – you must be completely frank with me. Uh . . . There's no need to pretend you committed the crime if in fact you didn't. Now I am going to ask you again, did you commit this offence?

Golightly. No, sir.

Counsel. I am so glad you have come out into the open with it.

Golightly. It's a great weight off my mind too, sir.

Counsel. Good good. Now then you have been accused of . . .

Golightly. . . . and wrongly and wickedly accused, sir.

Counsel. Wantonly accused . . .

Golightly. Yes, sir.

Counsel. Of loitering with intent to commit a felony. Now then Mr Golightly . . .

Golightly. Call me Fingers.

Counsel. Fingers, now that's an unusual nickname. Now why are you called that, is it perhaps something to do with your hands?

Golightly. Yes sir, I am told, sir, that I have very artistic hands and fingers.

Counsel. So you do.

Golightly. Yes, sir.

Counsel. The hands of an artist and sculptor. Well then, Fingers, have you any idea what your defence is going to be?

Golightly. Well, I didn't do it.

Counsel. Yes well . . . I think we can afford to fill that out a little. It's not in itself a cast-iron excuse.

Golightly. But I didn't do it, I didn't do it. I swear I didn't do it. And if I did, may God strike me dead on the spot, sir.

Counsel. Well, we shall just give him a moment, shall we?

(*Long pause.*)

Counsel. Good, good, well that's good. Well, unfortunately, the thing is, Fingers, that though the fact that God has held his hand satisfies me, I doubt very much that it's going to satisfy the jury and the judge.

Golightly. Well sir, I think I might try insanity, sir.

Counsel. Yes, well, ah, robbery while insane is not a common crime. I think we might have got by with that except for the fact that Mr Justice Trebizond was a trifle insane as a child. But he conquered the disability and as a result has been implacably opposed to insanity ever since.

Golightly. We can't use it.

Counsel. No, we can't really. Now it appears that you were observed on the night of September 12th loitering in a suspicious manner outside the residence of the widow, Mrs Edith Coddington.

Golightly. Yes sir.

Counsel. And loitering specifically on the sill of the third floor bathroom window . . .

Golightly. Yes sir.

Counsel. Now I am quite sure in my own mind that you have got a completely satisfactory explanation for this. Or if you haven't, it's just slipped below the surface of your mind, whence I, with my immense legal experience, will be able to retrieve it.

Golightly. Well, sir, I was not loitering, I was just doing my job, sir.

Counsel. Hum . . . well what job is that?

Golightly. Well sir, I am in business in a small way as a night repairer of bathroom windows.

Counsel. I see. It seems a trifle specialized to a layman like myself. What are the advantages being a night repairer?

Golightly. There is very little competition, for one thing. And on the night in question I was just doing a bit of freelance work outside of number 13, Scroggy Street.

Counsel. Were you looking *at* the window or *through* it?

Golightly. Oh at it, sir. Oh quite definitely at it, sir. In particular at the grouting of the window sir. The shocking grouting of the window. I was thinking what shocking grouting that is. Enough to aggravate a saint.

Counsel. I see. Did you happen to see, out of the corner of your eye, as it were, anybody come into the bath-room?

Golightly. Well sir, now you come to say it I do vaguely remember someone coming in. But I remember thinking what shocking grouting, oh what shocking grouting, ah here's the widow coming now to have her bath, oh what shocking grouting!

Counsel. Did you happen to notice what she was wearing or, failing that, what she was not wearing?

Golightly. Well, as a matter of fact, I did, sir. She was wearing some nylon stockings and some carpet slippers and a thick grey skirt and a green cardigan and a long voluminous coat down to her ankles, sir. That's all I can remember on the spur of the moment.

Counsel. I see. So when she says, as she does, in her statement, that she came into the bath-room clad only in her E-type knickers — she is lying?

Golightly. Down to the bottom of her black heart, sir, she's a mendacious woman, that Mrs Coddington. She lies like a stair carpet.

Counsel. I think that's all I want, Fingers, really. I shall, of course, try to discredit the character of widow Coddington and I notice she has got a Polish lodger, which in the eyes of the law is synonymous with moral laxity. It has not yet been made statutory. Well, I shall, of course, try to get these E-type knickers brought into evidence.

Golightly. And held against her, sir?

Counsel. Exactly. Now I hope we can have them passed around among the jury which will surely sway them against her.

Golightly. I'm sure they will.

Counsel. Yes.

Clerk. Your case has been called, sir.

Counsel. Good. Well come along, Fingers. I should have asked you perhaps earlier whether you have any other convictions of a similar nature. I don't suppose you have, have you?

Golightly. Well on one or two occasions I have been wrongly committed . . . accused sir, but I have only been convicted 27 times.

Counsel. Ah. I see, well, perhaps you had better just run through these as we go upstairs . . . (*They go upstairs.*)

Golightly. Well, sir, on the first occasion . . .

* * *

More waves of university writers and writer/performers arrived on the scene and began to give BBC radio comedy a new sound.

Here are sketches from a highly successful radio series which developed from a stage revue put on by members of the Cambridge Footlights Club, including John Cleese, Bill Oddie, Graeme Garden, Jo Kendall, Tim Brooke-Taylor and David Hatch. The series was *I'm Sorry I'll Read That Again.*

BBC BC

by Bill Oddie and John Cleese

Newsreader. Good even. Here beginneth the first verse of the news. It has come to pass that the seven elders of the seven tribes have now been abiding in Sodom for seven days and seven nights. There seems little hope of any early settlement. An official spokesman said this afternoon, 'Only a miracle can save us now.'

The walls of Jericho today suddenly collapsed, burying one Joshua and his seven-piece brass band who were passing beneath at the time. Scientists are working on the theory that soundwaves from the music may have disturbed the brickwork.

In the Sanhedrin today there was a wailing and gnashing of teeth in the public gallery when a certain Philistine was accused of writing on the wall at Balshazzar's feast a phrase including two four-letter words.

At the weigh-in for the big fight tomorrow, Goliath tipped the scales this even at 15 stone 3 lbs and David at 14 stone 3 lbs. David's manager said this even, 'The odd stone could make all the difference.'

News of a happy event. In Ramoth-Gilead, early this morning, Zebediah begat Naaman.

The news in brief: Lamentations 4, 18-22 and 11 Kings 14, 2-8. And now a look at the weather.

Weatherman. Good even. Well, it's been a pretty rough week in the Holy Land, hasn't it? Anyway, let's have a look at the scroll. Now we've got a plague of locusts moving in here from the north-west, they're going to be in the Tyre and Sidon area about lunchtime tomorrow. Scattered outbreaks of fire and brimstone up here in Tarsus and down here in Hebron. Oh, and possibly some mild thunderbolts, force two to three, in Gath. Down in the south, well, Egypt's have a pretty nasty spell recently. Seventeen or eighteen days ago it was frogs, followed by lice, flies, a murrain on the beasts, and last Tuesday locusts, and now, moving in from the south-south-east, boils. Further outlook for Egypt, well, two or three days of thick darkness lying over the face of the land and then death of the first-born. Sorry about that, Egypt.

Up here in the Eastern Mediterranean, we've got a pretty big depression. It's been building up here for some time now and that's being brought in towards the land by high almighty winds. So, further outlook in that area – well, continual rain for forty days and forty nights, followed by widespread flooding. So if you've got any gopher, well, I should start building your arks now. Good night.

Newsreader. Finally, here are two police messages. Would Moses, last heard of seven months ago on a hiking holiday in the wilderness, go at once to Egypt where his people are anxiously awaiting deliverance.

At the crossroads between Sodom and Gomorrah early this morning a Mrs Lot, of no fixed abode, was turned into a pillar of salt. Would anyone who saw the accident or can give any information, please ring Revelation 7777 . . .

* * *

JOHN AND MARY

by Bill Oddie and John Cleese

John. Ah, I love to be alone in the country.
Mary. John?
John. Yes.
Mary. I am with you.
John. I love to be alone in the country.
Mary. But, but John, you brought me with you.
John. I didn't, you hid in the back.
Mary. But you must have noticed?
John. Not at all, it's a very large tandem.
Mary. But John, when we fell off going down the stairs. . . . You must have seen?
John. I thought you were a hitch-hiker.
Mary. But I am your wife. You must have recognized me?
John. I didn't, Mary.
Mary. Why not?
John. Because you were disguised as a cactus.
Mary. Oh, John, John, talk to me. Say something to me. Say you hate me, say I am ugly.
John. Which?
Mary. Say I'm ugly.
John. You are ugly.
Mary. You are only saying that, you don't really mean it, you don't care, you never think about me. Up and down all night warming the milk, mashing the rusks, all the crying and bed-wetting. . . . .
John. Yes, I know, I know.
Mary. I wouldn't mind if we had a baby.
John. Well, I am sorry, but I prefer bison.
Mary. John, why don't you admit, you don't . . . . . don't love me anymore?
John. All right, I admit it.
Mary. John, once we had something that was pure and wonderful and good, what's happened to it?
John. You spent it all.
Mary. That's all that matters to you, isn't it? Money. I despise you, do you hear? I hate you, I don't know how I have been able to stand it, I . . . . . I suppose it's because I love you, I don't know. I do love you John, I love you more than I can say, I . . . need you John, I . . . please John, don't look at photographs of nude women when I am speaking to you.
John. All right, but, I know, you know . . .
Mary. You know?
John. Yes.
Mary. Oh God . . . . . . John?
John. Yes.
Mary. What do you know?
John. Well I could be wrong.

Mary. About me and Nigel?
John. Oh, oh, I was wrong. I thought it was Robert.
Mary. Yes, you are right, I can never remember names.
John. Anyway I do know about last Friday.
Mary. Last Friday?
John. Yes, he was in my bed wasn't he?
Mary. How do you know?
John. He kept pushing me out.
Mary. You mean you were there too?
John. You didn't even notice? Oh God!!
Mary. John, John, try to love me.
John. No Mary, it's no good, you somehow manage to hurt everyone you love.
Mary. Well, I'll take the cactus skin off.
John. No Mary, look there is something I have been meaning to tell you ......
Mary. What?
John. Cardinal Richelieu died in 1642.
Mary. All right, so mother was wrong. But can't we forget the past? I mean that's all history now, don't let's dig it up again.
John. You never liked me being an archaeologist did you?
Mary. I never said that.
John. You would have been happier if I had sharpened knives, or, or . . . sold ferrets.
Mary. Keep George out of this.
John. No, I am not going to keep George out of this. If you had to have a lover why did it have to be a ferret seller? Blasted ferrets all over the house for months. Why couldn't it have been a budgerigar man? At least budgerigars can sing beautifully. I can still remember waking up in the morning and hearing all those ferrets singing. It used to drive me mad, always the same tune.
Mary. Well ...... that's all over now, can't we forget, I mean, can't we start all over again, I mean go back and begin from the beginning?
John. I suppose we could try.
Mary. Please, John?
John. All right. ..... Ah, how I love to be alone in the country.
Mary. John?
John. Yes?
Mary. I am with you.
John. I love to be alone in the country.
Mary. But John, I ...... (*etc, etc . . .*)

* * *

THE DOCTOR
by Bill Oddie and John Cleese

(*A doctor's surgery*)

Nurse. Excuse me?
Patient. I want to see Doctor Cleese for my check up.
Nurse. Wait here until the doctor calls.
Patient. Thank you very much, thank you.

(*The* Doctor *enters.*)

Doctor. Next please, come along, come along, we haven't got all day, come along. Right — drop 'em! (*A crash.*) Ah, now take your trousers off.
Patient. They are, sir.
Doctor. So they are . . . yes . . . well, in that case your legs need pressing. Now, can you touch your toes?
Patient. No, sir.
Doctor. Well, how do you wash them then? You dirty little brute! Come grubbing round my surgery with filthy feet. *Ugh*! Well, if you can't touch your toes your arms must be too short. I'll just have to let them out a bit at the elbows.
Patient. Thank you, sir.
Doctor. Now, now, come over here. Now take this bottle — you know what to do with it, don't you?
Patient. Yes, sir, I do.
Doctor. Good. There is the ship and I want it finished by Tuesday. And if you find that too difficult, you can put the ship in the bottle. Right now, can you read this card?
Patient. Oh yes, sir.
Doctor. Well?
Patient. It says, 'A—B—G—X—R—I, 8—4—3—9, D—M—F—R—H.'
Doctor. It's from my aunt in Brighton, she must be out of her mind. She hasn't been the same since Mafeking. Right, well, thank you, off you go now then.
Patient. What about my check-up?
Doctor. Oh yes, oh yes. Ah, now, have you got a temperature?
Patient. Oh yes, sir, 106.
Doctor. Oh, that is a bit high, better call it 98. Now let's see . . . . . breathing — do you breathe?
Patient. Yes, quite frequently actually.
Doctor. Well breathe in, then. (Patient *takes a long breath in.*) Breathe out again. (*He does so.*) Breathe in, blow out, breathe in, blow out. In out, faster, in out, in out, keep going. Sorry I have to make you do this, but the electric fan has broken down. Right, that'll do. Now, how do you feel? Yes, that's quite normal, thank you. Now take your shirt off.
Patient. No, no, no, no, no!
Doctor. Yes, yes, I know it's embarrassing. Umm, I know, I will take mine off too. No, no, I have got a better idea — I will go behind this screen.
Patient. Thank you very very much, sir, thank you indeed.

Doctor (*behind the screen*). Is it off now?

Patient. Yes, sir.

Doctor. Well put it back on, I want to come out. Right now, ugh, eyes, feet, nose, ribs — I think you have got the full set.

Patient. Oh thank you, sir.

Doctor. Oh, I know, teeth. Open your mouth. Wider. Wider. (*Sounds of jaw stretching.*) Wider. (*A clatter of falling teeth.*) Well, pick 'em up, let me see 'em. Are they comfortable?

Patient. Oh yes, sir, very comfortable.

Doctor. Oh good, well, I think I will keep these then. (Patient *makes toothless protesting noises.*) No, no, don't worry, I'll put you on liquid food. Anyway, it'll do you good to diet, you've put on a bit of weight since I last saw you. What did I treat you for?

Patient. Nappy rash.

Doctor. Ah yes, that's it. Still troubling you?

Patient. No, no, no.

Doctor. Good. Anyway, you are far too fat. How much have you gained? Three pounds?

Patient. No, sir.

Doctor. Six pounds?

Patient. No, sir.

Doctor. Eleven pounds?

Patient. No, sir.

Doctor. Thirteen pounds?

Patient. No, sir.

Doctor. Thirteen pounds ten ounces?

Patient. No.

Doctor. All right then, open the box, Mr Oddie, you have turned down thirteen pounds ten ounces, so let's see what you have won. Mr Oddie, you have won Kenneth Wolstenholme! Well done, Mr Oddie . . . . . . Good night and that's all for this week and don't forget to join us next week when it may be your turn to beat the clock. Good night everyone.

*   *   *

POTS AND PUNS

by Douglas Young and Tim Brooke-Taylor

David. Television cookery experts have always been highly successful personalities. We wondered what it would be like, if they were ever cast in a radio play. Now I say that to justify the next sketch — but you and I know this is just an old excuse for lots of cookery puns. Listeners may be interested to know that the BBC's official entry for the Eurovision Pun Contest will be selected from the following playlet. Well, let's go then, and please remember — television cookery experts and radio plays. We start with the title of the play, 'Pots and Puns'.
Graeme. That was pun No. 1, that was pun No. 1.

(*Fade to* Woman *singing*)

Jo. Boiled beef and carrots, boiled beef and carrots, that's the stuff —

(*There is a knock on the door.*)

Jo. Who's there?
Tim. It's me, Lord Stilton. May I have entree to this joint?
Jo. Why, of course . . .

(*She opens the door.*)

Jo. . . . Oh my lard! You're dripping! You'll be kitchen your death of cold.
Tim. Thanks, I got caught in the reindeer.
Jo. Come toast yourself at the fire. Excuse my cooking apron.
Tim. You always look a tasty dish, Meg, whatever the dressing.
Jo. Oh, you menu! You're always flattering.
Tim. No, I mean it — you're a lovely bit of crackling. I could eat you all up!
Jo. Oh, can it, Lord Stilton!
Tim. Meg, why do you always adopt such a frigidair?
Jo. I mistrust men who are too fresh, they soon go off.
Tim. I admit it. In the past I was a loose liver.
Jo. You've certainly got an offal reputation.
Tim. But I've simmered down now. It's only when I'm with you my heart starts boiling over, Meg. Oh, Meg, you drive me off my nutmeg. Don't give me the cold shoulder.
Jo. Oh, you'll get over it. It's just a flash in the pan.
Tim. No, no! Lettuce get married. I'll beetroot to you to the endive my days!
Jo. This is so sardine. I'm afraid you're just not my cup of tea.
Tim. Oh you've got a cruel cold tongue. But all the same I love the tongue, I love the legs, I love the breas . . . but this is no time to talk of food. I suppose the truth is you've got other fish to fry.
Jo. As a matter of fact I have. You see I'm in love with Police Constable Dick Dangerfield. Yes I lost my heart the first day I spotted Dick.
Tim. Pah! The village copper! Use your loaf, sugar, he hasn't got a bean.
Jo. I know he only gets a small celery, but I'll run off with him whenever he cares to sago. You're nowhere in the rice.

Tim. So you turn me down for a penniless country dumpling!
Jo. If I make a hash of things, I'll just have to stew in my own juice, as my Marmite say.
Tim (threatening, lecherous). So you give me the raspberry, eh? Very well, then I shall have to start treating you like a tart.
Jo. Well, what sauce. Unhand me sir or ice-cream.
Tim. At last you get your desserts. And screaming won't help you, it'll only make me a little rasher. You *shall* be the mother of my child.
Jo. No, no I camembert it.

(*A knock at the door.*)

Tim. Curses, there's someone at the door.
Jo (shouting). Help! The door *is* open, just lift the ketchup!

(*The door opens.*)

Graeme. 'Ullo-ullo, there's something fishy going on here. What's cooking?
Jo. Dick, my darling.
Tim. Oh it's nothing, constable, the lady was just behaving like a custard.
Graeme. Behavin' like a custard?
Tim. Yes, getting upset over a trifle.
Jo. Ha! He nearly made mincemeat of me.
Graeme. A bit of a hot dog, eh? I've only got two words to say to you, sir . . . Irish Stew.
Tim. Irish Stew?
Graeme. Irish Stew for assault, battery and disturbing the peas.

Fade

* * *

Meanwhile, back on television the young man whom Ned Sherrin had chosen to introduce *That Was The Week That Was* and *Not So Much a Programme,* David Frost, proved to be so successful a presenter and interviewer that there followed a succession of television series, *The Frost Report, Frost On Sunday,* etc.

All of these programmes used plenty of sketches and had a strong team of actors to play them, including John Cleese, a large character actor named Ronnie Barker and a small comedian named Ronnie Corbett. The combination of a show whose style was to take a mocking but intelligent interest in topical issues, together with a fine cast of players resulted, as it always has done, in attracting the best writers to write for the shows.

Here is a selection of 'Frost' sketches, chosen with difficulty from hundreds.

NARCISSUS
by Bob Block

Announcer. There are many kinds of love, and few love affairs are perfect. But now and again, you come across some lucky person who is completely satisfied with the one he loves.

(A Man *admiring his appearance in the mirror.* A Woman *is watching him.*)

She. You shouldn't spend so much time admiring yourself, George. Sometimes I think you're getting a Narcissus complex.

He. Don't be so ridiculous, Gwen. A Narcissist is someone who's foolishly infatuated with himself.
She. Well, isn't that what *you* are?
He. No. With me it's the real thing.

(*He kisses his reflection in the mirror.*)

* * *

HENDON
by Michael Palin and Terry Jones

(*A party.* John *and* Ronnie *stand with glasses.* Ronnie *is chatty and* John *pleasantly tolerant if possible.*)

Ronnie. What do you do?
John. I'm the world's leading authority on impressionist painting.
Ronnie. Oh yes? I'm an accountant . . . chartered accountant.

(*Pause.*)

Ronnie. Where do you . . . er . . . live?
John. I live in a converted monastery in the Outer Hebrides.
Ronnie. Really? How interesting . . . I live in Hendon.

(*Pause.*)

Ronnie. Is your wife here tonight?
John. No . . . she's in Vietnam . . . fighting.
Ronnie. How fascinating . . . Do you know Hendon at all?
John. I passed through it once . . . when I was being kidnapped by Russian agents.
Ronnie. Really? Well I never! Where were they taking you?
John. Oh, they had a frigate waiting for me in the Thames estuary.
Ronnie (*excitedly*). Really! Then you must have gone down Ulverston Road! Past our house! D'you remember — just after the baths!

John. Well, I wouldn't know — they'd drugged me pretty heavily with Hypertalcin Metrathecane.
Ronnie. Good heavens . . . and what does that do?
John. It paralyses the memory.
Ronnie. Does it affect your eyesight?
John. Oh yes. You're totally unconscious.
Ronnie. Oh . . . then you probably didn't see our house. It's number 37 on the corner . . . You must drop in sometime.
John. Well, that's very kind of you, but I'm afraid I won't be able to. I'm going to prison.
Ronnie. Really? . . . Not anywhere in Hendon I suppose?
John. No, it's in Guatemala. It's just a currency offence I committed when I was over there investigating a man-eating cactus they'd discovered.
Ronnie. You went all the way to Guatemala to see cactuses?
John. Yes. I had some pretty horrible adventures. I was nearly trampled to death by a herd of rogue buffaloes.
Ronnie. Just looking for cactuses. If only I'd known . . . they've just had a display of them at Hendon Central Library.

(*Pause.*)

Ronnie. You know it's really fascinating talking to you, because it's not everyone that's interested in Hendon.
John. I'll show you something that'll interest you.

(John *pulls out a huge prayer mat or shawl.*)

Have you seen one of these before?
Ronnie. No, no, I haven't.
John. D'you know what it is?
Ronnie (*quite caught up by now*). No.
John. It's a Tibetan prayer-shawl. Do you know how I got it?
Ronnie (*engrossed*). No, I don't.
John. It was given to me by the chief slave-girl of the High Commander of the Tibetan Army. Oh! She was a beauty — her hair was black as a raven's wings, and one evening at the feast Ramsit Asi, the all-powerful God of Light, when 10,000 bullocks are sacrificed on the mountain, she crept into my room, filling it with a delicious fragrance, and she cast aside her tribal robe and her black hair spilled over her delicate pale skin . . . as she climbed into my bed . . .
Ronnie. Really?
John. Mmmmm . . . *She* came from Hendon.

* * *

ATTITUDES
by Robin Grove-White and Ian Davidson

Scene: A living room. Jo *and* Ronnie Corbett *embracing on the settee. There is a knock at the door.*

R.C. You'd better not be seen here with me. Go in the kitchen.

(*Exit* Jo. R.C. *opens the door.* Ronnie Barker *is there.*)

R.B. Good morning, good morning, good morning, sir. I'm the man who's come about the jokes.
R.C. Jokes?
R.B. Yes, sir, jokes. You sent in the coupon out of the TV Times. Gobsplitter Gags Limited. 'Get funny and socially successful in three days. Personal Tuition. Six Easy Lessons and One Hard One'.
R.C. Oh, yes, come in, come in.
R.B. (*presenting catalogue*). Now then, sir — what sort of things were you looking for? You have a browse through that catalogue and see what sort of things you fancy.
R.C. Boozy belters . . . cocktail quips . . . what about this one?
R.B. Which one, sir? 191? . . . (*from memory*) . . . I went up to the door . . . and the lady opens the door in her nightdress . . . funny place to have a door. Oh no, sir — that's your Cary Grant smoothie — that wouldn't suit you. The point is, where are you going to tell this first joke? I suggest over here by the door, so when your guests come in, 'What a smart man', they say — telling a joke soon as you come in the door like that.
R.C. Well, I feel more secure entertaining in the corner.
R.B. Over in the corner it shall be, sir. Here we go, then. Joke No. 1 coming up from the corner. 'My brother's name's Isaiah . . .'
R.C. Isaiah?
R.C. Yes, one eye's higher than the other. How do you like that one, sir?
R.C. One eye's higher than the other?
R.B. Yes, sir. One eye's higher than the other . . . Isaiah . . . Isaiah . . . Maybe that was a bit sophisticated. Now, sir, have you thought of how you're going to introduce these jokes of yours? I mean in a mixed bag of people.
R.C. Well, I thought of something like . . . Silence! . . . if you will. I'm sorry to interrupt the good time you're having but I have some jokes to tell.
R.B. No, sir, no. You need something punchy. They might be doing other things. You need something like Oi! You'll love this one . . . See, you're listening.
R.C. You know, I think something . . . stylish . . . polished.
R.B. There was this man fell into a vat of varnish. Terrible end. But lovely finish — how's that?
R.C. Well . . . Something artistic.
R.B. Artistic? . . . Musical?
R.C. Yes.
R.B. 'I was down the country cottage with the trouble and strife and there was this

flood. Four foot deep. I sailed out the front door on the mattress and my wife accompanied me on the piano.' That's musical.

R.C. Something more classical, I think.

R.B. Beethoven! You can't get more classical than that, can you? 'Beethoven's going down to Vienna with his old lady and she says to him, "If you're going on the booze again, Ludwig, I'm not coming with you." So he says, "Come on, my old darling, he says, you've gotta come 'cos you are my inspiration." So she says, "I am your inspiration." (*He laughs to the tune of Beethoven's Fifth.*) Hahahahaaaaaa . . . Hahahahaaaaaa . . . it's a musical joke you see, sir. Go on, you have a bash at that.

R.C. 'Beethoven's going down to Venice . . .

R.B. Venice, Venice, all right.

R.C. . . . and his wife says to him, "Wolfgang . . .

R.B. Ludwig, Ludwig. Get it right.

R.C. . . . Ludwig. I'm not coming with you, I'm going down the boozer." So he says to her, "That may be so, *my old darling* . . .

R.B. Good. Good.

R.C. . . . But you must come with me because you are my inspiration." Teeheeheeheehee.'

R.B. Well, that takes care of that joke. P'raps I was forcing the pace a bit. Cliches. Now we do recommend striking a note of seriousness in the middle of all this hilarity you will no doubt cause. To this end, cliches. Now, before I start, I should say that we are Cliche Suppliers by Appointment . . . 'My husband and I', 'God bless you all' . . . both ours.

R.C. Really?

R.B. There are three basic cliches for any occasion. 'Lovely weather for the time of year, isn't it?', 'What's a nice girl like you doing in a place like this?' and 'Your flies are undone'. With those you'll never be at a loss. Got them? Now. Repartee. Pretend I'm going and as I go, you shout — Oi, don't do anything I wouldn't do. O.K.?

(*He exits and reappears.*)

Come on. I was nearly on the bus out there. Now, good and loud when I get to the door.

R.C. Oi!

R.B. No, wait till I get to the door. Now, got the words? Take it slowly. (*Moves off slowly.*)

R.C. Stop! Don't do anything I wouldn't do.

R.B. That gives me a lot of scope. Haha. I didn't tell you, sir. There's a comeback to that one. Ah, well, you've gotta laugh . . . Look, why don't you have a look through this lot, and I'll sit over here with my head in my hands and have a bloody good cry.

(*Enter* Jo.)

Jo. Hello, hello, hello. You feel like a cup of tea?

R.C. Yes, please.

Jo. Well, you certainly don't look like one! Everytime a coconut! Whoopee!

R.B. Who was that lady?

R.C. That was the . . . er . . . lady I . . . er . . . was with last night.
R.B. That's no lady. That was my wife. I'm not playing second fiddle to you.
R.C. (*reading*). Second fiddle? You're lucky to be in the orchestra! 'When you're smiling . . .

(*Dances and sings from the book.*)

* * *

CHRISTMAS OATH
by Michael Palin

Scene: A courtroom. The Accused *enters the dock.* Clerk of the Court *leans over to him.*

Clerk. Would you read what is on the card?
Accused (*after brief look at* Clerk). May every Christmas wish come true
And joy this day be yours,
With mistletoe upon the tree
And holly on the doors —
Clerk (*in angry whisper*). The other side.
Accused. Oh! I swear to tell the truth, and nothing but the truth — love Denis and Mabel.

* * *

TENNIS
by Doug Fisher

RC. I didn't see you at the Derringtons' party last night.
R.B. No, I wasn't invited.
David (*off*). Fifteen — love.
R.B. No, as a matter of fact, I don't like them very much.
R.C. Oh, but I know them terribly well.
R.B. Yes I know them terribly well too, and I don't like them.
David. Fifteen — all.
R.B. Well, what have you been doing with yourself lately?
R.C. Well, I've been seeing quite a bit of Margaret recently — quite a bit.
R.B. Margaret, eh? Yes, I used to do quite a bit of that sort of thing — used to be pretty — randy.
David. Fault!
R.B. I mean I used to see quite a bit of Margaret in my philandering days.
David. Fifteen — thirty.

R.B. No, as a matter of fact, I think she's frigid!
R.C. Oh, no!
David. Thirty — all.
R.B. No, when I say frigid, I mean frigid in the same way as I'd say your sister's frigid.
David. Thirty — forty.
R.C. Have you seen Margaret at all recently?
R.B. Well I er er . . . etc . . .
R.C. Very nice flat she's got.
R.B. Yes . . .
R.C. Very nice — sofa!
David. Deuce!
R.B. Ah, yes, talking of that sofa, you didn't happen to find a pair of shoes of mine did you?
David. First service . . .
R.C. Em, light mauve chukka boots would they be?
R.B. Yes, those are they.
R.C. Yes, I think Margaret said something about — she'd thrown them in the garbage.

(R.B. *reaction*)

David. Advantage Corbett.
R.C. So you've seen Margaret recently have you?
R.B. Well . . . yes . . . last week — yesterday — for tea. Very good tea.
R.C. Very good tea!
R.B. Damn good seedy cake.
R.C. Damn good.
R.B. Damn good scones.
R.C. Damn good.
R.B. Damn good. You get a damn good tea . . .
R.C. Bloody awful breakfast.

(R.B. *reaction*)

David. Game, set and match to Corbett.

* * *

SANDWICH BOARD

by Peter Vincent

(Man *with blank sandwich board*)

Other Man. Excuse me — can you tell me why you're going around with a blank sandwich board?
Sandwich Man. It's my day off.

* * *

BUTTERLING

by John Cleese

Sheila. Head keeper to see you, sir. (*Enter* Keeper.)

John. Now when you joined us three weeks ago, Butterling, this was the second largest zoo in the whole of Europe. We had over 6,000 animals. All we have left are two hyaenas, a rhinoceros and a ferret with a wooden leg. Where are the others?

Keeper. I don't know, sir.

John. They're in the main street, Butterling, the main street. All except for the water buffalo.

Keeper. Where's the water buffalo, sir?

John. In my bathroom. My wife found it there early this morning. She's a nervous woman, Butterling. The police caught her just 40 minutes ago. She was over 100 miles away, still running. She doesn't remember anything, and she thinks she's a potato.

Keeper. I'm sorry, sir.

John. That's all right, I didn't like her anyway. But the town, Butterling, the town! It looks like a National Game Reserve, I mean, Butterling, how does anyone lose giraffes?

Keeper. People take them, sir.

John. What!

Keeper. I don't think they mean to steal them, sir, they just borrow them and forget to give them back.

John. You're lying, Butterling. I know all about your little agreement with the sausage factory.

Keeper. Ohhh!

John. And the aviary, Butterling, my little pride and joy the aviary. What have you done with it?

Keeper. I put all the birds in one cage, sir.

John. Well?

Keeper. The vulture's looking very well, sir.

John. Aaaarrghhh! I'm dismissing you as from tomorrow, Butterling. One of the baboons can take over for the time being. Now for the rest of the day, one, get the ferret out of the elephant's cage. It doesn't fool anyone. Two, Butterling, can you impersonate animals?

Keeper. Yes, sir.

John. Well?

Keeper. Cluck, cluck, sir.

John. What was that, Butterling?

Keeper. That was a chicken, sir. Woof, woof.

John. No, don't tell me, Butterling. Let me guess that one. That was a dog.

Keeper. Thank you very much, sir. Mooooooo!
John. This is a zoo, not a farm, Butterling. Get out. It's five to one. Go and feed the animals. The animal. Oh, and Butterling.
Keeper. Yes, sir?
John. If there's a potato waiting outside — tell her I love her.

* * *

FORGERY

by Michael Palin and Terry Jones

(Ronnie Barker *is examining a pound note for* Ronnie Corbett. R.C. *looks on anxiously.*)

R.B. It's a forgery!
R.C. How do you know?
R.B. Well, if you look closely you can see the base of the letter T is just cut out by the cross-hatching. And then that O isn't, d'you see? And look at that — the L A N are slightly closer together — oh by about a thousandth of a millimetre — but even so the trained eye can spot how it upsets the balance of the composition. It takes years of training to spot that one. And you probably can't tell but the texture of the D is wrong for the depth of ink on the Queen's face there — I mean only just. It's beautifully made, but to me all these minute points add up.
Anyway over there it says BANK OF TOYLAND.

* * *

REPORT ON THE VILLAGE FETE

by Michael Palin and Terry Jones

Churchwarden. Ladies and Gentlemen, members of the Tidworth Parish Council, I would like to thank all of you who worked so hard at our Annual Garden Fete on Saturday afternoon.

As you know, we had hoped to get the famous film star Marlon Brando to open it. I was on the phone to him in Hollywood only the day before, but unfortunately the pips went before he said anything. However, it was very good of Mr Thompson from the Library to step in at such short notice, and open the Fete for us . . . And give us such a masterly summing-up of the war in Vietnam.

And before I go any further, I must put a word of thanks to the village builders who put the marquee up so quickly and so often.

Miss Rubithorne's display of seasonal flowers in vases was a real joy again this year, and all thanks are due to the second Wolf Cub patrol for getting them back to the cemetery.

The Bran-Tub also made a good profit as there was nothing in it. Cleverly thought out, Mrs Grant.

A special word here for Mr Potter and his self-pedalling Magic Glider. A jolly good idea, and it was just unfortunate that his first trip coincided with the R.A.F. fly-past from Tidworth Aerodrome. He thanks you all for the get-well cards and hopes to be able to answer them all personally in a month or two.

Mr Marsden, our fortune teller, could not be with us this year, owing to unforeseen circumstances; but as usual, many of the villagers rallied round to entertain us. Mrs Hargreaves gave a recital of Gurkha War songs and fertility dances, and P.C. Rogers showed us how to make a typical arrest. Happily, Mrs Hargreaves was allowed to rejoin us later in the afternoon, after questioning.

Now we come to the problem of what to do with the proceeds. As you know, the money was to have gone to the 'Save the Village Hall' fund, but since the Hall was burnt down during the Fire Brigade's 'How to put out a simple grass-fire' demonstration, this fund is now closed, and the money will be put to our next social function, which is the Darby and Joan Club's performance of Swan Lake at the open-air baths.

Thank you.

*　　*　　*

SECRETARY

by Dick Vosburgh

Scene: An office. A smouldering sexy, busty Secretary *in tight sweater typing letter.* Employer *sits at desk. Typing stops.*

Employer. Finished, Miss Paisley?

Secretary (throatily). Yes, sir. (*Takes out letter and hands it to him.*)

Employer (reads). 'Messes Logan and Sins, Pringes Street, Ofinburgh. Gintlemen: Thamk you for your litter of the sextoonth. We shill be hippy to delover your oderr.' (*To* Secretary.) Miss Paisley?

Secretary. Yes, sir?

Employer. You're improving!

*　　*　　*

*   *   *

THE CHANCELLOR OF THE EXCHEQUER

by Barry Cryer

Good evening. I am here tonight to talk to you on a purely non-political, non-partisan, Labour party basis. I am the Chancellor of the Exchequer – so there. (*Blows raspberry*). Now, a lot of people have been saying recently that our economy is in really bad shape. Really? Yes. Bad? Yes. Shape? Perhaps. But really bad shape? (*Pause.*) Now then. Let's get down to brass tacks. The brass tax which I shall be imposing is an expedient necessity. It is essential, at this time, when our beloved country has its back to the wall, to realise how heartening that can be. Only with one's back to the wall can one go forward . . . to the next wall. People often come up to me in the street, which is in itself encouraging. They say, 'Look here, Smartypants' – and let us not forget that 'Look here, Smartypants' is what democracy is all about – 'Look here, what about the pound?' A fair question. A good question . . . and one that I intend to dispense with altogether tonight. I put the issues squarely before you. One, the pound is stable. The horse may have gone, but the pound is stable. Two, I wouldn't be doing this job if I were not a trained economist and mathematician. Five, my policy is one of non-alignment. I will not see Britain's money spent – on your behalf. Six, the Prime Minister is behind me – always. (*He looks round nervously.*) Seven, the trade index for the last fiscal year shows a trend that can only be described. And eight, figures prove nothing. That is why I say to you, this is a time for you, and I, and him, to tighten our belts, pull up our socks, square our shoulders . . . and try to relax. Every one of you can make some contribution. I shall be giving you the address later. May I conclude by saying I laugh at those who say this country is struggling. Ha, ha, ha. We can turn the corner, if only we can find it. We will confound the Jonahs, the backsliders, the dismal Jimmies and the rest of our great people, and prove to the world that there are bigger, better, greater crises ahead. Good night.

*   *   *

STRANGERS WHEN WE MEET

by Ian Davidson and Neil Shand

David. Very convenient to send the children away, but doesn't boarding school do harm? Doesn't it lead to estrangement of child from parent?

(*A knock at the door.* Ronnie Barker *opens it.* Michael *is there.*)

Michael. I'm sorry to bother you, but does Mr Ferguson live here?
Ronnie B. No, no, it isn't and anyway he's out.
Michael. If you see him, his son is looking for him.
Ronnie B. You're my son?
Michael. You're Mr Ferguson?
Ronnie B. Yes, yes, sorry about the fib. I thought you were a Jehovah's Witness.
Michael. Can I come in, sir?
Ronnie B. I suppose you'd better. (*They go inside.*)
Michael. Nice place you've got here, sir.
Ronnie. Yes, not bad, not bad. Look, you'll probably think I'm a bit of a silly so-and-so, but I didn't quite catch the name.
Michael. Sebastian.
Ronnie B. Sebastian?
Michael. Yes.
Ronnie B. We christened you Sebastian? My God, we must have been drunk. No, no, bloody rude of me. I'm very bad with names. Had to make sure, though — might have to introduce you to your mother. By the way, Sebastian what?
Michael. Ferguson.
Ronnie B. Of course, of course, on the tip of my tongue. Still, can't be too sure. I had this other wife, you know. Barnacle, her name was. Still, mustn't let me bore you. What do you do in life?
Michael. You sent me away to school, sir.
Ronnie B. I should have known. Remind me, what school is it?
Michael. Charterhouse.
Ronnie B. Good lord, I was there!
Michael. That's why you sent me, sir.
Ronnie B. You don't happen to know old Jimmy Forbes, do you?
Michael. No.
Ronnie B. Of course, silly of me. He was there when I was. Not very bright but he must have left by now. I am a State Registered Nurse — done any nursing yourself?
Michael. No.
Ronnie B. No, I didn't think so, really. Doesn't sound much fun — I know — but strangely exciting in its own way. Mustn't talk shop. What brings you to this neck of the woods, then?
Michael. It's the school holidays.
Ronnie B. Well, I hope the weather keeps fine for you. I won't ask when you're going back. A bit unkind to raise that subject on a fellow's first day of leave.
Michael. No, sir.

Ronnie B. When does school start again?
Michael. October the ninth.
Ronnie B. Three months. I suppose we'll be bumping into each other quite a lot.
Michael. Yes, sir.
Ronnie B. Sit down. We'll be seeing you around, then? Just one thing, there's four or five pretty girls around this house — don't get any funny ideas.
Michael. No?
Ronnie B. No. They're your sisters.

* * *

It has been said that everybody has one book in them. It could also be said that everybody has one sketch in them and the two Ronnies, Ronnie Barker and Ronnie Corbett, worked so well together that many listeners sent in sketches for consideration, some of which were good enough to be used.

One such came from a 'Gerald Wiley'. It was good enough for the Ronnies to play and it got its laugh. But then another arrived. This one, 'Doctor's Waiting Room' was very good indeed and was much talked about. As a string of further excellent sketches arrived from 'Gerald Wiley' it became clear that the name was a pseudonym for somebody who was no ordinary listener but a most skilful writer. As that series of *Frost On Sunday* drew to its close the excitement mounted as to who 'Gerald Wiley' would turn out to be. I was in charge of comedy programmes at London Weekend Television at the time and was highly delighted and flattered when rumour went round that I was the mysterious 'Gerald Wiley'. But I was not. At the end of the series the two Ronnies gave a party at a Chinese restaurant opposite the studios at Wembley and the secret was revealed.

'Gerald Wiley' was Ronnie Barker. He wanted to try his hand at writing sketches for the show and, typically, sent them in anonymously so that they would be judged on their merits and Ronnie Corbett would not feel that he *had* to perform them.

Here is the sketch which began 'Gerald Wiley's' highly successful writing career.

* * *

DOCTOR'S WAITING ROOM

by Gerald Wiley (Ronnie Barker)

Scene: A doctor's waiting room, full of patients. The doctor enters.

Doctor. Good morning.

(*He goes into the surgery. Enter* Ronnie Corbett.)

R.C. Good morning (*Silence.*) I said, Good Morning. (*Silence.*) Oh, so nobody's speaking, eh, isn't it amazing? Isn't it extraordinary how no-one ever talks to each other in a doctor's waiting room? Odd, isn't it? No, of course it's not odd. Oh, I thought it was. Well it's not, so keep quiet. Sorry. Don't mention it.

I see they are stopping all the tube trains tomorrow to let people get on and off.

Simple Simon met a pieman going to the fair.
Said Simple Simon to the pieman, Pray what have you there?
Said the pieman to Simple Simon, Pies, you fool.

Night and day, you are the one,
Only you beneath the moon and under the sun.
In the roaring traffic's boom,
In the silence of my lonely room,
I think of you, night and day.
Day and night, under the hide of me,
There's oh such a hungry yearning burning inside of me.
Whether near to me or far,
It's no matter, darling, where you are,
I dream of you,
Night and day.

Well, I've done my best. I can't think of anything else.

(Ronnie Barker *stands.*)

R.B. John has great big waterproof boots on;
John has a great big waterproof hat;
John has a great big waterproof mackintosh;
And that, says John, is that.
A. A. Milne.

R.C. Ah, that's more like it. Anyone else know anything?

(Jo *stands.*)

Jo. If you were the only boy in the world, and I were the only girl,
Nothing else would matter in the world today,
We could go on loving in the same old way . . .

Jo and R.C. A garden of Eden just made for two,
With nothing to mar our joy . . .

Jo, R.C. and R.B. I would say such wonderful things to you,
There would be such wonderful things to do . . .

All. If you were the only girl in the world,
And I was the only boy.

R.C. Wonderful, wonderful. Right, everybody conga. (*They join in a conga line.*) Aye aye Conga, aye aye Conga . . .

All. I came, I saw, I conga-ed,
I came, I saw, I conga-ed,
La la la la, la la la la.

R.C. Come on, everyone, back to my place. (*Exeunt in conga.* Doctor's Receptionist *enters from surgery.*)

Receptionist. Doctor, there's no-one here.

(Doctor *enters.*)

Doctor. Ah, I thought as much. That bloody little Dr Corbett has been here again and pinched all my private patients.

* * *

In the 60s the 'Liverpool scene', famous for its music and poetry, was represented in comedy by the Scaffold. Roger McGough, Mike McGear and John Gorman produced a lively mix of pop and eccentric humour.

TIM

by Roger McGough

(*Sound of dialling.*)

Man. T . . . I . . . M . . .

Voice. 14 precisely. (*bleep . . . bleep . . . bleep.*) At the third stroke it will be 8.14 and ten seconds. (*bleep . . . bleep . . . bleep.*)

Man. Mary, is that you? Mary?

Voice. At the third stroke, it will be 8.14 and twenty seconds. (*bleep . . . bleep . . . bleep.*) I told you never to ring me at work. At the third stroke it will be 8.14 and thirty seconds. (*bleep . . . bleep . . . bleep.*)

Man. Mary, can I see you tonight?

Voice. No.

Man. 'Ow about tomorrow night?

Voice. No.

Man. 'Ow about Thursday?

Voice. No. At the third stroke it will be 8.14 and forty seconds. (*bleep . . . bleep . . . bleep.*)

Man. Mary, why won't you see me again?

Voice. I haven't got the time.

* * *

The 60s and 70s were a fertile period for sketches. There were many radio and television programmes, apart from those we have already mentioned, which used the odd sketch. Even shows starring a singer often filled the time between big numbers with some sort of comedy, usually a sketch.

Here are four examples of self-contained sketches of that period, performable by anyone.

First Performance from *Four Degrees Over,* a musical stage revue of 1966, was the work of John Gould and David Wood. (The 'Four Degrees' of the show's title were those the cast had just taken at Oxford.)

Lost For Words was written, while he was still at Nottingham University, by Peter Spence, who later went on to create the hugely successful television series *To the Manor Born.*

Chippenham Wrexham by Russell Davies and Rob Buckman, a pair of 60s Cambridge Footlights who are now respectively a critic and a doctor/actor, shows that glee in playing with words has not vanished from the face of the earth.

Yes Folks, It's Obituary Time! is by Nigel Rees, another Oxford revue performer who went on to devise and present the radio series *Quote . . . Unquote* and is now a best-selling author.

FIRST PERFORMANCE

by John Gould and David Wood

B.B.C. Announcer (filling in during non-appearance of the performers). And now we welcome you to the Memorial Hall where we are broadcasting the first performance of a recently discovered fragment for piano and alto sackbut by the Bavarian composer Heinrich Danzig. Danzig was born in 1886 at Olsbrucke and died in Florence 10 years ago in 1957 at the age of 71. This fragment dates from 1909, when the composer was 23, and was written while he was on a holiday at Badesheim. The soloist tonight is Florence Brush, born in Danzig in 1926, when the composer was 40 years old, 31 years before his death in 1957 at the age of 71, and 17 years after the composition of this fragment in 1909 at Badesheim. Miss Brush later went to the Cockfosters School of Music in 1947, 21 years later at the age of 22, and as far as we know she is still alive. Her accompanist tonight is Feruccio Brangani, born in Cockfosters in 1927, when the composer was 41 and the soloist was nine months old, 18 years after this work was written in 1909 at Badesheim and 40 years before it is being performed tonight in the Memorial Hall, which was built in 1950, 17 years ago, 74 years after the composer was born, 34 years after the soloist was born, 41 years after this work was composed in 1909 at Badesheim and 2 years before my first wedding anniversary. The man selling the tickets is Albert Buttermold, born in 1904 – one year after . . . 1903 . . . And I am afraid that is all we have time for from tonight's concert, so I return you back to the studio. Goodnight.

* * *

LOST FOR WORDS
(for two under-rehearsed Shakespearean actors)
by Peter Spence

King. Herewith my subjects see me newly crowned
Their rightful king and ruler of this realm —
A title thus bestowed on this most Royal head.
And yet I fear that some contest my crown,
And thus besoak me in affairs of state. . . .

(*He starts reading from a sheaf of papers.*)

That I wit not whom mine adversaries are;
And now my bastard brother I suspect
At this same hour is . . .

(*He starts reading his lines from his hand.*)

. . . . firing rebelled frenzy
And cries to see me dead. See here he comes
and covetously peers he at my crown.

(Brother *enters and reads from* King's *crown.*)

Brother. Good day, Brother, and England's worthy king.
How fares his majesty today? See I bare my head
In homage to your crown.

(*He holds out his hat for* King *to read from.*)

King. Good day, brother. Why dost thou hang thy head upon such a joyful meeting?
Brother. Yes, why do I hang my head . . .

(*He puts on a pair of glasses, reads from the floor and then returns them to his pocket.*)

. . . . Ah yes! Because I am sad, brother, that you must die if I am to seize the throne.
King. My throne? Ah, my *throne.*

(*He has picked up his cue and takes up a position behind throne so that he can read from the back.*)

My throne, which I have barely held these three short days
And thou wouldst seek to steal it from me?
Brother. Yes.

(*He rushes into wings and reads off the flat.*)

I come to seize the throne and place the crown on my own head.

(King *rushes into other wing and does the same.*)

King. Has't thou raised an army to depose me?

(Brother *does not react. They look at each other each expecting it to be the other's line.*)

Has't thou raised an army?

(Brother *still doesn't move.*)

Would'st thou raise an *arm* . . . my?

(Brother *takes the cue and raises his arm so that the* King *then reads from his armpit.*)

To challenge my title to the throne.
Come now brother, kiss the royal ring
And make thy peace.

(*He extends his ringed hand for* Brother *to read off.*)

Brother. Then give me thy hand. . . . but only that I may bid you a last farewell.

(King *turns round — left side to audience — and reads from the ceiling.*)

King. Srats ho . . . . . .
That can't be right.

(*He looks up to ceiling again, and realising his mistake, he turns round — right side to audience — and reads from ceiling again.*)

Oh stars! That shine so brightly in the night
Send down the warm hand of fate to preserve my crown.

(Brother *draws his sword and reads from the hilt.*)

Brother. Wilkinson's Sword — makers of fine steel. . . . I beg your pardon. . . . Why do you draw your sword against your king?

(King *draws his sword and reads from it.*)

King. Because I covet your kingdom.

(*They angrily swap swords and repeat the same lines.*)

Why do you draw *your* sword against your king?
Brother. Because I covet *your* Kingdom. And I'll give my life to win it.

(*They then start fighting, all the sword play being done by the* King *while* Brother *holds his still to read from it.*)

Here, show us of your mettle if thou would'st be king
Strong enough to pierce this raging heart
Which once did beat within the very womb
Which makes us flesh and blood.

(*He bares his chest, but continues to read from the blade.*)

No, see you are a lily . . . . . . livered wretch.

(King *peers at bared chest and reads from it dramatically.*)

King. I love Mom — no, I'm sorry —

(*Still reading from chest.*)

Yes, I shall kill you if thereby
The rightful king shall keep his crown.

(*He thrusts sword at* Brother's *heart.* Brother *reads from end of* King's *sword.*)

Brother. Aaaaaaaahhhhh! You have but wounded me . . . . in the arm.

(*He takes the end of the sword and places it on his own arm.* King *rolls up* Brother's *sleeve and reads from forearm.*)

King. Come, roll up thy sleeve so that I may see
The cruel scar that I have drawn upon thee.
Aaaahhhhh; I am struck to the ground . . .

(*On this cue* Brother *pushes him to the ground, where he continues his line reading from the floor.*)

. . . . and the boot is on the other foot.
Brother. Yes, the boot is on the other foot. *The boot.*

(King *has not picked up his cue.* Brother *taps* King's *boot with end of sword, indicating that he should raise it, to show him his next line.* King *then does so.*)

Is on the *other* foot

(King *raises other leg, revealing line written on sole of shoe.*)

Thank you.
For now your choice is twain
Twixt death and abdication.

(He *places sword at* King's *throat where he can read from it.*)

King. The game is lost; the throne is thine.
I now cast off my royal seals, but let me live.
The crown is thine:

(*He has got up from the ground and taken off crown which he places on* Brother's *head and reads from it.*)

Good day, brother and England's worthy king.

(*He realizes he is reading from wrong side of crown, so angrily turns it round, and reads.*)

Good night, you bastard and vile usurper of my birthright. But be warned — soon it shall be mine again — for you have seen the writing on the wall.

(Brother *looks round at walls blankly. He cannot find his next line.*)

Brother. I see no writing on the wall.

(King *looks on other flat.*)

King. Nor this wall.
Both. Where's the writing on the wall?

(*They gallivant all over stage looking for writing.*)
Where's the bloody writing!

* * *

CHIPPENHAM WREXHAM

by Russell Davies and Rob Buckman

A. Soho!
B. This is
A. Solly Hull
B. and Sid Cup with a recipe guaranteed to
A. Brighton
B. every
A. Hove, Swiss Cottage
B. pie. First take a
A. Hull John O'Groats, Stornaway
B. in a warm
A. Kilburn
B. at Regulo Five, baste liberally with
A. Slough,
B. and add a couple of grated
A. Cleethorpes,
B. if you like that sort of
A. Tring.
B. Now take a large greased
A. Basingstoke,
B. the kind you use for
A. Melton Mowbray, Market Harborough
B. and fill it with lightly
A. Hampstead Blackfriars,
B. then absolutely
A. Faversham
B. with potted
A. Cowdenbeath
B. and green or
A. Stoke Poges.
B. Spend a good ten minutes
A. Birmingham
B. with
A. Chester Penge
B. of

A. Salisbury
B. and crushed
A. Pimlico,
B. then
A. Cookham
B. at the
A. Lowestoft
B. your
A. Chigwell Runnymede.
B. Then
A. Stow-on-the-Wold
B. until thoroughly
A. Goole.
B. Now comes the really
A. Tufnell Park,
B. if you are
A. Crawley
B. enough to
A. Penzance
B. an electric
A. Ilminster,
B. or one of those similar
A. Devizes,
B. then you're
A. Surbiton
B. on a
A. Wigan
A & B. ticket.
B. But don't forget when you
A. Deal
B. with the
A. Leeds, Oldham
B. very
A. Keighley
B. at the
A. Audley End, Nottingham Bristol
B. fashion around the appropriate
A. Halifax
B. which can be
A. Builth
B. quite
A. Cheapside
B. in your own
A. Worksop
B. or
A & B. Potters Bar.
B. I did have one, but the

A. Arundel
B. fell off. Now some of you may well be
A. Barking,
B. how
A. Much Wenlock
B. will
A. Uttoxeter
B. for a good
A. Firth o' Forth
B. helping. Well, you've certainly hit the
A. Walton-on-the-Naze
B. there. Remember
A. Morecambe
B. be made by
A. Dublin
B. the quantities. I've seen some really
A. Wapping Gorbals
B. of it in my time, but naturally it takes correspondingly
A. Leicester
B. make a
A. Littlehampton
B. of
A. Belsize
B. proportions. But careful with the
A. Grampians,
B. because
A. Chippenham
B. Wrexham. Vegetables, always
A. Clapham
B. in the
A. Dumfries.
B. You're certainly going to need a dozen
A. Cotswolds,
B. a pound of
A. Eccles,
B. a bunch of
A. Paisley,
B. a
A. Kettering
B. of
A. Norwich
B. oats, a
A. Hythe
B. of
A. Canterbury
B. sauce, and a stuffed
A. Lyme Regis.

B. Exeter, Exeter, Exeter . . . ermm . . . Surrey. Leatherhead!

A & B. But Hitchin next Wick for a Rhyll Bude recipe for your dandelion and Baldock, brought to you by Virginia Water, so for Dunoon, it's Killiecrankie and the Kyle of Lochalsh to you all!

* * *

YES, FOLKS, IT'S OBITUARY TIME!

by Nigel Rees

A memorial meeting. All sitting in a semi-circle.

Chairman. The death of A. B. Porter has plucked from our midst, in a very real sense, one of the greatest and most significant figures in twentieth century English literature. To anyone who, like me, was present at his deathbed, not to say *in* his deathbed, the loss is so much the greater, and — in a very real sense — frustrating, for his death occurred at the very pinnacle of his endeavour. Leading critic, David Cyril-Lord, you knew him well. Tell us about the A. B. Porter *you* knew.

Cyril-Lord. Well, I would say that the death of A. B. Porter has plucked from our midst, in a very real sense, one of the greatest and most significant figures in twentieth century English literature. (*Murmurs of agreement all round.*) I think above all he will be remembered as a writer. For he not only held a pen, but he also had a piece of paper, which he brought together in a most wondrous conjunction of spirits, usually neat gin. In fact, as Max Beerbohm said, he was a raving alcoholic.

Chairman. Before he died, A. B. Porter wrote over three hundred novels. In the three weeks since his death he hasn't written any novels at all. N. O. Holdsbard, you've been appointed his official biographer, tell us about the A. B. Porter *you* knew.

Holdsbard. I didn't know the bugger at all. I think that's probably why I was asked to write the bloody book. But if you really must, I'd hazard a guess, and say that his death has plucked from our midst one of the greatest and most significant figures in twentieth century English literature.

Chairman. . . . in a very real sense. (*Murmurs of agreement all round.*) Of course, A. B. Porter's *humility* was the subject of one of his most famous odes, dedicated to himself. Orson Cart, you knew A. B. Porter, tell us about the A. B. Porter *you* knew.

Cart. The A. B. Porter I knew was a Scottish policewoman in Dundee and one of the leading minds of her generation. Fearless in her fight for the one-legged trouser, outspoken in defence of lettuce, brilliant . . .

Chairman. Yes, yes. David — leading critic David Cyril-Lord, where would you put A. B. Porter in the pantheon of English letters?

Cyril-Lord. Well, I'm not really sure that he'd be terribly happy in the pantheon. Really I'd put him back on the streets where he belonged.

Chairman. Yes, perhaps we ought to point out to readers that A. B. Porter did have certain tendencies, not immediately apparent to the naked eye. Dame Helen Plumber, is that how you remember A. B. Porter, the A. B. Porter that *you* knew?

Plumber. Well, let me begin by saying that the death of A. B. Porter has plucked from our midst . . .

All. . . . in a very real sense . . .

Plumber. . . . one of the greatest and most significant figures etc., etc. (*Shouts of 'Hear, Hear'.*) But I'd just like to take up on one point you made. You said that A. B. Porter's homosexuality (*Murmurs of 'Gosh'*) was not immediately apparent. I found it out straight away! Anyone who saw him — as I did — in the spring of 1929 swinging through an orgy on a chandelier wearing a lovely yellow polka-dotted frock (which I believe he had knitted himself) worn over his gold-spangled leotards, will know exactly what I mean. On the other hand if they didn't see him, they won't have a clue what I'm talking about.

Cyril-Lord (*working up to a spasm and expiring*). That really is not true. Quite the contrary, as Max Beerbohm said, Porter had courage. And when I use the word courage I mean not only moral courage and intellectual, but physical courage, and above all sexual courage. I . . . I . . . I . . . (*Dies*)

(*All stand and look down at Cyril-Lord's body*)

Chairman. The death of David Cyril-Lord has plucked from our midst . . .

All. . . . in a very real sense . . .

Chairman. . . . one of the greatest and most commanding figures in twentieth century English literature . . .

Fade.

*   *   *

During the 1970s the two fine sketch performers, actor (and writer) Ronnie Barker and comedian Ronnie Corbett, were brought together and given their own television programme, *The Two Ronnies*, which has been running happily ever since.

As we have seen, when there is a successful show running which depends on good sketches and has a talented, versatile cast waiting to play them, the best writers respond and good sketches are forthcoming.

It is interesting to note that new sketch-writing techniques that have come up over the period we have covered have not obliterated the old but taken their place beside them. In the following seven successful sketches from *The Two Ronnies* programmes, four are based on word-play and could have been written in the 1920s (only perhaps not as well).

ORGY AND LESS

by David Nobbs and Peter Vincent

A party scene. There are no guests, but there are large numbers of glasses and a liberal display of canapes and snacks.

The Host *is dusting the canapes with a feather duster. The bell rings. He puts the feather duster away. The bell rings again.*

Host. All right, all right, no need to wear out the bell push. Bloody great thumbs all over it. (*Opens door.* Guest *enters.*) Hullo, hullo, come in. Step over the mat, would you, it's a new one.

(Guest *steps over the mat.*)

Guest. Hullo. Hope I'm not too late. (*Sees that there is nobody else there.*) Oh, am I early?
Host. No, we're in full swing. Come and join the fun.
Guest. Oh, thank you. Not very many people seem to have come.
Host. Oh, I don't know. It's a better turn out than last year. Not like in the old days, though. Sometimes we used to get as many as two or three all in one evening.
Guest. Oh, an orgy.
Host. Now, have a drink. What'll you have? There's water, or if you like something a bit stronger there's melted ice.
Guest. Oh, well, in that case . . . er . . . I think I'll plump for water.
Host. Right. Say when. (*Pours water.*)
Guest. When.

(Host *stops pouring.*)

Host. Anything with it?
Guest. Well have you anything to dilute it with — whisky, brandy, gin, to make it go further?
Host. No, I haven't. I thought you were going to bring a bottle. It *is* a bottle party.
Guest. Oh, I'm sorry. Well in that case I'll just have a dash of water with it.

(Host *gives him a dash of water.*)

Host. Cheers.
Guest. Cheers. (*They drink.*)
Host. That'll put hairs on your chest. (Guest *sits down.*) Look, I'm sorry, but I've forgotten your name. Awfully difficult to remember everyone's name at a party.
Guest. It's Wilfred.
Host. Of course. Look, Wilfred, one small thing, if you don't mind terribly. You are rather wearing out that chair.
Guest. Oh, I'm frightfully sorry. How thoughtless of me. (*Stands.*) Anyway, I prefer standing. I can't stand sitting down. I say, that's good, isn't it? I can't stand sitting down. Ha ha ha ha ha. Ha ha ha ha ha ha.
Host. Please don't laugh too much. It may seem a niggling point, but it uses up all the air.
Guest. Oh sorry, I must leave some for everyone else. After all, guests abhor a vacuum. Ha ha ha . . . sorry.
Host. That's all right, Wilfred. Come and have some solid refreshment.
Guest. Oh good, I haven't eaten all day . . . Mm, these look delicious. (*Takes a canape, bites, cries out.*)
Host. Nice?

Guest. Yes, it's . . . er . . . delicious . . . but it's made of wood, isn't it?
Host. That's right. I use the same one every year.
Guest. There's only one thing. I . . . er . . . bit of a fad, I suppose, but I don't eat wood a lot.
Host. Well they aren't all wooden. It'd be a funny party where all the food was wooden. There's one vol au vent that's real, but I've hidden it.
Guest. Oh, what fun. We'll play spot the vol au vent – and after that I can hide in a cupboard and play sardine.
Host. Oh, I think the party's going to be a success. Have another water.
Guest. No thanks, I'm driving.
Host. Go on, be a devil. Live a little.
Guest. Well, just a tiny one then. (Host *pours it.*)
Host. One tiny niggle, Wilfred. You are rather wearing out the carpet. Would you mind awfully standing on one leg?
Guest. Not at all. Which leg would you like me to stand on?
Host. Either leg, my dear fellow. This is a party. It's Liberty Hall.

(Guest *begins to hop.*)

Guest. I don't want to seem churlish, but aren't you using all your legs?
Host. Good point. You've got me there. I haven't got a leg to stand on. (*Also starts to hop.*)
Guest (*pointing at empty frame on wall*). I like your empty frame.
Host. It's an original. Here, have one of these. (*Hands* Guest *a paper hat, puts one on himself. They continue to hop.*)
Guest. Thank you. It's really warming up now.
Host. Good party, isn't it?
Guest. Much better than the local hop. Ha ha ha ha . . . sorry.
Host. Have one of these, go on. (*Hands him one of those things you blow out that writers never know the name of.*)
Guest. Thank you. (*They both work the blowers.*) I say, the frost's beginning to melt on your radiators.
Host. It never did that at all last year. It's you, making things go with a swing.
Guest. It's very kind of you to say so.
Host. It's true. You're the life and soul of the party.
Guest. Thank you.
Host. By the way, can I have my invitation back? I can use it again next year.
Guest (*ceasing to hop*). I haven't got one. I'm a gate-crasher.
Host. What? Get out, you filthy little worm. Abusing my hospitality. Get out. (*Pushes* Guest *towards door*) And mind the mat. (Guest *steps over mat.*)
Guest. I'm sorry, I only wanted a bit of fun.
Host. Get out – and try not to tread on too many of the stairs.

(Guest *exits. Enormous crash off.* Host *calls out.*)

Host. Thank you. (*Picks up* Guest's *glass.*) What a world we live in. He thinks he can barge in here any year just because he's my brother.

(*Carefully measures unused water back into the jug.*)

*   *   *

REPEATS

by David Nobbs

A party scene. Wilkins *approaches* Prothero.

Prothero. Hello.
Wilkins. Hello.
Prothero. Nice day.
Wilkins. Nice day.
Prothero. Warmer than yesterday.
Wilkins. Warmer than yesterday.
Prothero. Look, would you mind not repeating everything I say?
Wilkins. Sorry. Awfully sorry. My name's Arthur Wilkins by the way.
Prothero. Hello. I'm George Prothero.
Wilkins. Hello. I'm George Prothero.
Prothero. You said you were Arthur Wilkins.
Wilkins. You said you were Arthur Wilkins.
Prothero. Oh my God. You're doing it again.
Wilkins. Oh my God. You're doing it again.
Prothero. Look, would you mind not repeating everything I say? There are more repeats with you than with the BBC.
Wilkins. Sorry. Awfully sorry. (*Pause.*) I bought a colander in Tamworth yesterday.
Prothero. That's better.
Wilkins. That's better.
Prothero. Oh no.
Wilkins. Oh no.
Prothero. Stop it.
Wilkins. Stop it.
Prothero. Look, I may be unusual but I find it very irritating when you keep repeating what I say. It's not what I regard as the art of conversation.
Wilkins. Sorry. Awfully sorry. I have this nervous compulsion, you see. I repeat what people say three times, and then I don't repeat them once, and then I repeat them three times again, and then I don't repeat them once again, and then I repeat them three times again, and then I don't repeat them again.
Prothero. My God, that's awful.
Wilkins. My God, that's awful.
Prothero. The thing to do is to get through my next two remarks quickly. Knickers.
Wilkins. The thing to do is to get through my next two remarks quickly. Knickers.
Prothero. More knickers.
Wilkins. More knickers.
Prothero. Good. Now perhaps we can get some sense. How long has this dreadful complaint been going on?

Wilkins. Good. Now perhaps we can get some sense. How long has this dreadful complaint been going on?
Prothero. You've just repeated me a fourth time.
Wilkins. Yes. I think it must be getting worse.
Prothero. I believe you're a fraud.
Wilkins. I believe you're a fraud.
Prothero. I'll fox you. To escort an orang outang from Baden Baden to Wogga Wogga via Addis Ababa or vice versa is enough to make a Ghurka sherpa commit hari kiri.
Wilkins. I'll fox you. To escort an orang outang from Baden Baden to Wogga Wogga via Addis Ababa or vice versa is enough to make a Ghurka sherpa commit hari kiri.
Prothero. Rumanian dalmatians hate Tasmanian alsatians and Tasmanian dalmatians hate Rumanian alsatians. Tasmanian alsatians hate Rumanian dalmatians but Rumanian alsatians like Tasmanian dalmatians. Tasmanian alsatians hate Rumanian alsatians but Rumanian alsatians like Tasmanian alsatians. So Tasmanian alsatians hate Rumanian alsatians and dalmatians but Rumanian alsatians don't hate Tasmanian dalmatians or alsatians.
Wilkins (*after a pause*). Sometimes I only repeat things twice.
Prothero. You're a fake. I'm not talking to you.
Wilkins. You're a fake. I'm not talking to you.
Prothero (*to party at large*). That man's a fake.
All. That man's a fake.
Prothero. Oh no.
All. Oh no.

* * *

NOWS AT TON

by Barry Cryer and Peter Vincent

Newsreader. Good evening. Here is the News. (*The phone on his desk rings. He picks it up.*) Yes . . . Yes . . . Right. I see. Thank you. (*He puts the phone down.*)

I'm sorry about that. It appears we've had a slight problem with the News. Our new electronic typewriter has developed a minor fault and it's been typing 'O's instead of 'E's. I hope you'll bear with us . . . (*He picks up papers and starts to read.*)

Good ovoning. Horo is tho Nows at Ton.

At Choquors today, tho throo party loaders hold a mooting to discuss a coalition and this country's oxcoptionally sorious oconomic scono.

Tho conforonco was followod by an appotizing moal of roast boof and bootroot with jolly and croam. Aftorwards dologatos hoard a spooch by ox-Foroign Socrotary, Sir Aloc Douglas Homo. In a short addross Mistor Onoch Powoll said Sir Aloc had his koon support.

Hor Majosty the Quoon was at Homol Hompstoad today to unvoil a momorial to sovoral groat Onglish mon of lottors and poots, including Anthony Trollopo, H. G. Wolls and Hilairo Bolloc.

In Kow Gardons today, a Scotsman with a woodon log was caught hiding in the troos, aftor boing stung on tho knoos by a swarm of boos. Aftor his arrost for indocont oxposure ho statod ho was turning ovor a now loaf and changing his sox.

Sports Nows: Lato rosult: Cholsoa, throo. Loods, ono.

Tho woathor. Tomorrow's woather will bo wot . . . will be what? Ah . . . will bo wot . . with a touch of sloot.

Woll, that's all from mo. Ovor now to tho 'Wook in Wostminstor'. Oh God . . . (*Starts to woop . . .*)

Tho Ond

*   *   *

SKETCHERISM SPOON

by Dick Vosburgh

Pompous Theme Music.

Caption: Of Men and Words

Ronnie Corbett *at desk.*

R.C. Good evening. The Spoonerism. 'Of Men and Words' deals with a man who was born July 22, 1844. The Reverend William Archibald Spooner of New College, Oxford . . . the man who committed such inadvertent verbal transpositions as – 'Yes indeed, the Lord *is* a shoving leopard' and the immortal Royal toast: 'To the queer old Dean!' A new play opening next week deals with the home life of the spoon who invented the mannerism – er – man who invented the Spoonerism! Here is the opening scene of the play.

(*Cut to dining room of the 1880s/ 1890s.* Wife *is discovered making preparations for breakfast. Enter* Ronnie Barker *in dog collar.*)

Wife. Ah, there you are, William. Beautiful day, isn't it?
R.B. Quite so – the shine is sunning, the chirds are burping – lovers are killing and booing . . . It makes one glide to be a lav!
Wife. It's just as well you're in a good mood. (*She hands him a shirt.*) Because look what the laundry did to your best shirt.
R.B. Good Heavens. They've freed the slaves!
Wife. Frayed the sleeves, dear.
R.B. I did that, saidn't I?
Wife. They've also torn the collar and smashed all the buttons.
R.B. (*looking closer.*) Quite so! It never pains but it roars. Buttons, collar and sleeves at one swell foop! Well, I'll fight them nooth and tail! Naith and tool! I'll go down

and smith them to smashereens. (*Goes towards the door.*) I'm going to tump in a jaxi!

Wife. William — wait! Surely such a scene would be unseemly for a man of your calling?

R.B. (*returning to table*). You're quite right, my dear. After all, I *am* a clan of the moth. Better to let sleeping logs die. To hue is ermine. (*He sits.*)

Wife. That's better. Do you feel like some breakfast?

R.B. Indood I dee! A suggestion to warm the hartles of my — cockles of my heart. I rather fancy some hot toatered bust, a rasher of strakey beacon, and some of that cereal that goes pap, snockle and crap.

Wife. Very well, William. And while you're eating it, I shall be packing my trunk.

R.B. Tracking your punk?

Wife. Yes, William, you see, I'm leaving you.

R.B. Leaving me after 20 years of bedded wiss? (*Laughs nervously.*) This must be some rather jathetic poke. You can't mean suddenly to destroy my entire lay of wife!

Wife. I'm quite serious, William. I'm leaving and I'm not coming back.

R.B. But my dear, consider the word of the Highly Boble: 'What God hath joined together, let no son put Amanda.' Er . . . 'Let no pan soot amunder' . . . Dear me, I'm getting my tang all tungled!

Wife. Exactly. That's why I'm leaving you.

R.B. What do you mean?

Wife. It's quite simple, William. I can't spoon any more Standerisms! (*She realizes what she's said and screams shrilly.*) .

* * *

HELLO

by Michael Palin and Terry Jones

Party Music

Ronnie Barker *standing with drink.* Ronnie Corbett *comes up to him.*

R.C. Hello.
R.B. I'm sorry?
R.C. I just said 'Hello'.
R.B. Sorry? Sorry? I didn't catch it again.
R.C. Hello.
R.B. What?
R.C. Hello!
R.B. And . . .
R.C. And what?
R.B. And what else did you say besides 'hello'?

R.C. I didn't say anything else I just said 'hello'.
R.B. Not — 'Hello, you boring old git, who the hell invited you?'
R.C. No, I didn't say that.
R.B. Oh! I don't mean those exact words . . . I was only using them as an example . . . It might have been more on the lines of: 'Hello, you fat, ugly, mealy-mouthed sadist, I wish you were dead . . .'
R.C. No . . . I didn't say anything apart from 'Hello'.
R.B. Huh! I've only got your word for it.
R.C. Look . . . I was over the other side of the room, I saw nobody was talking to you, and I thought I'd just come over and say 'Hello'.
R.B. I never did!
R.C. What?
R.B. You implied that Dorothy and I were having a relationship.
R.C. When?
R.B. Just then! All that stuff about my car not being in the garage.
R.C. I didn't say anything about your car . . .
R.B. Oh no . . . but you *implied* it!
R.C. All I said was 'Hello'.
R.B. Oh yes, but look at the way you said it!
R.C. What?
R.B. You said it in that 'Hello! His-car-wasn't-in-the-garage-at-11.30-and-he-left-the-light-on-in-the-study-to-make-the-wife-think-he-was-working-late' — kind of way.
R.C. It wasn't meant to sound like that. It was just a 'Hello, how-are-you?'
R.B. Oh I see! 'Hello-how-*are*-you . . . going-to-explain-the-hotpants-in-the-glove-compartment-when-the-wife-gives-the-vicar-a-lift-on-Sunday?'
R.C. It was only 'Hello'.
R.B. Listen, sonny, if you go round talking to everybody the way you've been talking to me, I'm not surprised you haven't any friends.
R.C. I've got lots of friends.
R.B. Oh yes . . . but they all ran out on you and you had to come over and pick on me to heap abuse on!
R.C. I only said 'Hello'.
R.B. I mean, how was *I* to know it was loaded?
R.C. What?
R.B. The gun! The gun you said . . .
R.C. I said 'Hello'.
R.B. Anyway I was going to throw it away and never use it . . . it was Dorothy who wanted to have a look down the barrel and see how fast the bullets came out.
R.C. I just said 'Hello'.
R.B. I tried to stop her . . . But before I could, she'd pulled the trigger, jumped out of the car and buried herself under a bush on a lonely stretch of the A47 outside Stafford.
R.C. I was only using the word 'Hello' to start a little convers . . .
R.B. And now I come to think of it, I was in Glasgow at the time in any case — no, Frankfurt! . . . No! Even further away . . . er . . . Istanbul. I was in a cellar — chained — all by myself . . . (*Pause.*) except for the *witnesses* . . . lots of witnesses . . . Turks

. . . but they *write* in English . . . *They'd* testify . . . you could write to them . . . unless they're dead . . . oh come to think of it, I think they are dead! Yes I think I read about them being dead . . . pity . . . You've got to believe me! You've got to!

R.C. (*embarrassed.*). I only came up to him and said 'Hello'.

R.B. In any case I didn't mean to . . . but she kept on about the money and the divorce and the gambling and the bad breath . . . I just *had* to! (*His voice rising to a crescendo.*) All right I've been a fool! A bloody fool! I admit it!

R.C. A perfectly ordinary 'Hello' . . .

R.B. (*a manic glint in his eye.*) But you'll never take me alive!

(*Whips out a phial, tears off the top with his teeth and slips it in his martini and swigs it down, dying with many contortions and assorted terrible death convulsions. At last he lies dead at* R.C.'s *feet.* R.C. *looks over him anxiously . . .*)

R.C. Hello? . . . (*Cautiously.*) Hello? Hellooo? (*No reaction . . .* R.C. *stands up.*) Tut tut . . . Can't have a decent conversation with anyone nowadays . . .

(*Pull out fast to reveal* R.C. *standing alone amidst a roomful of dead guests. All have glasses, some are draped over tables, most are on the floor.*

R.C. *starts to pick his way through them, picking up the odd head with his foot, saying 'hello' hopefully and letting it drop again.*)

Fade.

* * *

HOW'S YOUR FATHER

by Chris Miller

A party

Ralph. Roger! It's Roger Davenport!

Roger. Good heavens! Ralph Clark. Haven't seen you since . . . oh, must be 1955.

Ralph. Those were the days, eh? What a time we had, chasing the girls. Remember when we took those two dollies to the Isle of Wight?

Roger. Shanklin?

Ralph. I think that's what we went for, yes.

Roger. Great days. How's life with you now?

Ralph. Oh, settled down. Family man. Two kids, both grown up. And you? Married?

Roger. No, never did. More fun single. You know. (*Wink.*) Take the girl I'm with now. Only twenty. Cor! (*Left hand on right arm bend gesture.*)

Ralph (*enviously*). You devil!

Roger. She likes things I thought only girls in books liked.

Ralph. And on the pill, I suppose?

Roger. Oh, yes. A real goer!

Ralph. I can't stand it!

Roger. She's here, actually, somewhere. Brought me along to meet her father.

Ralph. Really? My daughter asked me to come along this evening to meet her new boy friend.

(*They look at each other appalled.*)

Roger. Of course, when I saw she's a real goer, I mean that if I'm with her at 11 o'clock in the evening — never later — she invariably says to me, 'I must go now'. She always says that. She's a real goer.

Ralph. I see. Good. Because when I said, 'I can't stand it!', what I meant, of course, was: I won't stand for it.

Roger. Oh, quite, quite. When I said she liked things only girls in books liked, I was referring to . . . needlework . . . pony-trekking . . . playing lacrosse and so on.

Ralph. And when I said, 'On the pill, I suppose', I was merely inquiring whether she also played football.

Roger. No . . . no, she doesn't. You do realize, don't you, that when I went 'Cor!' (*Does gesture*) I was simply and solely paying tribute to her splendid muscular development. Not that she's muscular. Just very well-built. In the nice sense of the word. Oh, yes, she's quite capable of looking after herself, were any disgusting, filthy animal to try anything. Not that anyone would. Not that she's not enormously attractive. She is. But she's pure. Pure. So pure, she's . . . pure. And I admire and respect her for it.

Ralph. Good. Because when I said, 'You devil!', I meant: You devil!

(*Two girls appear, one at each man's shoulder.*)

Girl 1. Roger, darling, come and meet Daddy. He's over here.

Girl 2. Daddy, do come and talk to Simon. We've been waiting for you for ages.

(Ralph *and* Roger *smile at each other and relax.*)

Roger. Actually, when I went 'Cor!' (*Does gesture*), I meant *Cor!* (*Does gesture even more forcefully.*)

Ralph. And when I said, 'You devil!', I meant: you lucky devil! Cor! (*Does gesture.*)

Both. Cor! (*Both do gesture*)

* * *

MASTERMIND

by David Renwick

The 'Mastermind' set. R.C. *is sitting in the big chair.* R.B. *as Magnusson fires the questions.*

R.B. So on to our final contender. Good evening. Your name please.

R.C. Good evening.

R.B. In the first heat your chosen subject was Answering Questions Before They Were Asked. This time you've chosen to answer the question before last each time — is that correct?

R.C. Walter James Grebely.
R.B. And you have two minutes, Mr Grebely, on Answering the Question Before Last — starting from now. What is Palaeontology?
R.C. Yes, absolutely correct.
R.B. What's the name of the directory that lists members of the peerage?
R.C. A study of old fossils.
R.B. Correct — who are Len Murray and Sir Geoffrey Howe?
R.C. Burkes.
R.B. Correct — what's the difference between a donkey and an ass?
R.C. One's a trade union leader, the other's a member of the Cabinet.
R.B. Correct — complete the quotation 'To be or not to be —'
R.C. They're both the same.
R.B. Correct — what is Bernard Manning famous for?
R.C. 'That is the question'.
R.B. Correct — who is the present Archbishop of Canterbury?
R.C. He's a fat man who tells blue jokes.
R.B. Correct — what do people kneel on, in church?
R.C. The Most Reverend Robert Runcie.
R.B. Correct — what do tarantulas prey on?
R.C. Hassocks.
R.B. Correct — what would you use a ripcord to pull open?
R.C. Large flies.
R.B. Correct — what sort of person lived in Bedlam?
R.C. A parachute.
R.B. Correct — what is a jockstrap?
R.C. A nutcase.
R.B. Correct — for what purpose would a decorator use methylene chlorides?
R.C. A form of athletic support.
R.B. Correct — what did Henri de Toulouse-Lautrec do?
R.C. Paint strippers.
R.B. Correct — who is Dean Martin?
R.C. Is he a kind of artist?
R.B. Yes, what sort of artist?
R.C. Er . . . Pass.
R.B. Yes, that's near enough. What make of vehicle is the standard London bus?
R.C. A Singer.
R.B. Correct — in 1892 Brandon Thomas wrote a famous long-running English farce. What was it?
R.C. British Leyland.
R.B. Correct — complete the following quotation about Mrs Thatcher. 'Her heart may be in the right place, but her —'
R.C. Charlie's Aunt.
R.B. Correct. (*Bleeper noise*) And you have scored 18 points with no passes.

* * *

Index of Titles

Index of Authors